This book draws inspiration from a diverse array of cultures, histories and mythologies from around the world. While efforts have been made to respect and honour the rich tapestry of human heritage, it is essential to understand that this work is a product of fiction. Readers are encouraged to approach this book with an open mind and recognize that it is a work of creative expression. It is not the intention of the authors to diminish or misrepresent any culture, but rather to celebrate the diversity and richness of human storytelling traditions. Any resemblance to actual persons, living or dead, or actual events is purely coincidental.

CW01501582

HERETICS & HEARSAY

HERETICS & HEARSAY

HALEY ELLEFSON & DARIA K. DA SILVA

IngramSpark

THE FORSAKEN SEA

FALLDARE MEADOW

GRIMREE FIELDS

ABRAM WOODS

BRIGHES

THE ASHEN DOMAIN

OCHRORED

THE FORBIDDEN VALLEY

SLIMERT

TILVER

ALNOLA

CUDNOLA PEAKS

CARMINE LAGOON

ITESSONE

REALM OF ZEMERGAD

THE LUNAR AND SOLAR SANCTUM

THE WHILE ISLES

NEELEM

SURLISLE

THE TIDES OF TALTO

EMSIDEN

ARCHCOVE

THE RED SEA

EEPHIFER

KINGDOM OF EAD

WEREWOOD FOREST

MAYTIN BASIN

THE EX-ISLES

FOR US.

A Tale of the Past.

In the ancient world of Sumeria stands the Realm of Zemergad, land native to those who call themselves the Maidens of Lilith.

A powerful lineage are they, devoting their days to their Lady, who, upon her exile to Edom, could no longer walk within their physical realm.

It was prophesied that a child was to be born — one who would one day sacrifice themselves for her soul to inhabit their mortal body. This child was said to be the Hand of Lilith, and in their offering, their Lady would walk freely upon this world once more.

Abhorred by such a sentiment, the Kingdom of Ead confronted the Realm with hatred. They feared the Maidens, for they did not bleed the same scarlet red as them, they did not preach the same sermons. Eager to cleanse them of their religious zeal, the Kingdom attacked.

To them, there is only Adam, there is only Eve.

Their story we know all too well, and yet lurking in the shadows is Lilith, her story forbidden. They were the Kingdom's decided good and evil of this world. You were to pick your poisons.

Ead had long been ruled by the Royal Hyttenrauch family,

now at the power of Lionel Hyttenrauch. Himself and his wife, Queen Amabel, had been blessed with a daughter four years prior to the start of this tale, and now the Queen was in expectation again — only this time, it was not so easy.

It was as if she, herself, were snapping the cord, feeling the life inside of her die.

Writhing in her bedchamber, where she rot in agony, blood in place of sweat crowned her forehead; tears pooled into a conglomerate of the same bloody substance, blinding her. Not even the sigils of protection to ward off the Lady of Edom could help. It was not her crime.

Her screams ripped through her throat with a torment so virile and bitter, for someone to just save her boy.

King Lionel gathered the finest of his Knyghts to endure the blistering snow, his desperation seeking only the help of the Elders of Zemergad — the leaders of his sworn enemy — no matter the cost.

They galavanted through the palace grounds, crossed the bridge to the mainland with sheer strength and will, traveled through the far stretches of Surlisle, Neelem — even daring to venture through the thick woodlands of the Lunar and Solar Sanctum — and stormed through the Carmine Lagoon until they reached the border of the Realm.

The Elders, as taken aback as they were at such a request, had agreed to the Knyghts' pleas, but on one condition and one condition only: for the Kingdom to call a ceasefire on the annex of their homeland.

The Knyghts, as instructed, agreed on behalf of the King.

The journey back had not been easy, and by the time they

had made their way to the Kingdom, the Queen's conditions worsened, her skin now tinging deep shades of gray.

As the Elders stepped foot into her bedchambers, they felt the thud of the baby's heartbeat drive into a hammer once and for all before silencing completely — the Queen's heart following shortly after.

Sickened with grief, King Lionel buried his head against his wife's chest, one hand on her stomach, clutching her skin like one would the railing of a stair. Unwilling to let go, the Elders attempted to release his grip, the sharp edge of his nails digging into her, peeling away at her flesh. There sat an image of a distraught man, his tears mixing with his runny nose, gushing across her chest as he tried to push himself closer and closer to her, until there was not even the smallest bit of space left between them.

The Elders had known that it was their duty to do all they could for the sake of their land.

Ordering a gust of wind from the tips of their fingers, they blew it in the direction of the King, separating him from his wife in the impact. They began to chant in their long-forbidden tongue of Sumer, commanding ancient words of resurrection in an attempt to share their life force for the two in need, but it was too much. No heartbeat other than their own could be heard. Bringing back the Queen was too hard a task, feeling her defeat in their bones.

They knew what was to be done.

Searching the room for a sharp object — a dagger or a knife — the Elders happened upon a small ceremonial blade tucked under the pillow of the Queen. Wasting no time, they sliced through the layers of her stomach, hoping to find the form of a baby, curled up and bruised. They reached inside to pull out the limp figure, to rest him atop his mother, covered quickly with a blanket they had pulled from beneath her.

With great force, they chanted once more — begging, burning with the fire of revival. Ropes of purple light snaked their way from palm to fingertip, trailing over to the body of the boy. Rarely does their Lady give them access to such powers.

The Prince's veins, now protruding at the surface, filled with fuel. She must see the life of the boy as one of great necessity.

Exhausted, the Elders let go.

It had only been a few moments of silence before the boy opened his mouth to cough out bile the same hue of lavender that his blood now ran: the mark of a Maiden. He wailed as if he were a Banshee, crying out for his mother, for himself, for his father. He cried out for the new world around him and his now beating heart.

Charging through the door, King Lionel was beside himself in complete and utter awe. He noticed the rise and fall of his son's chest and rushed to his aid. The King picked him up, held him close and sobbed a noise so guttural, a noise so violent, he was yet to notice his wife unmoving, greening, spilling out.

The Elders explained they did all that they could — that they were sorry they could not save his wife. Whatever gratitude the King had shown the Elders had vanished, replaced by the anger of a thousand suns.

Reaching for the hilt of the knife, the King ordered the Elders to leave immediately, presenting them with a warning.

An eye for an eye.
They left, eager never to return.

The Kingdom kept their promise.
Zemergad thrived.
Two years later, they awaited the birth of their Hand.
It was said that Lilith came to a Maiden, deep in her slumber, asking her to be the one to bear the child. With willing devotion, the Maiden accepted such an honor. She had fallen pregnant, but she was not the only one.

Conceived and born mere minutes apart, a healthy girl and boy came into the world — the boy exiled for his demonic nature. Males native to the Realm were born as Night Demons, sent to live amongst the Howlers in the Lunar and Solar Sanctum. Such is the curse their kind bear.

The girl, raised to be the Hand, fruitfully saw her duties through. Her soul was one of gold carefully carved with compassion and light, adored by every stretch of her land. She was a bright and kind-natured young girl, someone who walked with a spring in her step, and a care within her true and strong. She was the one to serve them all.

She was only six when the Kingdom attacked.

It had been eight years of peace, of no fear, and yet the King's grief over his wife grew wilder every day. He had heard of the birth of the Hand through his Heathens, self-exiled Maidens, their magic rendered useless outside of the Realm.

The King had decided it would be best to let the girl grow up — to take her when the Maidens were least expecting it, much like the way his wife was ripped from his side, from the ribs that once covered his heart.

His patience grew thinner and thinner with each passing day, until, on the eighth year of his Queen's passing, he ordered a raid of the Realm, no matter the consequence.

Amplified in Zemergad's vicinity, the Heathens accessed the full range of their power against the Maidens, blasting down tombs, sanctuaries of prayer, devastating their villages: all this destruction for the Hand, sisters no longer.

Crumpled under a sand bunker, the girl wrapped herself with her arms in an attempt to make herself as small as she possibly could. In that moment, she wished nothing more than to be one of the grains of sand that surrounded her. Alas, the Heathens were far more skilled at wretched games of hide and seek.

Dragged by her hair, the girl kicked and flailed, screaming to draw attention from the Maidens, but they could not get to her.

The Knyghts sent by the Kingdom began their infiltration of Zemergad, raping the land with explosives. It took every bit of their power for the Maidens to call out to their Lady for strength. Though by the time Lilith granted them guidance, the girl was on her way to the Kingdom where she was to be held prisoner until her fate was decided.

The Maidens had eventually rid the land of outsiders, putting protective wards in place. Their land now inaccessible to anyone but their own — not even Heathens could enter.

The Maidens clung to one another in support and misery.

An eye for an eye, he had said.

PART ONE

—

"SOVEREIGN OF THE UNIVERSE! THE WOMAN YOU GAVE ME HAS RUN AWAY."

I
BEKA

The children arrive where a small patch of fig trees grow, our meeting spot, well before I do.

The trees are short, flourishing with purple and green pods. Petrus is crouched beneath the branches, swatting at the plump fruits as if they're a couple of flies. I wasn't sure if the children would join me on my journey to the orchard, but it seems the excitement for the harvest was well received. I can see their joy in the way Aravae dances around the bushels and in the wide grin Sarya gives me when she sees me walking towards them.

"Beka!" Petrus calls out. He ducks under the tree and bursts into a sprint, barreling towards me.

"Well, aren't you all a bunch of early birds?" I say, opening my arms up to engulf the boy in a hug.

"I got to the tree first!" Sarya brags. She's no older than eight with skin that clings to her bones like a wet sheet.

"We've been waiting for *hours*," Aravae, the eldest of the three, whines.

"I told you I was leaving at dawn," I smile down at them.

I attempt to move forward, but Petrus clings to my dress with his stubby fingers, wrapping his arms around my legs to keep me in place.

"The sun's nearly risen!" Sarya points out. She skips ahead, starting our walk to the orchards on the outskirts of our village.

A chuckle escapes my throat as I stumble, trying to move with Petrus's iron grip on my bottom half. "Pet— c'mon, let go."

"*Petrus has a crush on youuuuu,*" Aravae teases.

Petrus drops his grin and glares at the girl, unhooking himself from my legs. He scampers after Aravae with revenge on his mind. "I do *not*!"

I laugh as the three children chase each other, racing to the nearest tree. A gravel path weaves through the Grimfree fields all the way to the orchard, tall stalks of corn surrounding us. The roofs of cottages peek over the brush in the distance amidst flashes of yellows, oranges and reds. It's finally autumn, my favorite time of the year.

As cheeky as they are, the little ones are a joy to watch and their presence fills the absence of my regular helpers. I watch them scramble ahead, pushing one another in what seems to be a game of tag. Petrus gets his two hands on Aravae and shoves her into the brush, jumping up and down victoriously.

"Petrus! Don't shove her like that!" I scold, unable to hide my shock.

"She deserved it!"

To my surprise, only half of the trees in the orchard have reached full bloom, the others scarce in sweet abundance. Sarya, Aravae, Petrus and I scale through each row for hours, plucking whatever we can.

The orchard provides most of our income, but I try not to worry in front of the children.

Autumn is for the harvest.

Winter is for baking and staying close to an open fire.

Spring and summer are our busiest seasons by far, with farmers hurrying to get their crops in the ground ready for rainfall.

It was many years ago now when Emelyne brought me along to my first harvest.

She had been so excited. My ears rang as she riddled me with facts on seeds and planting patterns, pointing out the little caterpillars at the roots of trees waiting for fallen fruit. She handles her gardening with the utmost care, as she does with everything she loves. It rubbed off on me: my heart swells as the sight of these trees, red bulbs drooping from their branches.

Before leaving for the harvest, we had nothing but three empty wheelbarrows: now, all are generously filled. Petrus is barely able to push one on his own. Aravae and Sarya each take a side and work together on another. I stroll casually, pushing mine at a slow pace. Morning walks through the fields are my favorite, especially during this time of year — even if it took me a while to get used to the chill.

I balance my barrow beside a tree and step out into the grass. Here, if I stand still enough, I can pick out the faint sounds of crashing waves as the wind blows my stray hairs in every direction.

"Can I see?" Sarya's voice doesn't startle me.

"Of course, here." I reach my arms out to the girl and hoist her up onto my left shoulder.

Beyond the meadow and over the hills, the sea expands before us.

That first time Emelyne brought me here, she walked me down to the shores of the sea where I made my first sand castle. In the distance Sirens had wailed, and I remember crying into her arms for the first time. Not out of pain, but out of love.

I hear Sarya exhale. "It's so blue."

"Just like your eyes."

Sarya looks down at me with a toothy grin as Petrus and Aravae catch up to us, begging for a peek at the water too. The view captures their attention, so it takes some convincing to rally the children together for our walk back to Brighes. They abide, but only after I promise to take them to the shore someday to play in the sand and have a picnic.

We return to town during its busiest hour. The market bustles with chatter and encouraging gestures, beckoning curious eyes to linger by stalls where fresh crops are all the buzz. Corn and wheat typically fetch for a high price in the Isles, but here neighbors sell to neighbors. Wool is a fair trade for a sack of grain or even a few strips of beef. I spot a few peddlers weaving through the crowds, shoving tins of cinnamon and clove into the faces of unconvinced shoppers. We wheel past stalls loaded with brass and copper cooking vessels, candlesticks and spurs, horseshoes and nails. I glance over the stall loaded with fine fabrics, all of their silks and linen imported from the Isles — too expensive for a place like Brighes. Their merchants are scammers, anyway.

There are few Knyghts lingering in the mix, some running daily checks, others inspecting the market for supplies of their own. Rarely do they spend more than a day in the far stretches of the Domain. Lycidas says they get too hot underneath all that metal.

"Aye, nice pickings!" Miss Ysabelle hollers.

She stops her sweeping outside the bake house to marvel at the bounty the children and I are rolling in with. Petrus gleefully waves at his mother, bursting with pride. A few stalls down, Old Barnadas sits behind his table of fish, chewing a stale sliver of straw. The town Cleric, Elys, steps in our path as well, blessing the fruit with a quick prayer.

The rush of the market is behind us now as the wheels of our barrows rumble over the bridge, a thick slab of wood that passes over the stream. Emelyne is outside our cottage up ahead, setting up woven baskets for the harvest to fill up.

"Miss Emmy! Miss Emmy! Look at all the apples!" Petrus proclaims.

"Oh, how wonderful!" she claps her hands together, beaming at the sight of us. A gray shawl is pulled around her arms, swallowing her gaunt frame in its wool.

"I'm the best farmer there is," Petrus stamps his feet the last few yards, resting his barrow right beside the empty baskets.

"No, I am!" Sarya counters, pointing at her barrow.

"Well, every good farmer gets a reward for their efforts. I made a sweet treat for you all — why don't you go inside and grab it!"

The kids rush in a disorderly manner, roaring words of quick gratitude as they race through the door into our cottage. I gather the front of my dress and step around my barrow to approach Emelyne. She welcomes me into her thin arms.

"Petal, how was your day?"

"Perfect," I say, pulling back with a grin. "The leaves are changing."

"Autumn is here then," she hums, surveying the load. Her eyes are creased with content: three full barrows are plenty for the next few weeks. Business should be steady enough. "And the kids were helpful?"

"Oh, they were just fine. They aren't Lycidas, but any help is appreciated. I think I have some new helpers from now on."

"I don't think the pack has left just yet," Emelyne comments, eyeing the door to our cottage. "I'm going to go check on our little farmers. Petrus likes to play with his food."

She pats my shoulder before stalking off. I begin gathering apples in my arms to carry them over to the baskets for display.

"Ah, I came at the perfect time, didn't I?"

As if summoned by the mention of his name, Lycidas appears by my side, plunging one of his large hands into a barrow. He picks one out to hold it up like a prize.

"There you are!" I jump forward, locking him in a tight hug. My arms barely connect around his thick torso. He towers over me as most Howlers do.

Standing this close, I can smell the stale aroma of grain coating his body — he spends all day at the Granary, transferring wheat and corn from silo to silo.

Lycidas pulls away, a kind smile stretched across his stubbled mouth. "I had to see all these glorious apples for myself! It's all you ever talk about these days," he notes, going for a bite.

"Hey! Those are for *sale*," I tease, pinching his arm.

"What if these apples were poisoned? I'm merely sacrificing

myself to taste this fresh batch. Would you dare to let one of those youngins risk their life for the cause?" he jokes.

"I bet you Sarya would do it. She's pretty fierce, you know."

Lycidas ignores my comment and inspects the apple, rubbing his thumb against its skin. "I approve. Would make for some marvelous cider."

"You don't even *like* cider."

"But Rudi does! And everyone else. They trust my opinion," he crosses his arms.

"Fine, then I hope you don't mind helping me put the rest of the apples on display? Since you ditched me this year."

"So that's how it's gonna be, huh?" he huffs dramatically. "I guess I have some spare time on my hands."

We start unloading the barrows, careful not to bruise any of the fruits as we go. Lycidas shows off, gathering at least a dozen in one scoop, two of which nearly slip from his grasp and onto the gravel. I threaten him with a gentle kick to his shin.

"I hope this isn't how you treat those poor children when they help you," he feigns a gasp.

"Oh no, never," I sigh, placing one, two, three apples on display. "But you're no child."

Lycidas scoffs but doesn't argue back, opting instead to start a race of who can unload the barrows the quickest.

In no time at all, the work is done. I stand back with my hands on my hips, surveying the six filled baskets — Emelyne will be pleased.

"How soon do you leave?" I ask, glancing at Lycidas's getup. He's dressed for a journey: thick brown trousers, a loose shirt and a leather jacket that's cracking at the seams. A pack bursting with items rests on one of his shoulders, and in the center of his chest, sleeping against his brown skin, lies the translucent white of a Moonstone, wrapped about his neck with a thread of twine.

"A few left yesterday," he explains, a black curl falling over his face. "Rudi and I hadn't finished our rounds at the Granary until early this morning. We're heading out soon with the others."

I swivel my head and, sure enough, notice a small pack of Howlers walking about the village, picking up supplies before they leave. I spot a very tired looking Rudi amongst the pack, Lycidas's best friend. Seeing the lot of them together is a sight — not that they're uncommon, but just that they're drastically larger than any other being.

"You must be exhausted."

"Same old, same old," Lycidas merely shrugs.

"Every night, Emelyne insists on riding to the shore just to tuck you into bed herself."

"*Every* night? Oh, she worries too much! As do you — I'm okay!" he stresses.

"Alright, fine," I sigh. "But please, travel safe. Maybe you'll get some apple pie when you return."

He hums in approval.

"It's strange," he starts, changing the subject, "I seem to forget about time when I'm working, then all of a sudden my muscles start to ache, the gums in my teeth start to stretch."

"I can't imagine."

"Oh, you have *no* idea. I mean, it hurts a few days before, and yet, my goodness, Beka. I can't explain how it feels once it's here, shining down on me," he sighs.

"If only it were safe enough for you to Shift here."

"Right? Sure would save us a trip through Thessonne. That place is depressing."

"Better than going through the Peaks — I hear Harpies *love* the taste of grain," I tease. Lycidas just rolls his eyes. "And don't forget to bring back gems from the Sanctum. Petrus won't stop bugging me with his scheme to snatch your Moonstone."

"*That's* why he's been following me around. I *knew* Emelyne was teaching those kids to be thieves!" He's only poking fun, but to steal a Moonstone from a Howler is a cruel act to play. Without the stone, days that aren't blessed by the full moon are nearly unbearable for someone like Lycidas.

I laugh, embracing him one last time before he departs.

Once a month, when the moon is full, the Howlers across Sumeria cease their work and leave for the Lunar Sanctum — a portion of the woods granted to the Howlers. It's only on a full moon when their curse is released, allowing them to Shift into their most natural state. He's gone only a few days, but I miss him nonetheless.

Brighes isn't the same without him — he's family.

"You should come visit, you know. Nadine won't stop bothering me about seeing you again."

My heart stills slightly but I cover my hesitation with a smile.

"I wish I could, but Emelyne needs my help," I reason.

"It would be a short trip," he says, eyeing me. "But I get it. Harvesting season and all."

"I promise, maybe someday," I say, disheartened. "Nadine

can come back here anytime she'd like. I'd love to see Jeane as well."

"Nadine looks up to you, and she's been getting both painfully bored *and* on my nerves. Very easily, might I add. I blame you for the pest she's turned into."

"She has an older sister to learn from," I say.

Nadine and Jeane are the Shepard's daughters, the leader of the Lunar Sanctum. Lycidas has known them since he was just a cub, and it's always fun when they visit Brighes. I really do miss them, but I can't leave.

"Hey," he nudges my arm. My eyes focus back on his face, familiar and safe. "Take care, will ya?"

I nod. "You too."

He steps back to walk away, but not before plucking an apple from a basket and stuffing it in his pack.

"For good luck!" Lycidas cheers. I laugh at his silly gesture. Before I turn around, he quickly shouts after me, "Oh, Beka! I stopped by Inez's house earlier. She's not getting any better. Maybe you could drop by?"

"Oh, dear, still?" I mumble. "Thanks for letting me know."

Lycidas waves and then joins the rest of the Howlers in the square. A group of Knyghts are with them now, ready to take a headcount.

I spend no time watching the rest unfold.

I quickly gather a few apples and rush a few doors down.

All the cottages in our village are made of the same pale oak, hedged by cobblestone and topped with thatched roof tops. It's easy to mistake one neighbor for another, but I know Inez's place by the stone well placed in the front of her yard.

I knock on the front door where her sister, Gallienne, welcomes me inside.

"Oh, thank Eve!" She exclaims, taking the apples from my hands.

I stretch my neck past the girl, looking around their humble abode. Their house is clean, in similar set-up and shape as my own: wooden cabinets and tables, cloth draping over windows, and a blazing fire trapped behind iron. An emblem of the Kingdom hangs beside the fireplace: tree branches painted in gold, twisted into the image of a large tree with two figures standing on either side of its trunk. A man and a woman, their hands intertwined. Inez and I had shown the children at school how to make the same emblem with twigs foraged from the forest. This one I imagine Inez took home from our lessons.

"Lycidas told me Inez was still poorly. Is she alright?"

"She was getting better a few days ago, but now she's completely bedridden. She says it hurts too much to stand," Gallienne explains as I find my way to her sister's room.

Inez is there, lying in bed with a cloth over her forehead, her thin, brown hair splayed out on her pillow. She's tucked under multiple quilts, one of them I remember Emelyne stitching together with her frail hands.

"Inez," I whisper, falling to her side.

"Her fever broke two nights ago, so that's good. But she hasn't been able to keep any food down." Gallienne comes close to my side, looking down at her sister.

Inez stirs and opens her eyes.

"I'm not dead yet," she struggles to sit up, wincing in pain.

I reach out immediately to lie her back down. "I'm not dying, either, so please stop."

I sigh, feeling slight relief that my friend is able to find a way to antagonize us.

"Well, you don't *look* the greatest," Gallienne defends.

"You look just *fine*," I playfully retort, "but please, stay in bed until the pain goes away. I'll go to Emelyne and see what she has to say."

"Should we call a Haelend?"

"No!" I stand abruptly. Gallienne stares at me with incredulous eyes. "There's no need. You'll be okay, right?"

"Right," Inez affirms, followed by a low groan.

She glares at her sister and whines again, the pain causing her face to twist.

"I'll be back. Hold on tight," I say to Inez before fleeing their cottage and rushing towards my own.

I'm greeted by scattered crumbs across our meal table, remnants of Petrus, Aravae, and Sarya eating up the treats Emelyne made for them. I quickly swipe all the rubbish into my hand, ditching them out the door before striding across the room to the open fire. Emelyne sits in her rocking chair, knitting patterns from red yarn.

"Beka," she chimes. "Where had you gone off to?"

I take a seat on my chair beside Emelyne's. She sets her work down and reaches for my hand. I close the distance and rub her knuckles to relieve her joints.

"Inez is still sick. I went to check on her."

Emelyne's face falls just a touch at my distress. "Poor girl."

The wood crackles with heat, popping ash into the air. For a moment, I allow myself to rest and be present in my own body. During the day, I spend so much time busying myself that I forget to slow down.

"Petal, is she okay?" Her gentleness eases my mind, as always.

"She'll be fine, but her stomach is in knots. Are there any remedies you recommend?"

Emelyne's forehead pinches in thought. She's a very lovely lady, and sometimes I like to imagine what she looked like when she was my age of eighteen. I presume she was as beautiful as her face suggests now. Her hair must have been long and dark, whereas now it lies just above her shoulders, thick and gray with age.

"What about a Haelend? Can't they help?" Emelyne asks.

I shake my head, suppressing the urge to scream *no*.

It would be wise to call for a trained healer, but I fear that they will sense something more extreme happening that would require the presence of a Heathen. I simply can't risk it.

"Hmm," she ponders carefully. "Long ago, when I was pregnant, my favorite remedy was a mug of boiled ginger with a dash of honey. That should help with the aching."

"But she isn't pregnant," I insist. The very idea frightens me.

"It's not just for pregnant people, petal," Emelyne says, touching my cheek. "Don't worry too much or you'll wilt."

I sigh. I know, I *know* she mustn't be. I just can't handle the thought of encountering Heathens, or the stress that follows the ritual of birth.

"Then I'll bring her some right away."

"You are a lovely friend," Emelyne comments as I stand and make my way to our kitchen. I search our few cabinets until I find some fresh ginger root waiting just for me. "Stay with Inez as long as you need."

I flash her a small smile before heading out the door, crossing the path back to my friend.

"*Bleugh*," Inez coughs after one sip. "This is horrid."

"Come on," I persist, pushing the cup back to her lips. Her face twists in disgust, taking a chaste gulp of the liquid. "It's not so bad."

"You try it!" Inez whines, but further obeys my orders.

"You don't like ginger?"

She shakes her head dramatically, making me laugh.

"Are you feeling any better?" I ask.

Inez nods, very reluctantly draining the rest of her cup. I shift on my chair beside her bed to grab for the kettle.

"Gallienne was being dramatic, I think. I'm glad she listened to you and didn't call for a Haelend. Thanks to you, I'll be fresh in the morning," Inez says with a forced smile.

I shoot her a skeptical look, pouring her another glass. She recoils when I try to hand her the cup.

"Drink up!"

"Nope. You said *one* dose," Inez says, scrunching her nose.

"You can never have too much ginger tea," I sigh, nearly defeated.

"Oh, yes you definitely can," Inez deflates back into her pillow. "Why ginger anyway?"

"Helps with upset stomachs. Emelyne said she drank it when she was pregnant."

"I see," Inez voices, her eyes going placid as she stares at the bare wall.

There's a moment of awkward silence. The candlelight flickers by my side, its shadow moving in the space above my friend's head.

"You're not," I start, unsure what this pause could mean.

Inez snaps out of her daze.

"Hmm? Pregnant? No, of course not," Inez brushes off. "I mean, I couldn't be."

"I don't know what you get up to in your spare time. You could have a secret lover for all I know," I tease. "Have you been on the rag recently?"

If looks could kill.

"I'm not pregnant," she dismisses.

"I was just checking."

She sighs, "You would be the first to know of such a thing."

My eyes roll and Inez catches my nerves, reaching forward to grab my hand.

"Thank you for taking care of me."

"Always."

"I would do the same for you."

"I mean, I would hope so. You should get some rest," I say with a smile, cupping her cheek in my hand. Her skin is still damp, hot to the touch.

"If you say so."

It takes a while but Inez finally settles to sleep — I'm glad to see her eyes shut, tucking her away into a quiet slumber.

My thoughts have subdued to a tiny buzz, though they are relentless in reminding me of everything that could possibly go wrong.

I eventually fall asleep in the chair, back hunched with my head resting on the bed beside Inez's body.

I dream of Heathens, birthing rituals and angels — the angels she fears. Each with six feathered wings, their bodies guarded by interlocking rings adorned with all-seeing eyes.

But they can't hurt her.

Not with the chains of something much stronger than this world looping through each curve, tying them down to who knows what.

She's there too, smirking in the darkness of my own mind as I forget.

Forget all over again.

From miles away, the sound of a Banshee's cry is said to be agonizing. Like thunder ripping through the sky, its horrible wail has the ability to ricochet across Sumeria.

Perched on my shoulder, it submerges me. It's a piercing, gurgling sound that turns my brain to mush. I glue my palms to my ears, trying to block out the sound. Even after I think the screaming has ceased, I can still hear the echo of it pinging around in my head.

In a daze, I peel away my hands. They're covered in blood. *My* blood, and it's dripping down my jaw.

It's dark all around, inside and out. I scramble for a match to light the candle beside Inez's bed.

My heart sinks to my feet, and it crushes once my eyes adjust and find her in the flickering light. Her eyes are open, wide and bulging out of their sockets. The brown in them is broken, cracked with red lines. Her body is twisted with struggle: arms up by her head, legs open wide. The blankets that had been drawn over her body lay crumpled on the floor. I search for a sign of injury, but find none, and allow myself to accept the worst explanation for the blood soaking the cot beneath her legs.

I think I hear Gallienne enter the room, howling at the sight of her lifeless sister. She grips my forearm, her nails digging holes into my skin. In a frenzy, I pry her hands away, backing out of the room, stumbling on my numb feet. I pay Inez and her twisted face one last glance before I turn and dart for the door — my mind screaming at me to find help.

I burst out of the cottage and catch an image of the wailing woman, fading in and out of existence as her body trembles with warning. She's in all white, translucent like the fog that settles over Falldare Meadows. Her cry has summoned a few villagers out of their own homes, stumbling into the night. I lock eyes with Miss Ysabelle who, too, sees the Banshee before she vanishes into thin air, her work now finished.

2
AALIS

She's there in my dreams.

She's there in the darkness behind my closed eyes, her own filled with tears and terror. She's there when I reach out, touching the ghost of her presence between veils, immortalizing her. She's here now. Each stroke of my brush is proof that she exists — that she always has, even if only in my eyes. I stare at her face on my canvas and I'm met with beauty, fear, torture burning through the linen.

I try to remember.

I call out her name in my head, screaming in my thoughts until I feel the words throb like a vein, keeping the memory of her alive. I find myself talking to the moon every night, praying for her safety, begging for a sign that she lives on. I catch myself hoping that she's out there looking at the same stars and sky, finally safe, perched up against the blackthorn trees that border Tilver — where I told her to go.

There is a knock at my door followed by the cautious voice of my servant, Selova.

"Your Highness," she announces carefully from the hallway.

I snap out of my thoughts in an instant, feeling a rush of shame flood into my face. I cough awkwardly, realizing how carried away I'd gotten.

"Yes?" I call out, scurrying out of my seat to place my dirtied brushes in a jar of water.

I scramble to take the canvas off the easel and rest it against the far wall, the face of the girl turned from the prying eyes of the masses.

"The King has sent for you. He requires your presence and expects you to be dressed for the occasion in the next hour."

"What for?"

"The Princess' ball, your Highness," she drones.

I'd completely forgotten about Clement's birthday.

I hadn't even noticed the lack of sunlight coming in from the paneled window. I look down at the splatters of paint recklessly soiling my clothes, my pale hands stained with crusted smears of color. Creator, help me.

"Your Highness?"

Right.

"Yes, of course," I rip my eyes up and stride over to the door, swinging it open. "My apologies for keeping you waiting."

Selova shakes her head. We both know there's no need for me to apologize.

"Does the King happen to know where I've been?" I ask, not entirely sure why I should be concerned.

The King knows what my art means to me. It's the only corner of my life he is yet to invade. When I was younger, he used to post several guards outside my doors — both bed-chamber and drawing room, waiting to escort me around the castle. I've never, not once, even for a single second of my life so far, left the confines of the palace grounds.

After years of relentless begging — for trust, for freedom — the King finally let me have this for myself. This one thing.

"He's been asking for you for the last hour, your Highness."

On the surface, Selova is the picture of respect, but something like disdain tinges her voice whenever she has to deal with me.

I can't help but shift awkwardly on my feet. I am a Royal, yes, but many of the servants and Knyghts behave otherwise. They think I don't hear their taunts, their jeers, or see their sneers — the ones that hang, draw and quarter my spirit. They think I can't hear the way they spit my name out as if it were poison, as if it were some virulent sap on the tip of their tongue making them sick to their very core. They behave as though I am the laughing stock of the Kingdom: just a silly little thing who can't leave the castle. Their future King. I regard the wooden chair with wheels beside her now — the extent of my freedom. I glance back and forth between it and myself in the mirror, unkempt and bothered.

"I won't be needing that," I dismiss, offering her a weak smile.

I don't know why the King insists on me being carted around — my legs, my spine, my movement aren't the problem. I can walk just fine, but no matter how many times I protest, he insists nonetheless.

Too fragile, too costly, he always says, making me out to be sicker than I actually am.

My blood is not a plague, despite what he thinks. It's as if he wishes to wrap me in cotton and keep me locked up in the highest room of the tallest tower, never to feel the world beneath me with my own two feet.

Selova eyes me up, dubious as to why I've rejected the restraints of the chair, waiting for an explanation. Instead, I ask, "How much longer until the celebration?"

"It is in the next hour, your Highness," she repeats, clearly wishing she were elsewhere. "Hardly enough time to get you ready."

She looks at me with bated breath, awaiting my request of assistance, but I don't need her scorn. I'm not the helpless little creature they all make me out to be. I can do this myself.

"I'll go get ready, then," I murmur, feeling her disapproval drill into the back of my head as I turn to leave.

"And I shall go run your bath, sir," she grumbles.

Selova's steps, along with the churning of the chair, trail behind me as I walk in the direction of my bedchamber. As always, my steps are careful and slow with the strong thump of my heart. Too strong for a mere mortal like me.

I was still-born, pried out of my dead mother's stomach like a tumor. The Elders of Zemergad gave me a second chance at life, but at the cost of my human heart. I am human by every definition of the word save that precious organ. By that, I am impossibly Maiden. And it is too strong for me to handle.

I'm not particularly in the mood for a ball.

Though as it seems, my attendance not only matters to the King, but to my sister too — though they have always held little regard for what I want to do, who I want to be, and how I want to feel.

Growing up as I have, I've learnt to accept that I must at least act eager to do what I am told. I am watched for my every move, checked for my manners, and there is something constantly expected of me.

Within the stone walls of the castle, I do not belong to myself. I can't imagine I ever will. I can't imagine I'll ever even belong to Ead. Not with the blood that runs through my veins — a reminder that I could not even come to this life without someone's help. Painting is the only thing I know is mine. The drawing room is the only form of escape I have from daunting halls and damning chambers. What's in there is my own. At least that I have the power to control.

Red and gold.

Two colors I don't think look particularly great on me. They clash too much with my complexion, washing me out into a sickly gray. My hair is of a similar pallor, just a few shades away from the honey marigold of the suit jacket Selova has draped over my back.

Pushing each of my arms through the sleeves, I can't help but feel silly — I look less like a Prince and more like a doll. I fiddle with the tight cuffs that curl around my wrists, threatening to cut off my circulation. Selova comes up behind me and gives my forearm a slight smack before helping me adjust the buttons. I look down at the shining black shoes squeezing my toes. My tan trousers are a little short, exposing a sliver of skin above the ankle. How can I possibly be expected to behave and have fun when I feel so uncomfortable?

"My suit doesn't fit me well," I remark.

"You missed your fitting. This will have to do for now," Selova sighs. "At least *try* to smile," she adds. She's now on her knees, doing her best to tug the trousers over my peeping socks. "The celebration is for the Princess."

As if saying this will help?

Selova gives me a scornful glance through the mirror, as unamused by me as always.

Crimson red and marigold.

Not only must I wear them to any occasion open to the public, but I must also be forced to see no other colors but the two since they stand for the Kingdom of Ead.

Translations of them cover every inch of the ballroom in shimmering drapes hanging from the ceiling and silk cloths spilling over large tables. Even the gilded candelabras bleed red wax.

I spot the King at the far end of the room, sitting in his large throne of red velvet and *more* gold. His Royal advisor, Seth, stands diligently beside him with his hands behind his back. The King is dressed in a regal suit similar to mine, only adorned with precious jewels and the finest crystals Sumeria has to offer — most of them stolen from Zemergad.

A fur robe hugs at his shoulders, draping down his back, falling to the side of his throne. His beard is sharp and freshly cut, his crown fashioned with rubies resting securely atop his combed head. His observant eyes lock with mine as I stride towards him.

The ballroom is a circle lined with towering windows and a dome roof made of stone and marble: a magnificent place for a celebration. Servants mill all around me as I try to walk through with a straightened back and my chin held high, though my feigned authority quickly wavers with the ever growing presence of paralyzing anxiety. My foolish lungs feel as though they are going to run out of air at any given moment.

"If you had allowed yourself to be escorted in your chair, then maybe you would have gotten here in a timely manner," The King says calmly.

I bow before him and then take my seat to his left, a step lower than his throne.

"You know full well that I can walk just fine, sire," I sigh. "There is no need to worry."

"I will always worry," he replies, an edge to his tone. "You missed breakfast this morning."

"I was busy in the dr—"

"Your drawing chamber, of course. Will this continue to be a problem, Aalis? You cannot forfeit your duties."

"It was just breakfast."

"Breakfast or not, being late is one thing, but refusing to show up altogether? It is unacceptable. Do you think, had I behaved this way with my King, that I would have gotten away with it? It would have been a whip on the back. Your *condition* is no excuse. Or shall I ask the help to bolt the doors to your *drawing chamber*?" He sneers out the final couplet.

The rising hem at my ankles seems far more interesting than the eyes of the King. I shake my head, blond curls slipping across my bowed forehead.

"You are to rule Sumeria. An honor bestowed upon me by my King, and his King before him for generations you cannot deign to count. An honor from Adam himself," he remarks. He's not even looking at me: his eyes are on the entrance, awaiting the arrival of our guests. Nothing new here. "Do not disappoint him."

I huff, turning my gaze to the entrance where I watch my sister practically waltz in. At her arrival, the servants seize their actions, eyes blazing with admiration. Her beauty is undeniable, and the way she carries herself is truly something to marvel at. I sit up to fix my failing posture as she reaches the dais. Unlike my golden get-up, Princess Clement is dressed in a billowy, light pink gown — near blush — with delicate white flowers braided into her silken yellow hair. A ruby pendant the size of a baby's fist hangs across her throat, sitting in the space between her collarbones. Her skin is fair like mine, but it glows bright like porcelain, glazing her.

"Father," she beams, all performance, offering him a curtsy. "The ballroom looks marvelous!"

"Clement," he nods. "Take your seat."

She waits a moment for him to say more, but he doesn't. I roll my eyes at her desperation for approval to which she glares straight back before taking her seat to my left. I don't know why she even tries with him. Creator knows I don't.

"You look beautiful. Surely you'll find a suitor tonight," I say sincerely as guests mingle in groups.

"Your jacket is too tight," she mutters.

I expected nothing less from her.

The three of us sit quietly as the ballroom fills with idle chatter. A harpist strums a whimsical tune beside us. The song echoes throughout the hall, welcoming our guests, citizens of our Kingdom — most of them descendants of Adam and Eve. Also in the mix are wealthy shopkeepers and villagers from

Surlise and Eephifer, with even a few nomads from Neelem. *Our people*, as the King likes to call them.

The harpist fades to a stop and the room falls silent.

Approaching the dais in a sweeping movement is the Cain, ruler of the Great Church, formally known as the Arcadian Monastery, Knyghts flanking every side of him. His presence causes the ballroom to still and witness this rare public exchange.

"Your presence is always a pleasure and honor," the King bows. Clement and I mimic our father's gesture, a courteous welcome. "I thank you on behalf of the Kingdom for attending tonight's celebration."

The Cain dips his head slightly in acknowledgement. His face is covered by a sheer cloth, held down by a dainty, golden crown with spouting green leaves. Nobody knows of his age, and though his voice is stern and his authority vast, you just can't miss how young he sounds.

"Thank you, your Majesty. The pleasure is all mine," the Cain responds ardently.

Sumerians look at both the King and the Cain as the two highest powers.

The first Cain, the firstborn son of Adam and Eve, murderer of Abel, devoted his life to his parents. On his deathbed, he passed his title on to his firstborn son, who passed his title on, and so forth. The Hyttenrauch line was selected by the first Cain all those years ago, and since the beginning of our time, Church and State have always been one. So much so, that when the dreaded time comes, I will stand before the Cain as he performs a Divine Ceremony, tying my blood to the soil of Sumeria, crowning me as the ruler of the land. My stomach threatens to spill out at the thought.

Long have I argued with the King, with Clement, over this: never have I ever wanted this Empire — never have I wanted it to be mine. But as the Edenic faith does not allow for women to inherit the throne, it is my burden to bear, no matter if Clement is four years my senior. I realized it to be her main cause of resentment towards me some years ago, even if I believe she is far better suited for the throne.

I watch the King exchange words with the Cain. I can see the hint of contempt in his eyes. The King doesn't like to share. All it takes for him to feel utterly humiliated is being seen bowing to another port of power.

The Cain eventually stalks away toward his table, our guests following suit. The King stands and addresses the crowd once more but I fail to catch a single word he says, too busy playing with the cuffs of my sleeve, still trying to loosen the tight material.

Despite our distance, if it weren't for my sister, I'd be happily hiding away, drowning out my impending future as a serious, working noble. I do love her — I just find it hard to tell her when I know she no longer feels the same. It seems she has not cared for me since we were children. I am not her brother, but rather her burden.

"Happy birthday," I whisper over to her. Our eyes finally meet. Clement pays me no response, but I note a slight sheen coating her blue eyes, one so slight and easily missed, maybe one I will take as a 'thank you'.

It's the Princess's twenty-fourth birthday. Many would be surprised to hear that she's still unwed. I'm unsure if it's because the King could care less or if it's because Clement is too picky. Either way, Clement's always said that it didn't matter. Marriage has never been on her mind.

The ball is underway. I see her glowing in the center of the ballroom dancing with a handsome suitor. She looks like sunlight, beams of her beauty falling down on us all. Everyone's eyes shine as their gazes fall on her, as though we are in the presence of an angel. And here I am, hovering over the dessert table, shoving a sixth cake into my mouth. It's silly, really.

The cake slips from my mouth as a screech erupts in my ears.

I drop my plate onto the nearest table, enduring the noise as it fills every corner of my mind. It lasts only a few seconds, but my head feels as though it's been cleaved into dust.

I look around in shock, confused by everyone's behavior. The ballroom is still in full swing — people drinking and laughing and dancing. Did no one else hear that?

The sound continues echoing in my head, a relentless reverberation ringing from side to side. It's then I realize that this is no ring. Not even a scream, but a wail. I can't help but wail back.

The music has now stopped: all eyes are on me. I must've fallen, or at least stumbled, because I feel hands on me, forcing me to sit down in my chair. Someone must have fetched it. The King is standing before me, a strange expression written all over his face.

"Did anyone see what happened to him?" The King demands.

"Your Majesty, he looked very pale, and then I saw him stagger and almost collapse," a servant explains.

"Where is Celtis?" The King asks around.

I blink a few more times and feel my body slowly go back to normal. I turn my head and catch sight of Clement with her usual mask of disappointment.

I'm taken back to my bedchambers immediately. It takes five servants, the King and Celtis to escort me — the King insisting on watching Celtis perform an array of tests on me. Meanwhile, the servants bustle around, fetching water, medicine, and anything the King thinks I might need. I don't tell them that I feel fine. I don't tell them about the sound I heard. I don't ask if they heard it too. I barely have enough time to process what happened until everyone has left my room besides the Heathen.

"Make sure you drink the rest of that water before dozing off, your Highness," she advises.

Celtis is a small and beautiful woman, my personal Hae-lend, and most important to the King: a Heathen. Though her powers are now useless, her knowledge about my condition and how to treat it go beyond every head in the Kingdom. So I sit up to down the rest of the water.

"Is the celebration still underway?"

"People have started to leave," Celtis sighs.

"It wasn't a big deal, you know. I feel fine," I finish in a mumble.

"I know you *feel fine*, your Highness, but this is for your father's peace of mind."

Celtis walks forward to pour me another glass of water. "His Majesty will do anything to make sure you are well. I hope you understand why he takes so many precautions."

I have no choice but to drink up.

Celtis leaves after some time, bidding me good night. I try to get to sleep, but I eventually give up and stare at the ceiling. My beautiful, decadent ceiling, covered in scenes of Adam and Eve, my Kingdom's late saviors. I hadn't cared for it much until Clement. As a child, she would lay on my bed and stare at it for hours. Maybe this is where my love for art was born.

My mind is restless. I think I'm alright, and I do feel fine, but I can't shake the feeling of unease from my chest. The ringing lingers. It's unmissable.

I slip on a shaggy blouse and tug on some boots as the wooden clock beside the fireplace chimes with a faint song: it's long past midnight.

Opening the door to the hallway doesn't seem like an option, not when there are guards constantly posted there — and there's no way they'd let me leave after what happened at the ball. I turn into my closet and shove my way through with outstretched arms, my hands connecting with the back wall. I push my entire body up against the door built into the stone. It gives way, a secret entrance to a quaint little hall with another door hidden away at the far end — the door to my drawing room. Clement found this passageway years ago during a round of hide and seek. No one, save the two of us, know of it, but she wouldn't dare to come this way anymore.

I know something is off immediately upon entering the room.

The wick of the candle sitting on a nearby table looks freshly extinguished — tendrils of smoke curl through the air around it. It's not often I come in here to paint at night; I usually do my art in the daytime, relying more on the natural light streaming in through the window rather than the glow of a flame. It's a slight detail, but it's enough for me to panic.

My eyes snap over to my collection of paintings. The one I'd been painting earlier today has been moved, now resting face-up on a small table. I sneak over to the canvas and inspect it gingerly, looking for any signs of damage. My fingers lightly graze the face of the girl staring back at me, a hard tug pulling on my heart. How cruel to imprison her on my canvas out of the sheer desires of my heart.

"Right in here, your Majesty."

I freeze. Someone's outside the main entrance. I barely have enough time to sprint back over to the passageway and push it closed to hide me from plain sight, but it seems that luck is on my side. My heart drums against my ribcage as I hear the opening of the door — the padding of multiple feet.

"Are you certain?" the King's voice echoes. I cover my mouth, muffling my breathing.

"I wasn't going to bring it to your attention but," Selova's voice trails off.

I'm aware that she occasionally comes in here to clean, though I never thought her a snoop. I never thought she would bring the King in here like this, either.

"What have you found?"

"This is a waste of our time," another voice remarks, one I don't seem to recognize.

"*General!*" The King snaps. "What *are* you showing me, Selova?"

"I thought you should see this, your Majesty," Selova offers with a shaky voice. "It looks like her, doesn't it?"

Shit.

"Like *who*?" The other voice, the General, quips.

"I'm not suggesting that she's still alive because, *surely*, she couldn't have survived what happened during Lamya, but—"

"Why would my son paint this?" the King demands, anger slowly creeping into his voice.

"They're *all* of *her*, your Majesty."

A shiver rips through my spine.

"What exactly are you suggesting?" The King's voice is rigid.

The King detests the Maidens, that much is known by everyone. Ead and the Realm have a very long and tense history, one forbidden to discuss out of turn on this land. What's clear is that the Maidens stay in the Realm so long as the Kingdom doesn't interfere with their religious practices. Though that sort of peace is fragile, and I fear that he will be the one to shatter it.

"We don't have time for such senseless theories! The Dark Maid will continue to come for us if we don't act *now*."

"Bausan—"

"As discussed, we must work to purify the fallen village," the General declares.

"Send your troops out to Brighes, then! Go to Ochrore," the King snaps, exasperated. "I could care less what happens, so long as we work to eradicate her foul magic from our land for good."

"Yes, your Majesty, understood," Bausan snarls.

I remember who he is now: a famed commander. A jewel of Knyghthood. Once a nobody, now a somebody. *The* somebody. His success as a leader in the White Isles in the early stages of his career did not go unseen, hence his recent promotion to General of the entire Ashen Domain. The King seems to think his degree of discipline will influence the rest of the region — whatever that means. I see him sometimes at balls and celebrations, his appearance distinguished by his towering height and long, dark hair. The King speaks about him sometimes with a fondness akin to friendship, putting him in high regard within the Kingdom, something reserved for only a limited number of people.

"Have faith," he growls as heavy footsteps traipse across the room. The door slams shut and I know that he has left.

"My son knows something," the King speculates, nearly whispering.

"Your Majesty, she could still be out there. If I may suggest, I do believe that this incident with the Banshee is not coincidental," Selova says. I'm shocked by how she and the King speak so casually to one another. "It would not hurt to investigate, especially now that we've seen who your son has chosen as his muse."

"This must be kept at a hush. I don't want anyone knowing about these paintings. I must call upon our best scouts immediately."

Scouts?

There are a few muffled words exchanged between the two that I cannot understand, most likely whispers. I suppose it doesn't matter anymore — they have uncovered my biggest secret.

"I cannot pass on my reign until I know that wretched girl is dead," the King clamors.

Too afraid to hear anything else, I push away from the wall and rush back to my bedchamber.

I have no plan at all.

They'll let me sleep until morning, I presume. That gives me enough time. I rush around my room, retrieving an unused satchel from deep within my closet. I don't pack much.

I replace my undergarments and shuck on some black trousers. I stop in front of my mirror and comb my hair with my fingers, thinking about how long I've waited for this moment.

That sound I heard earlier, could it have been the scream of a Banshee? How could I have been the only one to hear it?

She might not even be in Ochrore for all I know, but if the King's troops go east, they could find her.

A white flash breaks my vision. I stumble, suddenly feeling faint, my heart on fire. I hadn't stopped to catch up with it.

I need to get to Domain quickly, though I wouldn't know the first thing about how. Despite not having ever left the palace grounds, my governess made sure I was well-read. I know I can't travel through the Sanctums unnoticed: there are guards posted on each border surrounding the forest. Going by horse would take too long and there's no way to cut around it. All I have is theory, no practice.

I walk over to my window and wonder. The waves of the sea crash against one another, sending water flying onto the side of the castle. Sometimes, if I'm really quiet, I can pick out the faraway songs of the Sirens: the daughters of Lilith and the fallen Samael. I've faintly heard their voices once before, full of desire. They never come on land — only ever close enough to return the body of a man sucked dry by seduction.

Then it hits me.

The *sea*.

It could work.

I hear ships come and go all the time full of supplies and plenty of fish for the Kingdom. I just need to follow the signs posted in the streets, wait by the docks until morning, and travel to the Ashen Domain from there.

Abeko, I yearn.

This could work.

3
ELIO

From where I'm perched, squeezed in the shadows between a frivolous tavern and scandalous brothel, I watch the clock tower, its hands welcoming in a new hour, singing to the depths of the townsquare and beyond.

I welcome the night, soothing the constant irritation of the sun against my body. Although late as it is, Eephifer is alive and running — Sumeria's Sleepless City.

With the rise of the moon begins the working day: taverns roar with music and laughter; street vendors prance around, trying to sell their stock to naive tourists; fellow Night Demons wander the streets and smile up at the dark sky.

I'm not smiling, though.

Oh no, I'm quite irritated.

I tap my foot and bite at my nail, bored and losing my patience.

I ventured out of my room at the inn not too long ago to stalk through the cobblestoned streets unbothered, searching for this agreed meeting spot. The brick is cool against my back as I lean against it; my hood draped over my head and shoulders, concealing myself from the public.

Those who needed to see me would.

It's the least I can do to not draw attention to myself,

which is a challenge in itself. I'm nearly the height of a Howler, which admittedly does have its benefits.

"Height is intimidating." Bea reasoned to me once. *"Although, you look more like a troll than a Howler if you ask me."*

Trolls don't even exist. Her insult didn't faze me in the slightest.

I figured it's fine: I still do my job better than anyone in the White Isles. Possibly in all of Sumeria. Still, I keep my head down.

I abandon my finger and pick at my trousers, pulling at a loose strand. I just bought these the other day and they're *already* fraying? I can't wait to leave Eephifier and go east where the textiles are far better quality. All people do here is gamble and carry bricks around. Fucking *bricks*. I even prefer the stone and cream marble of the Kingdom up north over the dull masonry fanatics here, thank you very much.

It's a quarter past one now and my client is late.

By now, people who ask for my assistance should know I don't appreciate tardiness. I don't wait for my payment. The threat should be simple enough and yet, here I am. Waiting outside a tavern like some desperate escort.

Bea would laugh at me if she were here, though I'm sure I'll receive her teasing when we meet later on. I already have my defense building up in my mind — this is a one time thing: you'll never catch me dead wasting minutes on a Kingdom Knyght ever again.

Personally, I think Knyghts are witless. Terribly gullible. Sometimes handsome, but for the most part rather dull-looking. Uninteresting. I often ramble Bea's ear off about my theories on what their training could possibly have looked liked. They swagger around with an unnecessary chip on their shoulder and shit-eating grins plastered on their faces. Some do their job, but most are far sketchier than the people they're supposed to enforce order upon. For a Knyght, one would expect they act with an ounce of authority. Most people seem convinced. However, all I see is a lame performance of unconvincing dominance and corruption.

I hear his footsteps long before he turns the corner to face me. I smirk at the ground, listening to his erratic heartbeat.

My client is finally here.

The Knyght takes a spot beside me against the brick wall, careful to leave space between us. I keep my head down and bite back the smirk forming on my face. There seems to be enough commotion going on in the square that I'm sure we'll go unnoticed.

"*Ahem*," he clears his throat after standing for a few silent moments. "I have your payment. But first, do you have as requested?"

I pick at my finger again. I listen to his heart threaten to burst through his chest. I push off the wall and stretch my arms out, pretending to yawn. The more of his time I can waste, the better. The buttons on my cloak loosen and pull apart, revealing my clothing. I'm wearing my favorite blouse: a deep emerald silk, the perfect color to compliment my red hair. Celestite dangles against my bare chest, the light of the moon catching its crystal fragments, making it glow.

I look back up at the Knyght and notice the details of his chained armor: the chunky silver plates married with a white and gray palette, the colors of the White Isles draped over his frame. A silver helmet conceals his face, leaving only two slivers of space for his eyes. For a second, I think of him to be an idiot for wearing his armor to a transaction with a thief. To each their own.

"Take the helmet off," I insist.

The Knyght hesitates. "But, this is supposed to be a *secret* operation."

I shrug, then begin to walk away from the wall. When I don't hear him following after me, I stop and beckon him over. We take a corner and stalk down an empty thorough-fare, only to turn again and land in another alley.

"There. No one will bother us, darling. Now, please, I prefer to exchange face to face."

The Knyght hesitates again before shucking his helmet off. His face is soft and his hair is tied back in a knot. I stand there nursing a coy smile. He's growing uncomfortable and oh-so selfishly impatient. The Knyght quirks his eyebrow at me, daring to look incredulous. The audacity.

"Well?" He chips at my silence.

I prowl forward and lean against the wall by his side, propping my elbow on the brick. I look him up and down, preying on his dwindling confidence. I must admit, he's one of the more handsome Knyghts I've worked for. He found me two nights ago to pitch his request, and I remember thinking about how much more attracted I'd be to him if he were a blond. His eyes are pretty, though. Green.

"You got a lot of nerve showing up here late and demand-ing things from me," I sigh, flashing a crooked smile to show off my pointed canines. "You saw that clock over there, right? It's big. Can't miss it."

The Knyght glances behind him and gulps. "I'm late. Forgive

me. I got caught up in Surlisle. Surely you've heard about the incident with the Banshee. Everyone's pretty alarmed."

I widen my eyes, feigning shock. "A wailing woman? It can't possibly be!"

The Knyght deadpans. "You think of it as a joke? Can't we just continue our business here?"

I chuckle and bring my hand forward to caress his cheek. He freezes. I swipe away the sweat beading on his forehead.

"I don't care about a bloody Banshee. I don't care about your excuse. I am a bit worried about your perception of time, though, for you ought to know that I have a strict hair routine," I pull away and draw my hood back, my hair falling down my shoulders in a raging fire. "I must brush it twelve times a day. However, it's only been cared for *ten* times today. While I've been waiting for you to arrive at a meeting *you* set up, I could have been brushing my beautiful locks. But I wasn't. I was withering away beside the ivy."

"Are you serious? You and your lot are so full of scum! I'm beginning to regret trusting—" he barely splutters before I snap forward and grab his neck with my hand. He's much smaller than me: I have at least five inches on him, and given my *certain* abilities, I'm stronger, regardless of his muscle. I drag him forward before slamming him against the wall, baring my fangs before his eyes. People pass us by on the street, seemingly unalarmed by the common scene of violence.

"My patience is thin. I warned you of this before," I sneer. "I got you those *damned* documents you were too afraid to get yourself. I barely batted an eye at the task. You doubt my skill for what I am? Let me remind you that I've heard all that shit before. At least I'll be a piece of *rich* scum, because I'm charging you extra for that one. And for being late."

The Knyght chokes out, his face turning a deep blue color. His eyes are practically bulging out of their sockets.

"Oh," I say, realizing I'm blocking his airway completely. "My bad." I release my grip on the Knyght and stand back, giving him room to heave, as he welcomes the air back into his lungs. His fighting coughs are music to my ears.

"I—" he starts. He coughs once more and stands back up, placing his hands against the wall to steady himself. "I wasn't—"

"By all means, take your time."

"I wasn't calling you scum for being a Night Demon. I hope you know that."

I could care less about what he thinks about my kind.

"I just, those documents. They're important. And if *anyone* finds out about this—"

"You'll be killed. Treason. Blah blah *blah*. Trust me, if anyone is going to kill you, it'll be me. I'll make sure of it."

"Thank you," he sucks in a huge breath.

"Pay me first," I demand.

The Knyght can now stand on his own. "How much?"

"Ten."

"Silver?"

"Gold."

His eyes go wide, "GOLD?! That wasn't our deal!"

"You were late. You called me scum. The amount is final and only fair," I shrug.

"I didn't bring that much," he admits, sullen.

This is my favorite part: this look Knyghts give me when

they are utterly defeated. This is what it feels like to be at the bottom.

"Well," I say, moving forward. The Knyght backs into the wall. "I have another form of payment that is just as precious as gold."

The Knyght chokes again. I'm not even touching him. "Are you— you're ridiculous! I'm not— I mean—"

"Oh, shut your trap! I don't want to sleep with you," I berate. The market these days. Shameful, truly. "I want to know your secrets."

"Secrets?"

"Precisely," I hum, close to his ear. He goes stiff under me. "What's so important about these documents, hm?"

"I'm surprised you didn't take a peek for yourself."

"I may be a thief but I don't pry," I lie. I can't technically read. At least not well. But he doesn't need to know that.

He shakes his head. "I can't. There's too much risk."

"Do I seem like someone who cares? C'mon, what in those documents has you so riled up?"

"I promise. I'll find you here tomorrow with proper payment. Please, just— I can't say. I'm sorry."

I hover over him for a long minute. I watch him struggle to leave my space and hide his worrying eyes. What a joke.

I did actually happen to peek at the documents, and of the words I did recognize. It seemed to be some sort of correspondence with a Commander in the Domain: it meant absolutely nothing to me.

"I'm not a very compromising guy, Iago," I drawl. My hands are on his sides now.

"How do you know my name?" he snaps.

I push away from him with a smirk. The weight in my hand feels like enough payment for now. In a swift movement, I snatch the parchment from the inside of my cloak and shove them at his chest. He stares at me in shock.

"You're boring. A secret or two could have created a lovely friendship between us."

"Wait! You—" he begins, surely finding that his pouch previously filled with gold is gone.

"You won't be seeing me," I wink before slinking off. "Good luck with those documents."

Of all the places Bea and I have stayed at, Eephifer is at the very bottom of my list.

It's not a terrible place, per say — I'd argue that it happens to be one of the cleanest districts in Sumeria. The night life is exciting and the streets are spotless by the time the sun comes up. Bea and I do spend most of our time here between jobs, even if it means having to scrape up some extra coins to pay for shelter, purely for convenience. The bricks here make for harder break-ins which reassures Bea when she's trying to get some sleep at night. Ironic since the nature of my work.

Eephifer sits in the very northwestern region of Sumeria, and although not directly connected to the Kingdom of Ead, it still ranks as the wealthiest district, gaining profit from masonry, lively taverns, and underground rogue operations. It's built upon red brick and cobblestone, a series of stone paths and buildings weaving like a gigantic maze.

Again, it's *nice*, and considered an opulence to reside in, but I can't shake the disgust that festers within me when I see Night Demons on their hands and knees scrubbing away at the stones, cleaning any imperfection, or seeing a Howler with scarred hands chipping away at old brick. This place depends on us Cursed Children for luxury. I'd love to see those bastard Knyghts live a day in our shoes. Maybe that's what makes the gold in my pocket feel so good. The privileged civilians and Knyghts think they have this place under their control. I go on letting them think that way.

It's well into the night now.

The streetlamps flicker with yellow flames as I make my way through the bustling atmosphere, sneaking through dancing crowds and avoiding chatty vendors. I'm seemingly calm, but my eyes are frantic, glancing here and there as I slip my hand in and out of tight spaces, the satchel at my side growing heavier.

It's a little too easy.

I descend down a stone staircase and duck under a wooden beam. A throng of Knyghts are gathered before the largest building in the district: the Guardian Headquarters. It's a tall looking thing adorned with even more currant-colored brick and pale asphalt, and brown wooden beams lining its sides. Just last night I slipped into the building unnoticed — the Knyghts are always so busy staring at the front gates that they forget the town is connected by rooftops. The metal of their helmets must have seeped into their brains.

The thing about all these regions in the White Isles is that the Kingdom entrusts their Knyghts to rule over the towns and people. Some do excellent jobs: Emsden is impenetrable when it comes to security. It's the one place I've actually gotten caught stealing. The Knyghts are far more intelligent there, but they also care for the people and treat them with a level of equity.

Here, the Knyghts are far more engrossed with their status. Bea says they all fantasize about getting Princess Clement's hand in marriage. She also says that *she'd* be the one to get to the Princess first, so they have no chance either way.

My point is, the level of authority here is nowhere near admirable.

Bea and I don't venture into the Ashen Domain as much, but I know it works a bit differently there. Alnola is really the only place where Knyghts have a level of jurisdiction: a strict one at that. The rest of the land beyond and around it rely on their people and community.

I arrive at a tavern called *The Dapper Jackal* and slip inside. It's dimly lit by hanging oil lamps and a fireplace or two strewn here and there. Rows of wooden tables are occupied by drunken civilians and criminals alike. A group of Knyghts rest at the bar top with their helmets off, carefree smiles streaking their faces. A woman sits atop a slab of open space in the back, humming an old tune while strumming a lute. I lock eyes with a stuffed black bear head, the tavern's prized ornament that hangs above the bar. I scale the walls, my arm sliding against it as I silently make my way to an alcove of tables and chairs away from the front. I find an empty chair and collapse in my seat, sliding down the wood and stretching out my long limbs. The long day dawns on me, and for once I consider letting myself fall into a deep sleep — not because I necessarily need it, but because some damned peace and quiet would be good for a change.

Instead, I wave over a young waitress and order a glass of

sour wine. She returns, placing the glass of red liquid before me. It's bitter, but not bitter in the way alcohol is to human folk. It's the fussy tongue of a Night Demon that makes any meal or drink besides blood taste like shit and charred ash — though, thankfully, not literally. We can stomach 'normal' food if needs truly be, but where's the bloody fun in that?

"Maybe it'll taste better if you sit up straighter," Bea jests, the sound of her chair scraping across the floor loud in my ears. She plops down across from me and sets her own drink on the table.

I pay her no mind. I touch my glass to my lips and empty the rest of the liquid freely into my mouth. It's absolutely revolting but I manage to choke it back with a smile.

"I happen to like the putrid taste of mundane liquor. It keeps me humble," I simply claim.

"Oh, because you're *so* humble?" she scoffs and levels my gaze, her obsidian eyes glimmering like topaz in the candle-light.

I shrug and clasp my hands together, leaning my elbows against the wood of the table. "I nearly broke my client's neck today with my fingers alone. I'd say I needed a drink."

Bea snorts and unbuttons her cloak, letting her hood fall back against her chair. Her thick, black locs fall in ropes around her shoulders, fanning around her leather armor. The silver scales of her breastplate look dull in the dim light.

"Now why," she starts before taking a large gulp of her drink, emptying half of her glass, "did you almost snap his neck?"

"He insulted me."

"What, did he make fun of your shirt?"

My face drops. "What's wrong with my shirt?" I press my palms against my blouse defensively.

She looks up at my hair. "Continue."

I look behind me, whining. "*What*?"

"Nothing."

"Well, no. I'm actually feeling a bit insecure about this," I pout.

Bea scowls, the charcoal around her eyes drowning her glare. Her expression doesn't scare me in the slightest, but if we hadn't been practically chained to one another since we crossed paths all those years ago, I would be completely terrified.

"Don't be a baby. Tell me about your job or I'll leave you out of my business," she threatens.

I sigh, deciding how long to wait before I share. Bea gets pissy when I beat around the bush.

"The prick called me ridiculous. And scum."

"Shocking!"

"He was also thirty minutes late."

"How *dare* he?"

"You're just mocking me now," I snap.

Bea just grins.

"Well, at least you got paid. Snuck into the Headquarters, too. Well done, Magpie," she winks, draining the rest of her drink.

"I hold your praise so near to my lifeless heart. I've told you that, right?"

"Oh, not since yesterday," she teases. I crack a smirk as we clink our now empty goblets.

She orders another round, and when my wine arrives, Bea

snatches it up before I can get my hands on it. Silently, she takes her dagger out of her belt and glides the tip across the skin of her palm. I turn away and glance around, watching the people of the tavern with keen eyes. I've trained myself to remember every detail of a room. My eyes find the small things — the ones so easily overlooked: a missing diamond in a woman's earlobe, the scars on the back of a Knyght's neck, the specks of rust on the chains holding the chandelier together. I look back at her and find my goblet in front of me again. I take it, barely regarding the darker red before taking a sip. The drink is still bitter, but it's now laced with a sweetness that replenishes a bit of my hollow stomach. My tongue sings with the sensation, and I silently thank her as I continue sipping. I ignore her fresh cut. Bea doesn't make a big deal of it so neither do I.

"Is there really something wrong with my shirt?" I ask again, only a little concerned.

"It's shit. Clashes with your hair," she shrugs.

I pinch the silk fabric between my fingers, stretching it out to catch her wandering eyes.

"This *shit* was too expensive for your attitude."

"Enough about your shirt. We'll be passing through Surlisle soon, anyways. You can get a new one there."

I ignore her back-handed comment and instead ask her about any new job opportunities. Bea seems happy to finally get to a topic regarding her work.

"I was sent a message from the King," she starts plainly.

I hardly conceal the shock in my expression: my head stretches forward and my eyes open wide, "*What?*"

"The *King* sent *me* a *message*," she enunciates as if I'm brain rot.

"I heard you. But, the King? Really?"

"I'm hurt by how surprised you sound."

"Well, I mean— it's the *King*. Sending *you* a direct message. That's not necessarily a typical occurrence for us. Or anyone, for the matter."

Bea just shrugs. "I don't know. I was scouted by some Knyghts from Surlisle. Remember we stayed there for a while last year? They must've been impressed by my work and recommended me for this job. They found me an hour ago and slipped me the message. It's a pretty top secret mission if you ask me."

"How top secret?"

"As top secret as receiving a handwritten message from the King can be, I suppose."

"Does he have nice handwriting? I feel like it would be obnoxiously fancy and swirly," I exclaim.

"That's far from the point. Do you know how *big* this is?" Bea says, and I can hear the slight shift in her tone — she sounds almost optimistic.

I drop my attitude and soften my face, something I do only for her. Living the lives we have, it's hard to know when we can finally stop worrying about being defensive and finally feel safe. If this is a request from the King himself, that only means a generous sum is to follow.

"We could get out of here for good," Bea allows herself to smile when she says it, eyes glazing over as if being submerged in a dream.

I don't remember a time when I wasn't with her and we

weren't fighting for a place in this world. Could this be our chance at starting a new life?

"So," I clear my throat and lean back, "he needs you to kill someone. You mentioned I have a role in this shenanigan?"

"That's the thing: he doesn't want me to kill anyone. He needs me to *find* someone. Capture and retreat," she explains.

Sometimes, when she speaks so casually about her position, I forget that she asks me to play with her hair when she falls asleep: she had once indulged that it reminds her of how her mother used to braid it.

"And we both know I'm a much better tracker than you," I add.

"Say whatever you want. You're coming with me regardless."

"Well, obviously. Where are we headed?"

Bea taps the side of her nostril twice as she stands, snatching her cloak and pinning it back around her shoulders.

Right, top secret.

I follow her out of the tavern, towering a whole foot over her brawny build.

"The message said we should start heading toward Ochrore. By dawn."

I nod, soaking in the information — who could the King possibly want from there?

We walk swiftly through the streets, the hubbub subsiding. It goes unsaid, but I know once we make it back to our shared room, we'll pack up immediately and head east. The idea of an adventure begins to excite me, but not nearly as much as the profit that's sure to follow.

"You think this has anything to do with the Banshee?" I say, keeping my voice low. "It happened a day or two ago, and word's been spreading like crazy. The Kingdom wets their trousers everytime something like this happens."

"I can't blame them."

"Whatever. They should concern themselves with other more important things, like the increasing population of Demons in the Ex-Isles, or the fucking labor laws torturing the Howlers, or—"

Bea freezes and pulls me to a stop, her hand tight on my wrist. "Oh, shut up, will you?" She looks at me with a wild stare: she's thrilled, and maybe the slightest bit smug. We back into an alley, and in the dark shadows, she whispers into the space between us, "it's the Hand."

"The Hand," I echo, dumbfounded. No one ever speaks about the Maidens as it is. Bringing up theories about their lost Hand is considered an act of treason within the Edenic Empire.

"Apparently she's alive," Bea marvels. "Or so it's been speculated."

"And apparently she died during the Battle of Lamya, however many years ago that was. You sure this isn't a fluke? Was this message really from the King?"

Bea shrugs, the irritation plain in her eyes. I'm one to know that she isn't easily deceived, so she takes the time to rummage through her satchel at her side and dig out a pearly white envelope. I snatch it from her hands and see that, sure enough, the letter is sealed with red and gold wax. The word *Capitan* is scribbled on the front, Bea's alias. I look up at her perplexed then tear it open. I recognise some words: *Magpie* — my alias, and '*The Hand, Capture, Return*' delicately described in curling black ink.

"The Maiden's precious Hand," I muse. "I suppose I wouldn't mind if those witches never got her back."

"Asshole," Bea smirks. I nudge her in the arm and guide her back out of the alley.

Within the hour, Bea and I gather up what little we have, all of it fitting into our personal satchels. We desert our small living space and head towards the main gates of Eephifer.

On our way through the stone streets, I quickly exchange items from my pack for more silver and gold, stopping along the way to buy some food and pickpocket other small necessities for our long journey ahead. I leave some extra coins for our carriage journey out of the White Isles and through the Sanctums.

Bea stops at the local armory to clean up her bow and sharpen our daggers. Once we're all prepared, I pay no good-bye to the Sleepless City.

4
BEKA

Three days pass before we bury Inez under a cloudless sky.

A cluster of village folk gather around where she lies still, her body covered by an inky cloth. A smaller wooden box lies beside her, sealed with a white ribbon. The morning sun peaks through the trees stretching over us, casting fingers of light over the burial site reaching down to pick up the fallen.

Everyone is wearing black, dabbing their cheeks with tear soaked rags. The Cleric is by the head of Inez's casket, reciting prayers from a book, blessing her afterlife with the promises of the true Eden. Gallienne is quiet beside me, her hand entwined with mine. She grips it aggressively, manifesting her grief into something physical.

I stare at Inez's hands, splayed beyond the cloth, staged across her belly: the skin around her fingers look fragile and oddly warm — the only part of her that wasn't rendered to a ghostly shade of gray.

"May our prayers bless her and her unborn on their journey to Eden."

Everyone closes their eyes, bowing their heads in prayer, but I keep my eyes glued to my friend, trying my very best to process this moment. I haven't slept since it happened. Every chance that my eyes close, anguish pierces my heart, suffocating me. I can't grasp the idea of Inez being gone, let alone accepting just how she left. I *want* to pray. I want to give her my words of protection; I want her to find peace and watch over her sister, but it would be no use. She shouldn't have left like this — not this soon.

"Step forth and offer her the gifts of life, death and prosperity."

Gallienne moves first. She places a necklace of thread with a silver pendant into the casket. She hovers over her sister's body for a painful moment. I hear her sniffle — I know that the necklace once belonged to their late mother.

Emelyne sits beside me, her lips quivering whilst giving me an encouraging nod. I move to take Gallienne's hand again and pull her back, engulfing her in a hug. She sobs into my shoulder, her tears cold against my skin. I watch the rest of the offerings in a daze. Some bring flowers from Falldare Meadow, with dainty yellow petals and strips of white blossoms — Sarya and Aravae place shiny rocks by Inez, someone places a wooden carving in the casket, and Barnabas follows in with the skeleton of a fish.

If Lycidas were here, I imagine he would have left a rose in her casket, or maybe a sliver of moonstone. Him and Inez have always been close, the three of us forming a tight bond over the past few years. He doesn't even know what's happened.

Gallienne continues to cry. I can't find the words to comfort her so I just caress her hair with my fingers. Elys holds up a vial of her blood, tracing it in the air to mimic the image of a sprouting tree: the Tree of Life. The village folk move to make an aisle for the Cleric, allowing him to walk towards a nearby stream. He empties Inez's blood into the water, letting it run through the brook.

"May our Adam and Eve embrace their souls. May our prayers guide them to the Garden forevermore."

Inez was always going to be a mother, a burden every woman of the Edenic faith bears. No matter how unwilling they are, the choice is not theirs. The scriptures of Eden say this is all we women are good for. But I know this wasn't what Inez wanted — at least not yet. My shoulders slump as I imagine my friend alive and full of joy, cradling a babe with eyes like hers. I can't help but wonder if she realized in her final moments quite what was happening.

As they close the lid of her casket, I squeeze Gallienne to my chest. What pains me more than grief is guilt, and no matter how many apologies sift through my head, none are enough to repair the damage that's been done. I don't know how to explain to Gallienne, and to the rest of our village, that Inez and her baby are dead because of me.

The walk back to Brighes is quiet.

Heavy.

Gallienne is yet to let go of my hand. Not even as we near her house.

It feels wrong when we walk in: the air thick with grief, the entryway cold. Gallienne perches on a stool by the dinner table, her eyes swollen and red.

"I'll make some tea," I offer, loath to pry my grip away.

My hands shake as I prepare the kettle.

It's mostly silent for a fair few moments, just a sniffle

here and there. A scream rips through the quiet and my heart bursts from my chest.

"Not again," I hear Gallienne wince, but it's just the boiling water taunting us.

A tiny knock sounds on the front door as I douse the stove's flame.

"I'll get it," my friend croaks.

I watch her open the door to an anxious Miss Ysabelle holding a covered wicker basket.

"Oh, Gallienne," the older woman says, reaching forward to embrace her.

"I'm alright," she mutters.

"I came by with some fresh loaves," Ysabelle says, placing the punnet on the table.

"Thank you, Miss. I feel that I should give you something in return for all your help," Gallienne replies, looking at the baked goods.

Ysabelle was the first person to reach Gallienne's house after the Banshee screamed. Gallienne and I were too full of shock, so she was the one who washed the bloody sheets and scrubbed the floors. Ysabelle also gathered some village folk to move Inez's body to a Haelend. I don't remember much of the last few days, but I remember Ysabelle doing these things and being very grateful for her kindness.

"No need to, dear. Why don't you lie down and rest?"

"Here, drink this," I say, handing a cup of warm tea to Gallienne.

"Beka, could I have a word with you?" Ysabelle asks, her eyes frantic.

I hum, following her out the door. Our village is empty:

none of the shops are open today, no one roams along our streets. Nobody says it outright, but something is very wrong. Inez's death wasn't normal, and the last time a Banshee was seen, the entire village of Thessonne was burnt down.

"How are you doing?" Ysabelle asks me. This close, I notice how similar she looks to her son, Petrus.

"Fine," I lie.

The woman nods, her gentle smile suddenly falling. Ysabelle drops her head into her hands and begins to cry. I grab her shoulders, hoping to steady her shaking.

"A poor, poor thing," Ysabelle sobs. "Inez was too young."

But she isn't pregnant, is she?

"I just— I don't understand. No one even knew," Ysabelle continues. I'm holding her to my chest now, my eyes drilling holes into the trees nearby.

"The Heathens should have been here. They would've blessed her and protected her! They could've saved her if we had just *known*."

I know I can't avoid Heathens forever. They come to Brighes on the occasion of birth. They're the ones who know how to set up the rituals: a means of defense to protect newborn children and mothers from Lilith. These rituals were put in place ever since Lilith was exiled to Edom. The Creator's most prized angels, Sanvi, Sansanvi and Semangelaf, had tracked her for years with word from him to bring Lilith back to Adam, or else send her to Hell.

She chose the latter.

Right before Lilith made her leave over the Carmine Lagoon, she swore that Adam would pay the price. This promise was one of revenge.

When asked in schools 'Who were the wives of Adam?', the name Lilith is not even uttered under bated breath — they are only taught of Eve. But the truth goes a little something like this: Lilith, Adam's first wife, had left his violent ways, seeking refuge in Southern Sumeria. The cause of his outrage? She had refused to bear his children, she had refused to bow down. She wished to be his equal, not his breeding pig, as they were made of the very same earth.

I am not of your rib, she would cry.

Upon her descent to Edom, Lilith screeched the ineffable name of the Creator, vowing that he, too, would come to regret this. She promised that one day, her Hand would come to save her — that she would reclaim her land and life once more. After all, what better revenge was there than to wage a war on Adam's bloodline, present and future?

The initial loss of children was devastating. It took some time for communities to adjust, but now, during times of birth, Heathens have learnt to surround expecting mothers with bowls lined with inscriptions of prayer; to place amulets around the mother's necks, and line silver daggers with ancient carvings around the bed; to write the names of the three angels above the mother's head. These traditions are necessary to ward her off, and they *always* work.

"Nobody knew," I murmur.

But *I* did. *I* had a feeling.

"A great evil killed her," Ysabelle weeps. "It was The Dark Maid."

I close my eyes, trying to pretend I'm by the sea, but a ghastly vision floods my mind instead. I see a temple made of sandstone, with women dressed in red and black. They're singing in an ancient tongue, songs of ascension and power. Offerings are piled on top of the altar, resting before a statue of a lady, her carved face sharp and ravishing. I'm standing in front of her with tears trickling down my face.

"I must go to the Cleric. We aren't taking things *seriously*," Ysabelle declares. I snap out of my thoughts as she pushes away from me. "Beka, are you sure you're alright?"

The wind blows, leaves clattering against one another across the branches above us. I look up and spot an owl with white and black feathers, and dark, pitted eyes that stare back at me, inspecting. Waiting.

"I don't know," I answer honestly. The rest of my breath gets caught in my throat.

"Come with me, then."

Over the past twelve years, I've been careful to limit my steps inside the Church. It's a holy space, divine to the Creator and the vessels who speak in his name.

Emelyne never questioned my reluctance, she never forced the Edenic practices on me — I can't say she's much of a believer herself. I've never desired a proposal, I've never fancied myself a bearer of children, even if I were something other than I am. So instead, I fell into the role of an old maid. A simple farmhand with shoddy excuses like offering to mind the little ones during weekly sermons. Thankfully, the Cleric appreciated my help. It seems he's too kind to have suspected something untoward from me.

Ysabelle leads me there now. Her fingernails dig into my skin as she tugs me along. I carefully resist, but it's no use.

The Church is the only building made of stone in Ochrore.

Brighes isn't wealthy enough to build entirely with stone, but the Kingdom and the Monastery bestowed every prominent village with temples for Clerics to preach in. It sticks out like an opal in a clump of dirt.

"I really should get back to Gallie," I say, halting before the entrance. This close, the etchings in the stone walls of the Church are clearly depicted: Adam and Eve, their hands entwined, standing beside the Tree of Life, not a snake in sight.

"No, we need clarity — *you* need protection. Elys can help you," she stresses, my hands between her own, quivering. She's borderline hysterical.

"His help? He's already done so much," I reply, biting at my tongue.

"Yes, dear, but," Ysabelle stops and looks around in a fit of paranoia. Her eyes harden as she brings me closer, whispering, "*She* could still be *here*." Ysabelle must feel my own hands tremble. "You were there when it happened. She comes in the form of anything, *anyone!*"

"Miss, I don't think," I stammer, but I know what she thinks and there is no changing her mind. I can see the terror in her eyes, the truth of what happened to Inez as strong as her faith.

There is nothing for me to say. I can't defend Lilith, not to Ysabelle, not to anyone.

"You *must* be cleansed, my dear," the woman pleads.

Ysabelle yanks me forward. I dig my feet into the ground, resisting her pull. She grits her teeth at my restraint, but before she can question it, the door to the Church swings open.

"Oh, what's going on here?" The Cleric implores.

"Elys! Please, help us! " Ysabelle cries.

"Has something happened?" The poor man looks ready to collapse. "Is this about Inez?"

"No, Elys please —"

"Our prayers were healing enough, Miss. Why don't we take a moment—"

"No! Her evil could still be here, sir. You know the tales, how her power flows through every river, every leaf — across our whole land. In our *homes*." Ysabelle wails. "Lilith is *everywhere*."

"Never say that name!" a voice snaps. A woman emerges from behind Elys: a Heathen, telltale by the white cloak wrapped around her body. "Be careful with the words you speak."

This Heathen can't possibly know who or what I am. Since they have cut ties Lilith, since they no longer feel the soil of our homeland, a Heathen cannot bear the magic of a Maiden. Through Lilith's gift, Maidens can feel that energy and power within their kin: they, *we*, are all connected. I've since learned how to hide it, my time away from the Realm aiding me, but I have cut no ties. Though my efforts were hardly valiant.

"I'm so sorry," Ysabelle frets.

"Miss, there is no need to worry," Elys assures. He breaks Ysabelle's hands away from mine to hold hers. She stares at him with big, hopeful eyes. "Word has traveled fast about our tragedy. Kymn came here as soon as she could."

The Heathen beside him nods.

"The Dark Maid attacked three nights ago. Her energy could very well be lingering within your village. Although anyone near the fallen should be alright, I have made sure of it," Kymn explains, carefully studying my face. "The Knyghts in Alnola are on their way now. Inspections will start in a few hours. They sent me ahead to appease your people. I can assure you all that Brighes will be cleansed. My hope is that your village will recover from this attack as soon as possible."

"You see? Everything will be alright," Elys says. "Would the two of you like to come in and pray?"

Miss Ysabelle nods and follows the Cleric into the Church. Kymn stands there, waiting for me to move.

"Thank you for the offer, but I need to get back to Gallienne," I say, my voice taut.

She watches me carefully, her eyes oddly familiar. There was once a time where I was constantly surrounded by women with features so crisp and enchanting. Seeing her brings up so many emotions I've ignored for a long time.

"What is your name?" Kymn demands.

"Tonis," I blurt. "Beka Tonis. My mother is Emelyne Tonis."

"I see," she nods. "The people say you were there when it happened."

"I was," I utter, taking a step back.

"So you saw what she's really capable of," Kymn states.

She knows, she knows, she knows.

I nod.

Kymn looks back to the Church, the rows of pews scattered with people bowing their heads. Ysabelle and Elys are among them, joining them in prayer.

"You are welcome to join. The Dark Maid cannot enter this space."

"Thank you, again, but I really must go," I stress.

I turn my back before she can force me to stay. The path

back home takes an eternity, my feet suddenly twice their weight. I feel bare, stripped from my garments down to the bone. The Knyghts could be here by sundown. I have until then to figure out a way to slip away unseen.

"What's bothering you, petal?"

Emelyne's eyes were on me from the moment I got home, prying to see if I was alright. I took to our dirty dishes, letting her eat in peace. Maybe that was telling enough.

"I'm just upset," I answer.

"I know you're upset, but why are you worried?"

"Knyghts from Alnola will be arriving soon to run an inspection."

"The Knyghts are coming?" Emelyne asks, dropping the spoon into her bowl.

"Yes, sometime later today."

"Well then, what a relief. The people could use some comfort," she offers.

"What happened the other night hasn't happened in a long time," I start, my thoughts drifting.

"Beka..."

"Everything is going to be fine."

"And yet?" Emelyne pushes, trying to knock down the wall that I've built up.

Her encouraging gaze commands me to move away from the dishes and join her by the fire. Here, my vulnerability creeps up behind me, like an unwanted shadow trailing my every step. My mouth falls open, the truth hanging on the tip of my tongue.

And yet it doesn't change the fact that it happened.

I imagine what I would say if I were to explain everything. If I were to be honest with her. Would she still love me if she knew who I really was?

"It's okay, you don't have to say anything," she responds to my silence. "Sometimes there isn't anything to say. If you want to sit here and watch the fire, then I will sit here and watch it with you."

Emelyne takes my hands and pulls me forward. I sink to my knees, dropping my head into her lap before I let myself cry. I want to tell her that this may be the last time she sees me. With the Knyghts on their way, it's only a matter of time before the life I have here is gone. Both sides of this ancient fight are coming for me. I can't bear the thought of Emelyne being caught up in the middle. It has to end somehow.

"Thank you," is all I manage to say.

She caresses my hair as I cry, the flames blurring into a red mess.

I don't know how long we stay like this, but I know I can't be bothered to move. I should go and pack my things, gather up what little I have and leave before Emelyne can notice, but really, where would I go then? How long can I run from this?

She wipes the skin beneath my eyes, a gentle touch before digging into a slice of bread.

Go now, the voice in my head urges, but it's too late.

Beyond the crackle of the fire, a cacophonous gaggle of cries erupt outside. I jolt at the sudden noise, anxiously exchanging a glance with Emelyne. The door of our cottage is ripped open, a flood of Knyghts infiltrating our space, shouting and grabbing at her before I can move to stand. I go to intercept their hands, but I'm knocked straight back to the ground, my arms held tightly behind my back. Their iron grips squeeze my skin, and I fear that Emelyne's bones will snap under such a hold. They don't listen to our questioning pleas. We're dragged out of the cottage, all the way into the main square of our village. Multiple rows of cages are set up, stationed around the center where a group of Knyghts are ushering people in behind the bars. I see Petrus and Miss Ysabelle squished into one along with other neighbors of mine. Knyghts are posted around the enclosures, pointing and yelling at everyone to stay in line.

I've lost sight of Emelyne.

I shriek and flail, trying to loosen the grips of the Knyghts holding my arms. They've come so much sooner than anticipated. Their armor is draped in navy and black cloth — the colors of the Ashen Domain, while several red and gold flags are leveled on posts, flapping above all our heads. I'm tossed into a cage at random where I hit the floor with a thud.

"Beka!" Sarya touches my arm. I scramble to my feet to embrace her, thankful she's in here with me.

"Stay close to me," I pull her in tight.

I want her to remember me as someone safe, someone she shouldn't be afraid of.

"Everyone remain calm!" It's Elys. He's standing in the middle of the square, arms up in defense. "Everything is going to be fine," he reassures, though he's the only one free of a cage.

The rest of us are herded behind bars. A Knyght stands beside him, one whose helmet is marked with a tassel made of red and gold: a Commander. The Cleric's words seem to stifle the hubbub for now. The Commander moves forward, shucking his helmet off to speak clearly.

"This is a necessary inspection ordered by the King himself," he announces. "Everyone will offer a sample of blood for numbers and be accounted for under the Kingdom of Ead."

Blood samples. I've heard of such documentation in the Isles, but never in the Domain. Especially not in Ochrore. Howlers are rounded up routinely for the King's records, but this is something entirely different.

"I'm scared," Sarya whimpers.

This is it.

They're going to find me.

I look around, but there's nothing I can do — not without being caught. Breaking out of the cage would be simple, but then what? There are Knyghts surrounding every inch of the square, blocking any opportunity for me to escape. They'd see me run off, or at least my attempt to.

The first round of villagers exit their cages. The Knyghts corral them in groups, sending them up to a station one by one to get their bloods done. There are five cages ahead of ours, and Emelyne is still nowhere in sight.

If I go up there for my turn, it will all be over within seconds. With one little prick of my finger, they'll know. My blood will spill like dark ink, a poison in their eyes, the plain and simple truth revealed. Maybe I should slit my wrists in the center of the square instead, smear my oozing blood on the front steps of the Church. At least that would be quick.

Death is a familiar foe but I'm scared all the same.

Sarya huddles closer to my chest, seeking the comfort of my arms.

At least this time I'm not alone.

5
AALIS

The Trawler wakes me up at dawn.

More specifically, it's the oily smell of fish that causes me to stir. I scrunch my nose and gag, the stench reminding me of why I never eat fish in the first place.

"The mornin's t'only time ya can catch some fresh herrin'," the Trawler informs. His accent is thick, his voice deep. "'Aven'cha e'er been fishin', boy?"

When did I fall asleep?

I sit up, rub the sleep from my eyes and yawn with a stretch, finally taking in my surroundings. I'm on a boat, but not the same one I hid on to travel from the Kingdom to Tilver.

It seems to be some time in the early morning, though it's hard to guess when, what with the slight overcast tinging the sky various shades of slate.

My back aches and I realize how uncomfortable I am after being crammed between two wooden barrels. I heave myself up, the rocking boat trying its best to knock me off my feet.

"Gon' tell me why yer on my property?" Thankfully, the Trawler doesn't sound too angry, but I think anyone would know better than to trespass on a fisherman's boat.

"I didn't mean to fall asleep."

What really happened went as smoothly as I could've hoped — truly.

I had no problem sneaking into the castle's port and onto a carrier filled with empty crates and barrels. The early transports rarely have many people on deck, so staying out of sight was simple enough.

The ride across the Forsaken Sea took about a day and a half. I watched the sun rise and set through a sliver of wood whilst my stomach rumbled incessantly. I listened to the crew talk of legends and exchange stories of their near-catastrophic encounters with Sirens — Succubi who live to seduce wayward men to the Realm for purposes of procreation. Though since the Battle of Lamya, rumor has it no child has been born to the Maidens.

The sailors spoke of how in Lilith's abandonment of Adam, just before her banishment, she seduced Fallen Angels to sire her demonic children. With Samael came the Sirens; with Sariel, the Harpies; and with Sahariel, the Howlers.

If this had been the Kingdom, the crew would have been hung for telling such tales.

We arrived in Tilver late last night. My plan was to stay hidden until midnight so I could roam around town unseen. Yet somehow, I ended up here.

"Boy?" The Trawler asks again. "If yer wantin' t'fish, go fer it, but I'm runnin' a business 'ere."

"I didn't mean to intrude," I reply, my voice wobbling.

"Go' anywhere else t'sleep?" The Trawler sounds almost empathetic.

"I was just looking for someone," I say.

"On my boat?"

The Trawler's boat seems to be docked near the edge of a town, the only one out along the pontoon. Maybe I could sneak into the town square before it gets too busy.

"Do you know a lot of people around here?" I press.

The older man gives me a funny look. If anything, he doesn't recognize me, which is all I can ask for.

"Like the back of my 'and," he says. I catch a glimpse of exposed skin on his neck which, under the lantern light, reflects a patch of shiny scales. He catches my eyeline and smirks. "Ya best get gone. Who yer lookin' for ain't 'ere."

Tilver is a watertown made up of wooden docks, bridges, and cottages held together by stilts. By all means, it's the complete opposite of the Kingdom — not to mention I've already seen more of Tilver than my home. A typical morning in the castle consists of quiet chambers and lonesome strolls through the hallways: maybe even a venture into the Garden alone if I'm really lucky. I don't love the fishy smell of Tilver, but it's better than being surrounded by four walls at all times. Even the Garden has its barriers.

The sun makes its welcome through the clouds as Tilver folk bustle around carrying barrels of fish, plenty of spears, and nets.

I pass by the Church, the only building not made of wood. It sits alone, no surrounding structures for company. I spot the Cleric, tell-tale by his cream colored robe and green sash, sweeping the stone outside the doorway. It's strange seeing a local Church like this one compared to the Monastery back home.

The castle and Arcadia sit on either side of the Garden of Eden, the Tree of Life at its very center. My family's relationship with the Edenic faith is very important to our tradition and rule. Every week, without fail, we would stroll through our Garden to attend the Cain's sermons, closing service with a bountiful feast. Fresh air and good food: my only incentive for going.

Apparently the Monasteries around the rest of the Northern Isles are wildly intimidating — from the buildings to the people, everything is pristine. Orthodox. The simplicity of Tilver is different and it fills me with jealousy.

I quite enjoy walking around, pretending I belong. No one stares or makes any snide comments. No one scolds me to stand up straighter or speak more eloquently. In fact, I don't think they know just who walks among them. I feel free: something I never thought I would reach beyond my canvas.

A startling sweet smell catches my attention. I stop and peek through the window of what looks to be a bakery, my stomach rumbling yet again, as if on cue. I step inside and glance at the rather bland looking treats displayed up front. A woman stands behind the counter, stocking loaves of bread into baskets. Another boy stands next to me, peering at jars of jam.

"I'll take two of those," I order, pointing at some eggy custard tarts. "And a fresh loaf of bread, please."

The woman runs her eyes over me before gathering all my items. I keep my head down as I pay her with the few silver coins I took.

"D'ya two boys 'ear 'bout the troops marchin' towards the meadows?" The woman asks.

Thankfully, the boy next to me speaks first.

"Tha's what Thaladah was talkin' 'bout!" He exclaims. Just

by his face, I can tell he's younger than me. Probably not by much, but surely no older than sixteen.

"I only e'er 'eard tales 'bout the 'aunted Maiden — a Banshee, as they say," the woman comments. The dialect here is much thicker than what I'm used to, but nothing too hard to understand. "Omens o' death, they are, cryin' out after the Dark Maid takes a life," she continues, shaking her head. "Dreadful things."

A girl busts into the bakery then, shaking the door as she swings it open.

"Another group o' Knyghts just left Alnola!" she exclaims. "I saw 'em back at the watchtower."

"More Knyghts?" The boy asks.

The girl nods her head. She has slick, silver hair and a pair of bright yellow eyes. A patch of teal scales wrap around her neck and along the side of her face. Apparently the offspring of a Siren and human aren't all that uncommon.

Demons, the King calls them. *Bloody demons.*

I've never seen someone like her before.

At that, she immediately turns her head towards me and cocks her eyebrows up. I snap my head down to my feet, embarrassed for staring.

"T'was only an 'our ago when I saw the first group," she continues.

"They must be doin' tons o' inspections. The Kingdom don't like those wretched 'eretics," the woman chides. "You kids know 'bout the Dark Lady? You know 'ow not t'anger 'er?"

I'm almost shocked by how openly these people are talking about this. My whole life I was told to never say her name —

to never speak of the Maidens, unless committing treason took my fancy.

"Ma says I shouldn't talk 'bout it," the boy replies.

"Come n' watch 'em with me!" the girl says, grabbing my arm, dragging me out of the bakery.

The girl pulls me through town towards the mainland, the boy following suit.

"What's your name?" I ask them as we rush through a line of cottages.

"I'm Thaladah. That's Graysen," the girl says. "You?"

"I— Adam," I blurt, making them giggle.

We reach the outskirts of the island, admiring the tall, stone watchtower that sits at the edge of the water.

"Are we allowed to go up there?" I wonder.

"'S abandoned," Thaladah shrugs.

"Yer not from 'round 'ere, are ya?" Graysen assumes. I trail behind them as we climb the spiral steps of the tower. "You sound funny."

"'E's got a nice satchel, too," Thaladah remarks.

"My father's a merchant. We travel around a lot."

"E'er been t'Neelem? Or Eephifer?" Graysen beams.

Only in books.

"A while ago," I lie.

A strong gust of wind blows me back as we reach the balcony. From here, I can see nothing but Tilver and the blue sea behind it. I walk around and notice, far out past an expanse of trees, the stone town of Alnola elevated on top of a hill, a mere dot on the map.

"Ya can just about see their banners over there — look!" Thaladah points out.

Sure enough, there they fly, small but mighty.

"You said this is the second group?" I confirm.

Thaladah nods. I notice that her lips are cracked and blue.

"Knyghts were 'ere last night, askin' 'bout the Banshee," Graysen recalls. "I ne'er thought I'd 'ear a noise like that."

"What did it sound like?" I ask, a little too eager.

Graysen's eyes widen. "Awful. It made my brain bounce 'round."

"I wonder who she killed," Thaladah whispers.

My jaw practically falls off.

"A Banshee only screams when an unprotected ma dies," Graysen states.

"I don't get it. O'course, everyone these days is careful n' prepared for birth, but I don't understand why this is such a big deal to the Knyghts. Or the Kingdom," Thaladah says. "Anythin' remotely unordinary is treated like a curse."

I watch Thaladah scratch at her scaled neck. I prop my arms against the stone, my heart breaking through my ribs. We're silent for a few moments, but I keep my eyes pinned on the flags in the distance.

"Do you happen to know a girl named Abeko?" I whisper hoarsely.

"*Ah—bek—oh?*" Graysen attempts to pronounce it with his harsh accent.

"Ne'er 'eard of 'er," Thaladah responds.

"Never mind," I mutter. She's not here. It was so long ago, I doubt she listened to me. "I need to follow those flags."

I give them both appreciative nods and step back into the stairwell.

"Is ya brain full o' saltwater?" Graysen squeaks after me. "'Ow are ya goin' ta catch up with 'em?"

He makes a good point.

It's likely that the Knyghts would make it to Ochrore well before I do, and if Abeko really is there, then I'd miss my shot at getting to her first.

Thaladah follows me down the stairs. "I'll get you an 'orse. 'S'a pasture not too far from 'ere. C'mon."

We exit the tower and duck under a cove of trees. Thaladah lightly jogs ahead of me. I follow along as quickly as I can.

The Siren girl leads me to an offshoot into the Forsaken Sea. I spot the pasture in question across the water, with dozens of horses roaming about.

"Right over there. The farmer won't mind. 'Is 'orses always find their way back." Thaladah points to the basin, "Tis the shallowest point of the stream, 'ere, you'll 'ave to cross it on foot."

"Thank you," I say, taking my first steps in the water. I can't help but shiver as it coats my calves.

"Yer not really a merchant, are ya?" Thaladah wonders.

"I'm just looking for someone," I admit.

"Does she love ya back? The girl ya mentioned. When ya asked about 'er, yer eyes twinkled."

Twelve years I've yearned to see her again in the flesh.

The first time I saw Abeko, she was caged behind the iron bars of a prison cell underneath the Kingdom's castle. She was frightened and scarred, crusted violet clinging to her skin.

She must have been no older than six when the Knyghts marched her into our land, victorious from their defeat over the Maidens. I don't remember being proud of the King and his Knyghts when they imprisoned her, although everyone else seemed to be.

Now they know how it feels, he spat.

Late one night, I had followed after the King down into the cells, cowering in the shadows, wanting to see his trophy for myself. Instead, I found a friend. I felt indebted to her, to someone who bled the same color as I did. I went there every night and ran back up to my chambers before the sun rose.

The Knyghts who were meant to be guarding the cell weren't doing a particularly good job, preferring to spend their nights in places more debaucherous than the dungeons.

I promised her I would get her out of there.

And once I did just that, I told her I'd find her again.

"I love her, and that's all that matters."

"Do you know the way 'round the Domain?" Thaladah muses.

Damn.

"You know, that's an excellent question."

Thaladah tuts as she reaches into one of her hidden pockets. She extends one of her scaly hands towards me, where between her fingers lies a small piece of parchment, scribbled on and ever so slightly torn. A map.

"'Ere, it's not much," she declares, "but it might 'elp you along the way. Though, truthfully, it should just be a straight line from 'ere."

"Are you sure you won't need this?"

"Nah, I took it from my da. Better 'e doesn't find out."

I pay Thaladah a nod of thanks, grabbing the flimsy sheet and tucking it into my satchel.

In no time, I reach the other side of the stream, glancing

back at the girl who's already running off, waving as she goes. I turn back and rush towards the grass ahead, hoisting myself up onto a horse and charging south.

I ride along the coast nonstop for the better part of a day, dipping into the occasional valley.

My knowledge of this region is based solely on diagrams and I'm only familiar with the names of a few of the towns. I do know that Ochrore provides a large bulk of grain and corn for Sumeria, as it's built upon rich soil and a hearty climate. Though I don't know how that fact will help me.

I spot a village in the near distance: oak cottages lined around a square, cloth huts held up by wooden beams, and large silos presumably filled with produce ready for trade.

According to Thaladah's map, this should be Brighes.

Exhausted, my horse trots up to a field of uniformed trees, apples littered below bare branches. I hop off and touch its snout, kindly asking it to stay put whilst I investigate, but something smushes under my weight, my foot sliding against it. I topple to the ground, straight on my tailbone, immediately winded. My horse whinnies at the sight, leaning down to dote over me. I grab hold of its reins to get myself up, grateful for the companion I have made. I wipe the soles of my soiled shoes on a patch of clean grass, chunks of sour-smelling mush falling away.

The deep rumble of shouting startles me. A group of Knyghts draped in their battle finery march towards the village ahead. I watch as a few of them assemble in the lines of trees, carrying torches in their wake. It's not even remotely close to sunset.

General Bausan is there too, ordering his Knyghts into position. He's intimidating in every way — as a General of the Knyghthood should be. Bausan bears no helmet, his eyes are sharp, and he wears his armor like a weightless silk.

"Light it up!" He barks, and I sit there frozen as the Knyghts lower their torches, setting the trees alight.

General Bausan doesn't mean to march through Brighes and inspect the citizens: he means to burn it all down.

One leg after another, I pull myself back onto the horse, pushing off into a gallop, a new spark lighting up in my chest.

This is history repeating itself all over again.

There once was a thriving village bordering the Sanctum called Thessonne. The town, although not the first to have had a run-in with Lilith, suffered the worst in all of Sumeria.

The King knew that the Maidens don't control who, what or when she attacks, but he ravaged the land nonetheless — burned it all in hopes of removing any trace of her presence. This event sparked a new vengeance in the King, causing him to gather up his best Knyghts and most loyal Heathens to attack the Realm and kidnap the Maidens' only hope. More lives were lost than saved, but he reasoned it at the time with the fear that purged his mind.

The King still blames the Maidens for the death of my mother, but he forgets that they were the ones to give me life.

I had hoped that he'd since learned from the tragedy of Thessonne. Then again, how well do I actually know him?

I'm at the brink of the village in no time, racing through the bordering trees, mostly concealed from sight. Squinting through the blurring branches, I notice more and more of Bausan's lethal troops advancing towards the poor village, its people screaming and shaking the shackles of the cages they're stuffed in. Small fires have erupted in patches all around the village, and from what I can gather, the Knyghts who were here first — the ones performing the initial inspections — are just as confused.

The Cleric stands out, what with his bright robe now stained and fraying sash. He's scrambling around the cages, shaking at the bars to release the people inside.

I feel like an idiot, unable to move as I watch these people suffer.

The Commander turns and spots the new group of Knyghts descending on the village. He moves to grab the Cleric, pushing him into the arms of two other Knyghts, taking him away.

Of *course* they only care about the Cleric.

Knyghts begin to back away, leaving innocent civilians stranded behind locked bars, and those who weren't shoved into cages fight relentlessly against their restraints.

At least the inspections have ceased.

I can't help myself as I dismount my horse, march out from beyond the brush, unabashedly hollering, "What are you doing? Why aren't you helping them?"

I yelp as a flaming arrow lands beside my feet, giving me barely any time to jump away. More and more rain from the sky, peppering the land in smoldering ash as they sink into the ground, some going straight through the chests of Dominians. I weave my way through the fires to face the Commander, who barely pays me any notice.

"As Prince and heir to the throne of the Kingdom of Ead, I demand you stop!" I squawk.

The Commander cocks his head. "The General informed me that when the inspections end, the fires start. His orders."

"To Edom with the General! These people will *die* if they stay in the cages," I argue.

The Commander turns his cheek. Does the King know about this?

"Because of The Dark Maid, these people are already cursed. There's no helping them now."

I'm tempted to lunge at him when an explosion shakes the village, sending me to the ground yet again. I watch in horror as a large silo bursts into flames, sprinkling all sorts of debris and detritus. A large chunk of its metal falls, crushing into a cage of people below it. Cries break out in every direction, swallowing the village in a chamber of fear.

The Kingdom will never see the horror of something like this. Protected by stone and status, the people there will never suffer — they will never feel this pain. They'll gossip over the news, discuss how it was the right thing to do after a visit from the Dark Maid, and move on with their cushy lives.

I'm losing whatever tenacity I had before.

The flames are hot as they devour the space around me in fervor. None of the Knyghts seem to care: they've all left the square to join the rest of their squadron on the sidelines.

Through the sparks of the explosion, as rubble drizzles down like water, my eyes suddenly catch on a face behind bars, one I've imagined far too many times to miss.

Surely not.

I blink once, twice, and the seeming mirage of her is tactile after all. There is no illusion before me. This scene is one of flames and anguish, yet there she is at the center of it all.

Abeko.

It's all too familiar, how we meet again in the same circumstances: her caged — a prisoner, and me standing there, watching her from a position of little power. It's hard to ignore the violent beat of my heart as I stick my hand into a dwindling patch of embers in search of an arrow. The heat sears my skin instantly. A string of curses spew from my mouth as my hand finds the neck of the bolt, clenching it hard in my fist. With a yelp, I pull it from the ground. Another explosion shakes the grounds as a second silo bursts into flames. I stumble across the square, eyes set on the farthest cage. It's all a blur, but I make it, falling down to my knees before the bars caging her in. I saved her before. I can do it again.

"Abeko," I gasp, frantically jamming the tip of the arrow into the lock of the cage.

She turns her head and it *is* her. It's *really* her. My heart swells, looking at her up close once again. Her face is just as I remembered, but all of it, the entire vision I've made up, is gone with the bewildered look crossing her face. Her brown eyes are swollen, cheeks glistening with tears, and her face is laced with utter confusion.

She has no idea who I am.

"How do you know my name?" she whispers in despair, clutching a girl in her arms.

I struggle to pick the lock apart. My hand stings from the hot metal as it eats away at my skin, the noise unbearable. If General Bausan sees me, it's over. It will have all been for nothing.

"I need to get you out of here," I stress, thrusting the point of the arrow into the metal with force: the lock is starting to break.

"I don't understand," Abeko cries.

"If they get to you, they'll bring you back to the Kingdom, just like before. They want you dead!" With one last jab, the arrow finally pierces through the lock. I rip it off the cage and fling the door open, desperately reaching for Abeko. She recoils, tucking the girl away from me and my open arms. "*Please*," I beg.

Abeko glares at me. "I can't just leave them!"

"The Knyghts are almost here! Abeko, please come—"

"How do you know my name?" She shouts.

A thousand words tangle into a knot at the base of my throat. After a few painful seconds, I see her face change, clarity glazing over her expression.

"Wait," she exclaims, "it's you. But how—?"

"Yes. It's me, it's Aalis. We have to go."

Abeko hesitates before picking the girl up and carrying her out of the cage. I grab her arm and lead her into the brush just as another wave of arrows fly into the square. My horse is waiting for us in the trees where Abeko wastes no time in raising the small girl onto its back.

"Sarya, listen to me," she hushes, her voice surprisingly calm. "You need to get far away from here. Ride to Thessonne and wait there. Lycidas and the others pass through after the full moon. He'll find you there. You understand? Find Lycidas."

The little girl, Sarya, has tears pouring out of her bloodshot eyes as she mutters, "No, Beka! Not without you!"

Beka?

"I'll find you again, okay?" Abeko starts crying.

"We need to go," I persist, reaching out for her arm, but she shakes my touch away. Her kind eyes stay on the girl.

"What about our picnic? You promised us we'd have a picnic by the sea," Sarya whimpers.

Abeko's face pinches, a swarm of tears streaming down her cheeks. She kisses the pad of her index finger and places it on the little girl's cheek.

"It'll be alright. I'll find you. Now *go*," Abeko demands, and the little girl nods before kicking the horse in the side, letting it take her north through the trees and away from us.

Abeko watches Sarya flee, and I stare at her.

"I know a safe place we can go," Abeko says, brushing past me.

"I, um—"

"Do you have any plan at all?"

"No," I hesitate. "My plan was to find you, Abeko, and I did! Honestly, I didn't think I'd get this far," I admit, shocked.

"I haven't been called Abeko in a long time," she whispers.

I go to respond, words ready to spill, but she starts moving fast, intent on creating as much distance between us and the village as possible. I stumble after her, trying my best to keep up.

Eventually, the trees thin out.

"Where are we going?" I pant, feeling ready to collapse.

"This way," she says, grabbing my arm and dragging me out of the brush and into sand.

A dozen or so cottages are lined up along the shore of what looks to be the Forsaken Sea. Abeko pulls me toward the third in the row. I search for her gaze when she turns her head back in my direction, but her eyes are frantic, scanning the area for any hidden danger.

"Is it safe here?" I plead, my vision blurring.

"For now."

We stop in front of the cottage — a small, wooden structure. Her hand slides away from my arm for a moment and I fear I may fall without her touch, without something to ground me.

"Abeko," I say, breathless.

I blink through the haze and catch her worry.

"What's wrong with you?"

My hand flies to my chest, the fabric of my shirt slipping between my fingers. Her hands are on my shoulders now, stabilizing me before I fall to my knees.

"Sorry— my, uh," I choke, unable to finish.

My chest feels thick and heavy. I'm panting for a chance to breathe, as if the fist of magic pumping my heart has vanished.

"Don't panic. Let's get inside," I hear her say, but my vision leaves me then and there. I have no strength left to fight it.

Abeko carries me inside the place, hoisting us through the front door.

"Here."

I feel her lower me onto the ground, setting my back against a wall. A blanket is placed over my body, before she moves to press her hand against my forehead.

"I'm okay. I swear," I murmur. I must look pathetic.

"Just sit here and rest. No one will find us. Not for now."

Her fingers leave my face. I reach out, but she is gone.

6
ELIO

"Let's say you and a Harpy get into a brawl, who comes out on top?"

Oh, Bea and her hypotheticals.

I mean, a Harpy could snap my neck and swallow me whole before I even think about unsheathing my dagger. Though *hypothetically*, I daresay I have an actual chance.

"Me, for sure," I decide.

Bea scoffs. I hold my finger up, determined to prove my point.

"Is it a night fight?" I ask.

"A *night* fight?"

"Y'know, dark sky, the moon is out. A fight at night."

"It's at any given moment. If you depend on a certain time of day to win then you should just surrender now," Bea chirps.

She sits across from me with her left hand instinctively resting on the small knife strapped to her belt. The rest of her weapons are staged neatly beside her folded cloak on the plush cushions of our carriage.

"I was only asking because I want it to be a fair fight," I reason. "They're blind in the dark, an advantage for me."

"They can fly."

"I have fangs."

"And when they pluck you from the ground?" Bea retorts, unconvinced.

"I'll poison them. I'll use that stuff we buy from Callos." I snap my fingers. "Instantly paralyzed."

"I don't trust Callos," Bea scowls.

"You don't trust anyone," I point out.

"Never mind. This is a fair fight," Bea says. "No poison."

"Capitan, oh, Capitan, you forget the one perk of my parentage. No Harpy can harm one born to the Realm."

"That's why I said *'hypothetical'*, asshole."

"Fine," I sigh, slumping back into the decadence of my seat. "How would *you* kill a Harpy?"

"Poison isn't a bad idea but I'd go for their talons first. Stick a few arrows in their wings. End it with a knife to the throat," she replies casually. Like it's that easy.

Well, for her it really would be.

Bea is skilled beyond anyone's reach. If she says she can kill someone or something, she's not lying. But that doesn't stop me from asking, "What about a dragon?"

She scoffs.

For the past two days, we've tried our best to not die of boredom. It's been a long and painful journey through the Sanctum. Long, given the land we had to cover, and painful because we had to keep our voices hushed.

The Howlers are immeasurably protective of their part of the forest, only granting travel through under strict circumstances. The Kingdom only tolerates their stubbornness because of the labor they provide.

I can count on one hand how many times I've been in this neck of Sumeria — the first being the most traumatic.

A male baby born of Heretic blood is born cursed: a Night Demon, and the Solar half of the Sanctum is where their oh-so esteemed Elders dump us, forcing us to forge our own path without so much as a blanket on our back or extra cloths to soil in.

Though, and not without struggle, most of us manage to find our way out, so the community here is usually small.

Tight.

I have no desire to be a part of it ever again.

I slump back in my chair, uncharacteristically quiet as the hours tick by.

I know Bea must relish the silence but I can't help but itch with impatience. I could talk my way out of a cloth gag soaked in poison. In all honesty, I think I'd rather suffer the wrath of the poison than keep my lips sealed for any longer.

"I'm tired of this."

"We should be in Alnola soon," Bea sighs dejectedly.

I mimic a gagging noise. "I despise that place."

"Don't be so dramatic. We won't be there long."

We discussed our plan of action back in Surlise when the Kingdom picked us up in our carriage. For two low-profile rogue operators, we're travelling in pretty high style. Our asses have been thoroughly wined and dined atop this gilded four seater coach. The cushions are plush, Bea has enough food to last her a month, and no one has the right mind to turn us away thanks to the Royal emblem.

The journey grants us the time to sort through our very many thoughts. Well, Bea's very many thoughts — I've never been one for thinking. Or knowing. Or wanting to think or know. I mostly just help Bea sieve through her feelings, occasionally nodding along or shaking my head. Real best friend stuff. Yet the more Bea rationalizes, the more *I* start to worry.

In all fairness, this whole ordeal seems very simple. Travel to the Domain, investigate the Banshee incident and track the Hand back to Ochrore — find the Hand, capture, retreat.

Simple.

Who am I to question that?

But now that we're actually on our way, the reality of the situation begins to dawn on me.

We're trying to find someone who's been missing for years — twelve, to be exact. We don't know what she looks like, if she's trained, where she actually, currently, *definitely* is, and how exactly she managed to stay hidden all this time?

I'm not one to get nervous but this clusterfuck makes me borderline feverish. I rest my dampening forehead against the carriage window, the cool glass keeping me calm and collected. I watch as our carriage crosses a small bridge out of the Peaks and officially into the Domain. Alnola can't be far now.

"Maybe after we find the Hand, the Royal family will formally thank us," I muster up, earning a glare from Bea.

"What, with a fancy ceremony or something?"

"Preferably. I want to walk down the aisle in the Great Hall, Knyghts bowing down to me with their heads on the ground. I want the King to kiss all my fingers and all my toes, and give me chests full of treasure."

"Right."

"I bet Princess Clement would even give you a kiss, thanking you for all your hard work," I tease.

Bea's eyes are scornful and roll with feigned annoyance, though the faintest grin plays on her lips.

"You'll be eaten by a Harpy before you get the chance to see that."

It's just after midday when our carriage finally stops just outside the gates of Alnola, where four Knyghts stand guard, wrapped in cloths of navy and black. Our coachman, a tall, slender man draped in brown opens the doors to usher us out.

Bea and I lock eyes, conspiring as we pull on the hoods of our cloaks, veiling them over our heads. I sheath my loose dagger as Bea grabs her bow and pulls another black cloth over her mouth.

She winks.

We're ready to start.

We thank the coachman silently and walk up to the entrance. I try to suppress the same slight panic tickling my body as we approach the Knyghts. I'm not afraid of them by any means, but entering different regions isn't particularly easy for someone like me.

"A Royal carriage: looks like we have some serious business here, boys," one of the Knyghts jokes. He's leaning back on a bench, legs outstretched and crossed in front of him at the ankle. I'd sock him square in the face if he wasn't wearing a helmet.

"We are here on business directly from the Kingdom. Just

passing through," Bea explains, her unwavering voice thick with authority.

I quirk a smug smirk watching the Knyghts tense up as she reaches into her pocket to retrieve a small token. She pulls out the golden hilt of a ceremonial blade, a silver tassel tied to its end: a symbol representing the rule of the King and the Cain, and our royal key to the city.

One of the Knyghts grabs the hilt, turning it over in his armored hands, inspecting it. Another Knyght steps forward, straightening his back to size me up.

"A Night Demon, no? Got those bloody eyes," he inspects. I lift my head slightly so he can see my glare. "A nasty bloodsucker like you belongs in the Ex-isles," another Knyght sneers. It's the one who greeted us — the punchable one. Fucker.

"Is this what you want to see?" I demand, reaching under my cloak and pulling out the Celestite around my neck.

The Knyghts shoulders bounce. He's chuckling.

"So eager to prove your innocence, aren't you?" He taunts.

I release the thread of my Celestite and step forward. "I'm eager to do a lot of things, starting with putting my foot up your—"

"Look, can we pass through or not?" Bea demands, nudging me back before I get us into any trouble.

The Knyght hands the token back to her, then he looks at me, "Name?"

At least someone here is doing their job.

"Elio."

"Elio what?" the punchable Knyght jeers.

I feel Bea's hand on the back of my elbow.

"Just Elio," I smile, devilishly. "Now, can we please move along?"

The other Knyght, the semi-decent one, nods as he jots something down on a piece of parchment — my name, most likely. The Kingdom loves keeping their tabs on the where-abouts of my kind. Howlers, too. We can't go anywhere in Sumeria without the Kingdom breathing down our necks. I'd love to breathe down their necks for a change. Maybe I could finally have a full feed.

"You two can go in. Commander Thierri is pushing orders until the General returns," he says, stepping out of our way.

The Knyght in front of me opens the lid of his helmet and spits on the ground, missing my shoes by a hair.

"Watch your step," he grits under his breath, "filth like you don't belong here."

Before I succumb to instinct and rip the bastard's head off, Bea grasps my forearm and pulls me forward. I burn my eyes into the Knyght, keeping my gaze set until they're behind us.

"We won't be here long," Bea reminds me. "In the mean-time, promise me you'll stay away from trouble."

"Admit it, you want me to hassle them."

"Elio, focus."

I breathe in, taming the heat boiling in my chest.

The Celestite proves that I can cross into any new territory and region — it holds me back on my innate nature of being a 'nasty fucking bloodsucker'. A Demon. With it, I'm treated as close to human as possible. I look and act like one too, despite my scarlet eyes, only needing a few samples of blood to keep my appetite at bay. It's what keeps me from being banished to the Ex-Isles. But when confronted by Knyghts who act like *that*, all proud and full of shit, I wish for nothing more than to succumb to my nature.

So I don't promise Bea anything.

Alnola is similar to Eephifer only in structure. They're both large towns built from rock and stone, although Alnola is darker, with hues of gray and black rock instead of crimson brick — merchants still litter the streets selling herbs, weapons, tapestries, cloth, and many other essential trading items. There's nothing that would be considered 'untoward' here.

The Knyghts roam the streets all the same no matter the region, but there's something different about their manner back in Eephifer. In the Sleepless City, the Knyghts do their job but they also know when to hang up their helmets. They drink and dance the night away at taverns and revels, partaking in all sorts of debauchery themselves.

Can't say the same for the stuck-up bastards here. With every corner we turn stands a Knyght, perched and poised, every bit the portrait of bullshit and bigotry.

As we walk, I see a Night Demon in the shadows being cornered by a Knyght tugging on his Celestite, yelling in his face. I feel that same innate instinct as before, running my blood hot, scorching with fury. There's truly nothing I hate more than the shit not only my kind, but everyone 'below' the belt of Royalty or militia deal with everyday.

"I really hate it here," I growl.

Bea grabs my hand, lacing our fingers, reminding me to stand down.

We swiftly weave through the streets, making our way towards the Guardian Headquarters. It's a tall building with a pointed roof: a black and navy tapestry, embroidered with the region's crest that hangs above the grand double doors.

"I'll do the talking," Bea says.

"What if *I* want to talk?"

"You're a burning powder keg," she counters. "As fun as it'd be to listen to you antagonize the Commander, I'd rather go in quick and finish this job."

Bea presents the token once again to get us through the doors of the Headquarters, a building of the Kingdom's design — nothing but white marble and weathered stone. Two Knyghts flank either side of us as we walk through the entryway. Our boots clip like rocks hitting water, echoing throughout the hall.

The Guardian Headquarter is considered a sacred building. Gilded and blessed, the walls are adorned with intricate paintings illustrating the lives of Adam and Eve; staged on surrounding pedestals and stored on wooden shelves are ancient ceremonial weapons. A Knyght is posted every few feet along the perimeter of the space, standing guard lest someone with my level of, let's say, *appreciation* gets too close.

The Knyghts escort us inside a spacious cabinet room where a man with a curly beard sits behind a table holding a lens up to one eye, the glass no doubt magnifying the multiple sheets of parchment scattered before him.

"Commander Thierri," a Knyght projects. "We have guests sent from the Kingdom."

"Welcome," he replies tonelessly, too deeply invested in his reading.

"We came on behalf of King Hyttenrauch himself, sent to capture and retrieve a missing person suspected to be in the

Ashen Domain," Bea begins. She steps forward, placing the token on the table. "My partner and I would like to ask some questions regarding the matter."

"I see," Commander Thierri says, still consumed in thought.

"Excuse me, sir, but we're up *here*," I jab, waving my hand to get his attention.

Bea pinches my arm, glaring at me to keep my mouth shut. Oh, if only she could read my mind — it's not like *I'm* the one being a dick.

The Commander finally looks up, pursing his lips. He scans us with one brown eye, the other one scarred, cloudy and gray, his expression incomprehensible.

"What do we call them?" he asks the Knyghts, as if we aren't standing right in front of him. Maybe I should blind him in his other eye, too.

"Capitan and Magpie, sir," a Knyght responds.

"Capitan?" He points to Bea, taking his guess. She nods. "You came here looking for Prince Aalis, no?"

"The Prince?" I blurt. Bea looks equally confused.

"His Royal Highness was privately reported missing two days ago, so I assumed you were here for that."

Since when did His Royal Highness ditch town?

"I'm an assassin," Bea states.

"Yeah, she kills people. I stand by and watch," I retort. Maybe Bea was right about me not speaking. "We are *not* here for the Prince."

"Oh, my apologies." The Commander clears his throat. He sounds worn out. "General Bausan set out for the town of Brighes to settle the incident with the Banshee," he resumes, "I'm sure he has all the information you need to know."

"But we're talking to you right now. What information do *you* know?" Bea admonishes.

Yeah, it's definitely a good thing she's doing the talking.

Commander Thierri waves the two Knyghts away. He waits for them to shut the door behind us before he sets the parchment down and sighs. He's fairly young, though the fatigue stretches wrinkles across his sun-rich skin, disguising that fact.

"Who is it the King wants you to find?" he inquires.

Bea hesitates, but there's no point in keeping it a secret if he knows something.

"The lost Hand, sir."

The Commander chokes back a laugh. "You are looking for a ghost, then."

"The King doesn't seem to think so," Bea insists.

"Then he is going off of information that no one else has. A Banshee screaming in a small town tucked away in Ochrore does not immediately suggest the location of the lost Hand," the Commander argues, pitching a fair point. "If the Hand is in fact still alive, and in Brighes, then we would know by blood samples taken from the villagers at the inspection earlier today," he continues. "Heretics have a special kind of blood pumping through them. She'd stand out like a sore thumb."

"When would those samples arrive?"

"By sundown, I presume." Commander Thierri shakes his head. "But General Bausan has no intention to thoroughly investigate the incident. He only wishes to rid the village of any cursed energy left by the Dark Maid. By the time they arrive back in Alnola, the amount of samples retrieved may be slim."

"So, what? The village is being burned down?" I jump in.

"It's very likely tha—"

"The General can't do that!" Bea snaps. I glance over at my friend, her eyes piercing through the slit between her mask and hood. "How could the Kingdom allow this after Thessonne?"

"It does not concern you," the Commander says, eyeing Bea's defensive stance.

"It concerns us if it jeopardizes our mission," I elicit. "The King would be very upset to learn that his most prized possession was burned alive in a very unnecessary raid."

The Commander sets his specs down and pushes away from the table. As he digs around on a shelf behind him, I sweep my eyes over the room once more, taking note of it all: weapons, paintings, some parchments scribbled with harsh ink, a map of Sumeria. But it's a particular piece of paper that catches my eye. It's folded four times over, wrinkled and stained by who knows what. I quietly pluck it from the table in front of me and stuff it into my satchel before the Commander spins back around, revealing the token with another tassel tied to the hilt. This one is navy.

"The King ordered the General to carry out his actions. He also gave you this mission, knowing that you can try and find her amidst the situation at hand." Now that the Commander is standing, I finally take in his build: his height is hindered by the hunch of his back, hanging low with broad shoulders. He points the golden hilt at the two of us. "You two seem smart. I can grant you access to the Domain and two horses for travel." He hands the token back to Bea. "But that's all I can offer you. For now."

Bea snatches the token from his outstretched hand.

"How generous," I say, dulled.

Commander Thierri sighs in defeat. He clearly wasn't expecting us and apparently couldn't care less about substituting for General Bausan. I can see we have overstayed our welcome as he stalks closer to the door.

"The General should be back soon." He places a calloused hand around the handle and opens it for us. "Best be on your way."

We leave without saying another word.

"I should've done the talking."

Bea ignores me, fuming. We've since left the Headquarters, now merging with the folk in the town. An overcast of clouds hover over the square like shadows in somber light.

I note that there aren't that many villagers walking about: mainly Knyghts and merchants. Though seeing as Alnola is more of a trading hub for a variety of vendors and a bridge to the rest of the Ashen Domain, it doesn't surprise me. It's not typically the first choice for a home or raising a family.

"We've got horses now. It's good enough," Bea grumbles. "We can ride to Ochrore and investigate more there."

"I want to get my hands on those blood samples."

"That's if there are any left," Bea adds. "Why do they even bother?"

We make our way to the edge of the town square in silence.

"I can't believe they're burning that village down," Bea mutters under her breath.

I shrug. "I expected as much."

It's barely there, but there's a glint of sorrow in her eyes. I suck in a breath and clap a hand on her back, derailing the thoughts I know are digging in her mind.

"Let's just worry about us," I suggest. "Hey! Like that prick said, we're smart. We very well might be chasing a dead person, but at least we have a place to start. If the King suspects that she's in Ochrore, then to Ochrore we go."

Bea's eyes crease, the slightest hint of a smile behind her mask.

"You're being strangely optimistic," she says.

"I have money on my mind. And freedom. We'll find her."

Bea nods, placing her hands on the stone barrier. She leans forward, her eyes falling again.

"Look at all that smoke," she notes. I follow her gaze far over the forest and see the fumes fading into the sky.

"C'mon," I say after a moment, grabbing her arm and tugging her away from the overlook. "I want to meet the infamous General Bausan."

It's sunset when we leave Alnola.

We exit out the eastern gates. They lead us on a cobblestone path along the town perimeter that dips down a hill near the bloodred shores of Carmine Lagoon. It's said that this is where the angels Sanvi, Sansanvi, and Semangelaf threatened to drown the bitch after refusing to return to Adam. Instead, she chose to go to Edom, staining the waters forevermore.

It's strange being this close to the Realm of Zemergad again.

The Lagoon expands far out south, separating the capital

of the Domain from the sacred, closed-off Realm that belongs to the Maidens of Lilith. It's been a long time since I've seen that crimson, murky water bubbling with who knows what.

Being this close reminds me of why we rarely ever venture into the Domain. So many sights, so many things I wish to forget. Bea too. She trots ahead of me on her white horse, quiet and focused. I can practically hear the cogs turn in her brain. Our meeting with Commander Thierri was more than infuriating. I know that she'd rather not talk about it — we're way past addressing our childhoods.

"I don't want to make a big scene," Bea says. "So, again, let me do the talking."

"You can't tell me what to do," I retort, shifting uncomfortably on the saddle. I couldn't figure out how to adjust the stirrups so my knees are practically up against my chest. It doesn't help that Bea can't stop giggling at the sight of me.

"Oh, stop it."

"You look ridiculous."

"These creatures are hardly cooperative," I grumble, trying to sit up straight.

"They'll never trust you if you talk shit," she says, brushing her hand through the horse's mane. It huffs appreciatively at her gentle touch. Show off. "You know, I plan to purchase my own steed after this is all over."

"That's a fair investment," I reason. "I'll be getting a new wardrobe."

The stone path ends, breaking off into grass and dirt. A dense cove of oak trees engulf us as we enter Abram Woods, the thick patch of forest between Alnola and Ochrore. The orange sky peeks ever so coyly through the branches.

Over the past few years, Capitan and Magpie have slowly, but surely, built up a notorious reputation in the underground world of fraudulent, debaucherous mishaps. Our clients range from nobles, commoners — even Knyghts who have all invested in us to handle their dirty work. And now that we've caught the attention of the King? It's a little ridiculous.

What sort of intel might he have in his poisonous grasp?

"Can't believe the Kingdom lost their Little Prince."

"He's a fragile thing," Bea chuckles. "Wherever he ran away to, he won't last long."

"Odd timing, isn't it?"

My question hangs in the air as Bea glances down at a map. If the Prince really did run away, might he be in the Ashen Domain? How does the Kingdom just *lose* him, though? Why would he even want to leave such a lifestyle? He lives in a shiny world with the promise of food and safety for the rest of his life, a giant fucking silver spoon in his stupid fucking little mouth. I can't imagine what pushed him to get out.

"What if someone kidnapped him?" I propose.

"Hmm? We don't need to worry about it," Bea dismisses.

"I'm not worrying," I defend. "Just curious."

"Yeah, a little *too* curious," Bea says, earning yet another scowl from me. She finally manages to look up from the map and squint. "The woods should cut off here soon."

We glide through the trees as the sun disappears, bathing Abram Woods in darkness. I eventually take the lead and guide us through the trees with Bea at my tail, listening to my horse's movements. In the night, my eyes adjust immediately, tracing the environment in cohesive lines that only I can see.

My vision enhances the more we break away from the dense trees, catching fragments of moonlight.

"Look," I point at a glimmer of light in the distance.

"Torches," she notes. "We're close."

We tear through the trees and are met with a vast terrain of tall grass and hills. A large group marches in our direction, the front line made up of metal-heads, small flames licking the tops of their torches, and a couple dozen seized civilians following suit in their hold. Behind them, smoke continues to simmer from the patch of land I presume to be the village of Brighes.

Bea guides her horse forward, and I follow behind her as we trot towards our new company. A Knyght calls out, having spotted us riding towards them.

"General Bausan!" Bea responds, gaining their full attention.

The Knyghts in the front line have all unsheathed their swords, defensive over our sudden approach. I slide off of my horse and put myself between Bea and the Knyghts.

"Who are you?" A gravelly voice erupts. The Knyghts move aside, making way for quite a large man. He wades through the mud before him, stomping and squelching with every step.

This man towers over me by a head or two, completely dissolving my dominance with a single glare, his eyes dark with specks that smolder like dwindling coal. His armor doubles his swollen build — a boulder beside my pebbled frame. His black hair is damp, curling at the top of his shoulders, and his clean cut beard wraps around the sneer that pulls at his lips, showing off his crooked teeth, and of course, in this moment of slight terror I feel looking at him, a laugh escapes from my mouth.

"*Elio*," Bea bites under her breath.

The man's jaw twitches and I wonder how hard it would be to crack him.

"I'm sorry, I mean no harm," I chuckle. I lift my hands up defensively. "You *must* be General Bausan."

The man grips the hilt of his sword and slides it out of his sheath with a scraping noise. He pushes it against my chest, the point digging into my blouse.

That simple, huh?

"Is this some sort of joke?" He growls. My hands are shaking, but the smile stays plastered to my face.

"No, sir," Bea replies hastily. She hops off her horse and pulls me aside, giving me an incredulous stare. The General keeps his sword on me. "We're here under the wishes of the King. I'd like to ask you a few questions and then we'll get out of your way."

The General almost doesn't seem real. He's no larger than a Howler, but I wouldn't be surprised if he could hold his own in a sparring match with one. I'd even bet my money on him taking down a Harpy with his fists alone.

"I don't care who you are."

"We spoke with Commander Thierri," Bea persists. "He said you might've gathered some blood samples from the villagers of Brighes. It's in both of our best interests that you allow my partner and I to inspect them."

"You and your partner don't concern me," The General retorts. It's now that I notice a smaller woman posted behind the General. She wears a crisp, white cloak around her body, her features telling. This woman is a Heathen.

"Respectfully," I spout, earning the tip of his sword pointed at me again. "You don't concern us, either."

"Is that so?" The General taunts, ice cold.

I nod, pinching the tip of his sword between my fingers, slicing the skin of my pointer. The General blinks, the slightest hint of bewilderment playing in his eyes.

"Indeed," I press, holding my finger up, the fire light catching the blood dripping from the small incision. "I don't care what you've done. We only ask for a peek at those blood samples and we'll be on our way. No harm, like I said. We're on the same team here, if it isn't obvious."

The General is silent whilst the Knyghts shift on their feet, waiting for their leader to act.

I glance at Bea, just to make sure she's alright. I tried my best to give her a moment to gather herself after having been berated by that piece of shit.

The General finally lowers his sword, lodging the point deep into the ground. His eyes stay sharp, sweeping over the audience that's gathered. Then, he looks at the Heathen and nods. She steps forward.

"We have no samples," she declares.

"Nothing?" Bea implores.

"Inspections are expendable — we simply do not have enough time, and the dark magic that has infected that town cannot be stopped by simply checking what lies within. They must be eradicated," the Heathen upholds.

"The survivors are with us now. Those who burned were sacrificed for the safety of the living," The General concludes.

"What business do you have with those samples, anyhow?" A stray Knyght wonders. He earns a glare from the General for speaking out of turn.

I don't answer, unsure of the General's intentions. Bea steps forward, her back straight, a hand tight around the hilt of her dagger.

"I'm the Capitan," she states. "If I'm sent on a mission, I will see it through. So, if you have any information from the villagers regarding the Maiden's lost Hand, tell me now. You do not want me as your enemy."

Realization hits the General, cracking through his grimace. The Heathen fashions a deadly scowl of her own.

"I see," he muses. The smirk on his mouth sends a shiver down my spine.

Our stand-off is interrupted by the sounds of commotion. Everyone's attention turns to the throng of screaming villagers as Knyghts bark at them, forcing them back into line.

"General! We have a runner!" A Knyght shouts, coming forward with a villager dangling in his grasp.

"Please!" she weeps. It's a dreadful old woman. Her dress garments are ripped and charred, scratches littering her beaten face. The General is piqued by her agonizing words, swinging around to face her. "Haven't you done enough?" she cries. The Knyght clutches her arm with vigor, the pain causing her to wince.

"What I've done is save you all," the General explains, unbothered by her pleas. "The Dark Maid and her evil magic had to burn."

"But my daughter! She's alive! She was left behind," she wails. "I must get back to her!"

The General studies the old woman, a predator stalking its prey. He shifts his gaze to Bea, clearly taunting her. I walk a few paces behind Bea, my hand at my side where my blade rests. Bea stalks toward the woman, her footsteps light and agile.

"Did you see your daughter flee from the raid?" Bea demands.

The old woman cries. The Knyght loosens his grip, pushing her to the ground, her palms digging into the dirt.

"She ran away, yes," she sobs. "I saw her."

Bea slowly takes out her dagger, keeping it low. "So she left. How could she leave you behind?"

The woman just shakes her head.

Seems like she was trying to save herself, I think.

"Everyone in that village should've been gathered up!" The General booms, addressing his Knyghts.

"That's right," Bea plays along. "Do you know where I can find her? To bring her back to you, safe and sound."

The woman whimpers in pain, though it isn't unlike anything I've seen before. I've watched people die, seen their blood spilled, drenched on Bea's armor. I've tortured people myself to get what I need: it's routine. Seeing this woman cower before my friend is nothing new.

I watch the General and Bea exchange a look. I guess we follow his orders now.

"She—" the woman sputters, "she would have gone to the shoreline. Please make sure she is safe."

"I will," Bea says.

I blink and Bea's dagger slashes the skin of the old woman's throat. Her body crumples to the ground, a pool of blood seeping into the land. The Knyght who was holding her steps back, resuming his duty behind the General. Bea towers over the fallen with her head down. I stare at the blood dripping from her blade. Some of the villagers scream, having seen the execution between the cracks of standing Knyghts.

"So much for not wanting to make a scene," I mumble to Bea.

I move my eyes to the Heathen, who has her head turned away from the body. She keeps her hands clasped in front of her, as poised and elegant as ever.

I turn towards the General, watching him divulge in the death of the old woman. He strikes a slimy smile at Bea — a look I'm not at all fond of.

"You have your answer, young assassin," Bausan grunts, kicking the body into the nearest pool of flames. "Now, carry on."

7
AALIS

I scratch my neck, staring at the ingredients in front of me.

My palms are slick with sweat as I pick up a dull knife and begin idly slicing a tomato. I grumble as the knife crushes through the thin skin. Red juice gushes into a mushy pile of seeds and liquid, splattering on my singed blouse.

How lovely.

I'm already embarrassed that Abeko practically dragged my unconscious body to this safe house, but I'm even more so now because I don't know how to prepare a meal.

I found myself lying on a mat by a fireplace after I'd come to my senses, covered by a knitted blanket with Abeko nowhere to be seen. I panicked at the unfamiliar surroundings, taking in the small cottage — just a small living space and kitchen, my satchel perched on the dining table. The only table. There was another room behind a closed door, and when I knocked on the wood, it was her voice in return telling me she would be out soon.

I had first assumed it was Abeko's home, but judging by the gigantic boots sitting by the front door and the unusually tall legs of the table, I soon figured it belonged to someone else — someone much larger.

I regret ever picking up the knife as I ineptly slaughter

yet another tomato. I don't even like tomatoes. I step back, wiping my hands on a shabby cloth. The skin on my palm is tender, small blisters forming from when I grabbed the scorching arrow out of the ground. Selova would throw a fit at the state I'm in: bruised and coated in filth.

There's a single window casting light into the cottage, along with some candles I presume Abeko lit whilst I was unconscious. I manage to catch a glimpse of the sunset, its colors reflecting across the bed of water outside. It seems I only ever got to witness such beauty from behind glass.

It must've been at least an hour since I last knocked on the door.

Do I check up on her again?

What if she's upset?

Would she want to be comforted?

Flashes of the raid resurface: the chaos, the screaming, the heat. The village is likely just a memory now, reduced to ashes and dust. I step away from the food, sick beyond belief, but some more rancid tomato guts dribble off the table, splattering straight onto the floor. I push the remains to the side and attempt to slice an onion. All seems well until my eyes start to burn, sending scalding tears streaming down my cheeks. I smack the tip of the blade deep into the countertop, my cries unwavering. I give my lids a rub to soothe the itch but by Edom, the damning burns only worsen. I bark quite the un-royal curse, slamming my hands down on the cutting board and tilting my head back to blink frantically at the ceiling.

"Are you alright?" Abeko's voice is sweet and full of concern, despite the startle.

Through my tears, I can make out the shape of her

silhouette — she's leaning against the door frame, somewhat hesitant. I most definitely look like a bloody fool, one at war with a stupid onion of all things, pointing at it accusingly.

"I was cutting that and *ah!* My *eyes*," I hiss. "Maybe we should just have the pastries from Tilver for supper."

Abeko pushes away from the door and approaches me. She takes the cloth on the table, grabs a wooden pitcher, and gently pours some water over it.

"Here," she offers, a worried smile playing on her lips.

I take the scrap from her hand, cool and heavy against my fingers. "Thank you."

She nods and steps in front of me, observing the vegetables splayed out on the table. I pat at my eyes with the damp rag, the stinging sensation slowly vanishing with each press.

"It looks like a lot of these vegetables are rotten, but I think we can salvage the rest," Abeko sighs, flitting from cupboard to cupboard laden with dust in search of, I assume, crockery. "Oh, Lycidas."

Lycidas? But I'm *Aalis*.

"I wanted to cook you something," I confess, a little more sheepishly than I intended. "I assumed you'd be hungry."

"That's very kind of you," she smiles while dumping the salvageable remnants into some clay bowls.

"I also meant to start a fire in order to actually cook something, but I—" I drift off, abashed yet again. "I don't know how to make one. Or how to cook. Sorry."

Abeko turns to face me. It's now that I try to study every feature on her face, and though my eyes seem to still simmer with the onion's rage, I take this moment and cherish it for what it's worth. It's all so bittersweet: the woman who stands before me, looking back at me with those same inquisitive eyes as she did years before. But now they drown in sorrow — a colorless, lifeless void where I can no longer tell iris from pupil. There is no more hope. It has all caught up with her.

We're both silent for a while and so, naturally, I immediately jump to the conclusion that she's probably going to start running for the hills any moment now, begging to be free of me and my silent staring — oh my, this is *not* going well. By Edom, my heart feels like it's about to burst free from my chest and splatter all over my shiny shoes, just like those poxy vegetables.

"Are you sure you're alright?" she asks, freeing me from torment.

"Yes, fine," I flash a strained smile. I even throw her an awkward double thumbs up.

Creator, you made me a walking nightmare.

"What about your hand?" she adds. I notice that her eyes are red and puffy. "I poured some of the cool water on it when you were unconscious to stop the swelling."

I lift my hand up, surveying the blister.

"It'll be okay. Thank you. I apologize for breaking down on you." For some reason, I can only bring myself to respond in staccato beats — it's either that or I fall to my knees and vomit up a confession.

"Don't worry about it," she waves. "And don't worry about a fire either. I don't think starting one is the smartest of ideas."

"Right!" I exclaim, "because the smoke would give us away."

"Well, it's a good thing I can make do with the ingredients we have. Did you bring this bread? It looks delicious."

"All the way from Tilver," I beam.

Abeko doesn't reply. She simply returns my grin as she continues filling the bowls. I stay out of her way as she moves around the kitchen, drifting from table to shelf in one fluid glide.

"So, is this your home?" I ask, itching to fill the silence.

She pauses from slicing a loaf of bread to shake her head. "No, it's my friend's. His name is Lycidas. He's gone to the Sanctum for the full moon."

Thank the Creator.

"So he's a Howler, then?"

I've never met a Howler — they're rarely in Ead, if at all. The Shepard has always avoided negotiating face to face with the King, and believe you me, I understand why.

"Yes. I figured that if he can meet Sarya in Thessonne, then maybe when he returns he can help me find somewhere to go," she says quietly.

Oh.

I hadn't really thought about our next move. Though admittedly, I really didn't think I would get this far. Some Knyght in shining armor I am. More like the Damsel in distress. Not that it matters. Abeko was planning on leaving, and she means to go alone.

"And you trust him? Your friend?" I don't really know why I push it.

Her eyes find mine, staring right through me, stripping me to my marrow.

"He's family. I don't know who else to trust."

My hand reaches out before I can stop myself, placing my fingers against her arm, desperately trying to find that connection we had years ago: one where she didn't freeze under my touch like she does now.

"You can trust me," I urge. Her eyes are wide, clearly still trying to process this whole situation herself. "Abeko—"

Her face pinches together, a minor flinch, recalling a bad memory. I pull away as if I were burned yet again, though this hurts twice as much.

"Please," she breathes, "just call me Beka."

I think I nod, my mouth drying. The smile she offers me is wry, it doesn't meet her ears, doesn't match her eyes, and wobbles ever so slightly.

Oh, bother.

She adds a few finishing touches to the bowls: some springs of something green here, a slice of something pungent there. She hands me one of the bowls along with a wooden spoon before making her way towards the barren fireplace. I follow in her step, quick and lithe, plopping down on the hard ground rather than spreading wide on the tartan chaise. Well, the 'chaise'. I sit a few feet away from her, criss-crossing my legs to use my knees as a table for my food. My stomach grumbles, the only noise save for the clammy chewing clacks. I'm not used to being in charge of making my own meals: they usually just show up at my door, or I'm reminded by a servant to come to the dining hall.

"Forgive me. I didn't mean to make you uncomfortable," I start.

"It's okay," she shrugs as she rips her bread into bite-size chunks. "I just haven't gone by that name in a long time."

I decide it's probably best for me to stay quiet. I don't want to pry anymore. I guess I imagined she was on some island this whole time, secluded and far from danger, living among the Sirens or something. I never thought she'd find her way into a community, living under the noses of the Kingdom and Knyghts, blending into the role of a farmhand so seamlessly.

"Is the food alright?" Beka asks.

I nod my head a little too enthusiastically. "Yes!" I shove a raw potato slice into my mouth. "The best I've had in a while."

"You're being too nice," Beka shakes her head, seeing right through my lie. "I'm sure the cooks in the castle are much better."

"They're not anything special." I mumble, scratching my neck. "There are these little cakes they bake, though. Sometimes they're filled with jam, but I prefer the chocolate ones. I swear I could eat five of them in one sitting."

"Five?" she grins.

"Maybe six on a good day," I rave. "They're borderline scandalous."

Again, Beka's smile vanishes as quickly as it had spread. She doesn't care about the cakes.

"I'm sorry. I'm not sure what to say," I confess.

"Me too. I can't really think about anything."

"Do you want to?"

She shakes her head. We sit and eat in silence.

Candles burn bright in the space around us, the sun now fully set for the night. Beka is bathed in a shadow, the orange glow of the flames confined within the living room. In the dim light she seems far away, nibbling on a carrot with a frown pulling at her lips.

"I never got the chance to thank you," Beka confesses.

I stop mid-motion, a piece of bread halfway in my mouth. "Hmm?"

"You saved my life back then," she adds. "I never understood why, but thank you."

I bite down on the bread and nod, mouth full of food.

"No need to thank me." I swallow as Beka eyes me suspiciously. "I don't regret doing it, if that's what you're wondering."

"You told me you would find me again," Beka mutters.

"Well—"

"Why are you here? Seriously?" Beka persists, her tone shifted. "You risked everything when you helped me before. Now you're here again, out of the blue, and I can't understand why."

"I just," I pause, choosing my words carefully.

How am I to explain to her that she's spent my every waking moment sat in my brain, perched behind my eyes, tingling the tips of my fingers, directing every movement of my paintbrush, dictating my every thought, without sounding like I had some sort of unhealthy, very creepy and very wrong infatuation with her?

"Everyone thought you were dead, but I knew the truth. The King announced that you were killed during the attack somehow. They assumed you died when the prisoner barracks were destroyed in the battle, but they never found a body. He tortured the Maidens with that knowledge regardless, and I've just been sitting in silence knowing it wasn't true. I gave you a chance to survive, and I've wondered the past twelve years where you went, hoping you were okay."

She refuses to make eye contact, instead picking at the

tassels of her ripped dress. I don't expect her to respond, at least not right away. She's probably recalling the events of that day just as I am.

Everyone remembers the Battle of Lamya.

Those who were there in the Kingdom bore the brunt of the fight, witnessing the collapse of the great bridge connecting Surlisle and the Kingdom together. The Maidens attacked ferociously with the heavy need on their shoulders to avenge. Their Hand was taken from them after being blindly ambushed by the Kingdom, murdering countless of their own. They just wanted her home. The Maidens didn't hold back, conjuring their darkest power to destroy the walkway and break through into Royal territory. The King sent me away to my chambers but I listened behind closed doors as Knyghts and servants bustled through the hallways.

The only thing on my mind at that moment was what they were going to do with the girl in the cell. No matter how the battle would end, someone was going to kill the Hand before she got the chance to live. Really live. It seemed so unfair, so unjust for a young girl to bear the brunt of a fight she didn't start. She couldn't help who she was, just like I couldn't help what color I bled. It was all down to circumstance of birth, something beyond our control.

That night, I fled to the prison. I descended through the dark halls with a single candlelight, managing to slip down unnoticed, all the way to the barracks. To my surprise, there were no Knyghts guarding the door. The King saw to it that they were rightfully punished.

"I was prepared to die," Beka whispers. "I couldn't believe that you wanted to help me."

I remember how terrified she was as I fiddled with the lock on her cell, the sounds of battle shaking the walls: swords clashing, magic ricocheting off the buildings. She'd ushered me to stand back, and once I did, a spark of energy erupted from her small hand, shattering the metal into pieces. *Magic*, I thought, amazed by the sight of it.

"Watching you suffer ripped me apart. I'd hate myself if I'd let you die."

Beka stares at me wildly, full of disbelief.

I think of the way I had taken her into the passageway after leaving the barracks, where we ran to the gardens stretching to the shores of the sea. The blue skies were stained with black and purple streaks, remnants of the powerful magic being materialized.

"You told me to go to Tilver. So I did."

"*How?*" I stress. "You couldn't have swam the entire way."

"It was the Sirens: they carried me through the sea. All the way to the docks on the other side. Seems as though their allegiance to the Lady is strong even to this day," Beka explains. We've both abandoned our meals. "I stayed in Tilver until the battle ended, then moved down to Ochrore."

"Huh," I sag.

We sit with the memories, a strange sense of nostalgia growing in the space between us.

"Why didn't you go back to Zemergad?" I hesitate, unsure if this is an appropriate thing to ask.

Beka considers the question. I'm relieved to finally talk about what happened; there's no one else that would be safe with the information we have.

"I guess," she starts, taking a moment to think, "I guess I

didn't go back because no one knew who I was in Ochrore, and I liked that." Beka brings her legs close to her chest, resting her chin between her knees. "A lovely woman named Emelyne found me and raised me as her own. She had a son once, but he had died before his first birthday — a sickly child. She had no husband, no wife, no partner. No one suspected anything of me, and I finally felt what it was like to just be a little girl. I was a daughter. I couldn't go back after having that sort of freedom.

"There was this duty given to me the moment I took my first breath. The Maidens are not cruel, and a life in the Realm would have been wonderful had I not been in this position. But they couldn't convince me that it was an honor being born to die. My eventual sacrifice was worth more than their own lives, and I was only a child."

"It's strange living a life that's already decided for you," I offer. "No matter what, I am the heir to the throne. My sister might be older than me, yet the crown will be put on my head. I can't change that."

Beka throws me an apologetic look. I've never told anyone this before — I'm sure she hasn't either.

"What about now? What does helping me mean for you?" Beka prompts.

I thought the same thing after I got Beka out of the cells the first time around.

I figured as long as I kept my story hidden, no one could truly know what happened to the Hand. The Kingdom would remember the Battle of Lamya as the day the Maidens got what they deserved. The Maidens would be haunted by the events, floating in a world that was once theirs that can never be reclaimed.

As far as the King knows, I was locked up in my room during the entire attack.

And now? Well, the King must know that I'm missing. Must know where my loyalties lie.

"I'm not really sure," I voice.

"You really have no plan at all?" Beka's eyes are suddenly frantic.

"I didn't have much time to think this through," I stress, every possible outcome of this suddenly flooding into my brain.

Beka sits back and gently smacks my arm. "Aalis," she reprimands, "what were you thinking?"

"I don't know! I overheard the King talking about everything — talking about the Banshee and the raid and about *you* and the possibility of you being alive. He wants you dead, and I figured that if I got to you first, we could find somewhere safe for you to go. I don't know, I just left!" I ramble, my breath uneven. Oh, I *really* didn't think this through at all.

"If people are after me, then we don't have as much time as I thought."

"The Kingdom is most likely searching for me as well."

"We can try and meet Lycidas halfway, maybe even stay in the Sanctum?" Beka suggests.

What happens if we're caught? Will the King put me on trial? He wants Beka dead, so there's no way he'd hesitate to make a show of it.

I groan, shoving my head into my hands. What kind of

person goes on a rescue mission and doesn't think about the escape plan? Me, apparently.

"Hey." I hear Beka shuffle closer to me, and suddenly she is leaning on my shoulder. I pull away from my hands, my eyes landing on her face. There's a scratch on her cheek, a thin line of purple blood, the slightest imperfection.

She's really here, sitting beside me. Her smile is gentle. Everything about her is, with the way her gaze envelops the things around her, embracing them with a single look.

"I'm such a fool," I whisper, her body close to mine.

Am I supposed to kiss her? Would that be totally presumptuous?

Beka frowns. "Yeah, kind of."

Did I say that out loud?

"I mean no offense," she counters, sliding off my shoulder, sitting back. "But we really should have a plan."

I sigh. "You're right. I suppose we're stuck in this together."

"But they mustn't know you're with me, helping me," Beka notes, tugging on a strand of her black hair. "Maybe if you leave me and go back now, you won't get in trouble."

"I'm not leaving you again," I protest. She's less surprised by my behavior now.

"Okay," she accepts after a pause. She's looking away from me, but I keep my gaze on her, waiting for another moment, hoping for another moment.

"Pastries?"

Beka stands up instead. I try to ignore the way my heart sinks.

"I think we should just rest for now."

I agree and from there we blanket ourselves in another

mutual silence, only this time not so painful. She floats grace-fully as we gather up the mess made in the kitchen. I find myself milling over our entire conversation, picking out each part I could've said differently.

Eventually we retreat to the single room. I offer to stay awake and keep watch, just in case. Beka takes the bed and dissolves into the abnormally large blankets, clearly exhausted from the day.

The full moon filters in through the square window, a soft light in the otherwise dark room. I sit in a chair by the door, keeping my head low, aching inside as she glows under the moonlight.

"Aalis?"

My head snaps up: I thought she'd already fallen asleep.

"Yes?" I feel my heart beat again.

"I'm glad you're here," Beka whispers.

It skips.

"Me too."

"If it's worth anything, I think you'll be a good King some-day." Her voice is quieter, looser. I feel the sting of tears pool in my eyes.

"Oh. Thank you." I find nothing else to say.

She doesn't reply, falling asleep moments later. I wipe a tear before it can drip off my eyelash. I don't expect myself to stay awake the entire night, but I try my very best to sit straight and stay alert. Though soon enough, my eyelids droop and my neck follows. I slouch into the chair and dream of this: of everything. Her smile, her voice, her presence. I dream that we're in a cottage of our own, cuddled up by the fire, eating our vegetables, reminiscing on our shared past. I show her my paintings and she kisses me, she tells me she's been waiting for me all this time, too. It's a good dream.

I wake up and that dream is gone.

There's something cold against my neck, and after I blink once, twice, I finally feel the stab of pain puncturing my skin.

"Little Prince," a shadowed figure says, pressing a knife below my chin. "What a lovely surprise."

8
ELIO

Bea and I don't plan to stay in Brighes for long.

We arrive at what used to be the town square, taking in the aftermath of Bausan's wrath. I hop off my horse and saunter around, keeping an eye out for anything valuable in the debris. In the pitch-black of the night, embers continue to cinder throughout the land, along with some spare torches burning for light around vast piles of ash. A metal silo has melted into a puddle, dripping through the scraps of what looks like the bars of a broken cage.

"I don't hear anyone. Let's keep moving," Bea says, still strapped onto her horse.

"I smell blood," I note, grimacing at the water of my mouth. "Human blood."

"No shit," Bea sounds exasperated. "The woman said she fled to the shoreline."

I turn away to poke at some detritus, finding nothing helpful whatsoever.

"There is a chance that this person has nothing to do with the Hand," I offer. I don't mean to doubt Bea at all, but it's something we have to consider. "They could be nobody."

"But they could be the Hand."

"I mean, that would be ideal, yes."

Bea's horse whinnies, shaking its head up and down in distress.

"If you find another lead, let me know," she says, soothing it with a gentle caress.

I make my way back to my own steed, careful not to puncture the makeshift peace between us. We don't dwell on the nature of our job. We were both there to see it happen, so why should we talk about it? If anything, we did the old lady a favor by putting her out of her misery before Bausan could have his way. But Bea is on edge, and that rarely ever happens — if ever.

"It just seems like a long shot," I grunt, pulling myself up. I wobble, nearly losing my balance as I try to stick my boot through the stirrup.

"We have no blood samples. Everyone else from the village was either killed or rallied up by the Knyghts. If there really were survivors unaccounted for, then that's who we need to find next," Bea explains, trotting up next to me.

"So grumpy!" I kick at her thigh.

Bea glares at me, winding her arm to smack me in the chest. In an attempt to avoid her attack, I nearly slip off my saddle. Bea turns her hand at the last second to grab the collar of my cloak, yanking me back into place.

"You need to work on your core," Bea smirks.

I swat her hand away and grab at my reins.

"We can rest if you want."

Bea shakes her head, but I can see the fatigue pulling at her face. She catches me staring and frowns, tugging her mask up to hide her mouth.

"I'm not tired," she grumbles. "I hate that you don't get tired."

"I have other things to do than worry about resting."

"Let's go, you bastard," Bea huffs with all the love in her heart.

I hear the crashing of waves before I see them.

The expanse of trees between the village and the shoreline is small. We ride for what seems like a few moments before our horses peek out of the brush and into the open. Bea and I slide off our horses and tie their reins to the trunks of the trees before stepping off the grass and onto a beach.

"Over there." Bea touches my arm and I follow her gaze in question.

To the right of where we stand, a colony of cottages stretches along the shore.

"They look abandoned," I muse.

Bea nods, her bow notched and ready to aim. When she managed to whip that out is anyone's guess. She's a wisp of a wraith: a shadow built of stealth and secrets with a tortured soul filled with enough hate to strike.

I move past her and inspect the ground, scanning the sand for any unusual tracks or recent imprints. Bea waits impatiently behind.

The air smells strictly of salt until it taints within half a beat. I stop, sniffing around, trying to find the hiccup.

"What is it?"

"Blood. Dried. Not human, either," I say.

Human blood is the type I drink most often. I know it better than my own. This scent, however, is completely foreign to me, and although I can't pin the taste of it on my tongue, I can only guess where it comes from.

"This is something new," I tell Bea.

That's all it takes for us to make a move.

We reach the first cottage: nothing. The second one is cleared out as well. We're rounding the side of the third cottage when the whine of a door opening and closing sounds. Bea and I freeze, gluing our backs to the wooden structure. I sniff the air again, my nose under siege by her scent. It has to be her: Maidens don't just waltz around outside of the Realm.

Bea stares at me, waiting. I mouth at her to *hold on*. I inch my way around the side of the cottage to peek out at the shore, and there, standing with her feet in the water, is the girl looking out at the sea. I meet Bea's gaze with a devilish grin. She sighs, pointing at the house, urging me to move.

"Go sweep the inside. I'll take care of things out here," she whispers.

I bring my hand up to my forehead, saluting her. "I won't let you down, Capitan."

Bea cracks the slightest smile, rolling her eyes. I patiently wait for her to react, and after huffing out a sigh, she puts her bow between her legs to free up her hands. She clasps them together in the shape of a bird, fluttering her fingers to mimic it flying away. For the finishing touch, she proudly sticks up both her middle fingers.

"Ass."

"Oh, off with you, Magpie."

It didn't fully click in my brain that I'd just put a knife

against the Crown Prince's throat even after he'd opened his eyes.

The Hyttenrauches have unmistakable features that coin them as the Royal Family — you just know when you're in the presence of their bloodline. From their tell-tale golden hair to the ocean blue of their eyes, no doubt a byproduct of centuries of incest, I'd gone my whole life so far without seeing one of them up close.

Until now, of course. And after hearing many a tale of these marks that distinguish them so, I was always told that if I was ever in the presence of those bastards, I'd know.

But the startled eyes staring back at me could belong to anyone.

With one tinted a pale blue and the other a faded brown, no part of me thought they were his — but there is no mistaking the woven-spun gold of his hair, or the copy of his mother's face on his: a portrait come to life.

I find myself prickling with triumph, because I, for one, was not expecting to find him here of all places. He must have a death wish. I was prepared to at least find either the Hand or a possible accomplice inside this cottage, but nothing could have stunned me more than to be met with *him*.

The first signs of dawn settle outside, the faintest rays of the rising sun peeking through the glass of the window. There weren't many spaces to investigate when I first walked into the cottage: just a simple living area and another door leading to this bedroom. Nothing interesting enough to snatch, either. Unless I want to stomp around in really big boots, which I can't say that I'm not totally tempted by. Well, not as tempted as I am by the now-squirming Little Prince.

I lift my knife from his neck so he doesn't slice his own throat trying to move, relishing in the foolish relief that stains his face. I can see the cogs turn in his head but, stupidly enough, he attempts to stand up, completely failing to realize that he has just pushed his throat back up against my blade.

Oh, on Adam's fucking grave. Why help anyone?

I stomp my boot down into his chest, knocking him back before he gets any Royal blood on my hands — a crime I cannot afford. To my surprise, he sinks back easily, his build crumbling under my force. Though, to be fair, I think even the wind could do him some damage.

"Tut, tut, tut." I click my tongue.

I'm aware that I just pushed Royalty with a muddy shoe, but who's here to stop me?

What surprises me most is that Prince Aalis allows himself to be held down, despite his frantic eyes darting between me and the unmade bed. I smirk as I take in the wrinkled sheets. The pure bewilderment in his expression tells me everything.

"Oh dear, were you supposed to be keeping watch?" I chuckle. This couldn't get any better.

"No," he croaks, the first time I've ever heard him speak.

"No?" I echo.

He shakes his head, golden hair brushing his cheeks.

"Who are you?" The Prince demands, aiming to sound intimidating.

Cute.

"If I remove my foot, you have to promise me you won't try and run off." I release some pressure from his chest, eyeing him for approval. Not so much for him, but more so for my cramping calf.

"Why should I promise you anything?"

I cock my head at his challenge, pressing my foot back down to showcase my advantage.

He winces at the return of pressure.

"Considering that I'm the one with the boot, you might want to do as I say."

The Prince pushes his hands out, scratching at my leg, but I don't budge. I thought it was a joke when I'd heard rumors of how weak the Hyttenrauch Prince was, but this clears up any of my doubts.

"You're wasting your breath," I sigh.

The Prince is clearly frustrated that he can't shove me away. I watch his energy drain, quickly at that, and he slowly comes to a stop, slumping back into the chair yet again.

"Okay," he surrenders, poking the toe of my shoe with his finger. He chokes up. "I can't br—"

I pull my foot back then. I watch the Prince gulp, soaking in a deep breath. He keeps his hand pressed against his chest.

"Wise choice, Little Prince," I muse. I step back to sit on the bed, my legs crossed and arms bearing my weight behind me: I'm sure he'll stay put. "Now we can chat."

"Who are you?" he repeats, earnest now.

"There's quite the fascinating story playing out here, don't you think?"

"Did the King send you?" The Prince asks. I can see the individual beads of nervous sweat rimming his hairline. I can smell it.

"Excellent guess," I respond, sitting up and uncrossing my legs.

"Did he send you to find me?"

I pout, shaking my head.

He holds my gaze for a couple moments, surely trying to come up with something to say. Then he jumps out of his seat and starts for the door again — but my knife makes it there first, hitting the door frame right in the center of his gaze. The Prince's eyes bulge, cringing at the close contact.

"What did I say about staying put, darling?"

The Prince snaps his head back at me. His cheeks flush a strange, lilac color.

Interesting.

I jut my chin out, gesturing to the chair.

"Sit," I demand.

I'm almost ready for the Prince to whip out some bull-shit excuse just to challenge me again, but to my surprise he simply bows his head and sits back down.

"Now, to answer your question, the King asked myself and my lovely partner to find a very special person. Luckily for us, it's been much easier than anticipated," I dawdle, standing from the bed to stalk around the room. "I thought we would face some difficulty in our search, considering she's been in hiding for twelve years." I stop in my tracks to flash the Prince a knowing look. "You know who I'm talking about. Isn't that right, Little Prince?"

"Did you take her?" he whimpers, giving me everything I want.

I stay silent, studying his expression. Behind those, admit-tedly gorgeous, eyes is a glint of terror: a look that reflects what I feel when I think of Bea in danger.

"Oh my," I exclaim, clapping my hands together. "This is

just, *wow*. I really am delighted with how this is going," I marvel, unable to help myself.

I left Bea outside with a hunch that the girl standing by the water was the Hand. Given our luck, it's evident to me now, based on the coincidental location of the Prince and his eagerness, that he knows something.

The Prince is stunned into silence. I almost want to pinch his cheeks with how thrilled I'm feeling.

"This *story*," I repeat, shaking my head. I walk over to the door frame and pluck my knife from the wall, blocking the exit with my body. I look down at him but he's avoiding my gaze. His blouse seems to be made of satin — that expensive woven shit I'm sure only Kingdom acolytes have access to, but it's ripped and charred, dusted with black smoke.

"I seriously almost didn't believe it was you," I admit, eyeing the rest of his build. He isn't anything special to look at, despite all the talk about how dazzling his sister Clement is. His hair is soiled and his cheeks still carry a layer of baby fat even at his grand age of twenty. Not that it's a problem.

Those eyes though.

"Well?" The Prince starts helplessly.

"*Well*, you're covered in filth! And you smell of fish. Some perfect picture of Royalty you have going on for yourself."

"What do you want?" he demands, obviously exhausted.

I stride towards him, crouching down to meet his eyes, getting in his face. He sinks further into his chair, eyes wide.

"Oh, no, no, no, the real question here is what do *you* want?" I supply. "Because at first, I was baffled to hear that the Prince of Ead, the heir to the throne, had gone missing. And then I thought about just how strange the timing was, since my partner and I are currently on a mission to find someone very valuable to the Kingdom, and there was just no explanation I could make up to justify you running away, either."

The Prince fails at keeping his face still — his cheeks slowly fall, a small sign of defeat.

I cannot wait to show Bea what I've found.

"So," I stress, smiling wide to expose my fangs. "Riddle me this: how *exactly* did you get yourself tangled up with the Kingdom's enemy?"

The Prince opens his mouth, but no words spill from his lips, only a strained breath, so I turn my head and cup the shell of my ear, winding him up as much as possible.

"Hmm? Oh, come on, darling, I'm just dying to know," I insist.

When it's apparent that I've stunned him too much, I sit back on the bed and cross my legs.

"You're a Night Demon,"

I quirk my eyebrow at him, scanning his face for any offense. I expect to see a nasty frown or a disgusted glare, but the Prince's face is only crossed with curiosity.

"And you're human, or so the tale goes. But regardless of what I am and the lack of what you have to say for yourself, this can really only go one of two ways."

"Where is sh—"

"One," I cut him off, holding up my index finger. "My partner and I take you and your friend back to the Kingdom. We're sure to receive a reward larger than initially promised — to bring back the Hand *and* the Prince?" A throaty laugh escapes from my mouth. "What a hoot."

Prince Aalis pays me no mind. He's fixated on his hands, fiddling with his fingers, picking at his skin.

"I'm tempted to just stick with that plan, actually," I taunt, fishing for a reaction worth my time.

He snaps his eyes back up at me, annoyed.

"What's option two?"

I grin, hopping back off the bed to pace in front of him again. I lift a second finger up to join the first.

"The second thing I can offer you — and this one I think you'll fancy a bit more — is actually a chance for you and I to have a very lovely friendship."

"*Friendship*?" Prince Aalis croaks. "I don't understand."

I stop in front of him again, leaning in real close. He freezes, instantly.

"I'm quite easy to get along with, although this would be purely transactional. No ties, unfortunately for you."

"What do you want?".

I lean in further, close enough for our breaths to mingle. The Prince's cheeks are flushed, his body shaking.

"To keep this secret of yours hidden," I whisper, "my partner and I carry out the rest of our mission — maybe even tell a story that the Hand kidnapped you and held you hostage. Play it out like we saved you." He still looks confused. I decide to sit back, suddenly feeling slightly flustered by our proximity as well. "You pay me a generous fortune and in return, I forget that I ever found you here helping the enemy. The choice is all yours."

The Prince seems to be running the options through his head, taking his sweet, sweet time.

"I can't imagine that it's a hard decision," I voice.

"I'm trying to figure out how to explain myself, given the position you've found me in."

"Sideways missionary?"

"What?"

Prude.

"I suggest you just take one of my offers."

"Well, it seems I'll have to politely decline, since your offers indicate that I'm aiding the enemy, which I am most definitely not," the Prince claims, shaking in that skimpy sheer silk of his.

"Oh? You *aren't*?" I goad.

The Prince carefully rises from the chair with his hands held up in defense. I notice that his right palm is scorched, blistering from a burn.

"Why would I come here and disobey the King? My *people*?" The Prince says. If he's trying to convince me he's telling the truth, he's doing a terrible job. Though I allow him to keep going, thoroughly entertained by his attempt. "I'm sure you already know that the respect I receive is little to none," he adds.

"I'm well aware," I say.

He frowns, but continues. "I overheard the King talking about sending people after the Hand. I thought, what better way for me to prove myself not only to him, but to the Kingdom as well, if I were the one to bring her back?"

I nod, playing along. It's a good story, too. Well, at least he seems to think so.

"And so you *magically* appeared here, *magically* found her, and *magically* plan to bring her back?"

"Yes, exactly! I'm doing just that! Listen, I can pay you and your partner off, more than you were offered by the King."

"That's cute," I sneer. "You're cute. This is quite adorable."

Prince Aalis forces a smile on his face. It pains me to watch.

Dare I play along with his little act?

"It's the truth," the Prince insists.

"Right! I forgot. *Manners*," I say, bowing my head the slightest before him. "Your Highness, everything you say is and always will be the truth. I must obey."

"Stop," he says, pushing on my shoulder. "I don't know who you or your partner are, but I can assure you we're on the same side."

"You know what," I start, watching his pupils dilate as I rise to tower over him. He's shorter than me by more than a few inches. "This whole time I've been thinking you were some coward, a lost cause to the Kingdom—"

"And who are *you*?" The Prince asks once more, this time the bite reaching his voice.

We're glaring at each other, and I can't help but hate the way his eyes have darkened while looking at me.

"Now if you had just waited a few seconds, I was about to compliment you," I say.

Prince Aalis's eyes soften the slightest.

"Do you believe me?" He quietly pleads.

I don't answer: something splatters against the window before I have a chance to think. We both whip around at the noise and see dirt scattered across the glass. A shout follows shortly after from outside, and I recognize that it's not Bea's.

"Beka," I hear Aalis mutter, and then he's sprinting out of the room.

9
BEKA

I keep my face turned towards the window, my back to Aalis.

I hope he thinks I'm asleep.

I want nothing more than peace, but every time I drift off for no longer than a second, it all comes flooding back to me. Every intrusive thought possible. Flashes of the raid, of the fires, of Emelyne being tugged away from sight. I can't bring myself to confront it. Not at all.

I peel my lids open, ignoring their sting. I can feel it deep in my bones — how they ache, how heavy my muscles sag. I know that I need to sleep, but I can't. I just can't.

One petal.

I twist my face at the scent that coats the sheets: my breath hitches at the comfort of Lycidas. My friend. It's subtle, but unmistakably his. Just the slight smell of grain.

I catch the full moon glaring through the panels: a pearl of light in the dark void. I don't dare to think of Emelyne. Of where she might be.

During my first few years of living with her, I would often break out in fits of tears, unable to control my feelings. I have never hated what I am. Could never hate it. It was the breaking away from my community, who I am, or rather, who

I *was*, that I mourned. I thought that, despite it all, I would not survive that pain.

But there she was: Emelyne always by my side, instructing me to count my breaths when it became too much.

One petal, two petal, three petal, in.

One petal, two petal, three petal, out.

I try now, but it is not the same without her. The weight of her absence crushes me, and I cannot bear to lie down any longer.

I sit up, fisting the sheets in terror. Lycidas' cottage seems very small now. With every breath I take, the walls move closer and closer together, and if I stay here, they will surely crush me.

Hesitantly, I release the linen crumpled between my fingers and spring off the bed as gently as possible. I hope Aalis doesn't wake to coddle me. He's slumped in the wooden chair beside the door, snoring. The floor creaks under my bare feet, but it thankfully doesn't rouse him.

With just a tug on the front door, the cool night air smothers me entirely. It tastes of saltwater, untying the knots in my chest. I sigh, walking toward the rippling shoreline where the moon's mirror so graciously dances. I spot the thin line of white foam that builds on the shallows of the shore, bubbling each time the waves roll back and forth across the sand. I inch closer, just enough to coat the tips of my toes in the dampening silt, just enough to feel the cooling kiss of the earth beneath me. A wave crashes in seconds later, submerging my feet to the ankle. The water is freezing, but it grounds me.

One petal, two petal, three petal, in.

One petal, two petal, three petal, out.

I let my eyes shut. My ears are filled with the sound of marrying waves, flowing into one another, stretching out on the shore. I think about the little crystals and pebbles under my feet, my skin rubbing against little slivers of shells. My heart is still racing but my thoughts are finally quiet, drowning in the loud song of the sea.

Aalis comes to mind.

I can't say I recognized him back at the raid. At least not at first glance. I remember him creaking his way down the steps to the prison. How he must have followed his father's shadow. I remember when he first set his gaze on me — gentle, unafraid. Some part of me knew he was my ally. In all the times he visited me, kept me company, malice never crossed his face. Not in the way the King's did. It seems the apple fell very far from the tree.

It took me some time to understand why he got me out during the Battle of Lamya, but after the exhaustion of reaching Tilver, I couldn't bring myself to think of the Kingdom again. Of my friend. And yet, there he was, the same sad scene from twelve years ago playing out before me once more.

He risked everything to save me. Again. He put his reputation on the line. For friendship. For justice. That is a debt I can never repay. But we have no plan. And even if I am to somehow meet with Lycidas, people are on our tail: time is against us. So what more can he do? I cannot bear to ask for refuge in the Sanctums. It isn't fair of me to impose on their land — especially since they have zero sympathy for Maidens.

The weight in my chest is back with a clattering thud.

I count my breaths, matching my rhythm with the waves;

the darkness behind my eyes no longer bleak, but rather a deep shade of the richest wine — a mulberry hue. There's a tickle on the tips of my fingers: a familiar sensation. One I used to willingly let consume me. It lingers, refusing to trespass until I let that feeling spark, until I let the heat spread from my hands to my heart. I see a palm unfold in mind, graceful and alluring. My hands extend towards the sea, invisible strings pulling them rigid. I selfishly ask for guidance after years of pushing her away. If there's any chance for Aalis and I to make it out alive, I need to gain my strength back, even if that means submitting to my past.

In this vulnerability, I welcome back her gift.

It overwhelms me. I try to reign it in, but in the void, all I see is her silhouette in the distance and no matter how far I reach, I can't get to her. I can't shut it down.

She's testing me.

I know it's just years of my own neglect, but I can't help but think that Lilith is punishing me. Ever since I was born, I was told I would have the greatest connection to the Lady of Edom. Our Elders locked me away to speak with Lilith, to offer her gifts in order to form a stronger bond with her. Since I am the chosen one, it was expected that I would connect with her on a deeper level than even that of the Elders — Maidens who had once walked the Earth with our Lady. But I never felt it, this connection that the Elders described to me time and time again. I always thought there might be something wrong with me. They said she should be visiting me in my dreams, talking to me day and night, raising me into the woman that is worthy of sacrifice. But Lilith would grant me only her gift, nothing else.

Maybe she knew I never wanted this.

I open my eyes, vision blurred with tears, feeling the burn of power from head to toe. I think about the conversation Aalis and I had earlier, how he said we're living lives that were destined for us. It seems that no matter how hard I try, I will never be good enough. With that, the fire winks out.

There's a noise behind me: the crunch of sand beneath someone's shoes. He's probably come to check up on me.

"I'm alright," I say, keeping my body turned to the water so he doesn't see my tears fall. "I just needed some fresh air."

There's no response. Only the point of something sharp poking into my back.

"Don't move," someone says, their voice almost a song. Feminine.

I can't help but shiver at the brush of her breath against my ear.

She digs deeper.

"Who—?" I croak.

"I'm not here to kill you," she rasps. "But I could. So you're going to have to cooperate."

"I'm not who you're looking for," I say, my voice shaking.

"Oh, I think you are." The point of the blade threatens to push even further. I yelp and jump forward, whipping around to see the intruder.

She's short and made mostly of muscle, legs bent in a position I can only imagine would strain the average thigh. The blade that was held to my back is now curled in front of her, angled skillfully, ready to attack. Her face is covered by her hood, cleverly draped over like a mask. I can't see anything but her locs sticking out from underneath as they fan out over a breastplate of armor, metal feathers lining the torso. I see a bow strung around her back, a bag of arrows, and multiple little knives strapped along their calf.

Lilith's silhouette surfaces again.

I can guarantee the assassin is waiting for me to make a run for it, but I am so tired. I almost call out for Aalis, but that would be stupid to let her know I'm not alone. My hands come up defensively as I back further into the body of water. It nips at my ankles again.

"Please, I'm not—"

My Lady's hand is closer this time, almost within reach.

"I spoke to your mother," she interjects, and my heart sinks. "She said you would be here."

I shake my head, unable to process her words.

"I'm not going to kill you," the assassin repeats. "The King wants you alive."

In my mind, I reach out just a little bit more, pleading. Begging until I feel her set the gift back in my hands, burrowing it deep within my soul.

She nods, and I explode.

I thrust my hands forward, commanding a blow. A current of water shoots out from the sea behind me, knocking my captor to the ground. I don't stand around and wait any longer.

My legs have since numbed but I urge them to move, sprinting away from the shore. But I'm not fast enough. Rounding the corner of the cottage, I steal a glance from behind and see her already on my tail.

"Please don't!" I shout.

Just when her hand is about to make contact with my

back, I conjure up the heat again and pull at the ground. With a flick of my wrist, sand and dirt blasts upward, spraying everywhere behind me.

By Edom, it feels amazing.

My time away from the Realm meant that I couldn't risk practicing my gifts. At least not often, and for no other reason than to prove something to myself. Some things were worth keeping. Emelyne would be amazed at how quick I could start a fire.

I race past the other cottages, nearing the treeline. I spot two horses tied up in the brush. I can take one of them and ride to Thessonne, find Sarya, and then meet up with Lycidas.

If the assassin spoke with Emelyne, then that means she's alive somewhere, and maybe I can find her. It could work.

For a moment I feel bad about leaving Aalis, but maybe this is the best option for the both of us. I never asked for him to get tangled up in my situation, and although I'm thankful for everything he's done for me, I can't allow myself to burden him anymore. He would understand. Besides, the assassin would never dare to kill the Crown Prince of Sumeria.

I break into the treeline when something sharp slices the skin near my ankle, sending me to the ground. Blood is gushing out of the gash in my leg, a stray arrow lodged into the tree beside me. My hands are shaking as I try to cover the cut, but I only end up smearing purple all over. I look up to see the assassin close by, her bow raised, loaded with another arrow.

I'm tired. I'm so tired. Lying won't get me out of this one anymore: the color of my blood gives me up without a doubt.

I crawl out of the treeline, a clear sign of surrender. The assassin doesn't lower her weapon, keeping the sharp point of the arrow trained on me as I approach.

"Are we finished here?" she asks.

I don't respond. My eyes catch on someone in the distance.

"Beka!" Aalis screams, toppling over his own feet as he sprints in our direction.

The assassin spins around fast, her arrow now aimed at the Prince.

"Don't shoot!" another voice shouts from behind Aalis. He's extremely tall and most definitely not dressed for the dark, not with that blouse. The assassin and I watch him tackle Aalis to the ground.

The assassin lowers her bow, clearly confused. She shakes her head, unsheathing a blade from a hilt on her thigh before turning around to face me again.

"Don't make me hurt you again," she warns.

The cut on my ankle continues to gush, no hope of me standing on my own. I have no choice but to offer up my wrists.

"Here," I say, wanting nothing more than to go back into Lycidas's bed and shut my eyes. "I won't fight."

The assassin moves to pin my arms around my back, tying my hands together with rope.

Aalis is on his feet now, disheveled and dirty, hands seized by the tall man. I avoid looking directly at him.

"Look who I found!" the man shrills, tugging Aalis forward to show him off.

Even in the dark, his hair blazes bright, a torch. He catches me staring and smirks, exposing a flash of his fangs.

He's a Night Demon, son of the Maidens.

"What's all this?" the assassin asks behind me, unamused. "What's *he* doing here?"

He chuckles, nudging Aalis forward. "Go on, Little Prince. Tell her what you told me."

I lock eyes with Aalis, searching for an answer. His lip twitches and my heart sinks.

"I—" he flinches, looking away from me and at the assassin. "I left the Kingdom with my own mission to find the Hand. To prove myself to the King."

My head falls, concealing the tears that once again fall down my face.

"He told me he'd pay us off. Give us more than what the King offered," the man chimes. He sounds like he's holding in a laugh.

"Precisely. Just let me take care of things here and you two can go home with more gold in your pockets than you could ever imagine," Aalis insists.

Was it really that easy for him to betray me? Even after telling me I could trust him, after everything he's done to get here?

Unless this is Aalis' way of trying to save us, or least himself.

"He's telling the truth," everyone turns to look at me. "The Prince knocked me out and brought me here after the raid," I lie.

The man's smile grows about ten times the size.

"This is—" the assassin sighs. She stalks forward, right in the Prince's face, eliciting a cower. "The fuck is wrong with you? Do you take me for some fool?"

The man walks around her to kneel down in front of me, sticking out a hand for me to shake.

Very funny.

"Lovely to meet you. I'm Magpie."

"Trust me! I mean no harm!" Aalis stresses to the assassin. A knife is pointed at his throat.

Magpie rolls his eyes. He brings his hand forward to push a strand of hair away from my face. I can't bring my eyes up to meet him.

"Happen to know my mother?" he taunts. It's clear that hating Maidens is still very high on a Night Demon's agenda.

I choose to stay silent.

"Splendid," Magpie clears his throat. He stands up and walks back over to the quarrel, patting the assassin on the head. "Leave him be. I already mentally agreed to his offer."

The assassin whips around, hands on her hips. "You can't be serious."

"Dead seri— why are you wet?"

Magpie and the assassin start bickering worse than Petrus and Aravae. Aalis steals this moment to creep forward until he's next to me. He drops down and inspects my ankle, eyes glowering at the sight of my blood.

"Are you alright?" he whispers.

"I don't think they'll believe you," I mutter, exhausted from speaking.

"Whatever it takes to keep you safe."

I sigh, relieved. "So *this* is your plan."

The assassin pushes away from Magpie and stomps over to the Prince. Aalis opens his mouth to reply, but the assassin slams her boot into his back, knocking him to the ground. He mutters something that sounds like the word 'again'. Magpie is right behind them, unwinding a thread of rope and twisting it around Aalis's wrists in the same position as my own.

"Sorry, darling," Magpie says, finishing the knot. "Looks like this is the only way we can all get along."

For a moment, I think about trying to break free, swimming into the sea with the hopes that the Sirens will help me out again. It might work, but I've lost a lot of blood already. I wouldn't get very far, and that's considering exhaustion will claim me before the waters will.

A tug on my restraints tells me that I'm being tied to a horse's saddle. At least I'm alongside Aalis. Magpie hops up onto his horse and takes the lead, forcing us to walk at a steady pace through the trees. The assassin trots behind us on her own horse, keeping her sharp eyes forward.

There's nothing left of me to give.

The only thing on my mind now is Emelyne.

"Is my mother alright?" I ask, breathless.

Magpie doesn't move and I'm afraid of what his silence means.

"We crossed paths with General Bausan, the Knyght who led the raid. She was among the surviving villagers with them, marching back to Alnola," the assassin explains.

"And she was alright?"

Again, silence hangs in the air.

A twig gets caught against my foot, and I stumble.

"Hey! She can barely walk! She's lost a lot of blood," Aalis scolds.

"And yet you still claim to be on some self-righteous

mission to win over the likes of your own father," the assassin goads.

"What good is it for a Heretic to have magic if they can't heal themselves?" Magpie adds.

He's a bit of a prick.

"Brighes is close," The assassin notes.

"Or what's left of it," Magpie mutters and my heart falls from my chest.

Magpie glances back at me, that smug smile still plastered on his face. How can he be enjoying this so much?

"It's cute what you two have going on here," he pouts, winking at Aalis.

"We want her alive, right?" Aalis counters. "I am a decent man."

"Of course you are," Magpie smirks.

I feel Aalis lean close to me, his breath hitting my ear.

"I won't let them hand you over to the King," Aalis whispers to me. "I promise."

Magpie gives a shout, "Night Demons hear all, darling!"

Heat kindles on my fingertips, simmering near depletion. I knew surrendering was my only choice, but if I let myself rest, I can build my strength back just enough to escape. I could use the gift to break free: to burn the rope and attack, run away and hide in Tilver. It could work.

It's like I'm watching myself from afar, hands tied and eyes void. Aalis's expression is hard to read but I can tell he's trying his very best to feign authority. The assassin sits straight on her horse's back, one hand resting at her side beside a sheathed dagger. Magpie shifts awkwardly against his saddle, grimacing. I can't imagine that I could walk all the way to the

Kingdom like this, and I wouldn't expect our captors to keep Aalis tied up, either.

I can see Brighes up ahead. Magpie's horse breaks out of the treeline and trots forward, forcing me to shuffle into a painful jog. What's left of my village tugs my body to a stop, the motion so abrupt that it rips my rope from Magpie's saddle. Aalis nearly trips over me as I fall to my knees and break away.

Miss Ysabelle's bakery is scorched.

The large silo beside the market is destroyed, remnants of its metal structure crushing other buildings beneath it.

What was once wood is now a pile of ash.

I choke when I think I see an arm poking out from underneath a fallen building, their skin charred to a crisp.

Someone is speaking to me, their words are muffled as if underwater. Or maybe I'm the one drowning, air no longer reaching past my throat. The screams coming out of my mouth are suffocating, the tears rendering me blind. I feel myself breaking, dissolving into the remains of the village that protected me, knowing I failed to do the same in return.

Lilith responds to my grief, her gift screeching in my bones as I dig my hands into the ashes of Brighes littering the ground. The ashes of my loved ones.

Aalis jumps back before the ground beneath me shakes, cracking until I snap, the plain sinking beneath me. I'm set ablaze with a fire of my own, the grief and anger and torture all consuming.

One petal, two petal, three—

This is all my fault.

Brighes is gone. Inez is dead. Emelyne is goodness knows where.

Is this what she wants? Is this her revenge for my absence? For the neglect of my duty?

Punish me then! I call out to the void. *Strip me of my worth. Let the Kingdom take me, skin the flesh from my bones and deliver it to the doorstep of the Realm. Take me yourself, you* coward!

Through the blur of tears, I see the sun peeking over the orchard in the distance. The apple trees are slain, lifeless and burnt, the meadow surrounding it no longer bursting with color.

I let myself scream.

I let myself cry.

The rest of my company is frozen, afraid to approach me as I sink deeper into the ground.

This is where I truly surrender, my heart now cold.

PART TWO

"IF SHE AGREES TO COME BACK, WHAT IS MADE IS GOOD."

LYCIDAS

I sit back on my hind legs and tip my snout upwards, taking in the sharp smell of pine.

The Sanctum is vast, separating the White Isles from the Ashen Domain with a blanket of dense wood, purple bulbs of wisteria coating the forest floor. The further south you head, the trees start to thin out, the forest eventually cutting off at a cliffside. At its edge, the Carmine Lagoon stretches out: one of my favorite views, especially at night. Under the dark sky, the water glows in patches scattered here and there with clusters of bright algae and herded sea urchins. Rudi and I occasionally run out there to catch a glimpse of their illuminations. Sometimes, if we're lucky, we'll even hear the songs of wailing Sirens, an echo of their eerie chorus.

I'm there now and the Realm of Zemergad is in the distance, a permanent shadow. It's a phenomenal sight, and I try, but often fail, to describe it when I'm back home in Brighes. Though not many people wish to hear of it, apart from Inez.

Inez listens to me ramble on and on — not just about the sea, but everything really. There was one story I told her about a Siren who lured a stray Howler to the shore. After convincing them to get into the water, the Siren screamed, turning its fur coat into a set of silver scales. It's nothing but a myth, but she liked it. It made her laugh, and I'd spin any tale, no matter how ridiculous, just to hear it right now. She even joked that she was the Siren, and I, the Howler of the tale, but promised she would never do such a thing to me. She spent the rest of the night showing me exactly what she'd do.

"It's like the full moon speaks to you," Inez whispered to me once.

I think of her, her words, as the moon frees me of my curse. It hangs low, dipping into the east: the sky changing from a deep black into a morning blue.

Nothing compares to this feeling. The freedom.

The Kingdom gives us this time, and this time only, to be free of our pains.

The ties of our society shackle us down. I don't mind working — in fact, I love my job. I love Brighes. The Granary gave me my closest friends, and the work is fulfilling enough. But this feeling, the moon, the radiance of the sea, the relief of pain from my body. Being here in the Sanctum is completely different, surrounded by my fellow Howlers. It's too sweet.

Even Emelyne's baked fruit pies don't come close, and I love her baking.

My ears flinch at the sound of a howl, calling me back to the Stronghold before dawn. I return the wail with my own, the sound ringing out of my throat and echoing into the night. I depart from the edge and merge into the trees, Rudi's scent not too far ahead of mine. Some of the pack emerge from my right, then my left, all of us banding together as we race through the trees, grasping onto these fleeting moments before we Shift back into a human cage of flesh and skin.

Just outside the entrance, Rudi pats my back as I vomit into the bushes.

"There you go, bud," he encourages, "let it out."

Shifting back is excruciating. Once the first streak of sunlight breaches the sky, our bodies instantly revert back into our human forms, causing our bones to break and twist and mold like a child playing with clay. The tearing from one form into another often causes sickness, which is why my innards are currently emptying themselves out onto a poor patch of grass.

"*Bleugh*," I spit, wiping my hand over my mouth with a grimace, still feeling my limbs stretch and straighten under my skin.

Rudi offers me a leather canteen, and I take it eagerly, pouring a flood of cool water down my throat.

"Sure, have all my water. I don't mind," Rudi says. He reaches for the canteen as I pull away, pushing him back as I continue to guzzle down the liquid. "That's enough."

"My mouth tastes like shit!"

Rudi, my beloved, yet *very* stoic friend, pinches his eyebrows together, a ridiculous expression painted across his chiseled face. He's a tad shorter than I, but all the more broad, and keeps his hair cut down to his scalp.

"Don't want to ask how you know..."

"You're a lucky dog, never getting sick after you Shift," I croak, ready to move again.

Other Howlers are slowly making their way here; though some are bare, looking for their clothes, others are dealing with Shifting sickness, and a few poor souls have to cope with both. Luckily, I'd managed to tug on my shirt and briefs before my insides turned against me. I return the canteen with only a few drops left.

"Dick," Rudi grunts, tipping his head back to tap the rest of the water into his mouth.

I wrap an arm around his shoulder and shake him close to my side. "Have I told you I love you? Very dearly?"

"Yeah, yeah." Rudi playfully shoves me away.

Once we reach the Stronghold, he runs off to find his clothes. I stop to stretch and wiggle my legs, attempting to ease the numbing pain in my joints.

The Lunar Sanctum can best be described as a canyon. After the army of evergreen trees, ropes of vines grow, snaking the forest floors, winding their way around until the abrupt dropoff in the ground, caving inward into a dried up quarry. Over time, the Howlers mined its walls to create a fortress of sorts: a meeting place for our kind during the full moon. Though many retired Howlers live here, too, along with the Shepard and her kin.

Humans don't travel this far into our territory, turning around when they reach the vines. They don't have the guts to carry on, typically too frightened that we'll Shift and rip them to pieces. Howlers can be dangerous, but only on a full moon, and very rarely. We're protective, and rightfully so, because the rock holding our Stronghold together is made of pure Moonstone — something we worship above all else.

The Solar side of the Sanctum is very similar, residing on the Western portion of the forest. The only difference is that instead of Moonstone, the Solar quarry is built with pure Celestite, and the Night Demons who reside there very rarely leave these days. Their community is small. Minuscule.

Contrary to popular belief, we have no tension between our communities. In fact, we work in tandem, and are quite happy to do so to keep the peace and sanctity of our home.

"Lycidas!"

I turn at the sound of my name. My friend Jeane runs up to me, dressed in a simple cloth shirt and brown trousers, her Moonstone necklace dangling from her neck with her curls all tangled. There's a scratch etched across her cheek.

"Nice face," I say, earning me a scowl.

"I was with Raven this morning. She got a little aggressive while Shifting back, nothing too crazy."

"I swear that kid's going to be bigger than me one day."

Raven is only eight, but she stands nearly eye to eye with her older sister, and like most young Howlers with growing pains, their force amplifies tenfold when they Shift.

"Mom worries about her sometimes. All she does is stay inside the Stronghold," Jeane comments as we walk down into the quarry, scaling the edge of the walls on makeshift stairs of mud and stone.

"Probably my fault. I told her a story about the flesh-eating bugs that fly around the pine trees' edge."

"You mean the mosquitoes?"

"Maybe."

"You're the worst," Jeane shoves me, grinning, as we make our way down the spiral staircase. "And don't even think about telling her that silly tale about the Siren turning a Howler into a fish. She'll have nightmares."

"But that's my favorite one," I groan. She shoves me again. "Alright, fine. I won't, cross my heart."

"Good. Where's Rudi? I saw him earlier."

Outlets start showing up as we descend, little openings scattered across the expanse of the walls. Families reside in some of the caves, others are used for storage or food. We inch closer to the center of the quarry: an open space crawling with Howlers preparing for our morning feast. It's tradition after the full moon to share a meal before everyone reports back to their homes and jobs across Sumeria.

"Ditched me to grab his clothes. As always, the bastard didn't get sick," I grumble.

"I don't get how he does it," she shakes her head, a smile tugging on her lips.

I smirk, knowing all too well about Jeane's feelings for Rudi. After growing up in the Sanctum with them and my family, I was assigned to the farms out east for work, and Rudi came with me. Jeane's mother is the Shepard, so she and her sisters stayed in the Sanctum to help out. She sees us every month when we come to Shift, or whenever she makes the trip to Brighes, but her interest in Rudi's presence has become obvious in recent months.

"Sit by him at the feast, yeah?" I tease.

The deeper we go down into the quarry, the brighter the Moonstone gets, its illumination divine.

Jeane blushes and pinches my arm. "Oh, shush. Tell me about your girl back at home."

It's my turn for my cheeks to flush. I'd been worrying about Inez since we left Brighes, having gone when she was feeling ill. I had nearly delayed my departure, but Rudi convinced me that she would be fine. It was no big deal. Gallienne and Beka were there to help her, so I knew everything would be fine.

"Who told you that?"

Jeane deadpans. "Who do you think?"

"Rudi?" I ask, not entirely sure if I ever told him about my relationship with Inez, being that it was supposed to be kept a secret.

"Lycie and Inez kissing in a tree," A voice chimes in song behind us. Jeane stumbles on a step as her other younger sister skips up in between us, hooking her arms around ours. "K-I-S-S-I-N-G!"

"How did you—?"

"Don't you remember? I accidentally walked in on you two—"

"I remember telling you to keep your mouth shut," I grit through my teeth, but Nadine just continues to laugh.

She looks just like her older sister, only her hair is chopped up to her chin. I sometimes forget that she's the same age as Beka, who acts far beyond the age of eighteen.

"Let's just drop it," Jeane concludes when Rudi appears at the end of the stairs, staring up at us with a small smile.

"I'm starving," he groans when we reach the floor. "Let's feast."

The tables in the center of the quarry sit far into the ground, the walls stretching high above, circling around us in shining Moonstone.

The feast displayed before us is abundant, ranging from freshly caught meat and fish, to raw vegetables recently pulled from the gardens. Everyone is sitting around long tables, chatting with each other, our food untouched until the Shepard comes to commence our meal. Rudi and Jeane sit across from Nadine and I, chatting and grinning at each other. Nadine elbows me and wiggles her eyebrows at how smitten her sister is with my friend. We giggle and whisper about them until they get annoyed and force us to join their conversation.

"You guys see Mel at all?" Rudi asks.

"He's still gone?" I muse, looking around.

Jeane shrugs. "It's been three months now. Kieran put in a word with the Knyghts in Tilver, but nothing else has happened since then."

"Theola is gone too," Nadine adds.

"That's four now," Rudi crosses his arms.

"I'm not too worried," I say, trying to lighten the mood. "You said Kasia was gonna chat with the General about it soon, yeah?"

Jeane nods. "Yeah, but when do the Knyghts ever make time for us? I only worry that they Shifted out in the open. We don't need any more conflict with the Eadens."

"Even then they'll still find something to hassle us for," Rudi scoffs.

"When do you want to leave for Brighes?" I ask him, redirecting the conversation.

Jeane turns her head, attempting to hide her disappointment at our departure. Well, mostly at Rudi's departure.

"Right after we eat, yeah? I don't wanna wait too long," he replies.

"You guys hear anything else about that Banshee?" Nadine says, her eyes gleaming with curiosity. "Mom was saying it came from Ochrore."

"They don't know that for sure," Jeane mutters, her voice hushed.

"But it came from that way. Mom said she heard it," Nadine speculates.

Rudi's eyes widen and I stay still, only having heard rumors after passing through Thessonne on our way here. Last I heard, no one was expecting a child.

"I'm sure everything is fine back home," I assure, my palms suddenly sweaty.

I wrap my hand around a mug of cider and inspect it, a sour aroma wafting off the liquid. Howlers love their cider, made fresh just outside of Tilver. The batch this year must've contained some blackberries, its usual honey color tainted with a faint hint of lilac.

I don't usually fancy the taste, so I pass the mug to Nadine.

"So Lilith really does just come out of nowhere in the night, taking anyone who isn't protected," Nadine says, taking a sip. "How barbaric."

"Hey! You're too young to be drinking that!" Jeane scolds, reaching across the table to pluck the mug from her sister's hands. Nadine sits back and sticks her tongue out.

"She's a monster and a murderer," Rudi remarks while looking at me, unbothered by the fighting sisters. He sips on his own mug as well. "Whatever happened, I hope she and her Maidens' pay for it."

I nod along. Howlers are always eager to slander the Dark Maid and her band of followers at any opportunity. It's the mutual hatred we share with the Kingdom that allows us to be seen as somewhat equal. We might not have the most luxurious of lives, and are often taken advantage of, but at least the Kingdom gave us the Sanctum and some form of freedom here.

Rudi looks about ready to say something else before the chattering amongst the Howlers dims. Our heads all snap over to the front of the table where Kasia, the Shepard, stands tall with her arms wide, a warm smile stretching across her wrinkled face. All of her daughters resemble her: charcoal black curls, eyes to match, dark olive skin, and square jaws.

"Have you seen Raven?" Jeane whispers, leaning over the table toward her sister.

Nadine looks around and shrugs.

"You were with her after you Shifted, right?" I inquire, keeping my voice hushed.

"Yeah, but she ran off afterwards. I thought she would've come here."

"My people, I'm so happy to see your faces," Kasia begins, directing our attention back to her. Yuri, her husband, sits beside, eyes glimmering with adoration. "Another month has passed, another full moon has blessed our kind, even if only for a short while. We, better than most, know how to cherish our freedom, whatever the cost."

All of the Howlers fix their unwavering attention on our leader.

The pride, the love we have for our community, for everything we endure, I feel it.

We all do.

"We are told that we are cursed, that what Lilith stole from us made us weak and damaged. It may be that we are no longer the same, but far from weak are we. We've managed to live in bodies that were not made for us for hundreds of years, and everyday we prosper. Everyday we thrive. Lilith may have taken the fabric of our souls, but she did not shake our pride.

Please, everyone, raise your glasses," Kasia instructs, and every Howler grabs ahold of their vessels, raising it before the Shepard. "To us!"

"To us!" everyone chants, thrusting their arms forward to clash mugs together, hooting and hollering with honor.

It's because of Lilith that we live as humans instead of our true forms. She created our kind, but as selfish as she is, when banished, she took our truth along with her. It's something we can never forgive, and even after asking the Maidens time and time again to help us, they've simply declined.

Nadine wears a devilish grin, sipping from the mug — *my mug* — she stole back from her sister's grasp. It seems Jeane's too worried over Raven to bother with Nadine anymore. She leaves her cider untouched.

"I'm sure she's here somewhere," I reassure.

"Yeah, you know how Raven is," Nadine adds, waving off her sister's distress.

Raven often stalks off alone, scurrying through weaving tunnels.

Jeane doesn't seem all too convinced but nods all the same.

The feast begins, filling the space with sounds of clicking plates, old tales, and calls for refills.

I laugh at Nadine as she tries to stick a whole chicken leg into her mouth and succeeds, cleaning the whole bone with one bite. Rudi chuckles while hunched over his plate, his shoulders fanning out, while Jeane nibbles on some freshly roasted carrots.

When my plate is clear, I excuse myself for a moment to find my father, Ad. He's perched at the far end of the table, chatting loudly with others. There are three empty mugs displayed around his plate, a fourth one in his hand. When his eyes land on me, he hurriedly moves to make space on the bench, squeezing me between himself and another older fellow.

"My boy! Finally here to see his old man," he beams. I duck my head as he welcomes me in with a firm grip on my shoulder. "How's work going?" he asks.

I look around at the other Howlers, noting their eager stares.

"It's good," I nod.

"I heard you have yourself a nice lady," one of the Howlers comments, draining his mug.

"I don't know what you mean," I laugh, trying to play it cool. *Nadine.*

"Word says she's quite the looker," another Howler chimes.

"It's not that serious," I dismiss, though it pains me to say it.

It's far from the truth.

Inez and I have always been friends. Beka, too. The three of us made an inseparable trio, but Inez and I somehow grew closer this past year, having shared our first kiss just outside my house. I had to bend down quite a bit to connect our lips, but she didn't mind — she never minds. For a few months, we saw each other regularly whenever I had a chance to break free from work. She was usually busy at the bakery helping Miss Ysabelle or giving lessons to the children in Brighes with Beka, so seconds together were few and far between. Though it never mattered to me.

"I would hope not," Ad grunts. "She isn't like us."

I nod, trying to suppress the disappointment on my face.

I knew he'd react like this. No human can carry the offspring of a Howler and live to tell the tale, but I didn't care so long as I was hers. With the strong sense of pride rooted in Howler culture, it means we intend to stay a thriving community, and to do that, procreating is necessary to our dying kind. But Inez is human, I knew that when I met her. I knew that when she stayed at my cottage the first time, when we shared our most intimate selves with each other, and I decided then that I loved her.

"How are you?" I turn to my father, changing the subject.

Ad shifts uncomfortably, reaching for another mug. His fifth.

"Same old," he shrugs, taking a sip.

"Have you gone to see mom lately?"

He shakes his head.

A memorial for my mother, Celine, rests in the Sanctum Cemetery a few yards north of the Stronghold. It's been a handful of years now since she passed. I busied myself with work as my father did with drink.

"It's okay. I'll bring her flowers on my way back to Brighes," I say, feeling the distance between us throb.

"Thanks, son," he says, eyeing me wearily.

"I'm gonna get back to Rudi and the others. I'll see you again soon?"

He nods, squeezing my shoulder again before I slide off the bench and walk back to my friends. I offer them a smile as I return, attempting to dull the ache in my heart.

Nadine follows me into the Chasm when it's clear that I'm intentionally ignoring her.

"Why won't you answer me? You're acting like Raven, and she's just a little pup. Are you a little pup, Lycidas?" she taunts from behind.

I shake my head, my body shivering as I enter the chill of the cave. I take what few stairs there are down, Nadine hot on my heels.

"Raven is not little," I reply matter-of-factly.

The Chasm is a vast space, complete with columns, spikes and a number of gemmed stalagmites and cites growing from both ceiling and ground. The floors are cold, drenched with tiny streams of water that trickle down to a small pond while soft lanterns perch on every nook, in every cranny.

"But she is a child, and you're acting like one," she grumbles, prodding me in the ribs.

I move towards the pond, kneeling to scan the water for chunks of Moonstone. Other Howlers are here doing the same thing, either stocking up or finding replacements.

"Help me find some stones, but nothing too big. Or too small," I say.

I figure that Petrus would most likely lose a gem smaller than an acorn, so something larger would be a wiser choice. I push my fingers through the silt, uncovering stones of all shapes and sizes.

"How is Beka?" Nadine asks, obviously trying to pry.

"She's well."

I'd been thinking of her after my talk with Ad.

My mom was killed when she was out working in Archove. An accident in the mines, though it went undocumented for months. The Knyghts wouldn't tell us much, didn't even let us see her body after they found what was left of it. It was tough. I was eager to leave the Sanctum after that.

Brighes was different and far away: exactly what I needed. I couldn't stand being stuck around my father, where he sulked and drank himself sick every night.

I met Beka when I was thirteen, a year after I'd moved to Brighes. She was a tiny thing, battered and bruised, walking along the shores of the sea when I found her. She didn't make a sound — mainly because she didn't speak our language, but we made it work. I brought her to Emelyne, who took her in and raised her into the kind soul she is today. I don't have any sisters by blood, or even a brother, but Beka is the closest thing I have to a sibling. Nadine and her sisters, too.

"I want to show her the Sanctum," Nadine groans, breaking me from my thoughts. "But she never leaves Brighes."

"She'll come if she wants to," I rasp.

Nadine keeps quiet while I continue rummaging around. I can tell that she's annoyed with my short responses, feeling her gaze drilling into me.

"I'm sorry," she huffs. " I didn't mean to tell everyone about Inez."

I look over and sigh. "It's fine."

"But you're upset."

"I'm allowed to be."

We drop the topic right after that. I don't want to talk about it, especially after Ad brought it up. Nadine flicks some water up in my face to break the tension, but not after I threaten to push her in.

"I wouldn't do that if I were you," Nadine threatens, shoving at my chest. "I've gotten a lot stronger, you know."

"Oh, have you now?" I laugh and sit back, picking at the water again.

Nadine scowls. "You don't believe me? That'll be your own mistake when I end up taking you down."

"Alright then. Next full moon, you versus me. If you win, I'll force Beka to come with me next time I visit," I offer, her eyes widening.

"And if I lose?"

"I'll consider forgiving you for telling everyone about my love life."

"Oh, come *on*, it slipped out!"

I stretch my hand out to her, waiting to make the deal. Nadine challenges me with a furrowed brow before taking my hand, squeezing it extra hard to prove her dominance.

"Are we good?" she asks.

"We're good."

It's bittersweet having to leave my pack for the month. I never know how to feel.

Ad stays back as I make my rounds saying goodbye. Nadine takes my hand and shakes it again, restating our deal with a smug grin. I hug Jeane after Rudi, her disappointment practically oozing. Someday I'll have to encourage her enough to tell him how she feels, but now doesn't seem like the right time.

Rudi and I bid farewell to the Stronghold.

We cross over the vines and enter the dense forest, set east with a pack of eleven Howlers. It's still morning, but the sun is lost behind the thick branches that stretch over our heads.

We adopt a slow pace, relishing the grounds of our homeland for as long as possible.

It's not long into our journey when Kieran, a fellow Howler who farms alongside me in Brighes, starts to stumble.

"Woah there, you alright?" I ask him.

He nods his head, but his sickly pallor tells me otherwise.

"I just feel a little funny," he says.

"Me too," Rudi agrees.

I look back at him and notice how much he's sweating, damp patches coating his paling chest.

"Do you need some water?" I take out a canteen, handing it to him.

Rudi sips some of the water, eyes glazed with nausea.

"It's probably the Shift catching up with me."

"And here I thought you were the toughest dog alive."

Rudi offers me the smallest smile. Him and Kieran are probably just feeling some side effects later on. No big deal.

"What's that smell?" Wynona, a Howler from Tilver, points out.

I sniff the air, catching something rotten. I hadn't noticed it until now.

"Did something die?" Kieran wonders.

Rudi grabs at my arm, his hand slick with sweat, unable to keep himself up.

"Rudi—?"

Wynona lets out a scream. I'm caught between holding Rudi up and snapping my head over to her standing beside a tree, hand smacked against her mouth. Kieran falls to the ground a few paces away from Wynona. Another Howler kneels beside him, desperately trying to figure out what's wrong. I drag Rudi with me to reach them, the smell growing stronger and stronger. Wynona steps back, eyes spilling with tears. I touch her shoulder carefully before looking down at what rests beneath our feet.

There, on the leaves of the forest floor, lies little Raven, her bottom half-Shifted: just tiny paws and black fur. The bones of her rib cage are gushing out of her skin, shriveled like the skin of rotten peel. Her eyes are foggy, purple oozing out of their sockets, her lips parted and raw.

"I'll go get the Shepard," I hear someone say.

Others are wailing, some have walked away, broken by the sight.

Wynona breaks down. Rudi falls down beside me, vomiting onto the leaves. Kieran is on his back, panting, unable to catch his breath, and I don't know how to move.

I hate that I can't rip my eyes away from Raven, lifeless and decaying. There are white, wilted blossoms stemming from the floor around her, outlining her body, some even *inside* of her. I fall to my knees and pick a blossom of the same pungent aroma as before, crushing it between my fingers.

"Lycidas—" Rudi croaks.

His face is whiter than the gem around his neck, his lips stained an awful blueish color, a pool of his vomit at his knees. He's pointing at something in the distance: a flash of red, stark in the green and brown of the forest.

An apple.

I scramble over to it. The very same stench wafts from the apple — a single, human bite taken from its otherwise perfect shape. Carefully, I pluck it from the ground with a large leaf. Eve knows what's wrong with it.

When I turn back to face the rest of my pack, Wynona and I are the only ones who stand. The rest have fallen to the ground, purple bile dripping from their gaping mouths.

II
CLEMENT

On the fourth day of chaos, I visit my father.

Heels clicking on the marble floor, I move briskly, holding the front of my gown, my shoulders back. Large windows line the wall to my left, filtering the afternoon light into strands of gold, lightly pecking my skin as I stride through, two Knyghts flanking my trail. Why must my father be so far secluded?

I have wanted to speak with him for days, but he has completely ignored me since the fiasco in Brighes. Nothing new there. I just wish he would stop for a second and worry not about the Maidens. I believe they had absolutely nothing to do with the Banshee scream. What's happened is completely out of their control — the Dark Maid is far too powerful to grapple with, and sooner or later we will face the punishment for our ignorance.

There is also the issue regarding my brother.

I did not see my father after Aalis passed out, but it was enough for my ball to deflate, my mood alongside. And just when I had thought things were already ruined, especially after word of the Banshee incident came through, Aalis, being the fool that he is, goes *missing*. Heir to the throne or not, I don't understand his behavior, but I can be sure that our father won't take any disciplinary action, should he ever come back. Though, if I were to be in my stupid sibling's foolish footsteps, best believe I would be on the receiving end of the executioner's ax.

Just steps away from the end of the hallway, the two Knyghts trotting behind halt at the sight of four more guarding the entrance to my father's bureau. Splitting evenly at the middle, they grant me access to the double doors made of withered, white oak. Embellished are they with the carvings of our blessed tales: etchings of Adam and Eve, their Garden of Eden and the Tree of Life.

"I am here to speak to my father," I tell them.

The guards nod, pushing the doors open without a single word.

His bureau is opulent, adorned with marvelous bookshelves stacked with thick, leather-bound parchments and maps. A striking stained glass window fans out from behind his table, bewitching a prysm of pigments to flit around the room. My father rests in his grand gilded chair plush with red velvet, head low and distracted by the work before him. His Royal advisor, Seth, stands quietly to the side, noting my presence. Some Knyghts take a close stand on either side of my father, protecting him from any visitor — even his own daughter, it seems.

"Clement," my father spits. He peeks his eyes up from the parchment, the slate of his eyebrows raised in a way I can only describe as distaste. "What is it that you need?"

"Father," I greet with a humble curtsy. "I wished to see how you fair."

I speak eloquently and smile after the words leave my

mouth: it is the least I can do to earn his ear for a few moments. He sighs, scratching at his trimmed beard littered with gray strands.

"There has been no word regarding your brother's where-abouts. I fear that he has been captured. The time of his disappearance concerns me for the world outside our gates is more dangerous at this hour. A full moon has just passed and the Dark Maid's attack on that village is more than enough to ail."

At the mention of the Dark Maid, his eyes darken, glazed with loathing and maybe even fear. His hatred for her, for her kind, are the vessel of his very being. It moves his body and betrays his mind, all consuming.

"He could have left on his own, for all we know," I urge, however meekly.

"So you think he's betrayed us?" My father asks wildly.

I step back, suddenly frightened. This could very well be his breaking point.

Things just haven't been the same since my mother died. She was the only one who could soothe his tempers, not that he would dare to raise his voice around her or even speak out of turn. Even his empire could not amount to my mother.

"It was simply an insinuation, father. I just thought—" I catch my tongue, knowing that my words mean nothing to him. "Forgive me, I know how much Aalis means to you."

"It's the Maidens and their bloody Hand. She's cast a spell on him, I'm sure of it," my father whispers the last few words to himself. "His paintings were all of that *girl*. Every. Single. One."

He is usually a very quiet and poised man, but in my

presence he releases all his demons, both inner and outer, along with all the secrets stored in his makeshift soul, or lack thereof. I never understood why, but it is as if I have the only needle and thread that can either stitch him up or pull at the fray. My mother died holding the thimble.

"Your Majesty," Seth interjects, offering the King a glass of water.

My father takes it and gingerly sips. I can see the worry playing on the Royal advisor's lips as he stares at the King. He's been my father's right hand man for years, growing with him as one would a sibling.

"Whatever do you mean, father?"

My stomach threatens to spill. Contrary to Aalis' beliefs, I do care for him. He is my brother, after all.

Father just sits back in his chair, holding his head in the palm of his heavily jeweled hand. The Knyghts shift with unease beside him, knowing how his fits of malaise corrupt his ability to act rationally.

"I have sent people to capture the Hand. I believe she's alive and I believe she is somewhere in the Ashen Domain. They left only a few dawns ago," he reveals. "She will be taken care of. The village of Brighes is under the inspection of General Bausan. Everything is under control. Surely, your brother will come back to us soon to celebrate your marriage."

My jaw flies open like a drawbridge.

"Clement, I've decided on a worthy suitor for your hand."

I seem to have lost touch with the beat of my heart.

I do not mind meeting men or speaking to them; I do not mind dancing with them, receiving compliments. I am quite experienced at the art of batting my eyelids, commanding myself to blush, all the skillful flirting, forced giggles and flashy teeth. But, I am twenty-four, and have no sense or idea what love is supposed to look like.

I saw it once, the memory now stained with sorrow and grief. I see the loss of that love everytime I look at my father. How he lacks that light inside of him, the one that used to burn so bright. It is a feeling I wish not to get acquainted with.

My mother's passing was devastating for the entire Kingdom, though with time, our people moved on. With me? Her death was a bruise — is still a bruise, one you find yourself pressing just to feel something and it swells when I think of how young she was, of how young I was to have lost her. Yet she lingers like a scab on the King — one he won't stop picking at: bloody and itchy, infected and refusing to heal.

Whatever suitor my father has chosen for me, I have no choice to accept.

It does not matter what I want. It never has, nor will it ever. When Aalis returns, he will still be the heir, he will marry, and he will rule Sumeria. I will not matter, no titles of mine could save me, but who I marry might.

"Forgive me, father, for my silence. Believe me when I say I am beyond pleased. Elated, by all means," I say, picking my words carefully; the smile on my lips painful as I stretch it across my face. I try to ignore the frown Seth is giving me from the corner of the room. "I just wasn't aware that you'd chosen so soon amidst such chaos unfolding."

"Our people need hope! A reason to celebrate! It is time for you to be wed," he huffs. "I've already spoken with the

Cain. Your marriage will be absolute in the coming month. The next full moon."

"Wonderful!" I exclaim, betraying my heart. "With whom am I to exchange such vows?"

"The honorable warrior, General Abel Bausan."

A chill runs down my spine. Nothing could have prepared me for that.

"General Bausan," I echo, trying to wrap my head around the thought.

"You don't approve?" My father asks furiously, a scowl clawing its way on his face.

"Yes, indeed," Seth nods along after a moment's hesitation. "The General is a renowned man and a wonderful leader. A fine choice for our fine Princess's hand."

I'm quick to reassure both of them despite the hollowness in my chest, though these words are not my own. "I cannot imagine anyone more respectable. I humbly accept."

I rack my brain for anything I can remember about the Knyght in question. I sometimes notice him at banquets and celebrations, always stern and observant. He trails my father around like a plague, constantly lurking in the shadows following his promotion to the Domain. He is at least a decade older than myself and he will be my husband in less than a month. The thought of it makes me sick.

"I'm glad you agree," my father smiles now. He rises from his chair to stand before me. "Worry about your marriage now. Aalis will be dealt with and brought home to us in no time."

"Of course," I squeak.

I hate how I wish to be held, just once. My father is

so close to me. I imagine that he reaches out and pulls me into his arms. I would hug him back and probably cry into his shoulder, releasing years of my loneliness into that single embrace. But he doesn't hold me. He hasn't since before Aalis was born.

"I suppose I should leave to prattle with the tailors."

"I leave for Alnola tonight," my father declares as I head for the doors. "There will be leftovers there from Brighes. I will be gone for a few days. General Bausan will follow me back to the Kingdom after that for the formal announcement of your betrothal."

I refrain from asking to come along.

As the Princess of Sumeria, I feel a strong sense of duty to give back to our people. However, it seems that my father believes I am best fit for busying myself with gowns and wedding plans opposed to aiding the people of our land, so all I say is, "Thank you, father."

The Knyghts follow me through the twisting halls even after I dismiss them.

I wish to be alone. I dig my fingers into the palms of my hand to cease their shaking. Servants and advisors stop to bow as I pass by, and it takes everything in me to keep my smile in place as my lips quiver. It is at times like this when I feel so completely pliant under the words of my father that I find myself understanding why my brother acts the way he does.

Aalis despises escorts, refuses to roam the halls with any sort of protection. He skips his lessons, paints all day in his room, and does Eve knows what. His behavior irritates me more than anything else, throwing away his duties just because *he* can, and *I* cannot.

I understand why, yet I still hate it.

I am exhausted, worn out, and I need to escape these prodding eyes for fear they'll see the tears that coat my lashes. My heels click against the floors once again as I rush through the halls and descend down a grand, marble staircase. It winds down to the foyer of a salon adorned with marble pillars and sparkling chandeliers. More servants are bustling around, cleaning floors and passing through carrying all sorts of things.

"Princess Clement," a servant, Selova, greets me. "The tailors have gathered the finest materials for your wedding gown. The King told us to start fitting you immediately."

Selova is kind, her voice encouraging. I am tempted to decline, to tell her that I must go to the stables or dining hall or anywhere that is not in this room. My smile wavers, but my body forces me to stay.

"That would be lovely," I say.

Selova claps her hands together, thrilled.

"Wonderful! Let us get you to your chambers straight away!"

I stand still in the center of my dressing room, arms above my head as I am stripped of my dress, bare save for the undergarments hugging my frame. I look much more delicate these days, bones prominently poking through my fair skin. The servants circle around me, measuring my limbs, my torso, my chest. They're ecstatic. That makes one of us.

I wonder about how the General will see me, how he will

touch me, how he will talk to me. I do not know him, but I have heard his voice, deep and assertive. I try to imagine how my name will sound on his lips and decide I hate it either way.

"I would like it tight around my waist," I instruct, tapping my midriff right where the hem should go. A servant shadows my fingers with a pin. "And then the skirt, I want it to be in our best ivory silk. The trail must be long as well, but not too many ruffles. Something classic."

If I'm going to give myself up, I might as well have the perfect dress.

The servants hurry to see my requests through. Some more material is pinned to my body as a rough draft, outlining the birth of an extravagant down.

"You are going to be the most beautiful bride," one of the servants marvels with watery eyes.

I imagine what my mother would think.

She would be more excited than me, eyes glittering with tears watching her daughter prepare for marriage. I think she would even step in, making her own arrangements, for she always had a brilliant eye. Or maybe she would protect me, and there would be no wedding at all.

"General Bausan is very handsome," a servant comments.

"He is our finest Knyght," another notes. "You are very lucky, your Highness."

"I hear that he's gone to Ochrore to handle the business with the Dark Maid," Selova remarks. She's got her hands on some sheer tulle, wrapping it around my waist. "He is very brave."

"Very brave, indeed," I reply.

"I just can't believe what's happened. Just to think, that foul creature killed a mother as young as you!" Selova says, shaking her head in distress. She always was a gossip. "Thankfully, you'll be under the best protection here in the Kingdom when you bear children."

I feel nauseous. All the tugging and pulling on my body makes my head spin.

"Imagine little Princes and Princesses running around the halls again," a servant says with more excitement than I could ever project.

How soon will the General want children? How much time do I have before I put my life second to others? When I marry the General, how much of a choice will I have? How much smaller can my voice get? How quiet must I continue to be? I want to put my privilege to work and make our lands better before I am tied down like this.

The servants continue to rave about my future, and the walls inch closer and closer. They say this marriage will change my life for the better — how it will give me a purpose, and my throat grows tighter and tighter. I spend a lot of time listening to the things said to me, but I don't absorb them, like watering a plant made of stone. I nod and smile.

Finally, after hours of measurements, notes and needles, the servants filter out of the chamber and leave me be.

I stand in front of the mirror for several moments, looking at myself in just my undergarments. I feel that General Bausan will think I am too small, fragile even. My cheeks ache from the persistent smile I wore all morning. I let it fall along with the tears in my eyes.

I cry for the loss of my freedom. I cry because my father doesn't care to listen to me. I cry because I wish my mother could've been here to see the fitting. I cry because I hate the color of the silk I chose.

Desperate to hide from my reflection in the mirror, I hop off the pedestal and cover my body with my dress from before. I nuzzle myself into the scratchy material and wipe my face with the sleeves. With no one to help me, I tie my corset myself. Part of me wants to see how far I can pull it. To see if my ribs break, or my lungs pop.

My eyes catch the outline of a long unused door covered by my other gowns, etched into the wall of my personal quarters. The door has no unique color shaded to blend into the wall. I place my hand where a handle should be and take a deep breath before pressing forward.

It takes some effort to pry it open: I haven't gone through for years. Aalis's room is just across the hall from mine. I could go to it through the main hallway, but there are Knyghts flanked outside, and I do not wish to be seen. Instead, I creep further into the passageway, surprisingly remembering my way around, taking three lefts until I hit the other end. In front of me is another door. I pull the handle and it takes me straight into my brother's room.

His chamber hasn't changed much from when we were younger, still eerily empty. I press my ear against his main entrance, eavesdropping on the servants. They talk of his closet in disarray, and how his sheets were crumpled and thrown on the floor the morning they found him missing. His room is clean and tidy now, but I try to imagine the scene for myself, wondering what my brother could possibly have been doing.

So you think he's betrayed us?

I no longer know my brother well enough to assume his intentions. I remember having somewhat of a bond with him until the Battle of Lamya. That day was a heavy hit for a lot of people in the Kingdom: homes were destroyed, civilians were killed, the bridge collapsed. For a while I thought the events scared Aalis away, as he was someone who feared conflict above all else. Though eventually, he stopped talking to me altogether, choosing to lock himself away.

I wouldn't be surprised to find out that Aalis left on his own accord. He thinks I do not see the way he dreads his impending coronation. As much as it angers me that he'll receive the crown with little effort and no desire, he is still my little brother, and I wish for him to be happy.

I wonder if he is happy now, outside of the walls he is confined to, free to be who he wants, relieved of his duties and expectations.

I mull over the rest of my conversation with my father as I step further into his room. I try to pick apart my father's thoughts — how he plans to deal with the chaos unfolding in our lands. A Banshee scream means that an innocent life was taken at the hands of the Dark Maid.

It's the Maidens and their bloody Hand. She's cast a spell on him, I'm sure of it.

The Battle of Lamya changed my father.

He expected the Maidens to attack the Kingdom some day, but he could have never prepared for the amount of force they brought upon our troops. They were angry, and rightfully so.

My mother died not because of the Maidens, but because

of her health, and he does not wish to believe it. She would not have made it whether Aalis lived or not. If anything, I was thankful that my brother survived. As for my father, that wasn't enough to calm him. He has long since been consumed with revenge, so I am not at all surprised to hear that he's blamed the Maidens for Aalis's disappearance as well.

I do not care much to worry myself with business regarding the women and their Hand. For far too long have I watched them torment my father and drive him insane. I want to believe that they are the enemies, that they are responsible for all the faults in Sumeria, but in the end, it was their land first, and we cannot compete with that.

I lay down on Aalis's bed and stare up at the ceiling: a retelling of the story of Adam and Eve painted in bountiful color above. I call out to them, waiting for a response — some sort of reassurance that everything will be alright, but I am met with silence.

There, my eyes grow heavy and I fall asleep, alone and cold.

12

BEA

I keep my eyes pinned on the gray sky as the Hand weeps, pressing my back hard into the trunk of a lone oak tree — one of the very few that survived the fire. My eyelids droop, lulling me into a light sleep.

"You're resting now?"

I nod, catching Elio's frown through my squint.

"What are we going to do with her?" Elio gawps, looking back at the girl. Her hands are pulling dirt from the ground as miserable cries spill from her mouth. "She won't shut *it*."

The aches in my body coax out a small moan as my spine pushes deeper against the bark.

"She's not going to go anywhere. If she moves, I'll put another arrow in her leg," I assert, not in the mood to argue with my companion. "Just let her cry."

Elio glares at the Hand, then leans down to my ear and whispers, "I think she's faking it."

"What about him?" I point at the Prince, who hasn't left the Hand's side. He's swaying, mewling soothing noises whilst he rubs her back. "How can you trust a *thing* that comes out of his prissy mouth?"

Elio scoffs. "Please, he's harmless. We'll get our money whether we believe him or not."

"He's a liability."

"He's my liability. Let me deal with him, alright?"

I shoo him off with my hand. "Just move him away from the girl or something. I can't stand to watch him anymore."

The Prince is lucky I didn't stick an arrow in him too.

"You got it." Elio salutes me and then spins around on the tip of his heel. "Oh, Little Prince!"

Prince Aalis snaps his head in our direction, alarmed.

"Don't bother with her, she'll be fine," Elio dismisses, walking towards our hostages. The Prince backs up defensively and the Hand doesn't look up at my companion. Instead, she chooses to keep her face smushed in her hands. "Come. Walk with me."

"But—"

Elio already has the Prince's ropes in his hands, yanking him forward. The Prince stumbles slightly but doesn't fight back.

"I'm not leaving her," he protests.

"We shan't be long," Elio promises. "It's a nice time for us to bond, darling. Don't you think?"

The Prince reluctantly follows my partner away from the Hand, tugging him along a path out of the main town square.

My eyes dart to the girl.

The ground beneath her is cracked and sunken in, stuffing her into a shallow pit. With the rise of the morning sun, the crisp remains of the village are on full display. Admittedly, seeing the charred structures brings back too many unsavory memories of my own.

I took my first life just two years after being orphaned.

He was a rich, filthy acolyte from Surlisle who had

adopted me from a small orphanage just south of Alnola. I hadn't planned on running away from him. I never fought or disobeyed, but when I saw the knife mere breaths away from me at the dinner table, I couldn't stop myself from grabbing it and sticking it into his throat.

It was that day that I learned I was good with a knife.

Little did I know, that would be the thing that keeps a roof over my head. Meeting Elio kept me above ground.

I don't feel bad about what I do: this job doesn't require the nuisance, nor the nuance, of emotion, and I'm the best for a reason.

Edom, I wasn't born this way — no one is. But I felt nothing when I killed that old woman. General Bausan was going to do it anyway. Better me than him.

"Excuse me?"

"What?" I demand, coldly.

"May I ask what it is you plan on doing with me?"

With some reluctance, I push myself up off the ground and stride over to the Hand, my mask reflexively draping over my mouth, an extension of myself. Dirt is smudged along her hands and knees; her dress torn, her face stained with filth, tears, and blood.

"The King requested that I bring you to him alive. What happens to you after that has nothing to do with me," I explain in 'Capitan Mode', as Elio calls it.

The Hand's face is struck with agony as she balls her hands into fists. I watch her brows furrow for a moment, the tension pooling over, and then she relaxes, her face entirely neutral: a sign of defeat. "We should leave, then. I do not want to be here any longer."

My legs teeter back and forth in surprise, the slightest hesitation in my movements as I decide my next steps.

There are many things I have long wondered of the coveted Hand, namely how she escaped the Kingdom in the first place. She was apprehended before the Battle of Lamya, though those were darker days. Then there's the Prince, and Edom knows what's going on in that half-witted brain of his.

Just a few days ago, I thought this mission would be the one to save us. It sounded simple enough: find, capture, hand her in, swim in gold, yet, "I'm sorry about your village."

The Hand's eyes finally meet mine, just as confused as my own.

"My mother. Please tell me she's alright," the Hand whispers, her voice hoarse.

"If you're ready to leave, then let's go."

I can't bring myself to sympathize with the devil, instead turning on my heel and making way to my horse.

"You said you spoke to her," the Hand whines.

Elio waltzes back into the square then, his tug demanding, the Prince tripping up in tow, and saving me from response.

"Good! You're done crying," Elio sweetly chimes.

"Time to go," I command, mounting my steed.

For once, I don't want to listen to Elio and his antics.

"Must you be so insensitive?" Prince Aalis glares at my partner.

Trust *him?* Yeah, right.

Elio rolls his eyes. "I only wish to part from such a depressing sight." He bends down in front of the Hand, prying into her space until she finally looks up at him. "Can you stand?"

She nods.

"Can you walk?"

Nothing.

"Well?" Elio presses.

"At least let her ride on the back of one of your horses," the Prince pleads. "She's bled too much."

"When will you realize that I do not care about her? Or you?" Elio jabs, clearly annoyed with his hostage.

I trot my horse up to them, stopping beside the Hand. "She may ride with me, I suppose. The King does want her back alive."

The Hand sighs, her body deflating with relief.

"Well then!" Elio exclaims in annoyance, dropping the rope tied to the Prince's hands. He stomps over to his horse and packs up his stuff as well. "Don't get any ideas, Little Prince."

Prince Aalis helps the Hand to her feet, handling her with the same fragility as glass.

"Thank you," she whispers.

I refrain from reaching my hand out to hoist her up. The Prince aids her tender leg as she climbs onto the horse, careful not to touch me.

"We spotted a throng of villagers headed this way. Scavengers from neighboring towns," Elio says as he rides over to us.

"I'm surprised they didn't arrive sooner," I counter.

I lead my horse out of the main square and onto a path, one that heads straight for the woods Elio and I ventured through this morning. I can't stand to be in Brighes anymore.

"Must I remain tied up?" The Prince inquires, holding his restrained hands up.

"It's just a knot. Surely you can free yourself if you so please." Elio looks down at the Prince, smirking. "And no, you still can't ride with me."

"Technically, these horses belong to the Kingdom, therefore they belong to *me*," Prince Aalis dares to bite.

I have to suppress my grin, knowing what his comment will unleash.

"Oh, I'm ever so sorry, your Majesty! Would you prefer to travel on your back as I race through the trees, your Majesty? Drag you like slimy herring on a hook through a stream, your *Majesty*?"

"Your Highness, actually," the Prince hisses under his breath.

"Like I give a fuck," Elio retorts.

"I didn't mean it like *that*."

"Like *what*?"

"Nothing," the Prince murmurs, our surroundings dimming with the promise of rain.

"So," Elio begins, yet again, looking pointedly at the Hand, "how are the Maidens these days?"

Here we go.

The Hand sniffles behind me. "I wouldn't know."

"I would applaud you for staying out of the Kingdom's reach all these years, though it wasn't entirely your doing, it seems. Practically everyone forgot about you. Choose ignorance or lose your head, which I believe is a beautiful and definitely *not* morally fucked up way to live." He studies her in moments between focusing on the path ahead. I often wonder what *doesn't* bother my friend. Even I, among many other things, tend to piss him off. "Regardless," he continues,

"I think you could have gotten as far as Neelem and lived a happy and unbothered life. I think you could have done whatever you wanted at nobody's benefit but your own. Not that you didn't try in that charnel house of a town, but you know. Guess you got unlucky."

I'll say.

"Is there a point to any of this?" the Prince barges in.

His cloying voice alone makes me consider tying a rag over his mouth.

"Might I finish?" Elio tuts. "As someone who enjoys some mess, I admire you for being, well, so unpredictable."

"You admire me?" she says.

He shakes his head dismissively. "Don't get it twisted, darling. I do *not* want to be you."

"I can't imagine anyone would," she says, slightly clipped.

"I'm just playing a little game in my head," he says, twiddling his fingers beside his temples. "I'm trying to imagine how much better the world would be if I were in your shoes. Can't you see it, Cap?"

"Yep," I hum, indulging in his imagination — for entertainment purposes only, of course. "You and your army of handsome Knyghts marching down the hill completely in the nude holding flags with your face flapping in the air."

Elio snaps his fingers, his crimson eyes beaming in the direction of the clearing ahead. At this pace, Abram Woods is no more than an hour away.

"They're chanting my name, telling every soul in Sumeria about their savior, the one who rescued them from their pitiful past lives!"

"Who would be naked?" asks the Hand, her soft voice surprising us all.

"Can't it be all of us, darling?" Elio winks.

"I do hope you're joking," Prince Aalis chides. "And would you leave her be? You don't know what she's been through."

Elio whips around to glare at the Prince. "I know she has power. She chose to hide when there could be some actual change for once. I'm no zealot of Lilith, but I don't suck the Creator off, either. The Kingdom shits on every being who isn't a precious acolyte and believer of the *divine* Adam and Eve = which, by the way, is all a fantastic illusion to sway the public from seeing how completely fucked the whole system actually is!"

The Prince's silence speaks for itself. I do love when Elio loses his temper.

"You're right: I could've done anything. I could escape at any moment," the Hand says after a beat. My hand flies to my belt. "And yet, here I am."

"Are you trying to convince me that you're special?"

"I don't think that you and I are all that different," she counters.

I turn my head from Elio, trying my best not to chortle.

"Enlighten me."

"I don't think I shall," she states. Elio grunts, losing interest in his conversation. "But whether I go with you or I go back to the Maidens, the fate of this world remains the same. Sumeria falls regardless."

"Whatever," he dismisses.

After that, everyone seems to agree that traveling in silence is best for our collective sanity. Though it's not long before another voice pesters my ears. The old woman's dying words creep into my mind, haunting me.

Please make sure she is safe, she rings and rings and rings.

"Hmm," Elio hums, digging into the pocket of his cloak. "I'd forgotten about this."

I glance at him holding a folded piece of parchment between his fingers, the lady now gone.

"What is it?"

"I took it from our good old friend, Thierri," Elio boasts, unfolding the paper.

"You *stole* something?" The Prince gasps.

Elio pinches his eyes, rolling them back again as he blinks them open, entirely spent by the Prince's naivety. "Don't you know it's improper to eavesdrop?"

"It's improper to steal," I hear the Prince murmur.

Elio scans through the content on the parchment while I wait full of impatience.

"Well?" I question when confusion stirs on my partner's face.

"It can't be—" he says under his breath.

A raindrop hits my hand, then another falls on top of my horse's mane.

"Elio, what is it?" I press.

"I don't know. I can't read," he chuckles, earning only a sigh of exasperation from me.

A painful screech rips through the air.

"Something's coming," the Hand whimpers.

My eyes snap forward, scanning the path before us, as above so below. There, squawking in chorus, is a whole flock of them, a dark mass in the clouds like a thick plume of smoke, headed straight for us.

"Elio," I grunt.

He looks up, eyes wide at the sight. The rain persists, falling down faster than before.

"Oh, shit," Elio curses, crushing the parchment in his fist while grabbing hold of his horse's reins again.

"Are those *birds*?" The Prince wonders, pointing at the creatures in the sky.

They're much larger now, barrelling towards us at an alarming rate. I count six of them, all bony bodies and feathered wings.

Some big fucking birds, Prince.

I feel a hand clutch my elbow, her grip as tight as iron as our horses pick up the pace, leaving the Prince racing behind, his hands still tied together.

"Bea!" Elio calls out, the rain now heavier. "They're *Harpies!*"

"Uh huh, yeah, I see that!"

"What are the bloody odds!" he says, almost laughing, surely recalling our game from before.

Elio takes both of his daggers out, ready for anything.

"Don't fall off," I urge the Hand as I unsheath my bow and load it with two arrows, pointing them up at the sky.

"Harpies never stray this far from the Peaks," she panics.

I've never seen one in person, only in books filled with drawings of the foul creatures and other species. I finally understand why many avoid passing through the mountains.

There's one flying faster than the rest of its flock — she screeches a shriveling sound akin to that of a Banshee, the resemblance almost uncanny. I trace the creature with the tips of my arrows, her wings brown and black, layers of tough, serrated feathers scaling her extensive limbs. Her face is all sharp and angular; cheeks sunken in, and a wide mouth decorated with rows of pointed teeth. And then there are her talons: those long, curled daggers that dangle beneath her body, her feathered toes clench as she sets her yellow eyes on a target.

"I can't—*hey!*" The Prince gasps behind us, tripping over his feet as he tries to keep up.

I'd nearly forgotten about him. The Hand screams behind me but it's too late: the first Harpy has already blown over my head and reached the Prince.

I release two arrows, burying them into her back, coaxing yet another piercing screech. The Hand turns around in the saddle and whimpers, watching the Harpy persist as she wraps her claws around the Prince's body.

My bow is reloaded within seconds, but it wasn't quick enough. They're hot on our trail.

"*Help!*" The Prince wails as the Harpy lifts him from the ground, taking him into the air.

Her talons slice the rope connecting him to Elio's horse. He dangles in her grasp, flying over our heads and past the flock. I shoot my arrows, but to no avail.

"For Edom's sake!" Elio shouts, yanking on his reins, propelling after the floating Prince.

"Elio!" I shout in warning.

A Harpy flaps above him, and I shoot three consecutive arrows at her chest, causing her to back away.

"Head to Alnola! I'll find you there, I promise!" He yells,

riding ahead, catching up to the Harpy and the flailing Prince.

I grit my teeth. I don't like splitting up.

I pull at my reins, driving myself and the Hand to the left, turning away from Elio's path. I shoot two more arrows, successfully catching the flock's attention as they barrel towards us.

"Can you fight?" I ask.

The rain continues to pour, drenching my cloak into dead weight. My mask flies away and my hair is exposed, flowing behind me like wings, my baby hairs curling with the damp.

"I don't know," she answers. "But I can try."

"Here," I say, handing her a spare knife.

She takes it and cuts her hands free.

The Harpies squawk, catching up with us in no time. One of them dips down to claw at my head, but I manage to shoot twice, the arrows landing at the nape of each of her wings. I'm worried I'll run out of arrows, and I think for a second that one of the creatures is going to catch me.

The rain suddenly shifts, forming into a single current, splashing forward in an unnatural motion, restraining the creature. The Hand's arms are outstretched, her wrists turned, moving the rain at her own will. I didn't appreciate her abilities when we fought before, but she's incredible. She seems in awe of her own powers, gasping with the rush of her attack. Two of the Harpies have fallen, disintegrating into piles of dirt.

They were created by Lilith centuries ago, official guardians of her land to fight off unwanted intruders and angels.

There aren't many of their kind left, which explains why they tend to keep to themselves in the Cudola Peaks.

The other three Harpies persevere, gushing purple from the wounds I've inflicted. They join together for a coordinated attack, screeching as they dive forward yet again. One goes for my poor horse, sending myself and the Hand to the ground. My body flattens against the grass as I tumble down a rocky hill. I push myself up just in time, snatching a dagger from my belt to fend off the three Harpies circling around me. I curse under my breath, unsure where my bow is. Without it, I suspect I won't last long against these three ancient creatures. I'm glad, at least, that they're only attacking me.

Harpies, in their service to Lilith, are not to harm those of the Realm, Night Demons included. I don't know where the Hand is and I don't expect her to come back for me. For once, the odds are in her favor.

I spin around, dodging a set of talons. My right arm thrusts forward, slicing the heel of the Harpy as I grapple at my belt and take another dagger into my left hand. This one I send flying into her chest. The Harpy screeches, calling the others for help. I slice through her other leg before rounding on the others barreling towards me. I slash at another talon, then the joint of the wing, but it's not enough. I'm knocked down again, the blow stealing the air from my lungs. I gasp, trying my best to stand back up, but they're closing in on me. I can't see the sky anymore. My back aches and I think I'm bleeding somewhere on my arm. My faith is quiet. I don't pray, at least not often enough to be called an acolyte.

In these moments, I think about Elio. I remember meeting him for the first time, curled in on himself, starving. If Eden is a place that wants me, then maybe I can watch over him still when I go. I hope he caught up to the Prince. I hope he comes back and finds the Hand and turns them both in. I hope he uses the reward to get him out of this place: to travel anywhere, no matter how far away, to be free. That's my final wish as I close my eyes and grip my dagger tight to my chest.

One of the Harpies reaches for me, but her talons don't connect with my chest. She's smacked away by a force of water and dirt, her wings crumpling under the weight, the other shortly following suit. I notice the Hand standing a few paces away, moving the rain with her fingers. She glances at me briefly before attacking again, sending the Harpies back, filling them with water, drowning them from the inside out. They try to fight off the unnatural force of the rain, the sight encouraging me to hoist myself back onto my feet and charge forward. I plunge my blade into the chest of one of the Harpies, slicing it all the way down until my feet hit the ground again. I tear the dagger from her body and fling it across the valley, sinking the tip of it into the neck of the last Harpy. She lets out a guttural cry before falling from the sky, shrinking into a mound of dust.

The Hand lets go of the water.

I stand there in awe, panting. Blood trailing from a cut in my arm where my armor is vulnerable. I tilt my head back and let the rain cover my face. It trickles down my cheeks, down my neck, past my breastplate.

"Your horse is wounded," The Hand says, her voice steady.

She's drenched as well: her long, dark hair damp as it sticks to her face like an ink spill. She's kneeling down in the grass, hovering beside the fallen animal.

I inch forward carefully, stepping over a pile of dirt — the remains of the desiccated Harpy. Its talons are all that's left.

The Hand is stroking the mane of the horse, soothing the animal as it whimpers. Its legs are broken and its face is slashed. Like the old woman, it won't make it. She's holding the knife I gave her in her other hand, resting it on the neck of the horse.

Please make sure she is safe.

"You did well," she whispers, patting the horse's head gently.

I close my eyes before she pokes the tip of the blade into its skin. The horse dies almost instantly, the rise and fall of its bulbous chest stilling after one final breath.

The Hand doesn't cry. She pets the animal well after it passes. I don't come any closer.

"Why did you help me?" I croak. The Hand doesn't look at me.

She shrugs, as if it were nothing. "You needed it."

"I don't need anything, especially not from the likes of you." I snap, defense always on the tip of my tongue. Even still, I can't help but add, "I captured you. I'm taking you to the Kingdom where they'll likely kill you. You didn't need to help."

The girl looks at me now, her eyes entirely void.

"I might as well do some good before I go."

It's quiet again. The rain falls loosely from the clouds above, hitting our faces like the soft caress of a lover.

"Okay, then. Let's go," I say, holding out my hand.

The girl looks at me: our eyes lock and it all feels very strange.

The Hand takes my hand in hers and allows herself to be pulled off the ground. Her skin is warm, startling me as I shiver from the cold. We move away from the horse. I find my bow in the tall grass, my hand still entwined with hers.

We don't talk about it.

We walk silently away from the valley and towards Alnola, my intentions as gray as the clouds in the sky.

13

ELIO

The Prince of Sumeria is in the air, dangling from the talons of a Harpy.

I don't wish to be insensitive, and yet, a laugh seems to bubble its way out of my mouth as my horse propels us through the rain. I'm bitter, and not usually one to flatter irony, but I'll give it to the damned Creator for pulling such an act.

"*Ahh!*" The Prince wails as purple expands along his shoulders and chest.

His Harpy flies low, a hideous creature with protruding bones and sharp feathers. I steal a glance behind me, expecting to find a murder of Harpies on my tail, but the valley curls away, and there is no other in the sky above us.

"Stop moving!" I yell at the squirming Prince.

He clocks me below, his jaw falling wide as the Harpy lifts them both higher. I curse, knowing I can't let her take him away.

No matter how little I care for the Kingdom, I'll never get my cash prize if the crown dies by my negligence. I don't suppose bringing him back to the King in shreds would call for celebration, or my freedom, for that matter. Well, maybe a celebration of my hanging but—

Aalis cuts through my thoughts with yet another shrieking wince.

"What a joke," I mumble.

I look around in search of our next steps, the Abram Woods in the near distance.

It's now or never.

I rip my feet from the stirrups and hoist them onto the saddle, my horse relentlessly blasting forward. I balance myself as best I can, burning my thighs with a low squat, but the Harpy lets out a painful screech, shattering my center.

"*Shit!*" I seethe, snatching back the reins.

Amidst the violent shatter of raindrop on rock, the roar of creature and rush of adrenaline, Aalis shouts something highly unintelligible. He is a pebble sinking in stormy waters, muffled and easily missed. I ignore him and hope for the best.

Too late for warnings, Little Prince.

It takes some time but I find my footing once more, ready enough to drop the reins. Abandoning ship, I push off my feet and jump, launching into the air with my arms stretched over my head, aiming for the Prince's legs: my bloody true north.

He yelps as I latch onto his lower half, my face meeting his torso, soaked by cold rain. The grip between us is wet and slippery — it takes everything I have to not slide away. Stupid silk blouse.

"Shut it," I grunt, feeling the loss of stability from underneath me.

Wind is whipping in every which way as my legs dangle loosely below. I hear my horse whinny, surely confused and maybe even frightened. *Definitely* frightened.

Aalis groans, my added weight causing him even more

pain: the Harpy has the Prince by the socket of his armpits, a set of talons clutching each shoulder, digging into his skin to keep him in her grasp, and for once, I am at a loss.

"Just hold on for now, yeah?" I shout.

I can't see much but he looks terribly gray, the flush in his cheeks staining like a bruise, and I'm scared he might vomit all over me and my poor shirt. The forest lies beneath us now, the tips of trees inches away from my toes. Alnola feels a world away.

"What does it want with us?" Aalis asks, his voice that of a trembling child.

"*Us?* She wants to eat *you*." The rain continues its blunder, forcing me to yell over the green-inducing gale.

It doesn't help that the dastardly creature is fast, throwing us over the enormity of the Domain at a speed far greater than the one Bea and I traveled at as if we were nothing but silly playthings. We may as well be a bag of feathers at the end of a stick hoisted over her shoulder.

"What about Beka?" The Prince shakes his head.

"Who?" I can barely hear him.

"The girl, the Hand!"

"What about her?"

"Well, your *friend*?" He shrieks.

"Trust me, your girl's in strong hands," I can't help but smirk.

Prince Aalis falls into a stifled silence: whether it is his lack of grasp, his definite exhaustion, or my calling the Hand 'his girl' that's made him finally cease his screams, I don't care enough to check.

Abram Woods is well behind us now, the Harpy flapping

diligently as we slip into the sprouting tips of the Peaks. The rain cuts off as the creature carries us under the curl of the mountains, through a wide tunnel. Her near-deafening caws echo off the walls, thundering like never before. I scramble for my next move with no chance of knowing that's to come.

And when they pluck you from the ground?

Of course Bea would come to me in my final moments. Most likely to say 'I told you so'. I sullenly recall our conversation from the night before, wishing my joke of poison was a possibility. I usually have a vial on me, or at least a few deadly bombs spare in my pockets, but, as luck would have it, I left those in my pack wrapped around my horse's saddle. We'd need to get down. Aalis might be just as useless on the ground as he is in the air, but at least he'd be out of the Harpy's claws.

Claws.

Bea said she'd attack their talons first: get rid of their sharp digits and go for their wings next. Though I don't have a bow — and even if I did, my shot isn't nearly as keen as my partner's — there are two daggers strapped to my thighs, and four smaller ones carefully littered around my calves. If I can cut the Prince away from her grasp, I could have a fair chance of lining my blades up with the tendons of her wings.

I peer ahead as best I can and spot a dim light at the end of the tunnel, but it's not the sentence of death.

The ground looks only a few feet away. Dropping now would be our best bet.

"You still with me?" I glance up at the Prince's.

His head is limp, lolling from side to side. I squeeze my

nails into his waist, applying just enough pressure to wake him up.

"*Hurts*," he mumbles.

"I'm going to cut you down. Get ready, okay?"

His eyes go wide. "Cut down? You want me to fall?"

"Just watch your head and you'll be fine!"

"Are you serious?"

Of course he has the nerve to argue. Why do I even bother?

The Harpy belts out an almighty wail as the tunnel comes to a near end. I panic as I stretch out one of my arms, inching my other up the Prince's body.

"Hey! I ca— wha—?" He wails.

"I'm trying to save you! Stop moving or we'll both fall."

He presses his palm into the space between my neck and shoulder, curling his fingers until they squeeze my skin.

"Promise it's not a far drop?" His words are small, hesitant and clipped.

"I can't promise you anything."

I wrap my hand around the base of the Harpy's foot, releasing my other hand from the Prince's waist to snatch a dagger from my belt, squeaking as I thrust my blade into the creature's ankle. She releases a foul cry as dark liquid spurts from the incision, coating our faces and chests. I hear the Prince gag as I indulgently stick my tongue out to lick at the ichor near my mouth and smirk, stabbing the creature's ankle again and again until her talons unlock, releasing the Prince's left shoulder. He splutters a slew of some very unroyal curses, now hanging in the air by a thread. My hand remains above the Harpy's damaged ankle — the other clutching the hilt of my blade still lodged in her foot.

"Are you ready?" I call out to Aalis.

"I'm going to *die*," the Prince weeps.

"You'll be fine," I reply earnestly, and just before we reach the end of the tunnel, I rip my dagger out of the Harpy's foot before jabbing it into the other, the attack freeing Aalis entirely from her grip.

I hold my breath as Aalis falls out of her grasp and plummets towards the ground at an alarming speed. I hear his impact with the stone, unable to look down, hoping for a few broken bones, not an already-rotting cadaver.

The Harpy is raging with fury, still bellowing at my assault. She flaps her wings with no mercy, lifting us higher from the ground toward a crater in the Peaks, neither Prince nor tunnel in sight.

In a single hack, her other foot slices clean off, rows of her hideously sharp teeth seething at my vitriol.

"You're a real beauty," I taunt, though I can barely catch my breath.

Desperate to throw me off, she shakes her gruesome body with great might, her severed flesh shedding in sheets, with trembling wings and all.

Wings.

Bea said the wings were next.

I lift the slick dagger to my face, and although the stench of ichor is repulsive, it doesn't stop me from bringing the blade to my tongue and lapping it up like a cat starved for milk. The blood may be foul, but it's just enough for me to regain some semblance of strength. I swing my hand back to lodge my dagger into her scale-covered stomach, greeted by her violent roar.

Bea was right to go for the talons first. With them cut away, the only weapon the Harpy truly has are her teeth, which can't reach me at the moment. I tug on the dagger snug in her flesh and lift my body, swiping my other blade and flinging my arm up at the muscle between her wing and shoulder. My face collides with her bulbous chest, taking a mouthful of black feathers in my teeth as I lodge another dagger into her socket.

With the loss of her winged mobility, our trajectory is diverted, and by diverted, I mean we dive straight into the side of the mountain. Thankfully, the Harpy's back connects with the stone first, blocking me from being squished under her weight. The crack of her spine is loud, and my head rings with the sound of her broken body. I rip the dagger from her stomach and deliver the killing blow to her throat.

I feel the urge to whoop, though I can't yet relish in the victory of this brawl; not while we're rapidly plunging toward the ground.

I definitely black out on the way down, though I assume, or hope, for only a moment. I don't remember hitting the stone floor, but when I come to, I'm shaking without end and the nausea is otherworldly. I push myself up with no time to spare. Beneath my splayed hands lies the Harpy, her bones crushed, her wigs snapped, and neck gushing with ichor. She slowly deteriorates into a gray ash, leaving me in a pile of her remains, save for a single talon I pocket.

All I do is laugh.

"*You!*" A voice calls out.

Fuck, the Prince. I turn my head and see him hobbling

over to me as he clutches at his heart — purple oozing from a gash on his forehead.

A part of me is very relieved to see him walk.

"*You*," he repeats.

"Did you see that? I took down a fucking *Harpy*," I announce. I continue to laugh, taking fists full of the ashes and chucking them into the air, letting the remains sprinkle down like the first fall of snow. "Just wait until Bea hears about this!"

"Excuse me?"

I sit up on my knees and point at the Prince, ignoring his attitude.

"You *must* vouch for me. I doubt Bea will believe I managed to take out one of these beasts on my own!"

Prince Aalis drops his arm and smacks my hand away.

"You just about got me killed! And yourself!"

"That Harpy almost ate you for dinner," I frown. "Please, allow me to appreciate myself and how I managed to save your life."

"Are you ever serious?"

"Are you ever grateful, your Highness? Or is the Royal scepter too far up your own ass?" I snap. "Not a single token of thanks from your bratty trap."

"Thank you, but I did not ask you to rescue me," he scoffs, fists balled at his sides.

"Oh, no, I'm ever so sorry, your Majesty! Seems like your gratitude is synonymous with being a twat." I jab, groaning as I stand. "But then again, what should I expect from a Prince?"

"You don't know anything about me," he bites back with bated breath.

"Oh, care to bet?" I stand to my full height, towering over him.

"What?" the Prince cocks his head: full of surprises, this one. "Assume I am some pretentious, Royal snob because I am a Hyttenrauch? Call me selfish and foolish, ill on my feet?"

"Well—"

"Yes, well, I have heard it all before."

I tsk, earning another scowl. "I don't think you understand just how much pleasure it would have given me to see that Harpy swallow you whole."

"Why save me then if you hate me so?"

"We have a transaction to uphold," I simply state.

Prince Aalis's hands smack against my chest, sending me backwards. I gasp, shocked that, although he isn't strong, I'm not entirely in the best shape to take a beating.

"You and your damn money! It's all you care about!" he shouts, striding forward to shove at me again.

I move back just enough so his fingertips barely touch the buttons of my shirt.

"Please, don't embarrass yourself any further," I sigh, unsure how to handle this turn. "You've already done so by trying to cover up why you're really here with the Hand, and it's pathetic." Nevertheless, Aalis stands his ground, rage cracking through his soft features, and out of my own twisted pleasure, I wish to watch him unravel. "Your attempt at deceiving myself and Bea was entertaining, but watching you fail time and time again just to cover up how desperately in love you are with that girl — it's sad! Brutal, even."

"You don't know what you're talking about."

"Don't I, Little Prince? Please, why else would you be here, sacrificing everything just to save some girl that you barely know? Tell me. Does your father know where you are?" I muse in a fit of pique, cornering him to the side of the mountain.

"I do not need someone as heartless as you to judge my reason for leaving the Kingdom," the Prince spits, any trace of his nobility momentarily tossed aside.

"If it is love that led you to betray the Kingdom, then you really are a lost cause to your people," I say, fueled by bad temper. "Once we hand her over to the King, her fate is none of my business, nor will it be yours. Best get over your little crush."

To my shock, he punches me.

Actually punches me.

I feel the bony knuckles of his fist connect with the hollows of my cheek, the blow knocking me off-balance. My face throbs as my fingers gently glide over the rising cushion of flesh, right where he made contact. I barely register what's happening until I feel the sharp strike of his shove against my chest, his force wringing my lungs dry of air, tackling me to the ground. I'm able to grab ahold of his wrists just before he manages to dig his claws into my face.

"This is, this is *far* from proper!" I reason, and although I'm winded, I ache, and I can already feel the twinge of my blood run to the surface, I release his hands with a wince and let him resume his thrashing.

Tears roll down his cheeks, and I feel their unwelcome sting when they drip onto me.

I doubt he's had any time to really process what he's done, how much his decision to leave has undoubtedly impacted the rest of his life. I wonder just how far his punishment will go when he returns home, or if he'll even have one at all.

Despite every new blow and hit to my chest, it quickly becomes apparent how the real pain I feel is one of hunger. From the moment I touched my tongue to the ichor, I felt my stomach twist and turn in disagreement. I need to feed, and as much as the Prince needs whatever this is that he's doing, I need to get him off me even more.

Gathering whatever strength I have left, I jolt my leg up from underneath him and swing it to clip at his ankles in one fluid movement. He loses his balance and I roll him over, this time being the one to pin him to the ground.

"You won't beat me," I say, my vision starting to blur.

"Release me!" The Prince lashes out. I quite like the view from here, holding him in place, watching him writhe beneath me.

"Are you finished?"

"You are so—"

"Handsome?" I flash him a smile.

A putrid taste begins to fashion on my tongue. Prince Aalis's eyes steady and he stops moving. I start to notice how close we are, how our breaths mingle together in the hot space between us, his cheeks suddenly flushing as I keep my eyes locked with his.

"Well?" I ask, feeling faint.

"You look ill," he notes, the rage evaporating from his body. "Are you alright?"

I fall to the side, setting him free. I'm able to scramble a few paces away before vomiting on the stone, nothing but bile. It tastes just as it had when swallowing the ichor: spoilt and rotten. Their blood the cousin of poison, burning my throat as it rips through my system.

"Elio?" I hear the Prince call. At the sound of my name, my stomach empties itself some more. "That is your name, right? What is *happening*?"

The last time I ate was in Eephifer, and although I can usually get by for several moons thanks to my Celestite, my body is trying to repair itself, and it can't do so malnourished. I attempt to stand but end up staggering, collapsing against the wall of the mountain. I press my back hard into the stone, just now feeling the deep gash in my side. I reach my hand down and press on the injury. My fingers pull away soaking wet. Wonderful.

"I'm hungry," I manage to croak.

"Oh, I..." the Prince searches for the right thing to say.

He kneels down in front of me, concern written all over his face, an expression I never thought would be from anyone other than Bea.

"It seems that Harpy blood does not agree with me," I explain.

I can't heal until I feed. I wish I had my satchel now: little vials of Bea's blood are packed in there, along with many other helpful resources.

"I am the same way with fish. I can't stand its dreadful smell, let alone the taste of it," the Prince mumbles.

"You should leave now," I say, avoiding his gaze. He's sitting far too close to me. "Go back through the tunnel and head for Alnola. Or go back to the Kingdom, I don't care."

"You speak as if you are dying."

"I very well might if I don't feed. Leave before more Harpies return to their nests."

Above all, hunger is my greatest enemy. Us Night Demons turn into motionless vessels, still breathing, but desiccated and cold as ice — as solid as the very stone I rest against.

All I can think about is blood. I'm on the tail-end of vision loss, everything dark and blurry, though I can feel the Prince's hand on my shoulder, the other pulling on my chin, urging my head up.

"What can I do?" he asks.

The sun peeks through the cracks of the mountain, turning his hair into woven gold.

"Be rid of me, I suppose. It's what you desire, no?"

Skin touches my lips. My mouth opens instinctively, teeth grazing the Prince's wrist.

"Allow me," he says, pushing his warm wrist further between my lips.

I want to bite, sink my teeth into his flesh and bleed him dry. I know I won't be able to stop.

"Come on," he urges. My vision focuses just enough to catch the brown in one eye and the blue in the other. "I need you," he admits, voice hushed. "We both know I won't make it out of here without you."

"I'll try to be careful."

I don't know why I tell him this.

The Prince shivers as I press my fangs into his wrist. I break into the vein and suck, my mouth watering as his blood flows onto my tongue. It tastes unlike anything I've ever had before, not crisp and dry like a normal human's, but that of honey — a smooth ambrosia of Eden.

I pull away, a question pleading to be asked.

"Your blood, it…"

"I know."

"So the tales are true."

"It would seem so."

So why would the Harpies go for him? I go to ask and I think he knows it because he brings his arm back to my mouth and forces my teeth to clamp. His blood is sweet wine and I am drunk on him. It blossoms and tastes like magic, my body restoring almost instantly. I grip at his arm and continue to guzzle.

"It's working," he marvels, breathlessly.

Our eyes meet and I can't look away. I'm unable to recall what we were fighting about just moments before. His blood is addicting and so is this look he's giving me, struck with wonder as he watches me, fascinated, unbothered by the pain I must be causing. Everything seems to amaze him. The wound in my back ceases its bleeding; exhaustion leaves my body and my vision returns.

It's only after I take my last gulp that an image of a woman flashes before my eyes. It's quick, but striking enough to leave me questioning if I'd just left my own body and gone elsewhere. She was what many consider beautiful, painfully so. Her hand was extended toward me, reaching for my touch, her face was twisted in desperation.

"Elio?" The Prince whispers, bringing me back to myself. I remove my mouth from his wrist and lick my lips. "Are you…?"

"Better. Feeling much better," I reply, attempting to stand.

The Prince steps back, sweating profusely. "We should get going."

"I think I," he frets, leaning back against the stone. He's awfully pale, most definitely from all the blood loss. "I think I need a moment."

"Very well," I declare.

Instead, I find a small pocket in the wall of the mountain: an indent of the stone that acts as a convenient shelter. The Prince falls asleep almost instantly, a soft snore rumbling from his lips. I can't help but notice his clotted forehead and collection of bruises that coat every inch of his exposed skin. I catch myself watching him deep into his slumber, struggling to tear my eyes away.

Submerged in darkness, I think of Bea. I wonder where she is now. I wonder if she's safe. We're no stranger to a deviated plan or an absurd situation, but nothing quite like this. As they say, there's a first for everything.

Will we even make it to Alnola in time? The Domain's capital is almost a day's straight worth of travel away. In my panic, I decide I'll wake the Prince a few hours before dawn, feeling nice enough to let him rest. Though I hope time moves fast. I hate sitting here in the dark with just myself and my mind.

I'd rather wish to forget the taste of the Prince's blood, how it danced on my tongue and left me salivating for more. In these dark hours, my desire to taste him again makes me blush. I clutch the Celestite wrapped around my neck in an attempt to purge my thoughts of any more satisfaction. It's almost as if I'm not wearing the damned gem.

Eventually, I am able to silence the noise, but I can't dismiss the strange, prickling sensation tickling my fingertips.

14
BEKA

The assassin insists we tend to the wound in my leg.

I tell her I'm fine but, as I've observed thus far, she is not so easily swayed.

"We won't make it to Alnola if you can't stand on your feet," she argues.

I shake my head in disagreement as I attempt to hobble along on my one good foot. Holding my own and limping in front of her is better than falling over and admitting she's right.

"I'm fine," I seethe, unsure if the drops falling on my face are cold rain or tears.

"It'll get infected. The King wants you alive, not ridden with disease," she reprimands, and I find myself complying, more for her convenience than mine.

I tell her of a village outside Ochrore, just south of Abram Woods. A collection of cottages and a small pasture home to three brown cows and a team of horses lined by the sprouting corn stalks that grow in Grimree Fields. I feel fingers tighten its grip on mine as I'm dragged swiftly along, a strong resistance in her hold whenever I try to pull away.

It's not like I can run away, I think.

My hand, uncomfortable and slick with sweat, eventually

gives up on trying to untangle the knot our fingers have tied. At the very least, this offers a bit of support for my hobble.

"There's a Haelend who lives here," I explain, feeling the wound swell on my leg.

The assassin eyes my injury, her expression just unreadable.

"I'm sorry I shot you," she says.

I stay quiet.

The sun has vanished over the horizon by the time we reach the village. The area deserted, not a single civilian in sight. I relieve myself from the assassin's grip, surprised for a slick release, to limp my way over to one cottage in particular. I recognized the white peonies planted beside the door: the sign of a healer.

I knock three times and wait.

The door creaks open a smidge, revealing the tired eyes of a girl. She's young. Probably not much younger than myself.

"Hello?"

"I'm sorry to bother, but I was just—" I drift off as she slowly trails her eyes down to my leg, noting my injury.

Her eyes are wide, surely surprised by the color of my blood.

"Were you attacked?" she inquires, stepping outside.

I look down at my torn and bloody garments: I look just as beaten as I feel.

"A flock of Harpies spotted us while we were traveling to Alnola. One of them got to my leg," I flinch at the memory.

"Oh, we saw them too! Everyone fled at first sight. I'm sorry you had nowhere safe to go," the Haelend sighs, her hands over her heart.

"Can you help her?" The assassin clips at my side, her voice rigid.

"I can do my best, though my mother is the Haeland of this household, not me," the girl admits.

"If it's too much trouble, we can leave."

"No, please. Come in," she steps aside eagerly.

To my surprise, the assassin helps me into the cottage, the space much smaller than the one I grew up in. There is a single table littered with herbs and piles of ripped cloth. Two narrow cots rest in the corner beside the lit fireplace, tendrils of flames wisping about in the cool air.

"Take a seat there. I can't do much yet, but I'm learning," she explains. "I'm Johna."

I sit down on the edge of the cot, and though it's rough, I relish in the comfort of her home. I haven't slept in what seems like days, but if I let myself go at this very moment, I would happily surrender to a deep slumber, wishing to never wake again.

"I'm Beka."

Johna nods and looks over at the assassin expectantly, though she doesn't seem to notice, refusing to pay attention. The girl moves to examine my wound.

"Your blood is quite dark," she says, puzzled.

My heart skips a beat but I'm quick to recover. "The talons of a Harpy must be venomous — I'm sure an infection is spreading."

"Thank the Creator you arrived when you did. My mother tells me few bleed like this," Johna comments, tone free of suspicion. "And your name?" she persists with a raised voice.

The assassin does a double take, surprised that the question is for her.

"My name?"

Johna nods. She has a few strips of cloths in one hand and a vial filled with a clear substance in the other.

"It's Bea."

Interesting.

"Bea. Is that short for something?" Johna presses, now kneeling at my feet.

"I think that's none of your business, Haelend."

Johna angles her head away, avoiding Bea's burning gaze. She dumps some of the liquid onto the cloth and grimaces.

"This should only sting a little bit."

I grip the sheets of the cot as Johna gently dabs the cloth around the cut, allowing myself a moment of weakness, my blood dying the material a rich stain of blackberry wine. I don't tell her that I've felt worse. The Haelends in the Kingdom were, and no doubt still are, beyond cruel. If it weren't for the King's no-kill orders, I'm sure they would've savored watching me die.

"How long will this take?" Bea demands.

Johna rubs my wound with some urgency now, her hands trembling.

"The gash needs stitching or the infection will grow," she explains. "But I can't stitch very well. Not yet."

"Where is your mother?" I whimper.

Johna sighs, bringing the tinted cloth away and into her lap.

"Alnola. She's with the survivors from Brighes, offering aid to their wounded. I'm not sure how long she'll be away."

My heart is in my throat. If Emelyne is in Alnola, then maybe I have a bit of fight left in me after all.

"Then I am lucky you are still here. Thank you for this," I say.

Johna looks up at me with bright, gracious eyes and nods.

"I might not be able to stitch you up, but I do know someone who can." Johna stands and walks around the table, away from Bea, and reaches for the door. "I'm sure she's still about. I'll be right back."

Bea turns to watch Johna close the door. I keep my eyes down and lean forward to grab the cloth from the ground, pressing it back onto my wound.

"I don't want to be here long. Once she's finished we leave," Bea asserts.

"Bea is a lovely name," I offer, filling the silence.

"Do *not* call me that," she barks.

I steal a glance in her direction, unsurprised that she is facing the door.

"Your partner calls you Bea. You two must be very close," I presume.

The floor creaks as she swivels around to face me: she looks as if she'd just been slapped.

"What does it matter to you?"

"I didn't mean to offend you," I sigh. "I'm sure he's fine. Aalis too, not that you care," I mumble that last part under my breath. "We'll finish your mission, just as you wish."

Truth be told, I hadn't really thought of Aalis since we parted ways, and I definitely haven't been thinking of Magpie. After all, the farther away Aalis is from me, the more of a chance he has at redeeming himself. As for Magpie — well, I don't think I've ever disliked anyone as much as I do him.

Bea's boots thrum against the floor as she stomps her way over to me. My eyes suddenly find interest in the ripped hem on my apron, the tension between us drawn out and uncertain.

"I highly doubt *you* go by *your* birth name either," Bea spits. "Aliases keep us hidden. My job requires a separate identity, and I take my job very seriously." I keep still, unsure what her point is. She's articulate, careful with her every word. Her tone, however, plays games with my mind. She taunts me. "Let it be very clear that I don't trust you, nor do I trust the Prince. When the Haelend is done with your wound, we will travel to Alnola where I will hand you over to the Kingdom. The Heretics are abominable, and turning you in will satisfy the King," Bea says, looking more like she's talking to herself.

"The King will be pleased, yes."

"And you don't care," she scoffs. "How is it that you are so intent on not fighting back?" Bea's voice suddenly rises, the slightest sliver of emotion breaking free.

"Believe me, I care," I raise, surprisingly firm. "You must think of me a coward. I suppose I am, hiding all these years, for betraying the Maidens and cooperating with you.

"Some luck that the Hand of Lilith is indifferent. The Creator must be having a laugh," she jokes, but it hurts all the same.

"I'm not indifferent. I am the Hand. That's who everyone is after. But it is not who I wish to be. I can't control that, but I can stay away from it."

"So, indifferent?" she probes, fighting for her point.

I just sigh.

"Sorry—" she starts, *again*, with the apologies.

"You're just doing your job."

"No, I just— I'm trying to make sense of this," Bea exhales, taking another step forward.

I peel my eyes away from my hem and find confidence in meeting her gaze. There is a tenderness in the way she looks at me and I'm reminded of the way her manners shifted after I put her horse down. It may be fear that she feels, and for someone like her with a profession so brutal, vulnerability is a liability. To feel any sympathy for me whatsoever could not only compromise her mission, but cost Bea her life. There is no common ground for us to stand on, and yet there was a split second after we were attacked where I thought that maybe, just maybe, we weren't so different.

That thought left as quickly as it came.

Bea inches lower towards my slouched frame, forcing me out of my head. She's watching me, her eyes noting my every breath, observing my every blink, tracking each of my hairs.

She opens her mouth, ready to speak, and after a hesitant pause, she asks, "Are all Maidens like you?"

The front door breaks the strain as it creaks open. I force my attention away from Bea and onto the young Haelend alongside the person she went to retrieve draped in a white cloak somewhat familiar to me. It isn't until she lowers her hood that I register she's a Heathen — one I've encountered before.

"This is Kymn. She was making her rounds in Ochrore just a few days ago. Thankfully, she was close by when the Harpies attacked," Johna explains.

The Heathen scans both Bea and I with knowing eyes. I can't seem to find the muscle in my throat to swallow, to push air in and out of my lungs. It's caught in my chest along with the ability to string along a sentence and it winds me.

"I know you," Kymn says, striding forward to stand before the two of us.

Unease eats me away at the grace, at the precision, of her movements. Her cloak moves like water, following the trail of her every movement. It looks as though she is gliding across the floor, not walking. I can't help but notice how Bea tenses, a small but unmissable twinge.

"Can you help her? I cleaned the wound as best I could with a remedy my mother concocted just days ago. It should have sanitized her skin well enough but—"

"Thank you, Johna," Kymn interrupts, her voice icy.

The girl snaps her mouth shut and nods. She shrinks into the corner of the room and perches herself on a stool, afraid to bother the Heathen any further.

It sets in now: how truly terrified I am of this woman. She stands there, observing the scene for seconds that seem to last a year. Bea approaches the cloaked woman, her hand flirting with the hilt of her dagger. Kymn simply glares at the assassin, holding her gaze until Bea stands down.

My bones seem to have calcified. I don't move — not even to breathe.

"I am here to heal her," Kymn claims, turning her head back to me.

She kneels down slowly, leveling our gazes. This close, I can see the pieces of our shared blood: the same hooded eyes and umber skin. How we share even the same coils of hair on our heads, down to the very same shade.

"A Harpy did not do this," Kymn smirks, hovering her fingers above my wound. "You are from Brighes, aren't you girl."

"Oh dear!" Johna exclaims. "You're from Brighes? It's awful, what happened."

"Quite," Kymn monotonously agrees.

"That Banshee scream sure gave everyone a fright," Johna shakes her head. "I feel ill when I think about it."

Inez. I'm not sure how much more my heart can bear the anguish of seeing her dead, of knowing I could've done something to stop it. Kymn's gaze is unrelenting, waiting for me to crack, though grief and fear are a powerful combination, and, quite frankly, I'm thankful they've left me mostly numb.

"Johna, how acquainted are you with the Maidens of Lilith?"

Johna stutters, apprehensive, surprised that the Heathen has addressed her again.

"They live in the Realm of Zemargad. No one knows how to enter it, and rarely do they venture into our lands."

"You are right. The Maidens bear no purpose to Sumeria but to sulk and complain, trapping themselves in their little 'oasis'," Kymn drones. She brings her pointer finger forward to graze my ankle. The touch is brief, but it's powerful. I can feel the raw presence inside of her, even dormant. "They have waited *years* for their Hand to be born, for one of their kind to be worthy enough to offer up their body to the Lady of Edom, the mother of Heretics and other cursed children of Sumeria," The Heathen continues. "They wait for her to take host inside that vessel to freely walk among us."

"But the Hand is dead. And the witch murders innocent people. She's a monster who kills mothers, just like that poor girl in Brighes," Johna whispers the last part.

She looks over at me sympathetically, but her face falls upon seeing the guilt crossing my face.

"And what do you think would happen if the Hand was not dead? What would happen to Sumeria if Lilith ascended into this world?" Kymn's voice is steady and calculated.

"We shouldn't be speaking of this..."

"How about you stitch this wound up and we carry on with our day?" Bea interrupts, earning a haunting glower from the Heathen.

"Very well," she says.

I've always wondered how Heathens managed without their connection to our lady. A Maiden is gifted their powers if they prove their devotion to Lilith, if they let her inside and allow her to guide them. A Heathen snaps the cord connecting them to Lilith's soul, severing that power, not their blood, but how do they go on?

"I'll need a needle and thread."

"Yes, of course!" Johna hops off her chair, itching to be of any assistance.

She snatches the items from the nearest table and places them in the Heathen's hand.

"Stay near. Watch me closely," Kymn tells Johna.

The young girl hovers behind, eyes glued on Kymn's hands, oblivious to the tension in the room. Kymn slides the thread into the top of the needle.

"This will hurt," the Heathen warns, but her tone lacks any compassion.

Kymn presses the needle against my skin and pushes it through, forcing a hiss out of my mouth. It stings, and I'm frightened.

"General Bausan was wrong about you," Kymn states, looking up at Bea. "He was confident in your loyalty."

"My loyalty remains the same," Bea affirms.

"The General keeps me at his side, for my judgment is far better than his. He considers your strength, but as for your intentions—"

The needle digs deep into my skin. I don't doubt that Kymn is a skilled healer, but she is not gentle with the way she weaves the thread in and out of my leg.

"I am bringing her to Alnola," Bea assures.

"And your demon friend? Where has he gone off to?"

"The Harpies separated us. We're meeting in Alnola."

Bea does not mention the Prince. I glance over at Johna, who is now less concerned with watching the suturing, and far more interested in the conversation.

"I will not interrupt your mission, then. As for its status, a report will be sent back to the General and the King. They will be happy to know that you have found and captured the Hand as requested."

I watch the cogs turn in Johna's brain. Her eyes widen, wild with the revelation. She backs away from me, horror twisting her face.

"You were right under our noses all along, weren't you?" Kymn spits. "Beka Tonis," she clicks her tongue, finishing the thread with a tie on its end. "Beautiful, you are, but I never thought of you clever."

"I won't fight."

From a young age, I was taught the Heathens were lost souls, adrift from the values of our kind. They found no honor in our culture, no value in worshiping an ancient Goddess whose destructive past promises more ruin than merit. I, too, have fallen astray, but only as a response to the fear buried within me. I only know how to cower at the hands of the Heathens whose devotion in life is to find and kill me. In my heart, I have cut no ties with our Lady.

After setting down both needle and thread, Kymn rises abruptly. She leans in, bringing her face close to mine. I hold my breath when I feel hers hit my cheeks.

"I should kill you myself."

Kymn steps back, turning to Bea, her hands wrapped within the pockets of her cloak. My ankle throbs, pulsing with the unfamiliar thread holding my skin together.

"If she's not in the Kingdom's custody by dusk tomorrow, then consider your mission a failure," Kymn warns. "The General is expecting you back in Alnola, and his patience is far thinner than my own. Do with that what you will."

Bea nods and steps between the two of us. "Understood."

Kymn doesn't seem convinced, raking her eyes over us once more before spinning around to face Johna. The girl is still in shock, frozen in place beside the table.

"My dear, gather the people. A new dawn is approaching for the future of Sumeria," Kymn instructs, her voice bellowing the farther she walks away from us. Johna nods and scrambles out of the cottage, afraid to look back. Kymn stops in front of the open door, smug and filled with pride. "I have eyes everywhere. Betray me, young assassin, and far worse things will fall upon you than death."

Kymn moves her gaze to me. There is disgust in the way she regards me, mixed with triumph that has been years in the making.

"Abeko, be gone."

The forbidden language sounds near foreign to me now, not having heard it since my time in the Realm. A single tear slides down my cheek, I feel it touch my lips, salty on my tongue.

The Heathen leaves without another word.

15
AALIS

The chill of the Cudnola Peaks bears through my bones, a wanton spirit haunting for foes.

The mountains tower high above, blocking out most of the sky. All I know is that it's night, and that I can't find my footing in the crags beneath my feet. Elio woke me up not too long ago, my mind still fuzzy with fatigue. I wrap my arms close to my chest, hugging my shaking frame. I damn myself for leaving my woolen garments in the Kingdom.

We huddle close to the stone walls, straying off the carriage path to better conceal ourselves despite the cover of the night.

No more Harpies, please. I don't think my heart can take it.

Elio healed far quicker than I could have imagined — it was almost instant. I watch him now, as he strides ahead, his hair flowing in flaming ropes with every bounce.

The ache that courses through my body is one I wouldn't wish upon my worst enemy. Admittedly, the drop wasn't too far, and I was lucky enough, if you can call that luck, to have landed on my side rather than my head, but it still hurt. A lot. Plus, my shoulder is still sore, bloody where the Harpy's talons pinched my skin. That hurts too.

We've fallen into a strange silence, Elio and I. He hasn't so much as said a word to me, not since he woke me up. My eyes sway with the swish of his hair.

"Don't scratch at it," he scolds.

I glance down. It seems as though I've been picking at the bite mark on my wrist — at the small two holes that have since clotted over, punctured into me. I hadn't even noticed what I was doing.

"Sorry."

Elio turns his head to look at me, his eyebrows raised.

"I've never—" I hesitate.

"Please don't. I figured as much," he finishes.

I mean, until the last day or so, I had never even been in the presence of a Night Demon, let alone seen one feed. If I'm honest, I'm not even sure why I offered him my arm. But, by Eden, the way it felt. I can't help but blush.

We continue the next leg through the mountains in a surprisingly comfortable silence. It gives me time to think. Time to think about being away from the Kingdom; away from the constant guarding, the nagging, the belief that I am incapable on my own. Oh, the sweet *relief* of not being under constant lock and key, or kept a close eye on by the gentry! Granted, yes, Elio and his partner breathing down my neck is far from ideal, but at least I am nobody to them. At least they have no time for the pity party I've been the guest of honor at for the last twenty years.

I think about the punch.

I try to feign embarrassment but, truthfully? I feel little of the sort. I don't know what came over me, but he deserved it — and who else can say that they've bested 'Magpie', or whatever his stupid name is. Though, admittedly, I hadn't quite thought past what would happen after. Evidently, consequences and I are not well acquainted.

I draw my mind back to Beka for a distraction, though it soon turns to nerves. I think about her now, wondering if she and the assassin were able to fight off the beasts on their own; if she's still tied up by the wrist, drained and bleeding from her wound. I think of her crying out for her lost village, sick knowing it was the very Kingdom who destroyed her home, not the workings of the Dark Maid.

I worry about what will happen when we make it to Alnola.

The rough glide of my nails along the cracks of my skin is the only noise between us. I curse ever so slightly at the cold breeze. I don't want to be the one to say it, but I can't stand it any longer.

"Listen, I'm sorry I punched you."

"He apologizes!" Elio throws his arms in the air, triumphant.

He swivels his body around and walks backwards on his toes. His swift movements amaze me, how light he is on his feet, like walking on water.

"And will *you* apologize?" I try to maintain a civil tone, but the irritation he provokes seeps through the cracks.

Elio's expression twists dramatically. "Oh, darling, whatever for?"

"For almost killing me?"

He hums, pretending to consider this before giving me a very definitive, "No. However, I *will* thank you for the blood. I'd be an ugly, rotting corpse if it wasn't for you," he says, pointing a long, slender finger at me, a glimmer of appreciation in his scarlett eyes.

He turns back around, this time slowing down to match my pace. We walk side by side, the tension dissolving. I catch myself reaching for my wrist yet again, forcing myself to stuff my hand in my pocket.

"Do you," I pause, "get donations often?" Elio quirks his eyebrow, and I shrug. "I don't really know how it all works."

"I don't go around biting people at random, if that's what you're wondering," he answers simply.

"Who usually feeds you then? Does your friend help you out?"

I don't know why I feel so awkward asking him. The knowledge I have of other species in Sumeria is both limited and censored: what's documented in books, and what the King has to say about them. Both redundant in their own ways.

"So many questions," Elio grumbles. "Just be quiet. *You* are *my* prisoner."

That I am.

"I won't bother you then," I reply, ducking my head down, fighting my disappointment.

This is the closest I've had to a normal conversation in years. His prisoner I may be, but is it strange to admit it's nice to talk?

"Wipe that look off your face. You're making me uncomfortable," Elio says.

"Sorry," I mumble.

I can't help but feel that this is all my fault: Beka being rediscovered by the King, being hunted down by Elio and his partner. If only he never found my paintings that night — if only I never painted them in the first place, then none of this would've happened.

Elio sighs, loud and exhausted. "The Capitan is tough, but, believe it or not, she's much nicer than me. Be happy that I'm with you and not your little girlfriend."

"She's not my girlfriend," I snap.

Elio has the audacity to hum again, smitten with knowing how easy it is to get under my skin. I allow him this indulgence before continuing somewhat bashfully, "I will court her first, of course."

The humming transforms into a hysterical chuckle, one he's unable to control. I tuck my arms tighter against my chest, feeling my cheeks tint yet again.

"*Right*," he snickers.

"You don't believe in the love I have for her?"

He puts his hands up defensively. We enter a dark cove inside the mountains, the light disappearing above the stone.

"I don't have to believe in anything. You think you're in love, but blindly so. Besides, she's a Heretic: they're seductive by nature."

"That's a generalization. She's not a Siren!" I counter, thankful for the darkness concealing my anger. "And what would *you* know?"

"You don't think I see the way people generalize me?"

"I didn't say that."

"Whatever. You want my honest opinion about your little love affair?"

I nod. Why, oh, *why* do I nod?

"You barely know the girl. She's a stranger. How could you be in love with a stranger?"

"She *isn't* a stranger," I assert, my heart thundering in my chest.

"An acquaintance at best," Elio clicks his tongue.

I feel his hand send shocks through mine as he guides me out of the cove and back onto the illuminated path.

"Love. Love is beautiful. It's art. What I feel for her moves me," I say, conflicted by his words. "I don't expect *you* to understand."

Elio shakes his head. "Well, what I understand is that true love is not one-sided."

I will not let his poor judgment best my feelings. From the moment I laid eyes on Beka, I knew I would do anything to keep her safe.

"I want her to live freely, happily, and I will do whatever I can to make that happen."

"And what if her happiness is not conditional on you?"

"Well—"

"Just saying, it's not all that worth it. Not one bit."

This makes me scoff. "Worth it? Have you ever been in love?"

"Not the kind you talk about," Elio replies, somewhat bitterly.

I stare at him, waiting for him to elaborate, but he keeps his eyes forward.

"How did you two even meet?" he asks.

"I'm the one who let her out during the Battle of Lamya," I reveal.

Elio freezes, jaw dropped. "You helped her escape?"

"I'm also the reason you're here now on this mission," Elio stares at me, waiting for some explanation. I shrug, feeling

the weight of guilt press down on me for betraying the Kingdom. Doesn't matter anymore, I guess. "It's because of me and
my ties to her that the King found out about Beka. That she's
somehow still alive."

"Well, shit," he laughs.

"I probably shouldn't be telling you this," I admit, although
I see no real point in keeping it a secret any longer.

"You surprise me, Little Prince," he sings, clapping a hand
against my back.

"Will you tell?"

"Who? Your daddy?" He taunts.

"I'm serious!"

"Now that you mention it, I bet this information is worth
quite a fortune."

"It's not for sale! Please, I beg you. Don't say a word," I
can't help but whine.

Elio continues forward, turning his face to send me a
wink. "Seven for a secret never to be told."

"What?"

He waves me off. "Never mind. A lot has changed now.
I'm still deciding what to do with you once we get to Alnola.
Let's keep moving. Pick up your pace."

At some point I try to convince Elio to let me rest again.

He eventually agrees but not without complaint. I sigh in
relief, pressing my back against the stone, sliding down to the
ground. My legs twitch and my head ceaselessly throbs.

"You get a few minutes." Elio orders.

My stomach rumbles, painfully coiling in hunger as flashes
of chocolate cakes, roasted ham and gelatinous pudding

torment my mind. I hate how I yearn for my Royal diet, to stuff my face with the best delicacies once again. It's only been three days. What a humbling trip.

"What are you grumbling about?" Elio inquiries.

"It's my stomach."

Elio snorts. I close my eyes and focus on gaining some strength. My hand travels to the mountain floor, all ashy pebbles and dirt. I move my fingers in the rubble, smoothing it into a canvas. I open my eyes and watch my fingers work, guiding the dregs into an image. It's not so different from using paints and a brush, and I find I quite enjoy the feeling of the grime against my skin.

"It's hideous," Elio says.

He's standing a few feet away, arms crossed impatiently.

I take it as a compliment, finishing the ripples of the Harpy wing with the tip of my finger, curving it inward three times. It feels good to make something again.

"So you're an artist," he comments.

I shrug, wiping my hand off against my trousers.

"A hobby. My mother loved to draw, or so I've been told," I say.

Elio doesn't say anything for a moment. I put my fingers back into the dirt and attempt to shade.

"I assume that my mother was some sort of whore, but that would be giving her way more credit than she deserves," Elio reveals.

I look up at him and find him distant. I glance down at the Celestite resting on his collar bone, taking note of the hints of blue trapped in its icy structure: the cold colors loud against the warmth of his brown skin.

"Do you think you're better for it?" he asks.

"What do you mean?"

"Like, are you better off not having known her at all?"

"In all honesty, I've never thought about it," I look to meet his gaze. "I didn't know her."

"Right."

"She gave her life for me," I add, considering his words. "I don't feel guilty, nor do I feel selfish in accepting that from her. I don't know, maybe if I were my sister I'd have thought about it more. All I know is that she is, in many ways, a part of me. Does that answer your question?"

"Not in the slightest," he mumbles, tearing his gaze from mine.

I can tell he's still uncomfortable. I return my eyes to the Harpy.

"I just wonder. You see, mother is merely a word to me, nothing more. Night Demons don't have parents, but Maidens have daughters. They toss my kind aside, basically orphaned the moment we take our first breath. Why even bother letting us live?" he spits — it's evident that where I've come to peace with my mother's absence, there is war plain in his soul.

"And that makes you better off?" It's my turn to ask.

"Can't mourn them if they never existed in the first place. I should be better off for that."

"I suppose," I shrug, in no mood to push the subject any further.

He chuckles and kicks away from the stone wall.

"Blasted Heretics," he curses to himself, then he turns to me. "Are you ready now?"

I tut and shakily hoist myself off the ground. Elio starts

walking as I take one last glance at the image of the Harpy. I swipe the sole of my boot over the drawing, mixing the dirt back into the ground, and hobble forward back onto the path.

We last about five minutes in silence before Elio skids to a stop, looking around suspiciously. My nerves spike as I watch him stand on alert. His arm reaches out in front of me, keeping me back as he scans the area, swearing under his breath.

"I smell blood," he says.

"Blood?"

"It's familiar."

In the near distance, I can see the light at the end of the Peaks where the sun is rising. We are so close to reaching Alnola, and yet with our damned luck, of course another obstacle would launch itself our way.

"Are you—"

"*Shh!*" he snaps.

I refrain from telling him that smelling requires his *nose*, not his *ears*.

Elio steps forward across the path, practically soundless. He hunches his back, preying like an animal, sniffing the air like a hound. He looks at me wearily before turning around the corner. I remain frozen, terrified of what he could be catching scent of.

"You have *got* to be joking!" Elio exclaims, throwing his arms in the air with his attention directed onto the ground.

"Darling, what a surprise." I hear a voice say, one that belongs to a man.

Elio glances at me, flushed, before bending down to pick

someone up. I make my way around the corner to see who the voice belongs to.

But I don't even manage to blink, and this person wraps Elio's tresses around his fist, closing the space between them — Elio trying to maintain some sort of distance, his arms tightly gripping the man's waist an elbow's length away. I feel out of place, as if their tension manifested into the tangible thickness of the soil beneath their feet, and I am suddenly trespassing. This man is digging for treasure in Elio's throat, his tongue tying a bow around the chest. I figure there's some sort of history between them.

Creator, I hope so.

I wish to move along, this impatience growing within me. It's not like I have any real reason to rush — all that's waiting is the inevitability of handing Beka over to the King, and then turning myself in. Yet I would rather shove my own tongue down danger's throat than watch Elio and this man.

I don't want to know who he is. I don't think I care enough. I just want to go.

I try to rip my eyes away from the scene, but there's this instinct eating away at the surface of my skin. It feels like an itch I can't scratch. Not like the bite mark, something entirely different, and I can't help but feel Elio's awkwardness radiate at this moment. If it weren't for the smacking sounds of their lips mushing together in a gross concoction of saliva, teeth and tongue, I swear I can hear his thoughts loud and clear as if they were my own, wanting to be free of this lip-locked state.

I watch him peel away.

Elio's look of bewilderment is almost comical, but now is

not the time to laugh. His eyes wide, hair tousled completely out of place. He just stands there, taken aback and pink lips plump; the rapid rise and fall of his chest the only indication that he has not, in fact, died of shock.

"Have you missed me?" The man asks.

Elio gulps loudly. "Hardly."

The man chuckles. He wipes the palm of his hand across his lips, as if the kiss were removable, then settles it against the stone wall to support himself against the mountain. His trousers are ripped and he's coated in blood, crimson seeping through his sheer blouse that's cinched at the waist by a char-coal corset. His hair is spiked in every direction, icy blond and soiled. He's in disarray, he's enchanting, and I hate him.

Elio attempts to gather himself rather quickly: his hands find their way to his hips, the shock on his face replaced with his usual smugness.

"What the fuck are you doing here?" Elio hounds at him, positively seething.

The man looks up at me — his emerald eyes bewitching, studying my body, dragging his gaze from my boots to my face in a somewhat teasing nature — and laughs. I feel like the butt of a joke. His eyes feel so familiar, like I've studied their hue before. I realize that I'm shamelessly gawking straight into his soul, to which he cocks his eyebrow up in amusement.

I really, really hate him.

"Who's your friend?" he says, charmed by my presence.

He has his other hand against his stomach, clutching what seems to be a giant bite mark in his side.

"I don't have time for this," Elio claims, turning away to curse at the sky.

"Brr. I was expecting a warmer reunion. It's been *months*, darling," the man says and attempts to move forward. He stumbles and winces in pain. I jump to help him back up to his feet. This close, his odor is absolutely foul: sour and tart, but with the strangest hint of something sweet. "You're a pretty little thing," he says, staring at my lips.

His words make me shudder. I release his arm to step away, and Elio is by my side in an instant. I suddenly realize where I've seen the green of that man's eyes before.

Elio is wearing it.

"I was busy hoping you were rotting in Edom," he bites. "It seems even you aren't welcome there."

"Oh, how you break my heart." The man grips the fabric covering his chest, tugging it aggressively.

"Care to explain your situation, Callos? Or would you rather just bleed out?"

"Why, want a taste? I know you dream of my blood on your tongue," the man, Callos, grins, showing off his blackened teeth.

Elio snaps. He pounces forward and snatches the collar of his blouse, crushing the fabric in his fists. He slams Callos into the mountain, lifting him off the ground, his feet dangling in the air. I knew Elio was strong, but this is something else.

I would really love to leave now.

"I dream of you dead," Elio burns, baring his fangs.

"You know that's not true," he grimaces, his breath moving the hair out of Elio's face. "Put me down, darling."

Elio releases him at once, letting him fall to his feet.

"Always so gentle," he mutters, stroking Elio's jaw. "I've missed you."

"Shut it," he swats at his hand. "Why are you even here?"

"I could ask you the same thing," Callos counters, gesturing at Elio's unusually disheveled appearance.

"Harpies."

"Ah, lovely creatures, aren't they?" Callos coughs, spitting up blood.

"What happened to you?" I ask.

Elio glares at me for speaking out of turn whilst Callos doubles over, falling back onto the ground.

"Howlers. Not so lovely."

"It's a full moon, what were you thinking?" Elio inquires, failing to cover his concern for the man.

I feel my heart pinch from exhaustion.

Callos sighs. "Things to do. Got lost. Yada, yada, then, *BAM*," he grips his injured hip, "little fucker took a bite out of my side, and here I am."

"I don't believe you."

"You never have."

"I'm sorry, how do you two know each other?" I blurt, embarrassed.

"We do business," Elio remarks at the same time Callos says: "We were lovers."

There is a moment of agonizing silence. Then, Callos shakes his head and pretends to stab his heart with an imaginary knife. "Whatever you say, darling."

"We need to move along," Elio declares, gesturing for me to start walking.

"You're not going to leave me here, are you?" Callos whines.

Elio pinches his nose and sucks in a large breath, stomping away before he can explode.

Callos rolls his eyes, landing them on me.

"He's so dramatic," he whispers.

"I can hear you. Get your ass up," Elio grumbles.

The three of us leave the Cudola Peaks together. Elio and I have Callos's arms wrapped around our shoulders, pulling his limp body along toward the fortified capital of the Ashen Domain, and I hate every second of it.

16

CLEMENT

I have always been subject to my father's tantrums.

Should he need to relieve himself of his ire, there I am. It is my Royal duty to catch his verbal blades, their edges wedging into the lines of my palms. His words the ivy that root their vines within me.

Aalis was always spared.

When we were younger, Aalis used to sneak me into his quarters after father had reprimanded me, demanding my confinement to my own chambers. We were never the closest of siblings, and yet he would pat down on his bed, gesturing for me to take a seat. I would awkwardly shift about until I eventually slid down his pillows, staring straight up at his ceiling. I would use that time facing away from him to blink away the tears. He wouldn't say much, save for several bouts of *shh*-ing: he would just perch quietly next to me.

Then we grew up.

I suspect father had started to weigh on him the importance of his legacy and tightened his watch on Aalis — his golden boy.

But I don't envy him. Father's coddling is just as bad as his admonition.

I lay there now, as I have for days and nights, uncomfortable in my gown, clutching a satin-cased pillow to my chest, weeping for no other reason than our father.

I imagine he'll be in Alnola soon.

I wish to waste away on this spread. I wish that no one but Aalis would find my body. The only times I left my station was to either relieve myself in the chamber pot or to steal food from the kitchens like a scavenger.

If I'm honest, I've lost count of how long it's been since I last saw my brother saunter and sulk about the palace halls, and yet his scent faintly lingers on his covers. It reminds me of our mother. I bury my nose deep into the fabric and fill my lungs with her. She rings in my ears, the memory unbearable from the restless nights spent on my back. I couldn't even move an inch without risking an assault from the underwire of my corset, refusing to have it prod and poke the tops of my ribs. I haven't even bothered to sink beneath the covers, to hide from the monsters of the world, because the only monster I know is on his way to the Ashen Domain and he is too far away to hurt me more.

I've spent every waking moment with my eyes glued to the ceiling. I could draw this mural from memory. I could paint it with my eyes closed. I could make my own version, my own translation, where my soon-to-be husband is Adam, but in the place of Eve, I would be the lowly Lilith. The wife Adam expected, docile and sweet. Maybe I'd paint myself pregnant, and instead of apples, babies would grow from the bushels before me. I would be pictured in a triptych, swollen with a babe in the first frame. The second would show me reaching up onto my tiptoes, plucking the ripened head of a sweet baby boy. And in the third, you'd see me unhinge my jaw — like that of a snake — and devour the child in one.

Creator, help me.

I swing my legs across the bed to find the floor, my shoes gently slipping on buckle after buckle, carrying me over to Aalis' washbasin: its water days old and lukewarm. But still, to feel the splash over my face — by Eden, it feels good.

It brings me back. I am a part of the world again.

I let the water air dry on my skin, catching a glimpse of my reflection in the vanity, admiring the sweet embrace of the droplets, unwilling to wipe them off. I perch on the stool and notice pages ripped askew tucked roughly into the covers of what looks like a sketchbook.

I slowly drag the book towards me, as if being watched, the loose sketches slipping out with ease. Some of them look unfinished, some of them are crossed out in charcoal over what looks like frustration. It seems as though the only thing they share is their prison-like nature: scribbles of cells, armed guards, even a captive.

Aalis' passion for art came by overnight, though our mother used to paint. He never spoke of his creative ambitions, he never made a fuss over it until — well, I'm not sure. I just remember one day eavesdropping on him begging father for canvases, paints and other art supplies.

He never let anyone see his work.

I had always expected for his room to be covered in it, though there is hardly a trace of him here.

It wasn't until several days ago that I dared to enter his chambers. Not since our last game of hide and seek all those years ago. I remember how I hid in his closet, my back pressed against what I thought was a wall, until it swung me through to some sort of passageway with a door at the end of the hall — just like the one in my room. I thought I had won that game for sure, until somehow, he found me.

Ah, the plague of nostalgia.

My curiosity bests me now, leading me straight to the back of Aalis' closet. My hands reach out for the stone wall in front of me, pushing ever so slightly with the hope I'll find the door I so desire.

Something in the wall gives way.

I inch my way forward, my hands stretched out in front of me, as I curse myself for not bringing a candle. I make contact with what feels like another door and push.

Before me is a room I have never seen: Aalis' gallery.

No wonder he spends so much time holed up in this place.

Lone easels are scattered by the singular window, and cloths drape over what resemble canvases in shape. Only one remains unsheathed, lying flat on the table. I tread over to it and notice an imprinted visage, careful not to rouse it as though its eyes will move and gouge out.

It's a girl, no older than Aalis. I notice his signature on the bottom of the canvas, and let out a whisper of a gasp as I trace over it. There's a tackiness behind my fingers, right on the pads, and I pull away to find stray pigment staining the tips.

I yank down the cotton cover of the canvas to my right, and in no state of surprise do I find the very same tender features gaze back at me. I raise my right hand to gingerly flit my fingers over the outline of her face. Any closer and I'll scratch it right off.

I pull down another one, and another, and another, all revealing the girl's face. The same brown skin of a reddish glow, the same tender eyes and soft cheeks.

Those sketches come to my mind.

The stress clings to my neck in sweat, buttering down any loose hairs. This time, I slide my thumb across the blush of her cheeks, admiring the gentle imprint I have made.

It is too hot in here.

My fingers rake through my hair and I can feel the color transfer with the damp caress of my forehead. I wipe my hands on my dress, the charcoal and dried oil paints marking their territory down my sides.

I know her.

I slam my shoulder into the room's main entrance — one I hope will lead me away from all things Aalis and hope that my feet will pick up the pace my head begs to set.

It can't be her.

I sniffle and shuffle my way desperately through the hallway, no destination in mind, grabbing fistfuls of my dress, careful not to trip.

How does he know her?

There is bitter panic salivating in my mouth, its taste akin to metal, and I can feel it crawl down into my lungs and fill me with worry. The deeper the breath I take, the tighter my corset binds. I fear I may burst.

Is that where he is now?

Between my arranged engagement, Aalis' disappearance, and my father's *duties*, I had not expected such a thread to weave through and stitch them all to Edom.

My fingers fumble with the ties behind my waist, grappling

at the loose ends but they hesitate to untie in the middle. I snag at the sides, wheezing as I try to push the boning down as far as it'll go.

He's on a suicide mission.

My hands rub red raw against the lacing, rough with the grain until I feel my palms sting. I wince and pull again, *rip-rip-ripping* until the grommets spill on the floor. The corset loosens, and I manage to shimmy it over my head, the fabric taut with tension.

That idiot.

I let the garment drop to the ground and charge straight for the double doors before me, crushing the grommets like bugs under my feet.

The doors lead me to the Garden.

There isn't a Knyght in sight; these grounds are far too sacred.

My mother used to let me splash about the stream when I was just a little thing, without ever letting me go. We were bound by those waters. She would guide me through the meandering bend, my other hand skimming the outside of the neighboring hedges, trapping thorns under my skin. My mother never shouted, she was never angry. She would just chuckle and sigh time after time as she pinched the splintered skin between her two fingers and relieved me of my pain. Those thorns don't compare to the ache of missing her. They don't even scratch the surface.

Right now, I want nothing less than to kick my shoes back off.

I break through their clasps, my bare feet squishing into the stones below and charge with every ounce of carefree childhood left within me towards the stream. The train of my dress soaks in the tender glory of the water. I let myself dwindle towards the ebbing of the surface, right at its skin before walking deeper into the stream, sinking further, until it comes up to my shoulders, up to my neck, smothering my chin. My head tilts back in its flow, the water clinging to me.

I think of my mother and smile, I close my eyes and float.

I lay there unbothered for what seems like a while, evident by the pruning of my fingers and toes. It's not until I hear footsteps etch their way through the grass that I realize I mightn't be alone.

I pry an eyelid open to see the Cain, all inquisitive.

"Oh, *Son of Adam*! You startled me!" I flail, struggling to keep my balance.

"My dear child, is something the matter? Whyever are you in the water?" he questions.

"It's nothing of concern, believe you me."

Utterly embarrassed, I manage to stand up — leaves and stray branches tangled up in my lace. What a picture of Royalty.

We sink into an awkward silence fueled by his disbelief.

"I find that walking through our sacred Garden is a great tonic for the soul," he eventually comments. "Perhaps you would like to accompany me through the grounds and we can have a chat? See if there's anything you would like to get off your mind."

I smile, dimples and all, still a babe in these waters.

"That would be lovely."

The Cain offers his gloved hand, but I manage just fine

on my own. He looks at me as if he expects me to run back towards the palace to change my dress, or to even put my discarded shoes on, his expression visible even through his sheer cloth covering.

But I have no time for that.

I know where he wishes to go.

I lead the way through the lawn, blades of grass stinging the space between my toes, following the curve of the stream ahead. Mania surges through me and it is much easier to embrace this flash of hysteria than it is to drown in pain.

"My child, slow down," the Cain complains from several paces behind.

"You wish to see the Tree, do you not?"

No response.

"Then hurry up," I gleefully retort.

I break into a light jog around the bend, bracing myself for the glory that is our Tree of Life. I am overcome with childish glee, positively giddy to see our miracle. The very one that Eve had been tempted by. Unless you ask a Maiden, of course, since they believe it was in fact Adam who had been so seduced by the apples, and blamed it on his poor wife when it all went awry. It is rumored that it was in fact Lilith who came to him as the snake to seek revenge.

In the Creator's foreboding of consumption, he cast both Adam and Eve to exile. Outside the Garden, they forged what we now know as our Kingdom of Ead. From there, they built up my family, established the Monastery, and slowly but surely crept back into the heart of Eden without ever having stepped foot in it again.

Just one more corner and—

I stop in my tracks, my feet calloused and blistered.

"My word, what has happened to the apples? Why are they all," I struggle to find the right word to describe them, "*rotten?*"

I know the Cain is ashamed of the sight, however blameless he is.

"Our Tree suffers as much as we do," he eulogizes as he steps towards it. "She bears the brunt of our conflict. Her roots are what connect us all together — Heretics, Sanctum dwellers, Eadens, Islers, and Domanians alike," he gently places his palm along the bark, presses his forehead to it and sighs. "She senses conflict: she mourns for her world," the Cain explains as he takes a step back. "At least we know that no one will be tempted by a bite," he attempts to joke but I do not laugh.

For the future of Sumeria, our poor Tree is *suffering*. My father and his 'savior complex' — he doesn't see the pain he puts our land through. The pain he puts our *people* through. To him, it is all in the name of Adam. All of it: his hatred of the Maidens, his grooming of Aalis for the throne, my engagement.

"Are you alright, child?" The Cain asks. "Why don't we venture inside the Monastery? We can move away from the tragedy."

It's almost comical. Wherever I'm concerned, I cannot escape tragedy. The throne is Aalis' legacy, misfortune is mine.

"I don't want to marry," I choke out.

A dropping pin would have made more noise.

"Pardon?"

"Son of Adam, I need to confess."

17
BEA

We ride through the thick and twisting trees of Abram Woods.

It smells of mildew and rich flora, coating the air with a layer of musty murk and petrichor. Blanketed by foliage, it's quiet for the most part. Peaceful even. I spot a few deer through the curled branches ready to run away at the first sight of danger.

The Hand behind me stirs, the saddle shifting as she sits up. I wish we could ride faster, but the branches are low in this part of the Woods, and I can't risk clipping our heads off.

"Look," she says.

I follow the finger she's pointed towards the trees. There, between the dense oak, is a small elk wandering around. It notices us after a few moments and barely bats an eye, continuing to explore the woods alone.

We haven't said much since we left early this morning. I would have preferred to leave immediately after Kymn fixed up Beka's wound, but we were both too tired to carry on. Johna never returned, though it hardly mattered once I dozed off. I woke to the sound of muffled sobs before dawn managed to break. Bek—the *Hand* was turned away from me, cradling her legs into her chest as she wept. I lasted a few minutes before the sound became torture. She had not slept at all.

There was a horse outside, saddled up and ready for us to take the rest of the way to Alnola, and we've been riding ever since, the sun slowly rising over us through the thick wooded trees.

"Do you need anything?" I ask.

She must be hungry.

"I'm fine," she blubbers, just as I thought she would.

At this pace, we should reach Alnola just after midday.

Right on time.

Today, the future of Sumeria depends on me. Kymn had made that quite clear.

I have eyes everywhere.

I don't doubt for a second that she followed Elio and I, or at the very least, stayed close to Brighes, assessing the progress of our mission. And if not her, then someone else. Maybe a loyal spy of hers, nimble and quiet enough to stay hidden from our keen eyes and sharp ears.

In theory, I am on the right track: I have the Hand as requested, I am taking her to the General in Alnola. But Elio is gone, so is the Prince, and this is not how this was supposed to go.

Since the first time Elio and I crossed paths nearly ten years ago, he has always listened to me. Trusted me. In all those years, not once have we parted like this — save for the few months he was tangled up with that bastard, Callos. Never will I let him live that down.

I just wish Elio had let it be and allowed the Prince to have been taken away, out of our hands, minds and business.

But, seeing as the Prince in our possession is worth more than gold, so fucking be it.

"There's another," the Hand purrs from behind.

A twig snaps and a second elk jumps up from the brush.

I dare to look back, a gentle smile pulling at her lips. I am bringing her to her death and yet she stares longingly at a baby elk.

Are all Maidens like you?

This is the person the King, that all of Sumeria are afraid of, and so my question stands. Her face drops when our eyes meet and I keep quiet, an understanding passing between us: Kymn's threat is final. I'm going to complete this mission once we arrive in Alnola.

No exceptions.

I rip my eyes away to stare straight ahead. There is no room for foolishness.

"I won't fight you," the Hand starts, "so if you'll let me, I'd like to say goodbye to my mother and friends when we arrive."

I don't flinch at her demand, but my heart recoils, plummeting into my stomach even so. I killed her so carelessly, without a second thought. She was pleading, worrying about her daughter, and I slashed her down. For what? So I could assert my dominance before General Bausan? So I could prove myself to the position, redeem the glittering title as the Kingdom's top assassin, the mighty Capitan?

I swallow back the lump in my throat.

"Okay."

The Hand sighs behind me. "Thank you."

"Anything else?"

"Tell the Prince that I am thankful," she says. "That he should not throw away his life defending me." I can't help but tut. The Hand considers this, then adds, "He may be a fool, but he is not a bad person."

"So it seems you do not feel the same for him as he obviously does for you," I press.

I had speculated the Prince's true intentions, as his story never did align with the way he looked at her, grossly yearning and full of desperation. It seems faith is sod's lore when it comes to love.

"I have thought about it but it wouldn't matter if I reciprocated or not."

"True," I say, teetering on whether or not to indulge in my own curiosity. "Doesn't mean your feelings are invalid."

The Hand takes her time to reply. We pass a large oak tree with a short stump and long, spider web-like branches twisted in all directions. An owl is perched on one of its thick limbs, its onyx eyes watching us as we trot by.

"I met him a long time ago. Despite his position, he chose to help me. Twice," she admits. "We do have a connection, and maybe I could — I don't know," she takes another moment to think. "I don't feel what he feels. I never have, not with anyone."

"Right." This conversation is dipping into forbidden territory.

"At the very least," she continues, "I hope you spare Aalis."

"That is not up to me," I respond, and I don't mean Elio will decide this either.

Once we get to Alnola, I am no longer in charge.

"Can I ask you a question?" She peruses after a moment's pause.

I would typically refuse, but, "What is it?"

"I'm just looking for a bit of," she halts, "perspective, I guess."

"On what?"

"Aalis is not a bad person. I don't believe you are, either."

"So?" I quip.

"I'm just wondering who you believe is right?"

"I don't think anyone is right," I blurt. "I'm here because I need money and I'm good at what I do." She scoffs, clearly disappointed. "People are scared," I continue, "and when they are scared, they will do anything to feel safe. I imagine that is how the King feels. Giving you to him will ensure safety for the rest of Sumeria."

"I understand."

"But I mean," I falter, "that's all I know. It's all I've been allowed to believe my whole life."

"I had hoped that maybe Aalis would take the crown before I was discovered again."

"Like *he* could do anything different than the rulers before him? It's not likely."

"You don't know that," she defends.

"If there's going to be any change in this damned world, then it definitely won't be done by anyone within the Kingdom walls."

"So you don't think the Kingdom is right, then."

"That's not what I'm saying—"

"Are you sorry then? For bringing me right to their front door?"

Her voice wavers on the brink of shattering, and it pierces my heart in a way I thought I had proper defense to deflect.

"It's not like you've done anything to stop me from doing so," I snap.

The silence that follows slices the tension between us, severing any hope that I'd had at having an agreeable end to our journey.

"Beka," I try again. Her name feels strange on my tongue, but I want to say it again, over and over until the muscle is numb. "I am sorry."

"It's fine," she dismisses.

"I mean it. It's not easy losing your home. I understand how you feel, and for that I am sorry."

"They are like me," she says, decidedly.

"What?"

"The Maidens. You asked me before."

"Oh, well I—"

"We don't want war. We don't want any of this. The murders, the curses. Any of it," Beka discloses.

She's picking at the rope bound around her wrists. I had loosened her ties before we departed this morning.

"But if Lilith comes back, war is inevitable," I wince.

As far as I know, the legend of Lilith and her Hand are tales of ruin. In her punishment, Lilith cursed the land alongside Adam's children, and even her own kin. The Kingdom and the Monastery swore that if she ever returned, she would offer no mercy to those who stand against her. I suppose it would make sense for Beka to stay hidden, to keep some sort of stalemate.

"It doesn't matter," is all she says.

"So you'd rather let me turn you in than help your own kind?" I debate.

"It's not that simple," she insists, her voice rigid.

"Then what is it?"

"Doesn't matter."

"It certainly matters if you're so intent on giving yourself up. They must not even know you're alive," I pose.

"I wouldn't underestimate them."

"Fine, but—"

"It's too late!" she bursts. "The King knows I'm alive, and it's like you said: war is inevitable. Destruction is inevitable, as long as I live. You needn't worry about the choices that I make. After everything, I deserve to die."

The woods no longer offer me a sense of peace. The birds aren't even chirping. I shouldn't even be speaking to her, and yet, a memory blares in the forefront of my mind. A nightmare.

"It's easier to blame ourselves for our own misfortune than to accept the pain of it. I imagine it feels better for you to do nothing than to fight and be reminded of everything that got you here. I was eight when Lilith came to our village. When the banshee screamed," I reveal, a hint of panic to my voice. "We thought the Kingdom would send aid. That's when the Knyghts came and burned Thessonne to the ground. I lost my parents and my younger brother in the fires."

I can still feel the ease in which my mother would tangle her fingers in my curls, separating the oiled coils before weaving them into countless little braids. We would sit before the kindling fire in our small cottage. I would listen to her hum an ancient tune as she worked, twirling strands of my hair.

She had been doing my hair that damned day, twisting them into little locs, the same ones I have now. My little brother was asleep on the cot beside the door, unmoving as my father stomped inside. His garments were coated in wood chippings and dust, sweat lining the curve of his eyebrow. After placing a kiss to my mother's forehead, he'd knelt down before me, his big, burly shoulders blocking the flames, replacing my view with his gentle smile.

He leveled his gaze, "How's the little Capitan today?"

"Not little," I grumbled, unable to stop the grin from forming on my face.

We hadn't heard the screaming outside. The fires caught on to our row of cottages first.

"Sometimes I wonder if people pray just so they don't blame themselves for the shit we do. It's just easier that way, to blame someone, something else for our own suffering," I blink the tears from my lashes, thankful Beka cannot see them falling.

"I see," she says benignly.

"But now," I halt, because what more could I possibly say?

My admission speaks loud enough for itself. That maybe, once I turn her in, I can finally put down my blade. That I can stop shedding blood in exchange for what was taken from me. That if Lilith really is the one to blame for my suffering, then maybe it will end when I know she can never come back to this world again. But if I'm wrong, if I can't finish this mission, then who else is there to point a finger at? The truth would mean that I've been wasting my time. Something so simple as changing sides feels weak. And I'm not weak.

"It's okay," she says, her words final, saving me from ruining everything. "This is just the way things are."

And she's right. She's *right*. How could I let myself think otherwise?

I seal my mouth shut for the rest of the ride.

Eventually, Abram Woods thins out.

The General awaits.

18

LYCIDAS

Jeane runs ahead of me leaving only a cloud of dust in her wake.

I duck to avoid the branches she pushes out of the way, the rest of them splicing the early morning rays of daylight into slivers. We hit the last batch of wisteria a few yards back as we move toward Thessonne in haste.

The Shepard told us to follow the scent. She told us to avoid the Peaks, to head east through the village. I'm fast enough on my own two legs, but it's moments like this where I wish I could Shift at will. Moving on four legs would cut the journey in half.

Someone's poisoned us, Kasia's words echo in my mind, pushing me to keep on going.

But no matter how fast I run, how hard I try to stay focused, I can't erase the image of little Raven dead in my arms.

I had carried her corpse back to the Sanctum where we were greeted by a cacophony of howling. Nadine clutched at her chest and fell to her knees in agony, screeching herself hoarse until she, too, threw up the purple bile. Apart from Jeane, the Shepard, a few other Howlers and myself, the rest have fallen ill. Just as Rudi did.

Six Howlers died overnight. Others are in critical condition, my father being amongst the ones who bore the brunt of whatever this is. I barely lasted a minute in the infirmary. Only the smallest of breaths escaped from his mouth, the same smear of vomit crusted around his lips. I couldn't possibly stay in the Sanctum and do nothing.

Jeane felt the same. She couldn't stand to watch her father, Nadine and Rudi writhe in pain. I don't think she's even allowed herself to cry over Raven yet. She's like her mother in that way, the oldest child for a reason — to lead by example, to stay calm in the face of horror.

"Howlers have been missing for months. Then a Banshee screams in Ochrore. Now—" Kasia had choked, her eyes dark, their usual spark simmered by unbearable grief. "Now my girl has been murdered, and others will die from this too."

Kasia had ruled out any possibility of this being a coincidence.

Howlers are just as susceptible as humans to the common cold, or a nasty bout of fleas, but nothing like this. This isn't a sickness. The apple I had found at the scene was spoiled. Rotten. There were other unusual scents at the scene: namely human blood and blossoms freshly bloomed, but nothing quite so threatening as the fruit of our Life.

Jeane and I volunteered to go investigate, to track down the scent and get answers, while another healthy group of Howlers set out to sweep the White Isles.

"Don't trust anyone out there, not even the Knyghts. Find whatever you can, anything. We need all the information we can get," Kasia ordered, bidding us farewell.

She sent us away after that, the entire fate of our pack on our shoulders.

Jeane refuses to stop for a break.

We've been running for hours. At this speed, we could make it to Thessonne just before sunrise, but I can't breathe.

"Jeane!" I shout. She spares a glance back at me, but carries on. "*Wait*— stop!"

She catches the trunk of a nearby tree to brace herself at the thunder of my command. I manage to catch up, panting beside her — my chest heaving, my throat thick.

"I'm sorry. I can't—" I gasp, reaching for her arm.

It starts with her shoulders. They shake as she catches her breath before releasing another sob. Eventually, she pushes away from the tree and stuffs herself into my arms.

"I shouldn't have left her alone," she croaks, pressing her face into my chest.

Raven's corpse was practically weightless, but the memory of her sits heavily on my heart. My father, Yuri, Nadine, Rudi, everyone else: they could be next.

"Whoever did this, we'll find them," I mutter close to her ear.

Jeane leans back and wipes her face with the back of her wrist.

"But *why* would anyone do this?" Jeane chokes, taking a breath between each word.

"I don't know," I sigh, bending down into a kneel.

"It couldn't be the Kingdom," she says. "We're too valuable to them."

"They tolerate us," I correct.

"It was a *human*."

"And what exactly were they trying to do?" I question,

looking up at my friend. Her eyes are swollen, the scratch on her cheek bright against her paled skin. "Poison us? *Kill* us? Round up the weak?"

"I don't know," Jeane sniffles, patting my back. "We should keep moving."

She's right. There's no time for this.

I straighten my legs, pushing up to a stand, before jumping back into a brisk jog, descending down a hill that thrusts us deeper into the forest.

"I just don't understand. We've negotiated with the Kingdom for centuries: labor in exchange for peace. It doesn't make sense," Jeane says.

Could it be that the Maidens had something to do with this? It wouldn't be too outrageous of a theory. Raven *did* bleed purple, and the apple has to mean something — though the Maidens are ones to keep to themselves. They don't like to leave the Realm, and if they were going to hurt us, they would send someone, some*thing* else to do the damage.

"Doesn't matter if it makes sense. We won't know anything unless we get answers. You still got the scent?"

"Barely," Jeane says. "It's faint, but I still have it."

"Good, because I don't."

As we race towards Thessonne, I worry that I will fall to the ground, just like the others, that I will bleed and bloom from the inside out.

It could happen, yet it doesn't, and I'm left wondering why I was spared.

After breaking through the thick wood of the Sanctum, we reach a colony of trees, all of them cut down to their trunks.

Jeane and I slow down, careful not to get our feet caught on the wood. There are a few stray axes too, their blades rusty and chipped.

Beyond the lumber yard, what once was a small market is now a makeshift den for scavengers, Night Demons, and other civilians who do not fear its damage. A few groups kneel around fires, others fixing the wooden beams of a fallen building, crafting a shelter from its remains. The only standing buildings are the Church and the old sawmill, both cemented in stone at the base, a feature that saved them from the fires years ago.

This is Thessonne, or what's left of it.

I was in the Sanctum when the Banshee screamed all those years ago, still a little pup. Kasia had gathered us all into the Chasm, trying to ease our shock. I remember her telling us that Sumeria was about to change, for better or worse.

Kasia is never to be doubted.

The result shocked all of Sumeria with the loss of a prominent village, one that harbored a great deal of lumber and sweet sap. Since then, Thessonne has been long forgotten.

Many believe Lilith and her magic still linger here to this day. As for those who don't, it's a fair place to reside if you've got the means.

"Where's your skiff?" Jeane asks once we enter the village.

"Just north, over there," I point past the Church where a river flows, dividing Thessonne from the rest of the Domain.

We pass a small family huddled together. There's a man roasting a squirrel on a stick next to a younger woman with a toddler in her lap. The child presses close to her chest, fear radiating from him as we walk by.

"Big pups strolling in I see," someone hollers — a Night Demon, posted atop a tree stump.

"Watch it," I warn, not in any mood to deal with snide remarks.

The Night Demon holds his hands up defensively, his fangs sticking over his bottom lip as he smiles.

"I mean no harm. Just observing. Say, crazy-pants over there has been waiting for your lot to pass through all day," he drawls, pointing at a man over by the Church.

"What?"

"Where's the rest of you?" I hear him say as I grab Jeane's hand to pull her along, leaving the Night Demon behind us.

In Thessonne, people come and go. I'm familiar with a few faces, Anselm being one of them. He's on his knees, barefoot, picking dandelions that grow wild beside the Church. The cloak he wears used to be a cream color, but it's soiled now and the green sash around his neck is frayed. Anselm looks up at us as we approach, flinching before recognizing me.

"Oh! You're here!" He rejoices, bouncing onto his feet. "I've been waiting for you."

Jeane raises her eyebrows and Anselm is standing with his cloak entirely open. He has nothing but a pair of sheer trousers on, not really the proper attire for a Cleric.

"We're in a bit of a hurry," I tell him.

Anselm, as I've learned, is chatty. I entertain him most times because I know how lonely he gets but now is not the time.

"No, no, no, this is important, you see, a little girl came by the Church today," he starts, pointing at the building. "I've never seen her before. She's a tiny, weepy thing, and I don't know what to do with her."

"Anselm."

"You heard about the Banshee scream, right? Brought back so many horrible memories."

I nod, losing patience. Jeane shifts on her feet beside me, eager to move along.

"Well, this poor girl was rambling on about it, crying about fires, saying that her friend told her to run away. She rode here all by herself!"

"Excuse me, sir, but we really don't have time for this," Jeane cuts in as sincerely as possible.

"I don't believe we've met!" he regards her, reaching out his hand. "I'm Anselm, Cleric of this Church."

"Hi." Jeane doesn't take his hand, turning to me instead. "We have to keep going."

"What's the rush?" he asks.

I really do feel for him. Anselm had managed to save a good number of children when Thessonne was raided by the Kingdom. He gathered them all inside the stone building, protected them from the flames that spread through the rest of the village.

Since then, most of the survivors have moved elsewhere but I don't think he'll ever be ready to leave this Church behind, so he stays and gives sermons to ghosts every seventh day or to anyone else who'll listen to him babble.

"The Howlers are sick," I explain, hinting at our departure by taking a few steps back. "Possibly from poison. We really have to go."

Anselm's jaw drops, and he moves to grab at my hand.

"Oh dear, I'm so sorry for bothering you," he shakes his head. "But please, this girl! She needs our help. *Your* help."

"My sister is *dead!*" Jeane snaps. Anselm recoils as she bares her canines. "We don't have time for this!"

The Cleric backs away, head in his hands, whispering his apologies over and over. I place my hands on Jeane's shoulders to hold her back from the man, but she shrugs them off and stalks away.

"You can't help everyone, Ly," she says to me.

I stand defeated between the two. Anselm continues to mumble, the dandelions crushed beneath his feet.

"I'm sorry," I mutter, jogging to follow Jeane.

The creaking doors of the Church swing wide open. I look back and see a silhouette of a small girl walking into the light. My heels dig into the ground.

"Sarya?"

The girl perks up in response.

I can barely believe it.

I sprint back to the Church with my arms extended, Sarya leaping into them as I reach the doors. She sobs against my shoulder, her tears dampening my shirt.

"What are you doing here?" I cry, pulling her back to wipe her face with my thumbs.

"Beka told me to find you," she pouts.

She's a mess: her garments charred, and blonde hair covered in soot.

"*Beka*? Why aren't you with her? Where's your mother?" I demand.

I hear Jeane come up behind me. Anselm remains with his head in his hands.

"I don't know," she cries. "We were in these cages and then Beka told me to come here and find you."

"Cages? What happened?"

"A Banshee, just like in the stories! Then the Knyghts showed up and they started attacking us!"

"Lycidas," Jeane says carefully. "We *need* to go."

I look frantically between the two, unsure of what to do. Brighes is now like Thessonne, I imagine: burnt to a crisp. Void of any life. I can see the despair in Sarya's eyes, the feeling clawing into my chest, hollowing it out.

"We'll bring her with us," Jeane sighs softly, offering the girl a small smile. "I'm Jeane. You'll be safe with us."

"I don't know what happened," Sarya sniffles as we walk away. "Things got scary after we buried Inez. Mama told me things were going to be very different, that we were all in danger."

In my peripherals, I see Jeane snap her head over to me. She's watching me, waiting for me to break. But I can't.

"It's okay," Jeane coos quietly. I can barely hear her. "It's going to be okay."

Now is not the time.

I move one foot in front of the other, trailing away from Church and heading towards my skiff. The red stream of the Carmine Lagoon bleeds through the land, all the way to the body of the sea. Anselm's murmurs have grown into shouts, his voice trembling with fear.

"She walks! She haunts! She preys on us all!" he wails, cursing the sky above. "The Dark Maid! Be afraid, for she seeks revenge by the will of her deadly Hand!"

Jeane is sitting with her legs crossed, poking at the strange water. Sarya stays by my side, clutching the fabric of my shirt. I focus on the movement of my arms as I plunge the ore deep into the Lagoon, like a knife to the heart. The ride is short, no more than an hour, and there's a sliver of land where I typically dock, just on the outskirts of Alnola. This is routine. This should be no problem, but between the motions, I hear a voice, faint in the back of my mind. It must be a demon, poking me, teasing me, waiting to be let in. It whispers her name, ever so gently.

Inez.

"The scent. It's getting stronger. Closer." Jeane says.

To us, a scent is more than just a smell; it has its own anatomy, one that swims through the air, forming a shape that ties it to its host, and this one in particular is dark. Not in color, but in nature, bending the space before my eyes. The more I focus, the more I can make out its direction.

"They must be in town. Or at least close by," I note, strained from exhaustive rowing.

Centuries ago, my ancestors built Alnola from the ground up, lugging materials from the Sanctum to the Domain. They hollowed out the giant body of rocks on which it's founded, carving deep, and starting from the ground up.

"Lycidas, look," Sarya gasps.

She's pointing downstream where the Lagoon extends into a larger body of water.

A flurry of storm clouds and fog seep through the atmosphere, dripping down to the bay's skin.

Something emerges from the darkness and the ore nearly slips from my hands.

"Jeane—" I start, gripping the plank tighter, turning us away from the fog.

"Lycidas, go!" She moves away from the edge of the skiff and pulls Sarya, holding her close.

I urge myself to keep my eyes on the shore, but I can't help but steal a glance.

Three large rafts drift into view, an unnatural force propelling the wood forward, the waves around them moving at a controlled speed. There has to be at least twenty of them. I snap my head away, giving the ore a few more swings before the sand of the shore catches at the bottom of our skiff.

"Hurry!" I yell.

Jeane lifts Sarya in her arms, wading through the shallow waters to rush into the forest directly ahead. I tug the skiff out of the water and drag it across the sand, setting it up against the trunk of a tree. Together, the three of us duck under the safety of the trees and watch, awestruck, as they glide with ease.

"Is that...?" Jeane trails off, suppressing a shriek.

"Yeah," I gawp, seeing now, through the fog, all the people aboard.

Their hands are pointed downwards, directing the water with their fingers, moving the rafts without any physical effort.

"This can't be good," Jeane says.

"I want my mama," Sarya cries, her body shaking with fear. I don't blame her.

The surrounding world of the Lagoon seems to welcome their dark magic. Birds chirp one by one in an eerie chorus, singing the most dreadful lullaby. The trees rustle, uneasy with the sway of the wind as they move closer to land.

It really is them, after all these years.

The Maidens of Lilith have left the Realm, and are headed straight for Alnola.

19

BEKA

"*You see that? The skin is soft and tender.*"

The apple looks massive in Emelyne's hand. I lean in closer to her side to get a better look at the fruit she plucked from the tree.

"Rotten," I say, still familiarizing myself with the language she speaks.

Emelyne gives me a soft smile, pleased with my learning. She nods and hands me the apple, allowing me to inspect it myself.

"Now, just because this apple is rotten does not mean the rest of them are," she explains, gesturing to the orchard.

We're in the middle of the field, our barrows filled halfway.

"Why rotten?" I ask, holding it up.

It's my first harvest. I've been curious about it ever since I wandered through the orchard months ago. I had run from Tilver with no destination in mind, set on getting as far away from the Kingdom as possible. I still don't know much about the farming in Ochrore, but it's different from what I grew up with in Zemergad. The Realm is dry — no green grass or trees, no rich soil or rain.

Emelyne turns the apple over in my hand, revealing a small hole. The crater is rimmed with black tissue, spoiling the flesh.

"A worm hole. Some apples are for us to eat, others are for insects and other animals, like elks and squirrels."

I nod and set the fruit down on the ground, "For animals."

Emelyne smiles down at me and grabs my hand, pulling me along through the rows of trees.

We spend hours plucking apples from their branches, stealing bites here and there. The juice drizzles down my chin, and I'm delighted by its taste. I've never had anything like it before.

At the end of the orchard is an overlook, the sea right at its doorstep. I reach my hand forward, stretching my hand out towards the water. It started out as childish play, but the second I felt the familiar tug, I slammed my arm down to my side.

"I was not supposed to be a farmer," Emelyne says. I feel her hand slide across my shoulder, hugging me into her side. "My family worked for the Monastery. I was meant to stay in Surlisle and marry into another family of acolytes."

"Why you left?"

Her entire body sighs. "I was expected to do so many things. I finally decided that I wouldn't let anyone tell me what to do, so I ran away."

I gasp, snapping my head away from the water to look at her. "They chase you?"

"Yes. There was a period of time where I thought I'd never be free. I spent years in a very dark place, and many people took advantage of me." I try my best to keep up with her words. "Eventually, I saw the Sea," she nods, and I return my gaze to the waves. According to Emelyne, towards the end of the Summer months, the waters grow aggressive with the changing of the wind, each strike thundering against the shores. I thought about calming them down. But that's all it was — a thought. "I dunked my head in the cold water, and I never turned back."

"You find hope?"

Emelyne kneels down in front of me. She brings her hand forward to cup my cheek, always so gentle.

"I found something else. A purpose."

"Purpose," I echo.

I don't know the word.

"A reason. I asked myself, 'Why am I here?' Only you can answer that question for yourself."

"Why am I here?" I recite, thinking the answer will pop up right before me.

"You do not need to ask yourself this yet," Emelyne chuckles and places a kiss on my forehead. "You are still growing up. Right now, you belong here with me."

The thought of getting comfortable in Brighes scared me.

It could've been at any moment that the Kingdom and their troops found me again. I didn't know if the Maidens were looking for me either. Eventually, it seemed as though everybody gave up.

I had twelve years of unbothered solitude, and though they were freeing, I missed home.

I remember the day I was taken from the land, the catastrophic attack that ripped me from the Maidens for good; the horror of it dominating all that I loved.

Sometimes, when I close my eyes, I can still see the blood-orange sunset, a flare in the dark. We would watch them nightly. Us Maidens would gather to roast hog and deer over chopped mesquite, where we would feast and sing and dance with abandon.

Our community was strong, and I remember thinking

how important it was for me to ascend, to solidify my people's place in our world once again.

I was six years old.

I can't help but wonder how they've managed without me. How they must've mourned me.

Maybe I should have just gone back — these thoughts intrude in bleak times.

I chose to stay with Emelyne for so long because in more ways than one, she reminded me of them. Of my home. She loved me without the knowledge of who I was. That, to me, felt like freedom. I hoped that maybe I could stay with her forever.

"Get ready to say your goodbyes and make it quick. We don't have long," Bea says, her voice a slap in the face.

How does someone say goodbye? I attempted it before the Knyghts raided Brighes, my mind set on getting out. But Emelyne had sensed something was wrong and it tore me to pieces knowing I could never be completely honest with her. That's what I want to be now. I want to be honest with her. I want to look her in the eyes. I want to tell her everything.

It's midday.

We scale the treeline beside the East Gate of Alnola, Abram Woods now behind us. The refuge camp is right outside the barrier, and suddenly I am six years old again, staring up at the Kingdom for the very first time.

I think of Aalis, slightly comforted knowing that he's not here to see this. I hope he continues with his charade. I don't want him risking his life for me anymore.

My chest aches, and what I feel deeper than hunger, deeper than pain, is exhaustion. I crane my neck to get a better look at the camp. Tents made of torn fabrics and shoddy wooden beams are scattered across the contained area, as if the Knyghts had nothing better to supply the survivors with. There are only a few people out and about tending to small fires.

My throat closes at the sight of it all.

Bea trots the horse up to the camp, stopping right before the first tent. The people milling around take notice of us and stop what they're doing.

"I just need a few minutes," I mutter. "Can you untie me, please? I don't want to alarm them." Bea gets off the horse in a graceful swoop, reaching out to help me down. Her hands pull on the ropes, easing me onto the ground. She stands close as she undoes the knots, head low. "Thank you," I say, rubbing my skin where it hurts.

She nods, avoiding my gaze.

The ground is littered with rubble and dirt, not a blade of grass to be found. It crunches beneath my feet as I slowly trek into the camp, eyes scanning the small crowd of people forming at the sight of my arrival. Every face is a familiar one. I see Barnabas, one of his arms in a sling; Aravae peeking her head out of a tent, her face smudged and covered with cuts. I spot Miss Ysabelle clutching a dirty rag between her fingers, dabbing at her eyes. I don't see Petrus, nor Emelyne, but when I notice the Miller standing there without his wife and three children instead of five, I'm hit with a deep sickness.

The Kingdom did this.

They tore these families apart, *they* murdered innocent children.

I turn to look at Bea, but her gaze continues to steer clear of mine.

"Beka?" Gallienne's voice is light. My head snaps, searching for the direction of the sound. "Beka!" I catch a glimpse of her before we collide in a melting embrace, our spilling sobs inciting a rumble of chatter amongst the surviving villagers. Relief swallows me whole. "You're *here*," she cries, shaking against my body. I caress her tangled hair. "Where have you been?"

"I'm so sorry," I mewl, leaning back to see her face.

Her grip on me is tight, she digs her fingers into my arms to solidify me, to confirm I really am here. Her eyes are desperate and I'm hit with more guilt, ashamed that I left in the first place.

"I thought you were *dead*," she blubbers.

How do I do this? How do I say goodbye?

I think of Inez. I think of everyone who isn't here, of everyone who didn't make it. There is an emptiness inside of me and I'm running out of time.

"Emelyne? Where is she?" I plead.

Gallienne's face pales, shaking her head once before resting her forehead on my shoulder.

"I wish you had been here," she weeps.

"*Gallienne*," my voice cracks. "Where is she?"

My friend steps away from me, her face telling me all I need to know.

"I'm sorry."

"She's not here?" My voice is fraught, breathy.

Bea told me she spoke with her. She has to be alive.

Gallienne shakes her head again, pushing her eyes into the palms of her hands.

I step back in a daze, circling around to scan the area. She has to be here *somewhere*.

"Tell me where she is," I demand.

"She—" Gallienne starts, but I've already turned away.

My eyes land on Bea, waiting for some sort of explanation. She refuses to meet my gaze, angling her body as if to exclude herself from the scene.

"Tell me!"

Bea won't look at me.

My voice rises. "You said you spoke to her."

"She's not here," Bea groans, head *still* turned away.

I take a step forward, my fingers tingling.

"So you've been lying to me," I snap, studying her with burning eyes.

"I did speak with your mother."

"Then where is she?" I shout, near predatory.

Bea, for once, shows more than a flicker of emotion. Her lips are downturned, her jaw clenched, trying to compress whatever it is she's wanting to say. A hand wraps around my wrist. I look over and see Gallienne at my side.

"It was *her*," my friend accuses, eyeing Bea. "She killed her," Gallienne weeps. "I saw it."

My fingers flare with energy and every time I blink, a hand is waiting there for me in the darkness.

Bea cowers before me but not enough to stop her fingers from hovering above a hilt strapped to the top of her thigh.

"General Bausan. He ordered me to do it," she reasons, filled with shame.

"You killed her."

I curse myself for being so surprised. Surprised that the assassin sent by the King for my capture, the assassin who had no business befriending me or becoming my ally, has slain the only love I've ever known.

I was always her enemy and now, it seems, she is mine.

The dagger is in her hand now. The very one I bet she used to strike Emelyne down, kill her like it was nothing, some animal up for slaughter.

I shake Gallienne's hand away from mine, prowling towards Bea. She must pay.

"Beka," she says wearily, pointing her dagger at me to stop. "Please, understand that I didn't want to."

"But you did."

"If only I had known—"

"Known *what*?"

"I don't know! Beka, we don't have to do this. We have to *go*." Bea commands with vigor.

"I'm not going with you," I shake my head.

"Beka, please."

That memory of Emelyne and I by the sea resurfaces. I'll never get to see her again.

I ask myself now, *why am I here?*

"You lied to me," I repeat, reaching out to the darkness.

"I couldn't, I didn't—I didn't know what to say. I didn't expect any of this to happen!" Bea backs away.

"You let me believe I could see her again and used that against me!" I growl.

I believed her so willingly. And she *knew*, even when she

held my hand in the field, even after I saved her from the Harpies, even though I ran with her.

"It was never my intention—"

"You still killed her!"

Lilith's face flashes before my eyes, pride and revenge fueling the hollowness inside me.

It's time I stopped running.

"The Knyghts burned down my village. *Your* village too. Do you think they meant to hurt our feelings?" I continue, harnessing my power. "I'm not going back to the Kingdom. Not with you."

The Maidens need me.

I grab at the air, moving the wind with the tips of my fingers, and turn it into a tangible weapon. Dirt and pebbles begin to swirl at my feet, rising up to my knees. Bea backs further away from me, jolted to find her horse has moved amidst the terror.

There are gasps from all around. Someone is saying my name, but I don't listen.

Bea attempts to lunge at me but I throw a gust of wind at her feet, pulling her to the ground. She's quick to recover, throwing her arm, the point of her dagger headed my way. I bend my finger at the last second, redirecting its path back to her own arm. It doesn't break through her armor, but I shock her nonetheless. We both know she's capable of killing me, but she won't. She can't. Bea is immobile, restrained by me, but she's fighting against it, and I don't want her to win. I make a fist, stripping her lungs of air. Suffocating her. The magic is keen on my fingers, and for the first time I'm accepting this gift with open arms.

"Beka, stop!" Gallienne's voice finally reaches my ears.

Darkness flickers beneath my lids, and Lilith's hand is gone. Bea collapses to the ground, out cold, and as I stare at her, I wait for a rush of shame.

It doesn't come.

My friend grabs my wrist and pulls me back, turning me in place to face her and the rest of the villagers, dousing my rage. I blink, taking in the people surrounding us now, having watched the fight play out. These are people I know, people I grew up with. These people raised me, but they're looking at me like I'm a stranger. An intruder. Someone dangerous.

Gallienne's eyes are glazed with confusion, but only momentarily. I watch them transition into a look of fear, widening with understanding. Of what I've just done and how I did it. She steps back, just as Johna did when she realized that I am a Maiden.

"It can't be," she mutters.

I feel a tear slide down my cheek. They are afraid of me. I spare a glance back at Bea, her body still motionless on the ground.

"She's one of them!" a lady shouts from the crowd. Miss Ysabelle steps forward, pointing a shaky finger at me. "A *Heretic*! Gallienne, step away from her!"

"Gallie—" I move towards her, but she recoils, yelping at my outstretched hand.

I flinch as the rest of the crowd joins in, screaming at Gallienne to get away.

"It was her!" someone else wails — Honora, the village weaver. "Beka *cursed* us!"

I let my friend go. Gallienne doesn't look back at me as she disappears behind the villagers.

"She brought Lilith to Brighes!" one yells.

"She's dangerous! Get back!" another shouts.

Miss Ysabelle is in the middle of it all, aggrieved. I think of all the times she stopped by our cottage, bringing round her fresh loaves, sharing hours of chatter and nights by warm fires.

She loads her arm back, a stone clenched in her fist.

I watch it hurtle toward me before it collides with my forehead and drops to the ground with a solid thud. The entire camp falls into an idle silence, my head throbbing under my palm.

"I don't want to hurt you," I say, my voice weak.

"Liar!" Miss Ysabelle screams, picking up yet another stone from the ground. "A Maiden cannot be trusted!"

She hurls it once more. I manage to step away this time, but not before someone else throws another my way, knocking into my side. The shouting starts up again as the villagers continue to close in on me. I know I could raise my hand at them, conjure up some power to fend off the attacks. And though I'm tempted to — I could snatch Bea's horse and retreat into the Woods, run away and get back to the Realm — these are people I care for, all of them looking at me with so much fear. I would hate to prove them right.

Miss Ysabelle throws another stone, this one grazing my stitches. The pain sends me to the ground.

They strike me from all directions.

A boot kicks into my stomach, another stomps down on my hip. I can't get myself up with all of them surrounding me, pelting me with anything they can scavenge off the grounds of the camp.

Behind all of their shouts, I think I hear someone call for a ceasefire.

Too late, I think, as a rock the size of my fist slams into my forehead.

My vision blurs and Emelyne is the last thing on my mind.

PART THREE

—

"I WILL NOT LIE BELOW."

20

ELIO

Bea tends to tell me that a heart is merely a muscle.

It has a job to do — much like how my fangs are carved for tearing, how my fingers are bent for snatching. My heart pumps, even when my tongue is dried up and I'm curled in on myself with agonizing hunger. It'll pump even when all else fails, even when my legs shrivel up like dried grapes and my body screams out for the bitch who created me to give me another chance. It's quite pathetic. And yet, I still remember the first time she found me and offered her wrist, whispering a little prayer for my heart to keep going no matter what.

You haven't finished your job, she had whispered that day.

I still felt pathetic, but at least I wasn't alone.

I hate charity. I hate how my existence depended on it. How people used to throw me scraps of fleshless animal hides and leftover goose bones as I crawled through the streets of whatever town felt kind enough to take me in. That was pathetic, too. Eadens think they do so much for us Cursed Children. They think they offer us such rich lives. They think they're the ones saving us from the roots from whence we came, giving us jobs and meager accommodations — as if that's enough to feel like we belong.

It's just a matter of charity for them. To be a good samaritan so that their Creator gives them promises of heaven. But for those like me, heaven is no place. The thin veil is so heavily guarded against creatures of Edom. Creatures like me.

This mission was supposed to be quick and painless, yet it's exhausted my patient coffers.

I mean, did I decide to entertain the Prince and his delusions? Maybe.

Is he a complete and utter liability? Truly.

Was it fun? Absolutely.

"You both reek, you know that?"

This, however, is far from okay.

It seems that Callos is *so* injured that he must drop all of his weight on us. His arms are wrapped around both our backs, his hands clenching our opposite shoulders for support. His legs are limp as we drag him along the path, nearing Alnola. It's been this way for hours.

Dick.

"I haven't exactly been able to enjoy the luxury of a steaming bath. I was too preoccupied with a grueling Harpy," I grunt. "Did I mention I slayed the beast?"

"Many times," Aalis sighs.

I look at him over Callos's spiked hair, silently struggling to hold him up.

"I'm curious as to why you were here in the first place," Callos muses.

"He was saving me," Aalis reveals. "One of them plucked me from the ground."

Callos chuckles, sweeping his eyes over to me with an incredulous look.

"Elio chose to save someone other than himself?" He feigns a gasp. "It seems you *have* changed."

"I would save anyone but you," I snap back.

"So what exactly are you doing right now then?"

He senses my hesitation, my failure to cover up how I truly feel. I feel him incline his neck forward to bring his lips close to my ear. The smell wafting off of him is hard to ignore.

I want to leave him for dead.

"Tell me," he whispers, "has your tongue soured completely at the sight of my face? Or do you still possess a craving for my sweet nectar?"

I'm reluctant to meet his gaze. I've let my guard down before these green eyes. I've allowed them to stare back at me, graze over my bare skin.

There was once a time where I would fall over and over into them, drowning in the riches of their emerald glow. But that was before. Now, I stare back repulsed. I feel nothing, only the anticipation of looking away. Aalis keeps his head low, staying out of the conversation.

"I'd rather join the courts and fancy myself a preacher than taste the likes of you again," I spit.

"Daggers. I know you're angry with me for how we left things, and I am sorry."

"Save the flattery. Whatever this is, you won't be seeing me once we reach town," I say, turning my eyes to the clearing before us.

"You heartbreaker."

"Now you know how it feels," I hiss with a blistering smile.

"I never thought I'd say this, but I sort of miss your little partner in crime. Bea, is it? She's so much nicer than you."

"She'd skewer you like a piece of meat."

"Where might she be now?" He asks, looking around dramatically. "The two of you are a package deal never to be separated! Should I be scared that she's nowhere in sight?"

"Oh, Bea's doing just fine. You can say hello to her yourself once we're in town."

Callos chuckles, the sound followed by a gurgling cough. Lovely.

It's dawn. The sky is a faint shade of blue, just bright enough to illuminate Alnola in the distance. Its stone fencing reaches far into the outskirts of the area, lining either side of the path we follow. The Peaks are far behind us now.

"We might want to think about finding a different entrance," Callos says. I've decided to ignore him. "It's just, we all smell, and we look terrible. I doubt the Knyghts at the gate will let us pass through like this."

"They'll let me in," Aalis says.

I give him a warning glance but it appears Callos has taken an interest.

"Who even are you?" he grills, rolling his head to whisper, "Seems hardly your type."

A bell sounds from the city center. It rings three times, echoing throughout the whole town and beyond. Callos digs his heels into the ground, forcing us to stop.

"I think I need to rest," he declares.

"Right now?"

"Oh, please," Callos insists, unlatching his arms from our shoulders as Aalis walks him over to the stone fence to lean on.

Aalis has his eyes closed, taking any moment of rest he can

get. Callos is clutching his side, blood still seeping through and spoiling his blouse, his face slack. Though it's only once he notices me staring that he winces in pain. I know better than to get any closer.

"How did you get away from the Howlers?" I interrogate.

He looks at me through hooded eyes.

"It was just a lone pup who attacked me. I was far enough from the Sanctum to escape," he explains casually, but the way he explains things is always the same — vague, devoid of any helpful information whatsoever. It pisses me off. *He* pisses me off. I study his features: a twitching eyebrow, a quivering lip, just waiting for the truth. He detects my suspicion and adds, "You don't believe me."

"You give me no reason to."

"We should keep moving," Aalis pants.

"I need a few more minutes," Callos huffs, touching his side tenderly. He holds my gaze for a moment before scraping it over to the Prince. "I never did catch your name. You know, whoever is a friend of Elio's is a friend of mine."

"What we are is purely transactional, and does not involve you."

A flash of disappointment seeps through the cracks on the Prince's face.

"Yeah, we are not friends," Aalis asserts from behind, albeit pathetically and with no spine whatsoever.

I plant my eyes firmly to the landscape beyond the fencing, trying my best to put a damper on my growing annoyance. The southern stretches of the Ashen Domain are rich in trees and rivers, all feeding into Carmine Lagoon. The tall shadows from the Peaks cascade over the land, leaving the water looking brown and muddy.

"What a shame," Callos clicks his tongue.

Further on south, the Lagoon dips into the Red Sea, and even further lies the Realm of Zemergad. It used to be connected to the mainland, but ever since the Hand was snatched from their possession, the Heretics destroyed any land that could access it. The Realm exists detached from everything else. It is said to be a land of tarnishing desert, sand ruins, and spiritual temples. You can't see it past the usual early morning fog, just a cluster of murky clouds in the space between us.

I stare intently at the area, squinting when I notice some movement. Down the slope, past the valley and over the Lagoon, a mass of smoke weaves across the water. The bell rings once again, undoubtedly calling everyone to the square. I wonder if Bea made it.

"We should go," I reiterate, my voice falling short.

What's down there in the water, it isn't natural. The smoke trespassing over the red water flirts with the grass along the shore of the Ashen Domain. My fingers throb with anxiety, hot on the tips, just as they had after I drank Aalis's blood.

"Don't move, darling."

Something sharp presses into the lower part of my neck. I bow my head, sucking in the chuckle that rumbles in my throat.

I hadn't even heard him move.

"I'll kill you," I spit.

Callos moves in closer behind me and I can smell Aalis' blood dripping off his blade onto my skin, dribbling down my back. Another dagger is pressed to my side: he has me trapped.

"You know I hate to do this."

"I'll *kill* you," I repeat, the words grating through my teeth.

"You have your business, darling, as do I. It's why we never worked out in the first place."

"Like you ever cared about us *working*," I bite.

"No need to fret, I see you have other people you care for now."

"Don't touch him," I seethe, just as I hear Aalis struggling, groaning in pain.

"It's too late for that. Envy often motivates me."

"What do you want?"

"Aren't we all in it for the same thing?" Callos whispers in my ear.

I could overpower him. He's wounded and far weaker than I am. I could rip his throat out with my fangs, and yet here I am, hesitating. Choking. Just like the last time I saw him.

"I have somewhere else to be," he remarks, the tip of his blade scaling up my neck, looping beneath the twine of my necklace.

"I'll hunt you down."

"You have far more important things to busy yourself with," Callos counters. His blade snips the twine in two, and he's quick to snatch the Celestite from my neck. "Like your friend over there, he's losing a *lot* of blood. I hope you can control yourself, *bloodsucker*."

I push away, ready to attack but he's jumped to the side, already out of reach, back peddling with a dirty smirk on his face. He waves with both his middle fingers before turning on his heels and dashing towards the city. I grunt, pulling myself together, and just when I think I might have a chance to catch up with him, he flings his body over the edge of the stone fence, disappearing into the valley below.

"I'll fucking kill you!" I shout, pounding my fists against my thighs.

Bea has always been right about him, and I was stupid enough to let my feelings cloud my judgment. Again.

"*Elio*," Aalis croaks.

He's on the ground slumped over and clutching his thigh with two bloody hands, lavender spreading rapidly down his leg.

He really takes this whole 'being a liability' thing to an extreme.

I take a step in his direction but stop short, feeling the effects of my missing Celestite. The smell of his blood wafts into my nose, up into my brain and sits with my thoughts. My mouth waters, and my stomach grumbles, empty and oh, *so* hungry.

"Just—" he gasps, his face paler than ever. "Get me to town."

I'm shaking my head. Celestite grounds me, stifles my hunger and allows me to tolerate sunlight. I haven't parted with the gem for years, always sure that it was tied around my neck securely. Since I was born a male in the Realm, I was instantly thrown aside. We are cursed like the Howlers, indefinitely sworn to the sun and whilst it won't harm us in the way of burning, living Celestite-less, under sunlight — it amplifies our most violent, animalistic tendencies. Now that it's gone, all I feel is the overwhelming sensation of wanting to dig my fangs into his skin and drain him dry.

I never thought I would fear for the Prince's life, but here I am, saliva dripping from my lips. I don't know what my body would do, how it would act if I got a taste of Aalis' blood right now. I just might tear him to shreds.

"Elio!" Aalis rasps.

"Well," I pause, gulping back the urge to pounce on him, "this can go one of two ways."

Aalis coughs again. He's losing blood fast.

"One," I hold my finger up, thinking back to when I found him a couple of days ago, asleep on the chair, failing miserably at keeping watch. "I leave you here while I go to town and find some Knyghts to help you. Our transaction will be terminated and we both keep our mouths shut about ever knowing each other."

"I'll bleed out before anyone makes it back to me."

He's right. I also doubt I'll be able to pass into Alnola without my Celestite.

I manage to take a step closer to him, fighting this war between my body and mind.

"That leaves the second option," I grit, daring to kneel beside him.

My hunger persists, and every cell in my body is yelling at me to dig my teeth into his flesh.

His eyes grow wide — he must sense my struggle.

"I'll get you to Alnola, but I might kill you in the process. By accident, of course."

"How reassuring," he winces.

"Is the cut deep?" I ask, thinking of a way to do this without harming him.

He shakes his head. "I can't feel much."

"That's not good."

I suck in a huge breath before sliding my hands underneath the Prince. With his body in my arms, I hoist him off the ground with a shaky leg. His face twists in agony as I scoop him up, his injured leg dangling off one side with his head resting against my chest.

His neck is right there, the skin soft and plush, and shit, shit, *shit*, I think this is it. I can feel the ache in my fangs, itching to break into his flesh. I crane my head forward, my jaw sliding open, ready to take a bite.

"You are no longer allowed to chastise me for how and who I love," Aalis breathes, managing to grin ever so slightly.

My head stops moving. I blink once, twice.

I notice now that his brown eye has flecks of gold in it. Just like his hair. And the other eye is not just any blue, but the deep blue of the Forsaken Sea. His tears ripple, a small wave crashing.

I blink again.

Scattered like constellations are pale clusters of freckles dusted over his cheeks and nose. His lips are cracked and dry, but they're the perfect shade of pink tinted with hues of purple. I'm wrapped in this trance — by my own delusional and fickle state, I do not know — as if I confessed to the Creator above and had all my sins forgiven. I feel that muscle in my chest seize as I inch away from his neck and lean towards his lips.

"You were right about one thing, though. True love is most definitely not one-sided."

I pull my head back, flushed. I don't think he seemed to notice.

"You think you're so funny," I goad, feeling a bit faint. My insides burning.

"That man is *awful*, and here you are ridiculing me for chasing after Beka," he chuckles.

"Not one word about this to Bea, understood?"

"Our transaction still upholds?" Aalis counters, colorless.

"So long as you stay alive," I say, feeling a slight pull on my cheeks.

"Then please get moving, and don't kill me. I know you want to."

That, I do. Now more than ever.

21
BEA

When I pull my head up off the ground, the camp is deserted.

I'm breathless, lying face down in the open field, shrapnels of dirt lining my tongue. I force out a cough, and think.

Beka nearly choked me to death.

Coward, I sneer, wishing for a moment that Beka's efforts in taking me down had succeeded. Now, I'm left stranded and empty handed. If it isn't me handing her over to the Kingdom, what then of my reward? Of my status?

I'm thinking about her. About the way she had looked at me. Maybe, her aggressive attack was my final reckoning, a sentence for my murderous sins. Despite everything, I wish there could have been some sort of goodbye between us. I fantasized a civil farewell and perhaps a longing glance as our time together ended — what foolish thinking this was.

I remember there were screams after we fought. There were so many voices, but they soon turned into echoes. Whether it was the Knyghts standing guard or the villagers themselves, they must've taken her away.

Something tickles my ankle. I groan as I lift my head to find my horse nibbling away at the grass beside my feet. It tenses as soon as it notices me stirring.

"Sorry," I croak.

Somewhere in the distance, a clock tower chimes three times — my cue to get up and move. The Knyghts must be summoning everyone to the town square. Why else would they ring the bell this early in the morning?

I hoist myself up from the ground, though not without difficulty, and take my time with mounting my steed.

What was I going to do when I got there? Watch? Interfere?

I barrel through the empty camp, undecided. It's the beginning of a warm day — the chaste rays of sun hinting at unseasonable heat. Sweat dribbles down my neck, the exhaustion of this journey now swiftly catching up.

A throng of Knyghts stand posted around the open gate to the city, perking up at my advance. The bell chimes another three times. I knock my foot against the horse's side to speed us along.

"Access into the Domain isn't granted unless, *hey*!" One of the Knyghts shouts when I show no signs of slowing down.

"I order you to stop!" Another yells as I charge between them, shaking the metal clinging onto their bodies.

"Wait! You can't—"

Their voices are lost behind me.

The paths up ahead are crowded with masses of people cramming in the streets. I pull on the reins, slowing my horse to a trotf before I crash into any civilians. Some of them take notice of my abrupt entrance, but most carry on pushing their way forward, whispering as I dismount.

"It's the Hand, they've found her."

"Is it really her, though?"

"I thought she was dead!"

"She's already attacked and killed someone at the refuge camp."

"The Knyghts are so brave, taking her on like that."

Beka killed someone? I can't imagine she'd lay a single hand on anyone. Then again, she had been the one to raise her hand at me.

"Move it," I bite.

The bell sounds again, rousing the people into a deeper panic. Through force of habit, I glance up at the rooftops, half-expecting to see Elio's slender frame loitering somewhere, but he's nowhere to be seen. Whispers turn to shouts the closer I get to the square, with people screaming threats, muttering prayers, and blessing the Knyghts for finding the enemy.

Not like they put in the work, I think to myself.

"After twelve long years, we can finally avenge our losses!" A voice rumbles from the center of the crowd. There's no opening for me to peek through, but I don't need to look to know who it belongs to. "Those ghastly Heretics plague our world, praying to a darkness so *vile,* so *violent* — one that reaps the light that we preach," General Bausan declares. His voice echoes off the stone buildings, booming loud for all to hear. "It's time we put our foot down. Let us end them once and for all."

The crowd erupts into a roar of cheers, elated and feverish with anticipation. With the way dampness coats my forehead, the only fever coursing through me is fear for Beka. Not of her.

My hands connect with the wall of a building, one of the many that corner the courtyard. I look around for anywhere to gain some higher ground, eventually lifting myself up onto a few stacked crates. The Guardian Headquarter rises over the crowd, the clock tower directly above it. A navy and black flag flaps on one side of the building, just below a larger one of red and gold. Down in the square, Knyghts trail around in three lines with their weapons drawn, holding civilians back from breaking into the clearing. Where it falls away, the crowd raves, pointing and shouting at Beka, who's right in the middle.

My heart sinks to my feet.

They're pulling at her limbs, securing her arms above her head, and her legs against a sturdy, wooden stake. She's gagged at the mouth, frowning around the cloth pulling her cheeks taut. I wince as they tie knots around her wrists and ankles, each tug surely breaking a bone.

This is a crucifixion.

"We will see with a draw of blood," General Bausan jeers, unsheathing his sword.

"Please! Don't hurt her!" A voice cries.

Knyghts are on the move immediately, tackling someone to the ground — a young girl. They tug her onto her feet, her face now swamped with the tie of a sack.

"Take her away," The General dismisses.

I watch Beka frantically fight against her restraints now, leaning toward her friend who's being forced from the square.

General Bausan brushes off the scene. He makes a show of his sword, tracing it in the air to commence a sequence of torture. The crowd falls silent, careful under his presence. He stalks toward Beka, the sword carelessly dragging on the ground by his feet. He's arrogant, and he knows he has her trapped. She can't escape this.

"How filthy is your blood?" he spits, lifting the blade to her bicep.

The General makes a careful incision across her skin, dragging the blade slowly along her arm. Her blood drips, thick like dye, oozing from the cut. He steps out of the way, revealing the evidence with his chin held high. Dark purple streams down her arm and wets her cheek as her head lulls from side to side. The crowd gasps in unison, their fear settling now they know for certain that a Heretic is within their reach.

"She is one of them!" he howls, igniting a slur of threats in response.

"Kill her!"

"Burn her to the ground!"

"Is she the Hand?"

The General lifts his sword, relishing in his triumph before slashing at her other arm, this cut landing deeper than the last. Her blood spills in ropes, coating her face, painting her. A baby wails in the distance.

"These Heretics are a poison. If we truly want peace — for the Kingdom, for Arcadia, for our children — then they must be eradicated from Sumeria for good! It is the Creator's will." The General presses his blade to her throat now, everyone screaming at him to finish her off.

"The Hand or not, I cannot stand to look at you any longer," he snorts.

He's going to kill her and the King is nowhere in sight. My mission was to bring her to him, to the Kingdom, not to the General for him to make a spectacle of her.

I load and release an arrow within seconds.

The General grunts, recoiling with the impact of my

strike. He glances at the arrow lodged into his forearm with a grim set of eyes, following the angle of the feathers all the way to my figure. His sword clatters to the ground, the only noise to come from the crowd. If he recognizes me, then he doesn't show it.

"Seize her!" a voice yells from the shadows.

My eyes quickly land on a Heathen standing by the doors to the Headquarters. It's Kymn, one of her boney fingers pointed straight for me. A group of Knyghts charge towards me, brought to an immediate halt when the General cries out for them to stand by.

He turns to face me and simply purrs, "Come forward."

All eyes are on me as I step down from the crates and make my way towards the square. It's mostly silent, save for the disgusting hacking and spitting of phlegm coming from the depths of Bausan's throat. There are a few whispers, a few jeers and points, all wondering who I might be. Out in the open, I am no assassin. Just a girl holding a knife.

"You can't kill her," I warn.

Even the gag around Beka's mouth cannot conceal the disbelief crossing her face.

The General scoffs. In one swift motion, he snaps the body of the arrow and casts it aside, his blood splattering on the cobblestone floor in a trail of bright red blots.

"I find it hard to believe that anyone would want her alive," he counters, reaching his uninjured arm out with an open palm. A Knyght moves behind him, grabbing Bausan's sword from the ground and placing it back in his grasp. He points it straight at my heart. "Only sympathizers and Heretics wish to see this girl live. Are you any one of those?"

"I'm following the orders of the King," I offer, as we circle one another, a dance of sorts. "He sent me to find the Hand and bring her back *alive*."

On the outside, I'm calm. Cool. Collected. I have my bow and arrows strapped on my back, both of my daggers in my hands. Inside, I'm terrified — like I've always been.

"I see," he replies, clearly amused.

I don't know what price I'll pay for shooting him, but I think it might be one I'm willing to cash out.

"How do you think the King would react if the Hand was murdered right here, right now, before his Majesty's judgment has been made?'

"There is nothing to discuss. She is born from evil, by spirit and blood."

I spare a glance at Beka. I think about what she said, about who I believe is right and wrong. She is not evil. She is just a girl whose home was taken from her by the Kingdom. The General studies me, looking between myself and Beka, and frowns.

"So you sympathize," he decides.

I can only shake my head.

"I'm just doing my job," I say, lunging towards him, my blade firmly in hand.

I'm quick enough to get the first move, throwing both my arms forward to knock his blade to the side and kick my right leg out to connect with his shoulder. Against any other opponent, the attack would've sent them to the ground. But Bausan is a large man with Edom knows how much experience, so I only manage to catch him by surprise. I dash behind Beka to swipe my blade along the back of the stake, attempting to slash through the ties binding her wrists, but Bausan's back on his feet and marching towards me before I can make the rope-killing blow. I attempt to get in front of her, but Bausan swings his sword at the last second, nicking at my shoulder plate. I can already feel my skin bruise and swell underneath the hit. The Knyghts surrounding us hesitate, anxious to get involved. It's clear that this fight is between the General and I alone.

"You can't possibly be defending her."

"I'm loyal to my job."

Bausan advances. I may be quick on my feet and a master with a blade or two, but I can't hold a flame to his power. I can't break through his armor with my strength alone, let alone kill him. He's waiting for me to make the first move, as if it'll be that easy to beat me. And it just might. He's already got me beat but I'm determined to make him work for it.

I take one last look at Beka, hoping she sees me trying, hoping that in the end, she might forgive me. I pounce, angling my body into a spin, before bringing my blades down one after the other. Bausan blocks the attack easily, but I'm quick to make the next jab once my feet land. My movements are swift and unpredictable, and even if he hits away every single swipe, I manage to overwhelm him with my determination. Bausan, despite almost tripping over, manages to block my attack but I'm running out of steam, and just when I think I'll be able to knock him over, he smirks, knocking my daggers away, holding me in a position where physical strength is the only way to win. His breath hits my face. There's nothing I can do. I'm stuck, gritting my teeth, pushing my arms as hard as I can to shove him away, but he just won't budge.

The General grins.
"I admire your spirit."
Mission failed.

22
ELIO

The clock tower rings yet again.

"I think we heard it the first time," I grumble, shifting Aalis in my arms.

"The morning bell chimes at least five times before I get out of bed," he slurs. "I miss morning tea almost everyday."

"Great. You're delirious."

"It's true. The King has a particular fixation with my attending meals. Especially breakfast."

"Aalis, you're bleeding profusely, and in a Night Demon's arms, might I add."

The entrance to Alnola is just up ahead, and I feel naked without my Celestite — and not the fun kind of naked.

I just hope the Prince is enough of a face card to convince the guards to let us pass through unbothered. I might even start praying.

"Sorry. I'm just hungry," he mumbles.

"Don't even get me started."

I should've torn into his flesh by now, what with his body so close to mine. His blood is everywhere — his shirt, his legs, my hands. I want him and I'm losing my fucking mind. The only thing keeping me from ravishing him dry is remembering how pissed off I am with Callos. This rage is the only thing keeping me together. I let it carry us towards the city gates. The very *guardless* gates. Typical bastard Knyghthood.

"There's no one here," I drone, unsurprised.

Aalis lifts his head to take a look. "How convenient."

"*Too* convenient," I wonder.

"It must be the bells," Aalis dribbles out, dropping his head back against my chest.

My hand holding his back slips, slick with blood.

"I don't like this," I heave, readjusting the Prince in my arms. "You're quite heavy, you know that?"

He just hums, looking ready to black out.

I shrug, cautiously stepping through the gated threshold. As I stalk through the empty alleyways, I catch cries from the city ahead. My path draped in shadows, the hubbub a distinct roar, hollering and shouting echoing in the air.

"What's all the noise?" Aalis squeaks.

I turn a corner onto another pathway and see the crowd some steps away — hundreds of people, all packed into the alleys leading into the square. There's no way I could get both of us through undetected.

"I should go check it out," I say, uneasy over what lies ahead.

I spot a lone, wooden chair perched against the wall, and move to place Aalis on it.

"Alone?" he perks up, tossing in my arms.

"Would you—" I snap, dropping him onto the chair. "Settle! I won't be long."

"I'm bleeding!"

"I'm illiterate, not blind," I scoff. "Besides, I can't walk into that crowd with you looking like *that*."

Aalis rolls his eyes, followed by a wince of pain.

"I can't believe you."

"You don't really think I can carry you in there, right? There's no way," I cross my arms.

"But if Beka's in trouble—"

"Oh, would you drop it?"

"She cannot *die.*"

"Aalis! Wake up," I snap. "There is no more helping her. You need to let her go."

"And then what? Without her, this means nothing," he fumes.

I take a step back, placing my hands on my hips, trying my best to ignore how bloody my clothes and hands are. It's infuriating, but he's right: without the Hand, whatever the Prince and I have matters no more than a courtesan stalking the Sleepless City.

"This was never going to work," he mumbles, defeated. "I lied, anyway."

"Well, obviously." I sneer. "You can't save her."

Aalis sighs, forlorn. I take a sharp breath, cooling my nerves.

"Listen, there isn't much we can do." I'm really trying to be sympathetic — *trying.*

"I promised her."

"We did what we could," I say, full of shit.

I never cared about the Hand, though my words seem to comfort him as he offers me the slightest look of appreciation.

"I really am foolish," he utters, dropping his head. "What good is love if it brings me here, regretting that I ever felt such a thing?"

"You're so soft," I dismiss but Callos crosses my mind.

"I'm serious."

"Well, regret it all you want. It won't change where we are now."

"It still hurts," he sniffles, bringing his hand to his chest.

I have to look away.

The crowd rumbles once again, reminding me that things aren't over just quite yet. I don't feel comfortable leaving Aalis alone, but I have no other choice.

"Listen. You're going to stay put, alright? I just need to check out what's going on over there."

Aalis takes a moment to look at his soaked hands.

"Okay," he nods, then looks up at me, his eyes glazed with tears. "Don't forget to come back. I don't want to die alone."

"Then don't die."

He shoots me an exasperated look.

"Forgive me. Only by your fangs may I have the permission to bleed out."

"You're starting to catch on, I see," I muse, rubbing my blood-slicked fingers together.

"Maybe, when this is all over, we can finally call each other friends."

"Now you've really lost it," I mutter, smiling, like an utter idiot.

The Prince grins and I suddenly become very interested in counting the cracks splitting the cobblestone under my feet.

"I'll, uh, make sure you get the reward I promised you. Both you and Bea will be generously compensated for bringing me home," he says.

I nod, my eyes trailing up from the ground to his throb-bing leg.

He should be dead, I think. *How am I resisting his blood?*

"Keep putting pressure on that," I point at his wound.

"I'll be okay," he says, glancing at me bashfully. "Thanks, you know, for um—"

"Don't mention it," I turn away, my cheeks warming up. Must be the heat. "I'll be right back."

As I approach the town center, it becomes very clear that I won't be able to push my way through to the front of the crowd. The street is packed enough that even with my height, I can't see the commotion happening in the square. I can hear it, though. The sounds of clasing weapons, the sounds of battle, and a voice I'd know even if I were deaf.

Bea.

With a quick lick, I lap up the blood soaking my hands. It sings on my tongue, sending a surge of newfound energy throughout my body. I hurry toward an empty alleyway, pouncing at the wall, my body near weightless. My feet instinctively find places to latch onto: the roof of a vendor stand, the arch of a stone entryway, an extension of rock. I climb my way up swiftly, grabbing onto anything to propel my body towards the rooftops. I pull my body over the ledge and steady myself above. I'm still close to the action, only an alley's length away from the square. I look behind me and see the rest of the Ashen Domain through a filter of clouds.

The highest point of Alnola is the Guardian Headquarters, the rest of the town declining behind me to ground level. I spring from rooftop to rooftop, the mass of people swarming below me a remarkable sight, though I'm not sure what I am expecting to see.

Knyghts line the perimeter of the square, leaving one slight area open for civilians to spill through and watch. The Hand is tied against a stake, bleeding out from her arms, limp and drained. She looks awful, though I can't say I'm surprised to see her.

What does surprise me, though, is right at the center of it all, defending the Hand, is Bea. Dueling Bausan.

The crowd is ballistic, gauding at the fight, spitting curses at the Hand. The Knyghts stand idly by with their weapons at the ready, waiting for some sort of command from the General, though Bea is holding her own, and pretty well too. She's faster than the General, her moves are smarter — much sharper than his. She manages to take the upper hand for a moment, her attacks strong enough to force the General to back up. But she's getting tired.

I make it to the bell tower on top of the Headquarters, keeping low to hide from any wandering eyes. I steady myself against the cool stone and look down, the Hand's body facing away from me. She's losing so much blood.

If she dies, will our mission be void? The King doesn't seem to be around, and surely he wants her dead — but how soon? Does the General have orders to do his dirty work and kill her on the spot? Or will he wait and torture her to insanity? Bea clearly has her reasons for challenging him, and that means those reasons are mine as well.

I stay close to the shadows as I figure out my next move. I should get back to Aalis, but that means leaving Bea. Bausan won't go down easy, and there's only so much fight left in her.

Their blades collide, eliciting quite the gasp from the crowd. Bausan has her locked — he's pressing her daggers down, bending her arms to her face, leaning forward to tower over her, and I can't bear to watch. Bausan disarms her seconds later, shoving her to the ground. The crowd cheers as a herd of Knyghts seize her. She's so worn out that she can't even put up a fight as they pin her arms to her back, forcing her to her knees.

"You see? You cannot defend these creatures!" Bausan roars, relishing in the chants. He raises his sword victoriously in the air, sweeping it between Bea and the Hand. "We are not safe from their mind games!"

Bea's head is low, defeated. Bausan takes a step toward her with his sword raised.

I inch my way down, my feet skidding across the cladding.

"You are cursed, young one. What a shame to lose a fire like you," Bausan recites.

He lifts his arms up, aiming for Bea's knelt body.

"NO!" I shout, reaching my hand out: a desperate, last attempt at getting to her side.

My vision goes dark then, a single hand waiting for me in the abyss.

I grab hold of it, and when I regain my sight, I'm plummeting to the ground.

23
LYCIDAS

"It's here," Jeane notes, pressing her palm flat against the stone. "They should be *here*."

We hadn't stayed long after spotting the Maidens of Lilith. Their rafts eventually sailed out of sight. We're standing before the towering wall of Alnola's fortress, the outskirts of the city. The scent we've been tracking led us all the way to this spot. Its shape seeps right into the stone, a dead end.

I have no answer — seems to be the case for everything at this point.

It's been hours now. More Howlers could be falling ill. More could be dead. Existentialism is not typically my thing, but I can't help it as it dawns on me more and more how nothing will be as it was from here on out. It was only a few days ago that I was back home in Brighes helping Beka sort the harvest into barrels. That I was gathering my things for my routine trip to the Sanctum. That I was with Inez.

"They have to be in Alnola," Jeane barks, ripping me from my thoughts.

"Dammit," I grit, knocking my fist into the stone.

This person couldn't be *inside* the damn wall. As far as I know, Alnola is nothing but solid rock. Yet, the trail of their scent runs right through the wall of the fortress, as if a door should magically appear in front of us, letting us pass on through. Jeane rests her hand on my back, thumbing the tight knots away.

"It's okay. We'll check out town and go from there," she offers. "We can even report to the Knyghts. I know my mom said to stay quiet, but maybe they know something. Maybe they can help."

"Maybe," I mutter, closing my eyes.

Her face is there behind my lids, sound asleep in my bed. Inez is there tugging on the threads of my heart.

"Ly, we should go," Jeane ushers, stepping closer, knowing exactly what's tormenting me.

"Come on, then," I nod, pushing away from the wall.

Sarya is behind us both, standing still as she clutches her arms into her chest.

"You doing okay?" I ask her, kneeling down to her level.

"I'm hungry," she mumbles.

Her blonde hair is slick with grease and sticks to her cheeks.

"We can get you something to eat soon," I promise.

Oh, the things I would do for a warm meal right now.

"And then we can go home?" Sarya says.

Brighes is very well gone with nothing but a cemetery to return to.

"Let's go through the West Gate," Jeane declares, starting for the path towards the city.

Sarya nods, keeping her head low. I hoist her up on my back, and we continue on.

The journey to the center is steep, but I welcome the burn

in my legs. Sarya keeps a firm grip on my shoulders, locking her hands around my neck to stay put. I want to ask her so many things, but I know I'll get answers eventually. Besides, she is just a child.

Jeane rushes up ahead of us, her legs moving twice as fast. I hear her muttering to herself, finding her own methods of distraction. We eventually reach the end of the trail, where Jeane peeks her head over a stone fence.

"Come on," she hisses, beckoning us forward.

I pull Sarya off my shoulders and hand her over to Jeane, who hoists her over the fence. Jeane and I follow suit. Once we're over, I find Sarya gazing at a valley in the distance. She points at the Maiden's canoes, now empty and cast aside on the shore.

Where the land dips low, left of the Lagoon, is the Forbidden Valley: a junkyard where the Maidens dump the men their Sirens bring through. It's a dreadful place, all life burned and left to char. There has been no life, flora, fauna or human, since the Kingdom invaded the Realm and took the Hand all those years ago. It used to connect the Realm to the Domain — as the remains of the bridge on the Sanctum's southern borders did — but the Maidens broke the ground free with their magic. No more trespassers.

"I smell blood," Jeane says, pulling away from the fence.

I call Sarya away from the edge, catching the metallic shift in the air as well.

"There's something off about it," I remark.

"Not quite human," Jeane adds.

"Look," I point at a smear of purple against the stone.

"Have they gone and poisoned someone else?"

There are splotches scattered like breadcrumbs all the way to the gate. Even from here, I can see that the entrance is left unguarded. Weird.

"Doesn't matter. I can smell them everywhere," I snarl, imprinting this scent in my mind. "They must be close."

As we follow the trail, a rumble of cheers ripple to my ears. Jeane and I exchange a look once we reach the abandoned gate. With nobody here to check our moonstones and mark our names for admission, why waste any more time?

I scoop Sarya into my arms as we enter the city. Stone walls are built up on either side of us, branching off into various alleyways that weave throughout the fortress. With a single glance down the main passage, abandoned in its entirety, it seems that everyone has flocked to the square.

"I don't like this, Ly," Jeane says, her steps light and cautious.

Another alley splits off to our left. The path is littered with vending tables of various trades — textiles, tapestries and clothes; patisserie stands with baked goods and corn; fruit tables littered with baskets of berries and assorted nuts.

"Over there," Jeane nods down the alleyway.

I pick up the scent from before, its shape settling beside the bread table.

Sure enough, as we lurk down the path, splotches of purple reemerge. We follow it all the way to the table where a pool of it stains the wood of an empty chair resting against the wall.

"It's fresh," Jeane says.

"Should we keep following it?"

"There isn't anything else to do," she sighs, nudging the chair with her foot.

Sarya's eyeing the bread table with a hungry look. I place her on the ground and step forward, snatching two rye loaves from display. She devours the thing within seconds of it leaving my hands.

Hungry myself, I rip the other loaf in two, offering one half to Jeane.

"Thanks," she mumbles, picking it apart before taking a bite.

Rye bread isn't my favorite and it's as dry as anything, but I'm starving — it's not so easy having the appetite that I do. There was one time, during one of my growth spurts, that I nearly cleaned Emelyne's whole cupboards out. She'd worried I might explode, prodding at my very bloated belly.

"Maybe we should split up," I suggest. Jeane looks ready to refuse, so I add, "I know. I'd rather stay together, but Alnola is huge, and we only have so much time until—"

"Okay," Jeane nods, finishing her share of the loaf. "We split up. But only for an hour. We'll meet back here after then."

"Can I come with you?" Sarya tugs on my shirt, crumbs sticking to her cracked lips.

"Of course. You stay by me," I tell her, pushing some of her hair back.

"Ly," Jeane pleads, her hand now on my shoulder. "Be careful, okay?"

"You too. If you find anything, run with it. We'll catch up soon enough."

For a moment, I really look at my friend: my first friend. My first crush, even. We were born just months apart, attached by the hip for most of my childhood before I left for work. We'd picked our first pieces of Moonstone together, having clicked our rocks against one another in cheers. I knew then how hard it would be to move away from home, but she remained a constant in my life — Nadine and Raven, too. And now, after all these years I've known Jeane, there's something different about her. Within a few days, the light behind her eyes has vanished. There is a deep sadness pulling at her face, the same kind wrenching my heart down into the ground, burying it into a place where no light can seep through. We're not children anymore.

Jeane says nothing else, but I can feel the weight of her silence, the burden that we both share. This loss is tying us together, now more than ever before, forcing us to keep going until we find whoever it is that hurt our family.

"I'll see you in an hour."

Maybe Sarya should have gone with Jeane instead.

Jeane had chosen to head back out the way we came, leaving us to make our way down the vendor's alley, and Sarya hasn't said much since we split our separate ways. The square is only getting louder, and I don't doubt Sarya has loads of questions — she's always been a curious girl. I could distract her with my own rambling, but I fear my words may shape into questions of my own. Ones even I'm not ready to hear the answers to.

I try my best to pinpoint any specific scent that could be of use as we lurk and loiter, but there are too many people gathered in the city. It feels silly to be walking around these empty streets with no lead other than the random blood from before.

"Do you think my mama's here?" Sarya finally speaks up, her hand clammy in mine.

"I don't know," I admit, distant.

I've kept my eyes trained on the path ahead of us — an unchanging pattern of dull stone. My head is sure to rot soon enough.

"Will we live here from now on?" she continues.

"I don't know, little one."

"I don't want to. I want to go home."

The path begins to bend. I keep Sarya to my right, closest to the wall as we round a smooth corner, another passage splitting off ahead. Sounds emerge from around the bend, muffles turning into voices: a girl screaming for help, her cries accompanied by the noises of clunking metal. Knyght's armor.

"Shut up!" a voice bellows.

A shadow of a figure is thrown to the ground, followed by a painful sob.

Sarya grips my arm tight.

"You better pray you make it into Eden after that stunt," another voice booms.

Another screech of armor, then a yelp.

"You might as well stay here and rot. Go join that wretched demon in Edom, traitor!"

I move around the corner, catching sight of a pair of Knyghts walking back down the alley they came from. Their armor is draped in the navy, black and silver of the Ashen Domain. For a second I think to chase after them and report the news of the Howlers, but there is a girl on the ground in front of me. She's dressed in a dirty chemise and brown tunic. A rag has been pulled over her face, her legs and arms littered with cuts and bruises. With some hesitation, I kneel down beside her, speaking before I do anything else.

"Are you alright?" She shakes her head, her sobs making it impossible to pull herself up. "They're gone," I say. "Let me help you."

The girl's head snaps up at my words. Seconds later, she's ripping the rag off her head.

Inez, my heart calls out too soon, mistaking these brown eyes for a pair I know too well — but these belong to her sister, tainted with a sick mix of terror and relief.

"Gallie!" Sarya jumps forward, throwing herself into my friend's arms.

Gallienne gasps, wrapping her arms around the girl.

"What—?" she exclaims, another sob ripping out of her mouth.

Her eyes lock with mine, and I, too, feel an immense relief. I step forward and join them on the ground, my arms concealing them both in my embrace. Something thick ripples up in my throat, choking me as I bite back a surge of tears.

"How are you here?" Gallienne wonders, pulling back the slightest to take the sight of us in. She looks exhausted, dread dripping from her slumped frame. "Oh, Sarya, I was so worried about you!"

"Beka told me to run away," Sarya explains.

At the mention of our friend's name, Gallienne releases a whimper, pulling the girl back into her arms, pressing a million little kisses on her forehead.

"What happened?" I demand.

"The General is performing a demonstration," Gallienne explains, looking down the alley.

"A demonstration?"

Gallienne hugs Sarya even tighter, placing her hands over the girl's ears.

"It's—" she breaks off, sniffing back a sob. "It's Beka."

"What?"

"She's one of them. A Maiden," Gallienne bows her head, rambling. "The General is going to kill her."

"Beka?"

In all the years I've known Beka, there were certain things I never asked her about. She arrived in Brighes just weeks after the Battle of Lamya. I've always been curious, but then I remember how terrified she was when I found her by the shores. She was around Sarya's age, frail and scared and desperate to get away from wherever she came from.

It took her a year to speak to me.

She would ask me about my work and beg me to tell her about the Lunar Sanctum. Her eyes glistened as I spoke, and she held onto my every word, clinging to them like a safety net. There were so many times where I wanted to ask her where she came from, but she made it known that it didn't matter. This was her new life, and she was never going to go back.

"I didn't know! She disappeared after the raid and I thought she was dead. We hadn't seen her for days. But then she came back, and it was like she was a completely different person. Now, the Kingdom, *everyone*, they blame *her*. It felt so wrong, watching her bleed out like that, and, *oh*, Lycidas.

I'm so sorry, but Brighes," she cuts herself off and all I can do is nod.

"I know." I lean back, feeling the nausea settle in as Gallienne weeps.

I hope it's the poison. I hope it kills me.

"Right after you left, Beka visited us," she continues. "She gave Inez medicine, but nobody knew about the baby." Her eyes search mine for an answer. "Did you?"

No.

"I should've guessed it, she's my sister for Eden's sake! I would know if she were pregnant, and yet," Gallienne reaches her hand out. "It was too late. Lilith came that night."

There is too much despair in her voice for me to bear, but now is the time to face it.

"Inez is dead," I whimper, my voice cracking.

Slowly, she nods, trying to pull herself together.

"And Brighes is gone."

Again, she nods.

"And Beka... Where is Emelyne?"

The weeping starts again, and it answers enough.

"Everything happened so quickly," Gallienne cries, grabbing my hand. "Our people turned on Beka, handed her over to the Knyghts. It makes sense to blame her. She was *there*. She's a *Maiden*. Then I saw her tied up in the square and I couldn't watch them kill her."

I couldn't lose her, too. She doesn't have to say it for me to hear it.

A thousand voices are churning in my head: screaming out, cursing Beka, damning Lilith for what she's taken from me, from Gallienne and everyone we love. But I know the truth of it all. Painfully, deep down, my own guilt points at me, laughing. As if this is all just some cruel joke. Gallienne is waiting for me to say something, anything, but I can't even meet her eyes.

Inez was pregnant.

I release her hand, afraid she'll see the crusted blood on my fingers and under my nails.

"You said Beka is in the square?" I'm already pushing myself up from the ground, backing away.

"Yes, but," Gallienne sits up, Sarya shifting in her lap. "You can't stop them, Lycidas! Please stay. I can't take it anymore."

"Stay with Sarya," I tell her, sparing her one last glance. "I'm so sorry."

The force of Gallienne's sobs blisters my ears.

My legs carry me down the alley, chasing the noises coming from the square. It's loud enough there to swallow the fortress, the echoing cheers and screams bouncing from wall to wall as I run away.

Gallienne can't know what I've done.

No one can.

24

AALIS

Elio leaves me, and I sit in the chair for only a minute or two before trailing after him.

I would've listened to him, and I know I should have, but am I supposed to just sit here and bleed out? I can't shake the feeling that *something* is happening. This feeling, it's born of the same fear that came after I heard the Banshee scream, and I refuse to let it hold me back.

I know Elio can see to it on his own, but that doesn't mean he has to.

A rush of adrenaline surges through me. I light the flame that threatens to ignite within my veins and lift myself up. I have never been so physically exerted. Well, nor have I ever been *stabbed* before, but semantics.

The King would surely catch his death at the sight of me.

Getting up was only the first part, walking is the second. My wound is still throbbing, my blood not yet clot. Wearily, I fumble for my belt, my fingers flimsy, tying a tourniquet around my thigh to stop the pooling and set off.

I keel over minutes later, straight onto a stone wall, my limbs limp. I use it to propel me forward, to bear my weight, as I struggle towards the crowd. Crawling would have been more dignifying at this rate.

I barely catch the flicker of motion above. I snap my head up to see a blur of red flaming over the ledge and onto the rooftops. I inhale a sharp breath and push away from the wall, hobbling as quickly as possible over to the first lot of people in the crowd.

"Excuse me," I press, placing a hand on a bystander's arm.

They jump, startled and clearly riled up by the gathering. It's a middle aged man, dressed in simple clothes and an apron.

"What's happened to *you*?" he questions, looking me up and down in horror.

"I just need to get through," I huff, dropping my head for a second to catch my breath.

He shrugs my hand off.

"Well, so do I! I can barely see the fight going on, let alone get a good look at that monstrous Heretic," he protests.

"But I'm the Prince. Prince Aalis," I explain desperately, reaching for his shoulder again.

He recoils from my touch, smirking. "Yeah, and I'm the bloody Cain. Seriously, you should've ran faster after the bell rang."

"I'm injured! Can't you see!" I don't have time to deal with bastards like this.

I catch myself mid-thought, taken aback. Maybe I'm more like my father than I thought. It makes me shudder.

Confront that another time, Aalis.

The crowd ebbs and flows in waves of erratic excitement, pushing and shoving to get a closer look. Getting to the center won't be easy. I ready myself for another jab from the bystander, but his eyes have grown wide, no longer looking

down on me, but past me. There isn't enough time for me
to turn around before I'm yanked from the ground. Someone
lifts me off my feet as if I'm a sack of dust, dragging me to the
side of the alley. My back slams into a wall, a burst of pain
shooting up my spine.

Oh, when will it end?

I'm met face to face with a very furious visage. A girl,
twice my size, has me pinned, her fist crushing the fabric of
my blouse. Her eyes are dark, her mouth slanted into a grim
scowl. The frizzy curls on her head resemble that of a mane,
and she looks about ready to gobble me up. She's strong,
nothing like that of a regular human. She must be a Howler.
Instinctively, I throw my hands up in defense. The bystander
is chuckling from behind.

"Who did this to you?" she growls, shaking my body with
her fists.

"What?"

"The cut on your leg. Was it poison? Or did you take a
blow when you were busy poisoning someone else?"

I really must be losing my mind.

"I—what? Poison? I don't understand!"

"Don't lie!" Her eyes coat with tears.

Clearly, this is a misunderstanding. I shoot a glance back
to the rooftops, but Elio is no longer in sight.

"It was a knife," I explain, recalling the moment Callos
stuck the damn thing in my leg.

"Who did this to you?" she repeats, her voice trembling.

"What's going on over here?" someone else inquires.

Both the Howler and I turn our heads at the voice,
·ting the tension between us. It's a Knyght, a young one,

approaching us from within the crowd. His helmet is off, exposing a head of closely shaved hair and dark skin. There is a pale scar over one of his eyelids, unable to open all the way. His other eye is narrowed, examining us.

"This is none of your business," the Howler hacks, fixing her deadly gaze back to me.

I look to the Knyght, pleading for him to intervene.

"Release His Highness," the Commander says, telltale by the tassel attached to his helmet.

Thank the Creator.

"*Highness*?" the Howler heaves, loosening her grip on my blouse.

"Please, let go of me," I squeak.

She's visibly torn. The layers of her wrath shed away almost instantly, as if she realized what she'd done, and to whom she had done it. Slowly, she backs away though her eyes are still furious, firm on my wound.

"Are we going to have any more issues here?" The Commander asks, inching closer to me.

"No," she says, hesitating. "I just thought—"

"His Highness must go, now," the Commander dismisses, grabbing hold of my arm.

"The Howlers," she chokes, "we need *help*."

"Find me later," the Commander dismisses, set on getting me away from everyone. "Things are a little busy here, if you can't tell."

He drags me away from the scene, leaving the Howler standing there at the brim of the crowd. I catch the sight of a boy, impossibly taller — taller than her — running up to her side. Another Howler. She points in our direction, then shoves her face into his arms.

"Where in Eden have you been, your Highness?" The Commander murmurs close to my ear, pushing us through the people.

"It's a long story," I groan as he lures me down an alley.

"You're going to need a good alibi, what with all the fuss the King has been throwing in your absence, sir."

"It's nothing, really."

He tugs me close, bringing his face inches from mine.

"Do you understand what's going on here?" he eyes me. I'm too stunned to speak.

"This is just the beginning," he continues. "General Bausan has been waiting years for this."

His words are surprising for a Commander.

"Waiting for what?"

"The King should be here soon," he looks around. "You need a Haelend."

"What I need is to get to the square," I say, ripping my arm for his hand. "If Beka is hurt then I—"

"*You* need to be very careful with what you say," he breathes harshly.

I lean back, unable to look away from his scarred eye.

A rumble of yelping sounds from the streets. The both of us jump, peering at the hollering crowd as commotion momentarily ceases in the square.

"Please," I beg him. "If you can get me to the front, I promise I can make things right."

"There's nothing you can do," he says plainly.

I grab his arm then, this time tugging him into *my* space. "What's your name?"

He hesitates. "Thierri."

"Well, Commander Thierri, in the past few days, I witnessed the town of Brighes burn to the ground. I saw innocent people die by the hands of *our* army. I saved a girl who's been hunted by us for years. I was threatened by a thief. I was dragged behind a horse and grabbed by a Harpy. I dropped ten feet in the air onto the cold, hard ground of the Cudnola Peaks. I was *stabbed*. I think I may be bleeding to death, so if there's one thing I wish to do before I can't stand anymore, that is for you to take me to the square so I can make all of this *worth* it." I take a long, deep breath, drained from every word that's left my mouth.

Commander Thierri pulls his arm away, only to place it upon my shoulder. He looks me dead in the eyes.

"You are not like your father."

I don't know what he expects me to say.

"I just want to save her," I admit. "We can't let her die."

"The Capitan will not win against Bausan," Thierri says, shaking his head. The *Capitan*? Bea is fighting the General? "How fast can you move?"

Without the Commander escorting me, I don't think people would have made any way for me to pass through.

They scoff and grumble at us at first glance, but when they spot Thierri, a pause settles. Then their eyes fall on my bloody state. Slowly the people move aside, creating a small aisle for us to walk through.

I've completely lost sight of Elio. I forgot to keep an eye

on the sky. I know I should've stayed put like he said, but sitting there would have done nothing. I can still feel the cut in my thigh. It burns like a brand, as if I were cattle being led to slaughter.

"You don't have much time. The King should be arriving shortly," Commander Thierri explains.

"Thank you," I murmur.

I hear the people in the crowd hush my name when they eventually recognize me. For once, I'm glad to be seen. For people to know who I am.

We make it to the front line in no time, my eyes landing on Bea and the General. He has his sword raised, ready to strike her kneeling frame down. Beka's behind them, slumped against a wooden stake, her eyes closed. Once more, I look to the skies and catch a flash of movement beside the clock tower.

He's sliding down the roof, stretching his arms as he cries, "NO!"

A strong gust of wind blows through the square, sending the General flying over the crowd. His body smacks directly into a stone wall. The world seems to pause for a moment, a flicker of confusion washing over everyone's faces. The chaos erupts into a piercing symphony as a Heathen steps out of the shadows and rushes toward the General. Alongside a handful of Knyghts, she ushers people away, making space as he lies limp on the cobblestone.

I turn my head back to where I spotted Elio, though now I can barely see his face. He's a gust of flames tumbling to the ground. He crashes into the Knyghts standing guard by the entrance to the Guardian Headquarters, falling in a wave of clashing metal and surprised grunts.

Commander Thierri blows straight past me, crossing the square in quick, long strides. I turn my head to Bea, who's staring desperately at her friend, visibly anguished. The Knyghts keep a tight grip on her. Our eyes meet as I wander into the center of the square. She quickly glances at my thigh, and then back up into my eyes, as if she can see the wash of Death's bitter waters drench me.

Through a blur of tears, I see the Knyghts seize Elio, lifting his slack body from the ground. Slowly, his eyes flutter open, and I take a breath of relief. He's *alive.*

A nearby groan grabs my attention.

Beka.

"Are you okay?" I hear myself say as I rush to her side.

My hands touch her lulling face, her blood smearing on my finger tips. A small whine escapes from her lips, her eyes still wound tightly shut. Her wrists have been rubbed raw, bruising where the ropes bind her. She won't make it much longer with all the blood loss.

"No," I mutter, shaking her shoulders now. "No, no, no, no, you *cannot* die. Please, you must stay with me."

"Aalis," she mumbles, lifting her head slightly.

Salty tears dribble into my mouth.

"I'm here. Everything's going to be okay, just please. Hold on a little longer."

She shakes her head, eyes peeling open a smidge before rolling to the back of her head in a faint daze.

I've painted those eyes so many times.

"Step back, Aalis," she croaks.

"I can help you," I plead. "I love you."

A sad smile forms on her face. My hands fall to my sides, realizing what I've just said.

I spare a glance back at the crowd mostly swarming around the General, now propped up against the wall, motionless. Others are staring at Bea and now Elio, who has been pulled into the light and forced to kneel beside his friend.

The rest stare at me. Even if they can't hear me, it's clear as night and day where I stand.

"You can't help me."

She isn't saying it back, I think.

"Beka," I whisper.

"You can't," she mouths, a single tear falls from her eyes before her head rolls to the side.

"Even half-dead her powers are still dangerous!" a civilian exclaims.

A mass of them reassemble their positions at the perimeter of the square.

"I will finish her," the same Heathen declares, stepping into the center. She makes a beeline for Beka, so consumed with rage that she startles upon seeing me within the square, standing between her and the stake. "Your Highness? Where did you—?"

"Call for a Haelend. She needs immediate medical attention," I order.

The Heathen glares at me, stubborn in her stance. No one moves a muscle.

"You don't know what you're doing," she snarls. Her white cloak is near luminescent in this light. She resembles Celtis and Beka in so many ways, save for the fury rooted in her eyes. "That girl is dangerous."

"I cannot let you operate an execution here without proper orders from the King," I say, eyeing a few Knyghts expectantly. "Am I not the Prince of Ead? Send a Haelend this way at once!"

I don't recognize my own voice. I catch Bea and Elio looking my way, astonished.

"You have no command here," the Heathen states as the Knyghts hesitate with what to do. "Beyond the King, jurisdiction remains with the General, and after the General it goes to—"

"Me," Commander Thierri enters the square now. "His Highness is right. If any more blood is shed in this square, we will all be subject as witnesses to unlawful discipline."

The Heathen steps back, stunned.

I send an appreciative glance toward the Commander. He's standing over Elio and Bea, a hint of amusement in his eyes.

"Everyone stand by," Thierri orders. "The King will be here shortly."

I drift to the side whilst the uproar dissipates.

General Bausan's unconscious body was escorted into the Guardian Headquarters. It seems his injuries are minor — just an incision in his right forearm and a severe concussion, but nothing he won't make a full recovery from. I can practically hear Elio calling him a bastard.

A Haelend has stepped forward to tend to Beka's wound though the ropes remain bound around her wrists. The Heathen, who I heard someone refer to by the name Kymn, stands guard beside the healer, and Commander Thierri tries his best to manage the crowd.

They call out to the Haelend, begging to leave Beka for dead, urging her to stop cleaning her cuts and let the enemy bleed out, though I know the only thing holding them back from finishing Beka off themselves is fear. The Knyghts posted around her shift on their feet, anxious as well. Maybe she'll strike again.

Instinctively, my eyes drift back to Elio. His head is angled towards Bea, most likely exchanging what little words they can with the Knyghts around. Bea notices me approaching first. Her eyes dart between Beka and I, obvious concern gushing from her gaze.

"Is she...?"

"Alive. She'll be okay," I nod.

"What the fu—" Elio starts.

"Are *you* guys okay?" I interrupt, eyeing the Knyghts, unsure if I should even be speaking to them.

"Fine," Bea says. "What happened to you?"

"Yeah, and why didn't you fucking listen to me? I told you to stay put!" Elio grumbles, his eyes glued to the wound on my thigh.

His face is freshly bruised, the skin around one of his eyes puffy and red.

"Who said I had to follow your orders?" I remark. "Besides, you two need me."

"Right," Bea deadpans.

"I will speak with the King and make sure you are generously compensated for your efforts," I promise.

"Right," Bea drawls.

"Your Highness, your wound requires tending to," one of the Knyghts comments.

I've avoided looking at it this whole time. My adrenaline is starting to evaporate, leaving me quite nauseous.

"I think he knows that, dipshit," Elio grunts under his breath.

"A Harpy didn't do that, did it?" Bea questions skeptically. Elio drops his head.

"It's nothing, really," I say, sharing Elio's shame.

"Doesn't look like nothing. What happened?"

More silence. Bea narrows her eyes at Elio suspiciously.

"Callos happened," Elio mumbles, suddenly sheepish. Bea's entire body slumps with disappointment. "I don't want to hear it," Elio dismisses. "Stop. Don't look at me like that!"

"You are a fucking idiot!"

"To be fair, he deceived the both of us," I add.

"Respectfully, your Highness, you are also a fucking idiot," Bea snides.

"I probably should go get it checked out," I mutter, glancing at the wound and my belt strapped above it.

"And that shoulder of yours — wouldn't want an infection from Harpy talons," Bea remarks.

"*Oh!*" Elio's eyes light up. "Tell her what I did, Aalis."

Her face twists, baffled by the casualty of my name on his tongue.

"I'm obliged to inform you that he did, in fact, kill a Harpy," I sigh, relieved that I am no longer plagued by Elio's tormenting ego, even if Bea looks far from convinced.

"On your own?"

"Well, *he* sure as Edom didn't do anything," Elio says.

"Bullshit."

"It's true," I defend.

This conversation seems totally inappropriate for our current situation, sensing the confusion from the Knyghts as we converse.

"On Adam's fucking *grave*—"

"Watch your mouth!" The Knyght holding Elio snaps.

After a gaudy eye roll, he resumes, more quietly. "I swear. I killed the beast. *Alone.*"

"Do you want a medal?" Bea chimes, sharing a smirk with me.

"I think he wants a medal," I agree.

"I can't believe you assholes," Elio grunts, giving up.

"Your Highness," one of the Knyghts coughs, clearly disturbed by my friendliness towards the captives, but I simply shrug off their stares.

"Ease up on them. They work for the King."

After a breath of hesitation, the Knyghts unanimously nod, loosening their grips on Elio and Bea. I flash the pair a cordial grin. I prowl off in search of a Haelend, but even from all the way across the town square, their bickering is all I can hear.

"I killed five."

"Five?"

"At least you tried."

"Fine. Whatever."

"I just can't take you seriously when you look like that."

"Is this another jab at my shirt?"

I can tell the Haelend currently working on my leg would

rather be elsewhere. She's an older woman, no doubt in disagreement with my actions from before.

With the click of her tongue, she starts unlooping my belt from my thigh. The release of pressure alone sends my vision into a haze. She inches my trousers farther up my leg for more space. Turns out I'd accomplished something with the tourniquet, cutting the blood off just in time. The wound is just about the length of my middle finger, and thankfully not as deep as I'd thought. I'll be fine. She dabs the wound clean with a sterilized cloth, forcing a hiss from my mouth. I pinch my eyes shut, trying to focus on anything but the pain.

"Who did this to you?" The Haelend asks, moving quickly with her stitching.

"He was nobody," I say.

That Howler had asked me the same thing. Why did it matter? I would really prefer to never think of that awful man ever again.

"Just about done here," she says under her breath.

I sigh, ready to leave this place.

The square has settled, somewhat, with people murmuring amongst each other in groups, and Beka in their constant peripherals.

I did the best that I could. Her wounds are cared for, and her eyes are shut. She must be resting. That's good. She'll be okay, for now. A brisk flapping of wings sound above me, and for a second, I think this was all some delirium-induced hallucination and that I'm still in the forsaken Peaks. I look up to see perched on the Headquarter's decorative gargoyles, not a Harpy, but a large owl with eyes as black as night.

"There," the Haelend says, sitting back from my leg. She's

finished. I move to touch the stitches, but she smacks my fingers away. "Leave it. You must rest now, your Highness."

"Thank you," I say, chastised.

The gentlest of coos grabs my attention. I crane my neck up to glance at the rooftops again, and find that the owl is still there. Still staring. I snap my head away at the sudden sound of Royal horns echoing through the square. The chatter of the crowd rises once again, Commander Thierri taking action, ordering the people to move out of the way. Quickly, the people divide to either side of the square, forging a path and stage. My heart stills at the sight of the Kingdom's flags flapping above.

The King is here.

The trumpeters walk ahead, heralding the arrival of the King's golden carriage. It wheels in after the fanfare ceases, carried by four white stallions dressed in the Kingdom's finest. The coachman is squished between two sizeable Knyghts, with another three posted at the rear. Thierri is there when it rolls to a stop. The door of the carriage opens up, and out comes the King's advisor, Seth. He's dressed in his usual beige tunic, a red shawl draped across his shoulders. It feels like a lifetime since I last saw him.

"His Royal Majesty, King Lional Micah Hyttenrauch the Third!" Seth announces, stepping aside.

The crowd bows as one, dipping their heads as the King emerges from the carriage. He steps into the light, fur cloak dragging in his wake, addressing the crowd with a curt nod. Thierri treads behind the King, slowly, trying not to disturb him as he absorbs the applause of the people. He's conscious of the crowd, speaking discreetly into the King's ear as the cheering continues. I watch his poised demeanor shift as Thierri informs him of the situation at hand.

Nobody really notices it — I mean, how could they? To the average person, the King looks beyond words, glimmering in his golden regalia. But, beneath the surface of his stern face, I know he's furious. Enraged. No doubt he's sifting through a whirlwind of conspiracies as he scans the area with bulging eyes. His wild gaze falls on me, and I'm compelled to rise up from the ground. The King cuts the distance between us, snagging my shoulders in his firm grip and pulls me into a tight and suffocating embrace.

"*Aalis*," he huffs, tense against my body.

I'm suddenly a young boy again, screaming for my father after a terrible nightmare, and I cannot help it. My eyes flood with tears.

"Aalis," he repeats, more grave. "Do not disappear like that again."

"I'm sorry."

"What happened to you?" he pulls back, a grimace set on his face.

My mouth opens, but the words catch in my throat.

The King's eyes settle on the figure behind me before I find the courage to speak. He steps back slowly, the color wiped from his face. The comfort his presence gave me is no longer there, gone as quickly as it had come. Terror takes its place as I watch the King watch *her*.

"Where did you say the General was?"

"Inside the Headquarters, your Majesty," Kymn chimes. "He was attacked by the Hand."

"General Bausan was performing an unsolicited execution,

Your Majesty," Commander Thierri advances, shooting Kymn a warning. "Allow me to further explain what happened, sir—"

"So that's her," the King notes, his voice surprisingly steady. "The Hand of Lilith."

"Indeed, she is," the Heathen confirms.

"As I was saying," Thierri starts, "the General was here before—"

"What of my scouts? Who brought her here?"

"Your Majesty," Bea says aloud, tugging herself up from the ground. She yanks her arms free from the Knyghts restraining her. "I am the Capitan, and as requested—"

"That *demon* there, was he in your accompaniment?" The King questions, glaring at Elio.

"Magpie, sir. He's my partner. You sent us both to retrieve the Hand."

"Take them away," the King orders, flicking his fingers in dismissal. The Knyghts yank Elio to his feet. "Your loyalties will be put on trial back in the Kingdom."

"But Your Majesty!" Bea pleads one last time as the Knygths grab her by the arms again, dragging the both of them toward the Guardian Headquarters.

"They found me! They are loyal to the crown," I try to explain.

"Enough!" he snaps. "Your efforts are spent already."

Nothing will appease him. Not while his attention is on Beka. Frantically, I look back at Elio, locking eyes with him one last time before they're out of sight. I nod, and he nods back: I made a promise, and I mean to keep it. The doors of the Headquarters slam shut, sealing Bea and Elio inside.

Seth walks into the center of the square, joining the King at his side.

"Your Majesty, what will you make of the Hand?" he asks, loud enough for the crowd to hear. "She is here, as real and alive as daylight. What say you of her fate?"

The King doesn't answer right away. He takes his time observing Beka before moving a step towards the stake. Then another. Slowly, he makes his way in front of her, sizing her up as they stand face to face. A moment passes where they just stare at each other. I can't see my father's expression, but his body is angled in defense, as if Beka could break free at any second and attack. The crowd is hushed, waiting for their King to speak.

"We meet again," he snarls, taking her jaw in his gloved grip, moving her head from side to side. "Does she resemble your art like you imagined she would, my son?"

My tongue is made of dust.

"Come on, speak!" the King barks, looking between the two of us. "I know of your faithless desires. You cannot hide them from me now."

The crowd may as well be gone. But they are not, and everyone here is waiting for me to say something.

"She is different," I croak.

"You love this creature, do you not?" My silence speaks for itself. "Can't you see? She's *seduced* you! Just as the wicked Sirens of her kind," the King spits, releasing the grip on her face with a shove. "Foolishly, she has brought herself right back to me. How *did* you slip from my grasp all those years ago?" Beka doesn't say anything. She doesn't look at me, either. The King dismisses her silence, whipping around on his heel to face the crowd. "It matters not where the bitch of Edom hid her. The Hand will die, but not here. At the Tree of Life, there awaits her demise."

The King's words are met with a rally of cheer: thunderous, joyful and triumphant.

"Let Sumeria be rid of the Dark Maid once and for all! Let us restore our world in the name of our divine ancestors, our Adam and Eve!" The King bellows, but his voice is muffled when it hits my ears.

The square seems to shrink around me.

I catch Beka glancing my way, her eyes strained and glimmering with tears. Her lips move and I make out one word.

Aalis.

The crowd starts taking notice, their cheers quieting into natters.

I hear it then, the sound of a shrill scream. Then another, and another, and another, and another — all coming from the depths of the alleyways. The air chills, the shadows darken, blanketing the square in a strange dimness, and the screams persist, growing louder and louder with each passing moment. Those closest to the passages begin to push and shove: whatever is in those caverns, they don't want any part of it.

"Your Majesty, I advise that you step back from the girl," a Knyght suggests, putting himself between Beka and the King.

"What is going on?" I demand, stepping closer to Commander Thierri, his face bleak.

Suddenly, the dim light turns violet, coating the square in a purple hue. The cobblestone beneath my feet starts to shift, every single piece of rock buzzing with energy.

"They're here," is all he says.

He does not need to specify who.

"You," the King points a shaking finger at Beka's fettered body. "*Stop*! Stop this sorcery!"

But Beka is tied up, near death. She couldn't possibly be conjuring anything this powerful.

"Stop this!" The King lunges forward, digging his trembling fingers into her frame.

The ground rumbles beneath my feet before I can move to push him away from her. I lose all balance, staggering to the side as the King falls backwards from the sheer force of the rift.

The blaring screams continue to siren, leading the crowd into a frenzy, dispersing from the streets and fleeing as the quaking continues. The horses hooked to the Royal carriage squeal and buck, terrified. Even the Knyghts break formation and scatter.

All at once, the alleyways that intersect into the square split down the middle, collapsing in on themselves, their cracks reaching the center. From these cracks, jagged spikes of rock and dirt shoot up, splicing the air. The ground breaks in a wave, the spikes pushing the crowd back, barricading us all inside the square.

"Everyone get back!" Thierri hollers, grabbing arms and pulling bodies out of the way as the cobblestone tears open.

The King looks as if he is frozen in time, his body between Beka and the threat of the rocks, and standing before us all are the Maidens of Lilith.

There are at least five dozen of them, dressed from head to toe in black cloaks, their trims embroidered with scarlet lace. Their hoods are drawn over their heads, wraith-like, and a force to be reckoned with. Their arms are exposed, hands moving in a dance as they manipulate the earth beneath the cobblestone, ready to defend themselves. But there is no one who is willing to go against them. The Knyghts, out of their own fear, have fled.

"Your Majesty!" I hear someone scream.

There are Knyghts pulling at my arms as well, trapping me from the scene at hand. A long, sharp point of torn stone charges for the King, still unmoved from his spot, but before it can touch him, Seth shoves him to the side, the spear piercing straight through his own chest in one clean sweep. Silence follows, save the sound of Seth choking, gurgling on his own blood. From where he lays sprawled on the ground, the King stares up at Seth's punctured frame, screaming with all his might. Unable to watch, I turn away, the sight twisting my stomach into all sorts of knots. The Maidens have infiltrated the square, surrounding what little remaining Knyghts we have, the rest of the crowd cowering away in the corners.

We are completely defenseless.

Two Maidens step forward, different from the rest. Instead of a hood, their cloaks are fixed with a sheer, black cloth that drapes over their faces. There is no red lining on their cloaks. They move like wind, elegant and delicate. Through the cloth, their pitted eyes fix on me.

"Your Highness," the one on the left speaks, addressing *me*.

The King wails, crawling on his hands and feet. "You cursed Heretics!"

"It is a sight to see you alive," they continue, ignoring his pain. "Many years have passed."

"You are the Elders," Commander Thierri states, cautious.

"I am Ayil, this is Odem," the Elder explains, gesturing to their counterpart.

They move another step closer and unveil their sheer coverings. Their brown skin hugs the bones of their face tight, wrinkling the area around their mouth. I cannot stop staring at their eyes that pierce the crowd. They are hauntingly beautiful, and exude so much grace — I couldn't even guess their exact age. Pulling himself to his feet, the King approaches them at a threatening speed.

"Demons!" he rasps.

But he barely makes it to them: the Maidens on the outskirts thrust their arms out as a unit, grabbing hold of the King with an invisible force. It seizes him, tugging him backwards against the side of a protruded sliver of stone, the impact sending his crown clattering to the ground.

"We do not want any more bloodshed," Ayil explains. "But you have left us with no choice."

I have never seen the King so disheveled. Our eyes meet and he squirms. He's startled, his usual pride exchanged for humiliation. Without his crown, he might as well be nobody.

"I do not wish for bloodshed, either," I whimper, voice trembling.

I keep my eyes on the King, avoiding Seth's unmoving body.

"An eye for an eye, then," Ayil recites.

The Elders move their gaze over my head, in the direction of where Beka is posted on the stake. Kymn suddenly slips around a corner of spiked rock, charging for the Elders.

"You have no jurisdiction here!" she yells, not making it another step.

Odem moves, their arm snapping into sight, fingers curled inward. Kymn is lifted from the ground, suspended in the air like a white dove. She's choking, gasping for a breath. Odem's lips are twisted into a cat-like grin, whilst Ayil eyes them cautiously.

"Enough," I say.

Kymn is completely immobile, her legs entirely slack as she struggles for air.

"We'll do as you wish!" Commander Thierri implores. "So long as you release her."

Odem lowers their hand, freeing Kymn from their hold. The Heathen drops to the ground with a loud *thud*. Nobody dares to move to her aid.

"We have nothing to lose," Odem says, the tenor of their voice nothing short of authority. "We will kill anyone who doesn't mean to cooperate. Even you, *sister*."

The threat is clear. They are not afraid. Like Odem said: there is nothing else the Kingdom can possibly take from them. We've stolen their land, their freedom, and their Hand.

This is it.

"How did you know she was here?" Thierri voices, unafraid.

I wonder the same thing.

Ayil shrugs, stepping closer to put themself between us and the King.

"Our Lady has eyes everywhere," is all they say, turning to face me. "Prince Aalis, untie the Hand and bring her to me."

"Aalis—" the King coughs, his voice cut off.

He's writhing against the stone, struggling for air. They're choking him too.

Maybe I'm hallucinating: it's quite possible an infection has spread across my thigh, and has since reached my brain and scrambled my every thought. I glance at Seth, slumped, his blood pooling against the rock. This is most definitely real.

I walk forward, all eyes on me.

The Knyghts that had been standing guard around Beka are gone, the spiked rock blocking any chance for a decent barricade. I tread carefully around the stone, reaching out for her. It's just the two of us again.

"Beka," I whisper. "I'm going to untie you, okay?"

"Okay," she groans.

I'm careful with the knots, starting with the ropes around her feet, before moving to her wrists.

"Hurts," she mumbles.

"It's going to be alright," I tell her.

Once she's free, I move quickly to prop her up. We take our time shuffling across the square, avoiding the wreckage as much as we can.

"What's happening?"

"It's time to go home," I wince. It feels as though I've swallowed a handful of broken glass, the tiny pieces piercing the confines of my heart from every direction.

"My home is gone," Beka mutters. Her eyes are not yet open all the way.

"I'm so sorry," I tell her, my words eaten up by the sob ripping through my throat.

Beka doesn't say anything back — she's spotted Ayil now, whatever color she had left draining from her face. She wobbles for a moment, but once she forces her balance, her back straightens. Her head is held high. For once, I do not see this girl from my dreams. She is no painting, either. Beka is a prisoner to this land. I cannot trap her in my mind with a canvas and a set of paints any longer.

Elio's voice rings in my head, *Don't regret it.*

I don't regret helping her. I never have. But this feeling, it pokes at my chest as I watch her walk away from me. Nothing, not even death, could relieve me from this pain.

She doesn't look at me when I let go of her.

"*Abeko,*" Ayil exclaims, taking her hands with care.

The Elder caresses her face with their slim fingers, their pitted eyes softening almost immediately. They guide her away from the center, the Maidens opening up their formation to let Beka slip through. Odem steps in front of her defensively, concealing her frame from sight.

"Nature has balanced itself in this exchange," Odem commences. "When Adam banished our Lady, it was he who bewitched this land. Not her. I suggest you learn from his mistakes."

The King fights against the forces holding him back.

"You lie! Your Lady is not righteous, she's *jealous.* She lashes out, murdering and punishing our people! Adam could have never loved someone as *rotten* as her—"

"If you think you can cross into our lands without such consequences, then your faith misleads you, and will continue to mislead you, blindly, until you are nothing more than a fragile man too proud to accept his own demise," Odem warns, their words reaching every ear in the square. "You men are fools. Any words of peace will not be heard. Not anymore."

One by one, the Maidens take their leave. Slowly, their

hooded figures drift back through a singular passageway, one spared from the destruction, dispersing from the square.

The King is released from their clutches. He falls to his knees, gasping. Odem looks down at him, a smirk pulling at their lips.

"His Majesty is tormented by a storm. It thrashes in his mind, sweeping up his deranged thoughts. I pity him, and I pity the lies in which their foundation is built up," Odem sneers, moving their darkened gaze to me. "Prepare yourself, young Hyttenrauch, for you will inherit a dead Kingdom. Let's hope you can survive it."

With one final sweep of the square, Odem retreats, joining the rest of the Maidens as they head out of the city. Once they depart, the violet tint in the air vanishes and the sunlight returns, though things are not as they once were.

Chaos ensues.

Commander Thierri may be speaking to me, but I can't hear a word. The Knyghts flood the square, taking in the measure of destruction — rock irreversibly protruding out from the ground in all directions, their spikes sharp and jagged. Another group is out helping the King up, placing the crown back on his head, while another horde of Knyghts situate themselves around Seth, ready to carry his body away. I hear the crowd's uproar as they scream for mercy, fearful of the event that just took place.

"Aalis!" The King hisses, ashamed. "Their evil has pierced your heart. The damned creatures underestimate the strength of our faith!" He stirs, glaring up at his skewered advisor, his only true friend.

Eadens are taught from a young age the story of our

Kingdom: that Adam is good, that his word is right, and that Lilith can never come back to this world. As Adam's acolytes, it falls on us to see his wishes through, to push back against her sinister power and keep her in the dark. I don't see how that kind of thinking can go on any longer, but here the King stands. In validating his own torment, he ignites a rage born of fear — he recognizes the weakness of our people, of our system and land, and wields this flame. It kindles, a mere blow away from consuming the square in hot flames.

"You have heard it said, 'an eye for an eye'." His audience, his people, they look to him as if he were Adam himself, emerging with the promise of everlasting life dribbling from his lips. "If they strike you on the cheek, turn to them the other," he booms loud for all to hear, but says it directly looking at me.

A foreboding for war.

Let's hope you can survive it.

25
BEKA

I fall in and out of consciousness as the Maidens march me back to the Realm.

Blood pulses underneath my stitches. Every inch of my body aches. The Maidens are gentle with where they touch me, four of them carrying my limp body down to the shores of Carmine Lagoon. Every now and then, my eyelids flutter open, watching the Maidens cast a tight formation around me, smothering my frame in the mass of their dark robes. They talk amongst themselves in our native tongue as they ease me onto a skiff, their voices muffled as it reaches my ears. It's rhythmic, their triumph filling the cracks between each moving body with a semblance of hope.

I didn't think I'd make it. Not after the General slit my arms, and especially not after the King arrived in the square. I'd thought I really passed on after Aalis came to my aid. After his confession. In those last moments, it wasn't love that I felt — I was far from it, but at least it was him by my side then. He deserves better.

The wooden base of the canoe is solid, and I curl into myself, cradling my knees to my chest. The rocking of the waves eases my mind and I am grateful to be lying down. As we glide across the Lagoon, I am cursed with the plague of remembering. I think of the meadow and all its changing colors. I see the orchard, ripe apples dangling from the tree branches. The Forsaken Sea crashing in the distance, a blue and absent embrace.

A Maiden says something to me, sitting me up. A cloak has been wrapped around my shoulders, a canister pressed to my lips, and when I open my mouth, a flood of water hits my dry throat. I violently guzzle it down.

"Eat this. You'll feel much better."

I don't register what it is until I bite down and chew. A soft dough melts between my teeth, breaking into the middle where a paste of ginger and cinnamon salves my tongue in bitter sweetness. I know this flavor, my childhood coming back to me in just one bite.

"You're awake," Ayil exclaims, carefully stepping over to me so as not to tip the canoe.

I nod, my neck stiff.

Ayil kneels down, meeting me at eye level.

"How did you find me?" I whisper.

Talking is a great effort.

"We grieved you for so long," they start, gently. "But then we felt it again, felt *you*. It was as if you were calling out to us. As if you were reborn."

I can still feel the power that surged through me the moment I snapped at Bea, waking up feelings I had never thought I was capable of. Anger. Betrayal. Revenge. Those same feelings spark inside me still, a thrum of new energy. Purpose.

"There are those still loyal to our Lady amongst the

Kingdom, all across Sumeria," Odem explains, emerging from behind Ayil.

Where one Elder is, the other is always close to follow. They once walked the same ground as Lilith, her friends. They are two of the most powerful Maidens, second only to the Hand. To me.

"We received word that you'd been spotted riding towards Alnola. Even if it weren't true, we couldn't abandon the possibility," Ayil continues, reaching out to caress my cheek and I fight the urge to recoil. "You are safe now. Do not fear my touch."

I don't move. Lilith's energy is so strong within them — but it's strong inside me too. I used to fear this feeling, afraid that it would reject me and cast me aside, deem me unworthy of its power. I still fear it, but not as much as I fear feeling powerless. I've seen what my indifference can do. All the paralyzing guilt and anger and pain from before cushions my weight, comforting me, and I embrace it.

Ayil's hand falls from my face as I rise from the floor of the canoe. The Carmine Lagoon is behind us now, and the blue sky above fades into a violet fog. We pass through a layer of protective wards as we ready our entry into the Realm. Enemies stop here, no longer able to navigate our lands. Sirens illuminate the direction of our path ahead, as towers of sandy rock poke out of the water, forming an aisle that drifts our canoes towards the entrance into the Realm of Zemergad.

A hand smoothes my hair down, tucking a few strands behind my ear. I look over and see Odem there beside me. Their eyes are less inviting than Ayil's, but familiar all the same.

"Welcome home, *Abeko*."

TO BE CONTINUED...
HER MAIDEN'S DESOLATION

Glossary

Eadens — People who follow the Edenic faith of Adam and Eve.

Haeland — A trained healer.

Harpy — Daughters of Lilith and the Fallen Angel Sariel. They are ancient creatures sworn to protect those who are Maiden-born.

Heathen — A self-exiled Maiden who has cut ties with Lilith, severing their ability to possess magic. They have converted to the Edenic faith.

Heretic — A derogatory term used to describe the Maidens of Lilith.

Howler — Children of Lilith and the Fallen Angel Sahariel. They are considered 'Cursed Children' and Shift once every full moon into their natural forms. They must wear Moonstone to ease the pain of their human forms.

Maiden of Lilith — A follower of Lilith who resides in the Realm of Zemergad.

Night Demon — The male-born offspring of Maidens of Lilith who are exiled upon birth. They are considered 'Cursed Children' and rely on blood to survive. They must wear Celestite to reduce their cravings and face the sun with ease.

Siren — Daughters of Lilith and the Fallen Angel Samael. They reside in the waters of Sumeria and lure sailors to the Realm to procreate with Maidens.

Acknowledgements.

Daria —
Before I start, a poem comes to mind. I wish to share it with you all.

> *Of Adam's first wife, Lilith it is told*
> *(The witch he loved before the gift of Eve,)*
> *There, ere the snake's, her sweet tongue could deceive,*
> *And her enchanted hair was the first gold.*
> *And still she sits, young while the earth is old,*
> *And, subtly of herself contemplative,*
> *Draws men to watch the bright web she can weave,*
> *Till heart and body and life are in its hold.*
> *The rose and poppy are her flowers; for where*
> *Is he not found, O Lilith, whom shed scent*
> *And soft-shed kisses and soft sleep shall snare?*
> *Lo! as that youth's eyes burned at thine, so went*
> *Thy spell through him, and left his straight neck bent*
> *And round his heart one strangling golden hair.*
> — Lady Lilith, Dante Gabriel Rossetti.

First and and foremost, I'd like to thank Haley.
There are a million things I would like to say but no word in any language could truly convey the gratitude, the love, the

admiration I hold for you in my heart and soul. If I could do this with anyone, I would pick you every time.

Secondly, I'd like to thank Dr. Lewis, my high school English teacher. She is why I do what I do. She lit the fuse all those years ago and kept the flame kindling. It is now a wildfire of passion, and I would be nowhere without her.

I'd also like to extend my gratitude to every single person who has shown even just an ounce of interest, or a smidgen of support. Your kind words and excitement helped push this project to where it is now. There are too many of you to name, but you know who you are (with special mentions to Tom, Jennifer, Lindsey and Jane).

My parents, sister and pups: I love you. я люблю тебе. Eu te amo. Woof woof woof.

To Halsey and *'If I Can't Have Love, I Want Power'* — you changed lives with that album. Oh, and Every Hozier Song Ever. Thank you, Andrew.

Project Darley forever.

Haley —
Where to begin.

I want to start off by thanking my family, Ted, Angie, Elin, and Karin (and the dogs) for the endless amounts of support since I first started my writing journey at six years old. I had written a story called 'Lily of the Rainbow' — a tale about a horse named Lily who gathered intel from other farm animals about the different colors in a rainbow. I didn't know then how passionate I was about creating stories, but my mom could see it. She'd scanned and printed out all those silly pages for me to look back on. Thank you, mom, for always believing in me and being the first to read and critique 'Heretics & Hearsay.'

This entire project means the absolute world to me. I want to extend my thanks to anyone who ever shared an interest in learning about the story (you know who you are). The simplest of questions and conversations about it will truly stay in my heart forever. I could talk about it for hours, so I also apologize to anyone who endured my rambling. A huge thank you to the handful of readers who were among the first to experience Sumeria and send feedback to Daria and I. Thanks to Aunt Kari for always showing me your enthusiasm about my writing. Thanks to Lindsey for drawing our characters and bringing them to life — I am forever thankful for you and our shared creative pursuits. Thanks to Karin for helping with advertisement and creating promotional content. Thanks to Greta and Macy for being by my side for anything, through

369

everything. Thanks to Tom and Jennifer for aiding Daria and I as we ventured into not only the publishing world, but the business world as well. A special thanks to Mable and Willow: without you, I probably wouldn't be where I am today.

Hey, Daria, can you believe we did it? We have a baby! When I think back to 2018, I smile as I recall the girls we used to be. Just two pen pals against the world. Your friendship has felt like an enormous gift, one that I cherish so close to my heart. When I came to you with the scraps of the idea for 'Heretics & Hearsay,' your passion and commitment were instant. You challenge me. You make me a better writer. Together, I truly feel that we can accomplish anything, and I thank you endlessly. The Capitan to my Magpie, forever and ever and ever and ever...

Daria is based in London, where she works as an Editor. She holds a BA in English Literature and Language from the University of Westminster. To no-one's surprise, she is quite the reader and takes a lot of pride in her personal library. Occasionally, Daria goes by Daisy J. Wilde, and her solo writing can be found on tumblr.com/daisyjwilde. 'Heretics & Hearsay' is her debut novel.

Haley wrote her first story at the age of 6 and, since then, has always had one churning in her mind. Growing up, she wrote under a pseudonym and started many novels, all inspired by the popular Young Adult books of her time. Her fiery passion for storytelling showed no signs of fading; instead, flourishing in the creation of 'Heretics & Hearsay', her debut novel. Born and raised in Minnesota, Haley lives in Minneapolis with her best friend and their cat, Louanne. When she isn't writing — which is not often — Haley enjoys reading, going on walks, playing Wizard 101, and spending time with family and friends.

In 2018, Haley and Daria met on Instagram through their mutual interests. What started out as months of penpalling turned into years of video chats and texting, the connection between the two blossoming into a deep and loyal friendship. The girls have met in person only twice, with Haley being from the United States, and Daria from the United Kingdom. In 2021, Project Darley was formed. After a series of very long zoom calls, cooperating with a six hour difference in time zones, and drafting multiple manuscripts, the dynamic pair is ready to share their creative genius with the world. You can find them on Instagram and TikTok @projectdarley or on their website at https://projectdarley.wixsite.com/projectdarley.

Milton Keynes UK
Ingram Content Group UK Ltd.
UKHW021950191124
451425UK00011B/101

9 798869 345851